Apothecary 709

By Cristen E. Rose

Happy Cat Press

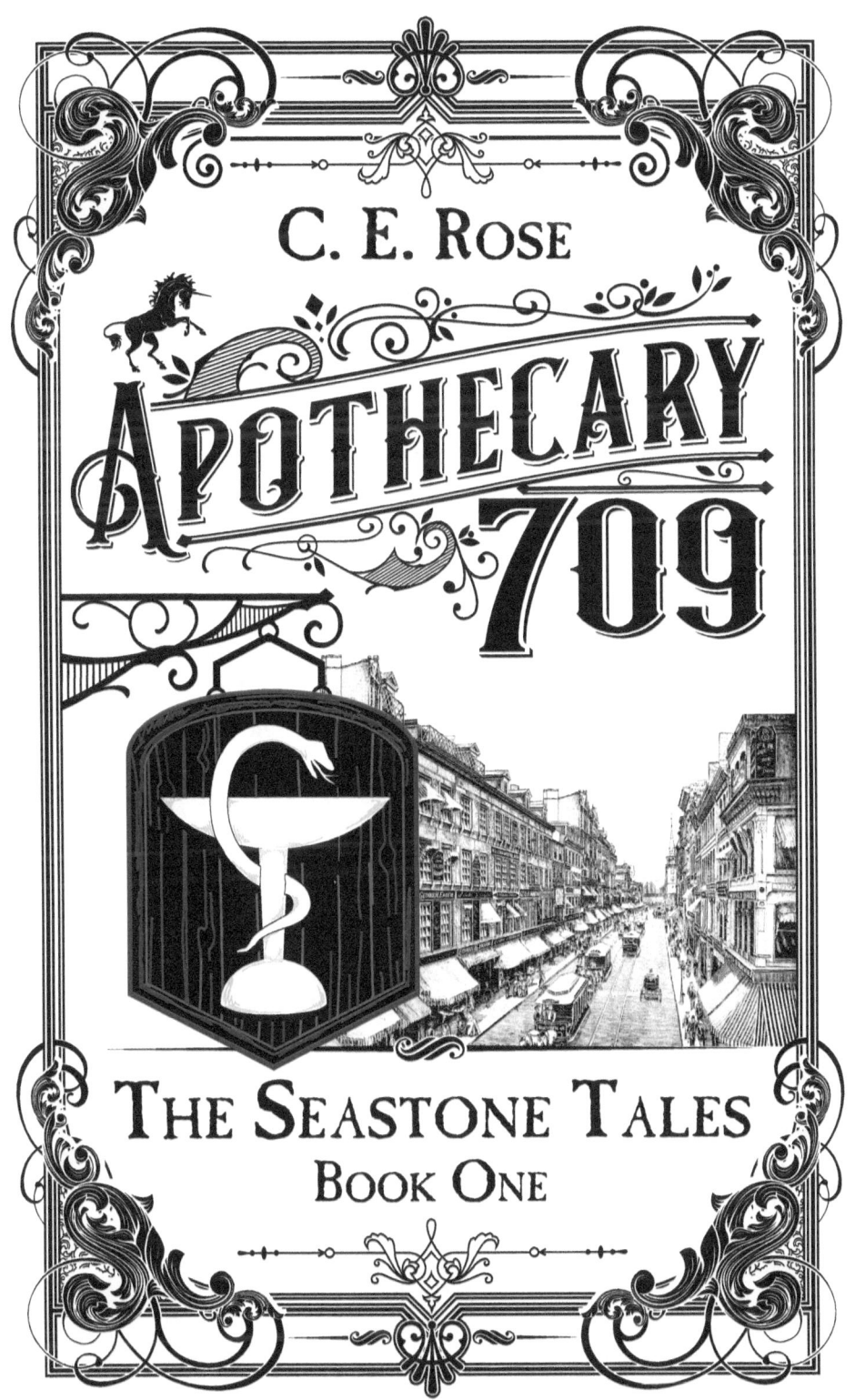

C. E. ROSE

APOTHECARY 709

THE SEASTONE TALES
BOOK ONE

First publication date: September 2023

ISBN (Paperback): 979-8-9885159-0-6

Cover and book interior design by Babski Creative Studios

Published by:
Happy Cat Press
Tallahassee, Florida
www.happycatpress.com

Author website: www.cristenerose.com

*For my husband John, my partner in
our real-life magical adventures.*

Content Advisory

This book is intended for an adult audience and includes adult language, violence, sexual content, as well as discussions of mental illness, suicide, and kidnapping.

Herbal potions described in this book are for entertainment purposes only. Plant medicines are powerful and can be harmful if used incorrectly. Please consult a qualified herbalist and/or physician before taking any herbal medications.

All characters, events, and places in this book are entirely fictional.

"One does not become enlightened by imagining figures of light,
but by making the darkness conscious."

—Carl Gustav Jung

PART 1

THE SHADOW

CHAPTER 1
A Tea Shop

The Sovereign Kingdom of Seastone
Wednesday, 10 July 1907
New Moon

 *on't look down.* Too bad I rarely took my own advice. The rain puddle's reflective surface proved too tempting. It snared my gaze. Colors and light slid over that living canvas, halting my steps. In the inverse world, seagulls swam through blue sky. Shining hands of the clock tower above marked backwards time below, framed by a dun-colored bank of clouds far under my feet. The puddle rippled in a breeze.

Images swirled. A familiar sensation itched the back of my brain, holding me in thrall. A void of shadow, darker than a moonless night, coalesced in their midst, as I knew it would.

"Violet, watch out!"

A horn blared. Mrs. H grabbed my arm and pulled me backwards. I stumbled to catch my balance. Right where I had stood, a motorcar whizzed by on the cobblestone street.

Mrs. H shook her fist at the goggle-wearing motorist. "Hey! Watch where you're going!"

He didn't even glance back at his near-victims, but careened around a wagon at the end of the block. Horses whinnied and spooked, earning a worried *whoa there* from anxious drivers.

My puddle now churned and muddy, the illusion vanished. I sucked in a breath, tainted by foul-smelling engine smoke.

"Automobile." I coughed. "The wretched things should be banned. They're a public nuisance."

"Well, there's your scientific progress, I suppose." Agnes smirked, trying to make me laugh, no doubt. This topic was our usual sparring ground—her belief in magic and superstition and my insistence on provable fact, which we had debated yet again on the walk into town that morning, though it was a good distraction from my anxiety. This ridiculous walking excursion was my housekeeper's idea, and I had given in to her meddling. She often pushed me to test my limits. True, I hadn't left the house in months, buy why should that matter? At home, I was comfortable and safe.

I couldn't draw enough air. My hands trembled. My heart raced. My corset was too tight. This was ridiculous. Why was I even out here?

I'd nearly been killed. Because of my infernal obsessions. My illness.

I closed my eyes and visualized what might have been. My mangled body sprawled on the cobblestones, my face spattered with blood and muddy water. I cringed.

No. It's not real. I whispered to myself, "It's only fear. My mind will clear."

But the mantra, given to me by one of the many well-meaning alienists who had found me a noteworthy specimen since childhood, proved little comfort. Despite the July heat, ice crawled my spine. My vision began to tunnel. I had to get out of here. I needed to be home.

The new headache which throbbed in the back of my skull was genuine enough.

Agnes grabbed my arm and hauled me the rest of the way across the street. "Are you all right, dear? Didn't you hear it coming?"

"I don't know. No." Then I saw the mud—actual mud—splattered on my skirts. "Oh, blast it all."

Mrs. H noticed it too. "Well, it's not too bad." She sighed. "It'll wash out. The important thing is you are fine. Come on. There's a lemonade stand up ahead. We'll stop and rest in the shade for a bit."

"No. I'm not... I can't go any farther, Mrs. H. I'm sorry. I need to head back home. This was a bad idea."

Agnes smiled, all rosy cheeks and bright hazel eyes under her perfect gray chignon and wide-brimmed hat. My housekeeper knew my inner battle better than anyone else in this life, even my father, though I had not told her everything.

"Nonsense," she said. "You've come so far. It'll be a waste to turn back now. We've only a few more blocks to go, then we'll head back home. I promise."

On that crowded boardwalk, my drama had attracted unwanted attention. Before I made a further scene, I nodded and said, "All right."

We pressed on. One footstep at a time. One breath after another. Soon enough, I convinced myself I wasn't going to die on this ordinary Wednesday morning. The headache, however, had found familiar purchase in my defective brain, and would not be so easily placated.

We stopped first at Mrs. H's favorite pastry shop. I tried to follow her up the tiled steps, past the chalkboard sign advertising the day's specials, but my legs froze, as if I'd hit an invisible wall. Cold dread pressed the air from my lungs. I did the only sensible thing—pretended I'd forgotten something and turned around.

All my life, some doorways were just *off limits*. My phobias had decided I could enter certain places with no trouble, while others caused panic. I couldn't control or predict it. Life was just easier when I avoided them all.

On a wooden bench outside, I sat and watched the harbor through headache-hazed vision. I nodded to passers-by, trying to hide my face under the wide brim of my hat, in hopes I wouldn't be recognized. Thanks to my ex-fiancé and a stay in that terrible asylum, my name had been drug through the mud in this small town, sure as the puddle water which dried to chalk-colored smears on skirts. I was grateful my handful of art students overlooked my past—fortunate any of my paintings ever sold at all.

Fishing ships caught the morning light on distant sunlit sails, a contrast to heavy clouds on the indigo horizon. An airship sailed through the summer haze—a passenger ship, moving inland to the air docks. Had I canvas and paints, I might have captured the golden light on that colorful, hydrogen-filled envelope before the ship flew out of view. It had been ages since I felt well enough to bring a field easel this far into town to paint, though I used to do it so often when I was young. How had I once been so free of these invisible chains?

I glanced at Mrs. H through the bakery's display windows, piled high with plaster replicas of cakes and pies. She returned with a waxed-paper bundle tucked under an arm, smiling as though nothing at all was amiss.

We proceeded to Seastone's open air market—a gathering of tents and costermonger stalls tucked between a few older warehouses and the shipyards. People milled about, haggling for various goods. Someone played an accordion, though not as well as our butler, Mr. Travers. I convinced myself to stop for a cup of lemonade, and while the spiced griddle cakes smelled divine, my nerves were too riled to abide the idea of food. Mrs. H introduced me as 'her employer, the artist' to a shawl-wrapped basket-weaver who had made several of the pieces in service at our house. I met a soap-maker, a few

3

fishmongers, and a woman peddling hand-knotted rugs—of the same design which had appeared in our kitchen. Agnes had never asked Father or me for reimbursement for any of these items. I supposed she knew Father would never approve.

We'd not gone another half-block down Harbor Street before an electric-powered tram plowed through the crowd. Its clanging bell drove spikes through my aching skull. I clenched my trembling fists as it rumbled by.

A tugboat bellowed, maneuvering near the seawall. I wondered if the ship wouldn't scrape the boulders connected to the embankment upon which we stood. If the tug sank, surely there would be time enough for passengers to escape, and the road might not be torn asunder before we all slid into the sea.

Soon we neared a flower stall tucked under a millinery shop's red and white awning. Mrs. H declared we must stop and inspect the dahlias.

A purple spiral with a yellow center caught my eye, and despite my protests, Mrs. H helped the salesgirl pin two of them to my straw hat, along with a sprig of jasmine for scent. I refused to let my housekeeper pay for them, though I normally wouldn't have spent the money on such a trifle.

"Isn't the color a bit loud?" I asked her afterward.

"Think of it this way, my dear—nobody will notice the mud on your skirt if they're looking at your hat. Besides, I know the girl's family. They could use the money."

"Quite the philanthropist you've become, Agnes."

"Oh, hush now. It looks beautiful."

The gaudy flowers did have a nice fragrance, which masked the dockyard stench.

We pressed on, despite my unceasing anxiety. Storm-weathered wood of an old warehouse loomed to our left, a harbor of rusting and barnacle-encrusted fishing boats to our right. Schooners and tugboats worked the glittering bay. A line of rain approached, like angled brushstrokes on the southeastern horizon. Weather was moving in fast; sweltering heat pushed ahead of the transition.

"We're going to be soaked," I said. "We forgot an umbrella."

"No. It won't rain today."

"Let me guess, you read it in your tea leaves this morning?"

Agnes was wont to consult her omens and auguries for all manner of daily decisions. One never knew what nonsense she might bring home from her spiritualist meetings, entertaining though it all was.

"And what if I did?" She grinned like she knew a wonderful secret. At least her delusions gave her comfort instead of torment. I was envious.

"Well, the rain will cool us, at least." I blotted my forehead with a hand-kerchief. "Where are we headed now?"

"You know that new favorite tea of yours?"

"A tea shop?"

"Yes. Well, you'll see." With that mischievous gleam in her eye, she was up to something. But I trusted her more than I trusted myself out here, even if she displayed an alarming lack of concern for the panoply of dangers surrounding us.

"How much farther is it?" Would I be able to step inside was the real question.

"Just a couple more blocks. We're nearly there. I promise it'll be worth a gander." Again, that wicked grin.

Gone were the shopping crowds from this industrial zone. A few dock workers and fishermen tended their boats. One old man sat slumped on a barrel beside the road. Bald, he had a mess of yellow-gray beard, eyes white with cataracts, and he smoked a pipe that smelled like rum. He held out an empty tin cup as we approached.

Mrs. H stopped and dug a few coins out of her purse to toss in the beggar's cup. She even gave him one of her bakery-purchased currant scones. Something about this fellow crawled my nerves. I mentally scolded myself for such heartless thoughts and bit my tongue.

The man nodded and thanked us, staring with blind eyes.

We turned town a deserted alleyway.

"I don't like this side of town," I whispered, glancing up at a broken ware-house window. "Where did you hear about this place?"

"It came highly recommended by one of my associates, and I must say I wasn't disappointed. You'll love it. I promise. Ah, here we are."

"Do you mean the suffragettes or your Mystical Sisterhood?" Either way, this could be interesting.

"You'll see."

We turned onto another lonely passageway between old brick buildings. A slant angle of morning sunlight washed one side of the swayback brick pavement. We had not far to go before reaching our destination—a sagging green portico beside a wooden placard which read, *Apothecary ~709~*. Flakes of gold paint marked a weather-worn shield behind a carved chalice and serpent—the time-honored emblem for apothecaries the world over. While it lacked the fancy filigree of the newer shop signs in town, the antique symbol felt more honest. At least the shop's windows looked to have been dusted, even if they only allowed a glimpse of indistinct interior gloom.

Unmistakable mewing sounds issued from beside a concrete stoop. I quickened my pace to find a basket containing a mother cat and her five nursing young.

"Oh, Agnes! Kittens."

I knelt beside them. The mother watched me but didn't flinch. She and her brood lay on a clean rag blanket beside a half-full saucer of cream, a plate of fish bones, and a gnawed-upon mackerel head. Two of the kittens were of their mother's striped gray, two orange and one black. The mother purred. Those slender golden eyes held what must have been pride. *Aren't they beautiful—my precious children?* I imagined her saying.

"They *are* beautiful," I answered.

"Do be careful, dear. Wharf-cats are full of fleas."

When I stood, the black kitten turned its tiny face toward me and watched me climb the stairs.

Mrs. H had gone ahead, but of course I faltered, staring at the dreaded threshold. The door creaked open. Smells from the shop hit me first—a moldering mixture of organics—a hint of incense. The interior air, cool and earthy like a cellar, promised respite from the July heat. I crossed my fingers and stepped forward.

Half-expecting that same old paralyzing panic, instead I took another step. Mrs. H closed the door behind us, jangling an assembly of silver and tin bells which hung from the inside handle. I exhaled in relief.

Nothing too unusual in the space's architecture. It might have been a converted old warehouse. The weirdness accosting my olfactory senses ebbed and flowed as we explored the dim shelves. Rows of glass and earthenware vessels contained sundries in time-dulled colors—dehydrated leaves and mushrooms, crystalline honey and tree resins, mysterious powders and liquids—most labeled with cryptic symbols or Latin. Brass and leather implements (to their macabre purpose I cared not hazard a guess) perched like menacing metallic birds which might hop among the dried botanicals were they not immobilized. Whitened bones, perhaps from cattle or livestock, peeked from the rims of chipped ceramic crocks; I had not the willingness or scientific expertise to imagine them human.

In the back of the room, I spotted a shelf of antique books. I approached what was surely the proprietor's collection of reference material on varied subjects—herbalism, botany, biology, phrenology, astrology, and others unidentifiable. A few volumes looked centuries old. Embossed in gold leaf on the spine of one black tome were bizarre symbols like dots and circles connected with lines. Another bore silver glyphs showing eight phases of the moon.

Then it was her spiritualist friends who'd recommended the place. I might have guessed.

While Mrs. H compared jars of tea, I leaned over the countertop to more closely inspect the books. A silent apparition moved within shadows of a nearby doorway. The human-sized figure materialized from the gloom. It was the height of a tall man, but with two large bulbous eyes and a hooked bird's beak.

I blinked. Still there. Gooseflesh crawled my skin.

It uttered a muffled sound, like a word pressed behind a feather pillow, and moved into the light, revealing a person wearing a mask. I stepped backward, catching myself with a hand on the countertop. Before my racing thoughts formulated any words to say, he removed his leather gloves and laid them at one end of the counter. He unfastened the mask behind his head and pulled it away, snagging a few locks of his long hair, and set the monstrosity on the counter.

"Terribly sorry if I startled you. I'd forgotten I had it on, if you can believe it." He approached me in the flickering gaslight, extending a bare hand. "Hello. I'm Roger Gale." He smiled.

I blinked, staring at this stranger like a mute idiot. He seemed familiar, but I had not met him before, I was almost certain.

I cleared my throat. "Violet Morgen." I shook his outstretched hand, as though I had never done such a thing in my life, wishing I had worn my better gloves.

Handsome did not begin to describe Mr. Gale, though he possessed all the classic hallmarks. High cheekbones, firm jawline, and well-formed lips. Eyes as green as the Welterwood forest. Shoulder-length hair a few shades darker than my own—nearly a lustrous black. Some quality of his bearing drew me more than his beauty. I could not help but imagine regal princes in storybooks. Classical heroes of myth. Little did it matter that in real life, the man wore plain clothing and a shopkeep's apron. A more brazen version of myself might have invited him to sit for me in my studio while I sketched his features for hours. *Damn.*

"Delighted, Miss Morgen. How may I help you?"

Double damned if his velvety voice wasn't equally charming. What was he asking again? I blinked.

Right. I was a customer. In his shop. But how he had guessed correctly that a woman my age was a Miss and not a Missus? I suspected Mrs. H had told him too much of my personal history.

"Well, ah… Mr. Gale, might I inquire about that dreadful mask?"

Did I imagine he looked flustered? I might have embarrassed him.

7

"Certainly."

He stepped toward me, holding the object out for my inspection. Glass-domed eyes, riveted above the hooked leather beak with brass pins, were darkened by corrosion and age.

"It's an antique I've modified." He pointed at the beak's underside. "This is an air filter. At the time it was made, it would have been filled with herbs and roses, thought to impede foul odors which spread the plague. For my needs, I've replaced that with gauze and carbon to protect against dust particles. Quite useful when I'm mixing preparations, but not the best attire for greeting customers, I'm afraid. Please forgive my rudeness."

"Perhaps I was startled, but you weren't rude. I mean… it's fascinating. I've always been fond of antiques. I've never seen anything like it… your mask, that is. Or your shop, for that matter." And I was going to drop straight through these old creaky floorboards for mortification.

I tapped my fingers on the countertop, bit my lower lip, and glanced away from those green eyes.

Mrs. H appeared, bearing several earthenware jars in her sturdy arms and sporting a devilish smirk. Yes, we'd found something *worth a gander* in this little tea shop, indeed.

I tried not to laugh.

My fingers went to the brim of my hat, worrying at the flowers. I turned away, adjusted a stray lock of hair, and folded my hands at my waist—cheeks burning.

"Mr. Gale," crooned Mrs. H, "I see you've met my dear Miss Morgen. Like a daughter she is."

"Indeed. It's quite my honor." If the man wanted to add another few words, they failed him. Mr. Gale's expression cooled.

"Well…" My traitorous housekeeper maneuvered her way to the counter. "I'll have two ounces each of Orange Pekoe and Dragon's Gaze, if you please. And more of the special calming tea you blended for us."

The apothecary went to work weighing and mixing her order. I stood nearby, watching the unwitting grace of his movements. The focus in his composure was remarkable. What ridiculous magic did Mrs. H expect was at work in this tea? Not that the man needed anything other than his looks to sell tea in this town.

"It's become Violet's favorite, in fact," she continued. "Helps her sleep better too, if she doesn't mind me saying."

"Is that so?" He didn't look up from his scales, though a shapely eyebrow arched, and the corner of those fine lips might have curled in amusement.

"Oh." Was he talking to me? "I suppose it has, thank you."

"Wonderful. I'm always glad to hear of a satisfied client."

Hmm. I'd bet. But I cleared my throat and said, "It must be rewarding. Helping people, I mean."

I had to get out of here. I was a mess, and my head was going to split in two. I massaged the back of my neck while pretending to examine a row of spice jars.

As though he read my mind, Mr. Gale said, "Headache?"

I nodded, wishing I hadn't been so transparent.

"Do you suffer them often?"

"I'm afraid so."

He turned to another shelf behind his counter and selected a small bottle from amongst a collection of various concoctions. He approached me, took my gloved hand, and placed it in my palm. "Here. On the house. Take two or three drops in a cup of water or milk and it should ease your pain."

"Thank you, but I can't accept this for free."

"Nonsense." He returned to his prior work. "Your family is a loyal customer. It's the least I can do."

I inspected the bottle. The brown glass contained what appeared to be an alcohol tincture. The foil-stamped label read:

ᴵᴺ HEADACHE TONIC ᴺᵎ
· Including extracts of Willow, Mint, Cannabis Indica & Cramp-Bark ·
For Headaches, Rheumatism, Female Complaints, and general Bone Pain.
☞ Do not exceed 10 drops Per Day. Do not administer if Fever is present.

Well, it didn't look like an absurd magic potion. Just a typical herbal preparation. A good sign.

Mrs. H turned to me with a smile. "Cat got your tongue, dearie?"

"Cats?" Yes, that might fill the awkward silence. "That reminds me. Mr. Gale, are those your kittens outside?"

"Not exactly. I feed them, but the mother cat's a free spirit. Many nearby shops set out food for her. I call her Maggie, though I wouldn't doubt she has a few other names besides."

I pretended not to notice Agnes' smug expression and inched closer to Mr. Gale as he wrapped tins in brown paper. If I'd expected any reaction to my nearness, I'd have been disappointed.

"Have you named the kittens too?" I asked as he bagged our order.

"Not yet. Hmm… Miss Morgen, why don't you do the honors?" He gestured to the doorway with a half-bow. Taking the cue, I led the way.

Outside, Maggie lay in her basket, having a feline-style bath. Her charges played in wobbles around her. One pounced on its sibling's ear, while another hid under the blanket as a means of ambush. The black one mewed at me, watching with tiny eyes of sea-green.

"Mr. Gale," I said. "I believe a name is of lasting importance. If I were going to name these cats, I should like to get to know them better. Their personalities would inspire me, I think." As soon as the hasty words came spilling from my mouth, I regretted it. Naming a fellow creature was a serious matter, but I realized how presumptuous I must sound. Mrs. H beamed, while I huffed in frustration.

"What a perfect suggestion. In that case, Violet, now that you're acquainted with the shop, you can pick up our next order. That will give you more time to name the cats."

Mr. Gale seemed to want to speak, but Mrs. H cleared her throat and gave him a conspiratorial look. He grinned and clasped his hands behind his back, staring at the brick pavement.

What could I say but, "Perhaps I shall?"

After we took our leave, I couldn't disappear from the man's view fast enough. My boots clattering on uneven bricks, headache pounding in my skull, I didn't even speak a word to Mrs. H. When we neared the end of the alleyway, I glanced over my shoulder, but he'd gone inside.

On Harbor Street, the beggar still sat beside the rusting row of boats. He laughed.

Mrs. H shrugged, but I turned to look. Those blind, white eyes stared nowhere. Still, I thought he laughed at *us*.

The cackling old sailor stood. Impossibly, the shadow below his shoes did not fall in line with the sun's rays, not parallel with the barrel's shadow, nor those of the posts along the harbor wall. His shadow rested askew from reality.

The hair on the back of my neck stood on end. A tickling sensation cracked in the back of my brain.

The shadow arm lengthened. It snaked toward me over *dry* cobblestones (no reflective water in sight), fingers outstretched, though the man had not moved his hands an inch.

I quickened my pace, tugging Mrs. H along with me.

"What's wrong?" She asked.

"Nothing," I lied. "I need to return home. Right away."

I couldn't remember if a hallucination like this, one free of a mirrored surface, had ever manifested in the light of day.

CHAPTER 2
AN INVITATION

Friday, 20 September 1907
Waxing Gibbous Moon

ummer slipped on, turning gilt at the edges, ripening soon into fall. One morning in September, I peered over the seawall in Crestfield Park and considered tossing Father's unopened letter down to the churning waves. The linen paper, folded enough to ensure opacity from prying eyes, rustled in the sea breeze. He'd sealed the envelope with a medallion of crimson wax, stamped with a family signet ring he rarely used.

Father had made it clear he didn't like my now-frequent visits to town. He had suspected, when I bought myself a new dress, when I smiled more freely than I should, that I had found another man bent on ruining my life. When he pressed me on the topic, Roger's name seemed to trouble him. I didn't know what could have set Father so against a man he'd never even met.

Over breakfast that morning, Father divulged he'd once had dealings with Roger's own family, the nature of which he would not reveal. He'd dispatched me with a letter and a dinner invitation to deliver to Mr. Gale. Judging by the tone of his voice, the meeting between them would not be a friendly one.

If I had to guess what Father had written—no doubt it was an ostensibly well-meaning disclosure of his daughter's mental shortcomings, disguised as an apology for her brazen forwardness. In sum—a warning to the gentleman to stay away.

Blast it all.

A flock of gulls sailed overhead, chattering on their way toward some weathered pier. They cast shadow *M*s on the crushed shell pathway. Pelicans perched upon marble mermaids in the park's central fountain. Colorful kites dotted a cloudy sky, steered by laughing children and attendant mothers.

Sighing, I opened my sketchbook, intending to tuck the envelope in the back. Wind rustled the pages, flipping through my visual journal of these monumental weeks since July. Seagulls. A block of shops. Fishing ships. Things I had not allowed myself to sketch in so many years, because I had lived as a recluse, hiding from the world. I turned another page to find studies of Maggie and her kittens. Rows of apothecary jars. Roger as he mixed an order of tea. Roger, sitting on a bench across from me, on that afternoon he'd closed the shop early to take me for a stroll down to Bayshore Park. We'd bought ice cream in waffle cones and sat under the shade of elm trees, listening to the music of the carousel. He told me more about his past that day. He'd lost his mother and sister when he was young, and his father just a few years ago. I couldn't imagine being all alone in this world, as he was. But we had also laughed, and I smiled until I thought my face would crack. My heart had felt lighter than the colorful ships' sails in the bay, even if the words left unsaid between us pulled like an undertow.

Mr. Gale's friendship had awakened within me a flame too long dormant. This gorgeous man and his miraculous medicines helped me remember what fullness of life I had forgotten. My paintings had become more vivid. My compositions more full of hope. Roger was my Muse.

I didn't want this pretend love affair of mine to end, yet it had always been doomed.

I snapped the book closed, my eyes stinging from more than the wind. Soon these pages would pass into the myth of what my life might have been.

Determined to see this through, I pressed on and bid my usual good morning to the open-air market vendors, though I didn't linger. By the time I reached the flower stall beside Mrs. Tremble's millinery, I decided today might be my last such chance, so I bought two wine-colored peonies and a spray of asters for my hat.

In the alleyway leading to Roger's shop, Maggie and her growing brood greeted me with their usual eagerness, but I had no heart to stay longer than a moment with them. I would miss them too.

I gathered my wits and opened the door, inhaling the aroma of dried herbs and sundries I loved. Today, my heart was heavy as stone.

Roger stood from where he had been arranging tins on a low shelf and tucked a pair of glasses into his apron pocket. When his gaze met mine, he smiled—a sight that never failed to make my breath catch.

"You have a shadow today, Miss Morgen."

"What?" I froze. I'd never mentioned my night terrors or my Shadow. I'd not even told Mrs. H.

Roger pointed to my feet. The black kitten from Maggie's litter pounced at the hem of my skirt.

"Oh! So I do." I knelt to pick up the squirming ball of fur. "Your mother will miss you, little trickster."

My eyes stung, but I pushed the emotion away.

The kitten flattened his ears when Roger drew near, but soon enough, he purred.

"I've never been able to catch one of them." Roger peered down at the creature with patient inquiry. "They tolerate me when I bring food, but always run if I get too close. You must have the magic touch."

The way he said the word *touch* made me flush. I was glad for the temporary distraction of his flirtation. Yet, today, it cut like a knife.

"Did you want to hold him?" I swallowed the words I wasn't ready to say.

Roger offered a hand to the cat's inspection. The kitten's eyes widened—ears tilted back.

"There now, little fellow." He stroked its tiny chin. The cat appeared to relax, but his purring ceased.

"You've never owned any pets?"

In all our visits, my friend had never stood this close before. I was conscious of every motion of his hands, every glance of his eyes, even his warmth.

"Not cats," he said, as if he'd not noticed a thing. "We had a pack of hunting dogs when I was a boy, but they weren't pets. Mother once kept finches. I was not overly fond of them."

"That may be your problem." The kitten wriggled, eager to set tiny paws on *terra firma* once more. And I needed to pull myself together. "Let me take him outside."

I opened the door and placed the cat on the top step. He hopped down to be with his siblings before the brass latch clicked again in place.

With a twinkle in his eyes, Roger indicated the flowers on my hat. "They're lovely."

"Oh, thank you." My cheeks flushed. I feigned interest in a nearby jar of what turned out to be calendula.

"One moment and I'll have your order ready."

I nodded. How would I even begin to say goodbye?

My apothecary retreated behind his shop's counter-top, putting proper distance between us once again. I gathered my courage with a shaky breath. I loved—I would miss—watching him work. He'd assembled a collection of jars and crocks and began to measure various ingredients for Mrs. H's usual order. At the opposite end of the counter, I approached a time-worn leather-bound volume entitled *Herbal* beside a wooden rack containing small bottles.

An old bottle read, *Artemisia * WORMWOOD*, bordered in filigree on a corroded foil label. Paper tags on cotton strings dangled from the necks of a few newer vials. On them were hand-written names. Pine. Lilac. Geranium. Rosemary. Belladonna. Deer's Tongue.

"Is it safe to open these?" I picked up Briar Rose.

"Yes. Just don't get any on your skin."

I uncapped the glass and lifted it to my nose. The concentrated floral smell danced delightfully but carried a bitter undertone of alcohol preservative.

"Blue Lotus?" I asked, picking up the next bottle. "Sounds intriguing."

"Ah. It has calming properties and was known to the ancient Egyptians for its hallucinogenic and aphrodisiac effects."

"Hmm." I set it down. "What's a gentleman doing with such a thing in his collection?"

"Only filling the occasional custom order, I assure you."

He winked, and I blushed, but I remembered my purpose today and sighed.

"Is something the matter?"

I shook my head. "It's nothing." My trembling fingers landed on the old book. I opened it, finding hand-written notes on the front papers, like a recipe for some tincture or tonic.

Roger glanced at me with concern on his often-inscrutable expression.

I flipped through yellowed pages, nearly two centuries old if I read the title plate correctly.

"What a charming book. The engravings alone are delightful. How did you come by such a treasure?"

"Well, it's been here in Father's shop for as long as I can remember. I think it was my grandmother's."

I found the section for Violas. *Heartsease,* printed in old letterpress, followed by a list of ailments it would alleviate. I didn't know my namesake was also medicine. I turned the page to another wood-cut illustration and the hand-written Latin name *Viola odorata.* The book might have predated even that classification system. A folded piece of loose paper fell from between the leaves. I held it up to the light of dim windows, discerning the faint outline of a pressed flower.

"Oh, this must have been here for ages. It's so delicate."

Roger left off his work and walked to me, though he wouldn't meet my eyes. I handed him the paper, and he frowned, placing it over an engraved illustration depicting wild violets.

"My sister collected it long ago. I'd forgotten it was there." His thoughts seemed a thousand miles away. Had I already managed to hurt his feelings? He shut the volume.

Roger turned and quietly re-shelved the book. I got the message. He didn't want any more company. I didn't want to make it any worse.

At that, I determined to abandon my task and be done with the entire business. I paced toward the door before he said, "Don't go. Please" He sighed. "It's just… Felicity took her own life. They say time heals all wounds, but it isn't true."

I turned around, mortified. "I'm so sorry. I know what you mean. Some things you never forget."

How was I so obtuse as to think I could relate to the loss of a sibling when I had none? I needed to make a graceful exit posthaste.

Roger's approaching footsteps brought me back.

He stood beside me. "Your order is almost ready. If you can wait a moment…" He wanted to say something else but didn't find the words.

I nodded, swallowing an ache that clawed its way up from my chest to my throat. A wave of emotion enveloped me, beautiful and terrible. I yearned to touch him, and wished he would hold me. I knew he saw it. Needing to flee, I took another step toward the door.

"Wait. Violet."

He caught my hand and slipped his bare fingers around my gloved ones. He had never before used my given name. Oh, that he would not have! The memory of it spoken in his resonant voice would become a new torment.

"Will you please tell me what's wrong? Have I offended you?"

"No, you haven't, Mr. Gale, but I…" My heart fluttered like a caged bird.

"You know, I look forward to our visits," he said. "More than perhaps I let on. I should have told you so before."

I fumbled in my shoulder bag for the blasted letter. "My father asked me to give this to you. And… I'm also here to deliver a dinner invitation."

He raised an eyebrow and took the offered envelope. I never noticed the thin band of paler flesh on his right ring finger before. I didn't recall him ever wearing a ring.

"You don't have to accept." I cleared my throat. "Father seems to think you're obligated to him because he knew your family. I know it's presumptuous. Father is ill and finds it difficult to leave the house these days; otherwise, he might simply have come here to harass you in person. The truth is, he

15

doesn't approve of our visits. I don't know what he wrote to you, but if it's half as rude as I expect, please accept my apologies in advance."

"Oh. I see." Roger tapped the wax seal on the envelope, before he tucked it, unopened, into an apron pocket. His expression grew cold.

"So, ah, listen… I, too, enjoy our visits. Very much so. But I respect my father's wishes, and if you want to see me again, you must speak with him. I don't know what he'll say, but it won't be pleasant. I'm sorry." My half-hearted grin only made me feel lower. "If you can't come, honestly, I'll understand. And I'm grateful… for everything."

He said nothing, but he stared at my hand in his.

"I'll give him your regrets." I wanted to escape before I did any more damage, but he held my hand fast, and I didn't have the heart to pull away.

"There's no reason for you to apologize. If your father was acquainted with my family, I should like to meet him. However, that's not the most important question."

"Oh?"

"Do *you* wish me to accept this invitation?"

I don't know why I didn't lie. "Yes."

"I would be honored to join you for dinner. Just say when."

"Don't you want to read the letter first?"

"No need."

"Sunday at four o'clock?"

He glanced upward for only an instant, as though calculating some unspoken cost. "I'll be there."

One way or the other, it was too late to turn back. If we played this game and lost, I would forfeit a friend. Truthfully, I already had. That was enough to kill any foolish hope which might have bloomed in this nearness to him, in the way he pressed my hand. Then he nodded and let it slip from his.

While Roger finished preparing my tea, I paced the shop's rows. Under the crinkle of brown wrapping paper, and the tread of my boots on creaky wooden floors, I heard a shuffling sound. Had another patron been lurking in the shop all the while, eavesdropping? I craned my neck to look over the shelves, searching for the source of the noise, but found nothing.

There it was again.

"Did you hear a noise?" I asked from across the room.

Roger shook his head. "Could be rats?"

"Excuse me?"

The sound—louder this time. A shuffling bump, coming from below, as if someone stirred in the basement. "Those would be rather large rats."

"So it seems." He resumed measuring scoops of dried herbs onto the brass scales with uncharacteristic haste. A sickening dread grabbed my gut when I realized it might be in my ears only. *Was that why he reacted so strangely? He can't hear anything.*

How long had it been since I heard a phantom noise? A disembodied voice? I thought I had been cured of that torment. But even as I stood, I was sinking down into some dark chasm, and the sound itched at the back of my brain.

I blinked. My inner vision showed a flash of gleaming white—like satin in the sunlight. No, it wasn't fabric, it was… a wild living thing. I rubbed my eyes, and a new headache threatened. Dizzy, I caught my balance on a nearby shelf, rattling the crockery. Whitened bones filled one glass jar. Small fragments, like the legs of animals, or perhaps fingers or toes. Printed on its label was a jagged rune encircled by a compass rose. The design seemed to crack with a warning. *Dreadful magic.*

That phantom sound broke the silence again. In my head or not, it pressed like a vice.

Roger bagged my order and strode out from behind the counter. He gestured to the door.

"I haven't paid you yet," I protested.

"We can settle up later." He wouldn't look at me. "I must go see what damage they may have caused."

"The rats?"

"Er, yes." In a rather poor attempt at courtesy, he swung open the door.

I grabbed my tea and brushed past him.

The taut muscles in his jaw—the way his eyes darted from mine—left me with the distinct impression he'd spoken an untruth. Had he read the letter and calculated I was not worth the trouble?

Stepping outside, I spied Maggie not three yards away, her posture guarded, ears back. "You should employ your friends here as ratcatchers. Make them earn their keep."

"Perhaps. Good day, Miss Morgen." He shut the door.

That was all. No 'See you Sunday,' or 'until we meet again,' or any other such nicety a woman might desire after offering her fearful heart on a dusty lace sleeve.

I turned with my aching head high, choosing to ignore the obvious— what Mrs. H called *positive presence.*

Maggie crouched at a street-level window, which must have connected to Roger's shop. She yowled, as I'd never seen her do. Light issued from one grimy pane of glass, the others having been painted opaque. When I spoke her name, Maggie hissed and ran away.

Bright white flashed behind my eyelids. I stumbled, grabbing the brick building for support, soiling my gloves. I tried to steady my labored breath. Thunder boomed across the bay. A massive headache pressed my skull.

What a fine time for an episode.

The sky darkened with impending rain, and I had no strength left to walk home. That meant I had little recourse but to hire a hansom cab or take the trolley. The latter thought sent a shiver down my spine.

Chapter 3
The Cards of Fate

own the road from Roger's shop, I waited for the trolley. Soon enough, a cacophony of metal wheels on steel tracks, tethered to overhead cables by insect-like antennae, came chuffing dirty breath. The infernal contraption vented a screeching hiss of steam and rumbled to a stop.

Other passengers boarded without pause, but I lingered until I forced myself up the dreaded steps. No lack of will could derail me from facing this old phobia of mine, nor my worsening headache, or the sting of electricity which somehow conducted itself into my hand through the support rail. I was determined to win just one minor battle that morning, or consign the whole day to another failure. I gritted my teeth and chose a seat beside a normal, unconcerned citizen before the iron cage jolted forward. Shops and carriages careened by—a jumble of umbrella-bearing pedestrians, ships, docks, harbor. All a foggy blur through the rain-obscured window, until an old nightmare slithered into view. My Shadow materialized on the pane of glass beside me, that foul manifestation of my disease—my personal holographic torment. It would not leave, even when I closed my eyes and whispered my mantra. *It's only fear. My mind will clear.*

Even with my eyes shut to ignore it, my headache was a knife like to split my skull in two. This was no use. I was going to be sick, and I couldn't do that in front of these people.

I stood up, grabbing a brass railing to keep from tumbling, and begged to be let off that farcical ride, claiming I'd forgotten something important.

It wasn't a lie. I'd forgotten I was a coward.

I made my disgraceful exit from the infernal machine. Quickening rain slicked cobblestone streets, deteriorating the state of my hat and clothing beyond any pretense of propriety. My sketchbook had remained dry enough in my leather bag, along with the day's packages. Another woman would have chided herself for such foolishness as I'd displayed on the trolley, but that would be a pointless waste of effort. At least I'd kept my breakfast down.

I hastened toward the shelter of a confectionary's striped awning, one of Mrs. H's favorite shops. I'd never been able to enter the place, of course, since my illness had deemed this doorway off-limits.

On a dry stone bench, I shook off my waterlogged hat, readjusted the soaked peonies, and wrung out my cape. I measured my breathing—a technique I'd found somewhat effective in combating such episodes. At the moment, the exercise only filled my lungs with the aroma of roasted toffee from the shop's forbidden interior. My headache raging, the less I moved, the better I could manage the pain. If only I'd brought along some of Roger's headache tonic.

Rain washed the road in windswept torrents. Gutters poured and tin rooftops rattled. Muddy water splashed under the wheels of passing carriages, the churning puddles too chaotic to reflect anything. Out in the bay, ships continued in their purpose, undaunted. Gray waves roiled below the heavy sky, mixing freshwater and salt. Did ocean fish taste the transition seeping down to their underwater domain?

Perhaps I could still hire a hansom cab if the rain did not let up soon. They'd never much frightened me. But such old-fashioned conveyances were fewer and farther between these days, replaced by wretched automobiles.

Would I ever change, or would I remain at the mercy of my fears forever?

A man in a black longcoat walked alongside the sea wall, one of several other pedestrians caught in this downpour. The man's long hair, tall build, and purposeful stride seemed familiar, though a large umbrella obscured his features. He noticed me and waited for a line of carriages to pass before he crossed the street.

Roger. The sight of him heading toward me did not engender the warmth in my soul that perhaps it might have on some other day.

"Mr. Gale." I stood.

He stopped just before my shelter, so as not to splash me with water from his umbrella, I suppose. Under a raindrop-misted wool coat, he wore a tweed waistcoat over a band-collared shirt. Now that he'd shed his ubiquitous shop's apron, I could see a gold watch chain draped from his waistcoat pockets. A black fedora hat looked newer than the rest of his ensemble; the latter, though it was well-tailored and handsome, seemed some years out of fashion.

"Violet. Please, may I join you here for a moment?" He gestured to the bench.

He spoke my given name again. Damn him.

"Were you following me?"

"No. Well, in truth, I was headed to your house, but I was lucky to spot you sitting here. I'm glad I found you. I must apologize for my earlier rudeness."

"And if I should ask you to leave?"

His shoulders slumped, hopeful expression transformed to one of resigned defeat, which pulled on my heart. "Then I would go."

Before he turned away, I placed a sodden glove on his dry coat-sleeve.

"Since you've found me, I might appreciate an escort home."

He nodded. "Good."

He joined me under the awning, shook off the umbrella, leaned it against the bench, and turned to me with hopeful eyes and that beguiling grin of his. "Your cape is soaked. Please, may I exchange it for my coat?"

"You're going to wear my cape?"

"Well, I am quite fond of capes."

Despite my miserable state, I laughed.

I unclasped the soggy velveteen. Roger slipped his dry longcoat over my damp shirtwaist. The warm wool carried a hint of his shop's aromatic spices.

He draped my cape over his arm. "Oh, I nearly forgot again. If you'll look in the right front pocket, there's something for you."

Between layers of black silk, I found a small box wrapped in brown paper and twine. "More tea?"

"Not exactly. A birthday gift. It's today, is it not?"

"Yes. But I don't celebrate such trivial things." *Too many bad memories.*

"So your Mrs. H told me. To be honest, I haven't celebrated a birthday in ages either, but for you, I couldn't resist. Perhaps another apology is in order?"

I smiled. "No. This is very kind, thank you."

"I meant to give it to you earlier, but I'm afraid my mind was elsewhere."

I'd already unwound the twine and torn the wrapping. The small paper-board box contained a pendant of natural rock crystal—clear as diamond, set with fine gold filigree, suspended from a thin chain. Mysterious symbols decorated the setting. I squinted but couldn't distinguish them well under the pressure in my aching head.

"This is…" *too much*, I wanted to say, but I swore some thread of illumination emanated from within the mineral, though it must have been only a trick of my eyes. "Beautiful." I laid it against my blouse and tried to fasten it behind my neck.

"Here… Allow me."

He fixed the clasp and tucked the chain below the ruffled lace collar of my shirtwaist. The light touch of his fingers on my skin evoked images such as a proper lady should not call to mind.

"What do the symbols mean?"

"They're an ancient magical language. Known only to a few. I have a book or two in my library. Perhaps you'd care to study them sometime?"

"Was that an invitation to your home?" I didn't like to talk about his superstitious ways, but for this thought, I'd forgive him.

"Hmm. We'll have to see how Sunday goes first." But he smiled, and it gave me foolish hope.

Wanting to change the subject, I touched the pendant and asked, "Do you sell these at your shop?"

I suspected it was some backward folk charm, but it was beautiful. Something about its design thrilled me, and seemed familiar, though I could not place it.

"No. This piece has been in my family for a long time. With little purpose until now."

"Oh. Surely, I can't accept this." Was he serious or exaggerating for my amusement? Still, it was a kind of him, though a bit lavish.

"Please do. You might say it spoke to me and wanted to be yours." He shifted his weight and clasped his hands together. Who was nervous now?

"In that case, I thank you, Roger, for this lovely gift." If he was going to use my first name, I would take the same liberty.

"You're welcome, Violet." The joy in his usually restrained expression was perhaps enough of an answer to my unspoken questions. Retrieving his umbrella, he presented his arm, and we stepped out into the rain.

It was not until after we'd crossed the street and found our path beside the seawall, that I noticed my headache had subsided. Water cascaded over our umbrella, drumming a symphony on black oilcloth, veiling the way before us. With myself wrapped in his wonderful coat, Roger walked at a scandalous proximity, so that I had enough shelter to stay dry, despite how inappropriate it might look to public eyes.

I was a fool for not telling him this was hopeless. For not turning him and his gifts away before things got worse. I was selfish, because being with him felt so good.

When we neared Crestfield Park, the rain dissipated. Dolphins and water nymphs frolicked in the central fountain, although the storm had driven away their usual audience. Only a group of pelicans perched in windswept cedars. Roger closed the umbrella, and they took flight into a calmer sky, dark clouds broken by azure.

We neared the little hillside borough where I lived, visible now from our vantage point. Terrain sloped upward, from the gravel road beside the seawall to an elm-shaded lane of Victorian homes. Old society ladies they were, skirted in porches, crowned with diminutive turrets, and bedecked with gingerbread trim. Human progress had yet spared them the invasion of electricity and telegraph poles which went up like mad eagles' nests in town. No doubt it was only a matter of time.

We trekked uphill through an orchard that bordered our neighborhood, past an old standing stone I'd often sketched. The hillside menhir, eroded and covered in lichens, must have stood sentry for thousands of years. Such monuments made by ancient ancestors dotted our island, dedicated to long forgotten gods.

I caught my breath in the shade of an apple tree—its branches low with ripening fruit. Asters and goldenrod shed drops of rain, their fragrance earthy and alive. My headache, dulled though it was, echoed my elevated pulse.

Roger leaned the umbrella on the split-rail fence and tucked a lock of hair behind an ear—a nervous habit of his I found so endearing.

"Violet, there are things about me… I should like to explain. They will take some time. Perhaps after dinner on Sunday we might speak in private."

I wasn't sure how to answer. I didn't expect him to stick around that long, or that Father would let this friendship continue. My eyes darted down the drive toward my home, still obscured by a row of elms. I hugged Roger's coat tighter to me as a sea breeze crested our hill.

He stepped closer. "I am… afraid you may not like what I have to tell you. You won't think of me in the same way after you learn my secrets, but… you must know my past if we're to have any future together."

"Are we?" I asked. "I mean…" I exhaled a shaky breath, glancing at the soaked hems of my skirts.

"Well, you did invite me to dinner." A nervous grin before he shook his head and added, "I'm sorry. The truth is, I think highly of you. And often. You're a dear friend, regardless of anything more. I wish to share who I am with you. I would lay all my cards at your feet for you to read as you will."

"Fair enough."

Anything more. Was it possible someone as normal, and charming, as Mr. Roger Gale had feelings for me? Or was he only playing with my heart, like the last person who had said such sweet words, before they soured? My pulse sped. My cheeks flushed, though the chilly wind might have been sufficient excuse.

"You're not going to tell me you're married, are you? Estranged from a wretched match forced upon you by cruel fate? Anything of that sort?" I saw no ring on his hand where I'd noticed the pale mark before.

"No." He almost laughed. "I'm not married. Nor have I ever been."

He edged a little nearer. I didn't back away. Alone on this rain-washed stretch of road, we had only apple trees for witness. More the scandal if anyone should happen by, but I didn't care.

"I might also share a few secrets of my own," I said. "I'm... *unwell.* I've lived through... some difficult things." I'd shared some of my struggles with mental health, but he did not know I'd been hospitalized. No one knew the dark visions which haunted me. I was not so pure and innocent a shrinking flower as my namesake. "You may not like what I must tell you either, Mr. Gale. In fact, I'd be surprised if some of it isn't written in that letter from Father. Did you read it?"

"Not yet. I'm saddened to hear you speak so of yourself, but... I don't believe there is anything you or he can say which would change my opinion of you."

"You're sure?"

"Quite." He inched closer.

My heart nearly fled my chest. I gulped for air and smelled the spice which always clung to him. I didn't look away from those eyes, green as the storm-shadowed hills. He touched my cheek, with so light a caress it made my breath catch, before he kissed me. I lost all awareness of self, but for the place where our lips connected. I could have been floating, weightless. He tasted like a forbidden wine, imbued with a yearning for an unknown home.

Too soon, he broke the spell and whispered beside my cheek. "I'd better walk you the rest of the way home."

My pulse throbbed... everywhere. Even in places where it had no good business. A new, though not unpleasant, sensation flooded my nervous system on quickened blood. I felt strong enough to run. I'd not been well enough for such a thing in years.

"I'll be fine." No doubt, I smiled like an idiot. "My house is just up the road." I pointed down the shady lane, my hand shaking. "I'd rather go on alone, if you don't mind."

My arrival with Roger's escort would require obligatory social niceties. Mrs. H would want to invite him in for tea. He would likely be expected to greet my ailing father, and that might ruin everything.

Roger nodded. Perhaps he understood more than I intended.

Insisting he take back his coat, I draped my damp cape over an arm and traveled the lonely gravel drive toward our private acres. Only once or twice did I turn to see him walking down the hill.

Through the wooden gate to our property, the latch clicked behind me, and I exhaled. Once again, I was safe where I belonged. I greeted our two horses in their summer pasture beside our small carriage house, where our butler, Mr. Travers, had a second-story apartment. Their whinnies, bright eyes, and soft noses always calmed me. I fed them sprigs of out-of-reach clover. Not until I'd ascended our creaky front porch steps did I realize I'd never heard a satisfactory explanation of what real trouble in Roger's basement caused him to shove me out his shop's door with a lie.

Perhaps the noise had only been in my head.

Bewildered, exhausted, and over the moon, I sat in our kitchen, wrapped in a dry blanket over wet clothes, drinking a cup of Roger's tea. I held the crystal pendant to the late afternoon light. The mineral's natural geometry, grown inside the earth, fascinated me. Strange motifs circled the gold setting. A *magical language*, he had said. Ridiculous. Yet it pulled at my imagination like a forgotten dream.

Worse than that, I was now obsessed with a man who harbored secrets. Things he promised to confess, which he swore would damage my views of him once revealed. Perhaps he was as mad as me. Fitting.

But that kiss. *Damn.* I'd never been kissed like that in my life. Granted, there were scant few in my frame of reference, but I couldn't stop thinking about it.

My musings were cut short by Mrs. H's return from one of her society meetings.

Sighing, I tucked the crystal pendant below my damp shirtwaist, so only a hint of the gold chain was visible.

Agnes opened the door to the kitchen, humming an old folk tune like a hymn. She'd styled her silver hair in a fancy chignon and wore sea foam green day dress—one she'd sewn herself. Her black hat laden with guinea feathers proved a smart complement.

"Dear me, you were caught in the rain, I see." She planted both hands on sturdy hips. "What else happened, eh?" A knowing gleam shone in her eyes.

"Not a thing." I gulped my tea to hide a foolish grin.

She laughed, unpinned her hat, and hung it on the kitchen's apron rack. She was glad when I told her Mr. Gale was coming on Sunday, and we didn't speak of Father's rude insistence that I deliver his letter that morning. Over tea, she filled me in on the latest gossip from her Suffragette's Assembly. Like always, she invited me to the next meeting, and as always, I declined, though even to my own ears, my dedication to avoiding all social events was wearing thin. Afterward, she asked me to follow her upstairs.

Under the eaves on the third floor, Agnes had carved out a sewing nook, while my art studio bordered a southeast window for more light. Here, on a treadle-powered sewing machine (the sight of which still gave me unease), she crafted much of her wardrobe and a few pieces of mine. When she was young, she'd been a seamstress for a living, and still took on the occasional commissioned job.

I had paid little attention to her latest project, other than a cursory glance, when she tucked a few strands of moss between the layers of green and black tartan. She'd even placed a row of gossamer bees' wings between the folded hems. I'd guessed her client must also have been eccentric.

My side of the attic was filled with dusty canvases. These days, I spent most of my painting time with my few remaining students on the first floor in our converted music room, or in the garden when we painted *en plein air*. I'd largely neglected my own art for years. That had all changed when I met my Muse a few months ago. Now a new still life was clipped to my easel, full of bright color and captured light.

Mrs. H gestured for me to follow her past a worktable laden with bolts of muslin and broadcloth. She lifted an old bedsheet away from one of her dress forms—this one adjusted to fit my own measurements not long ago when I needed a new painting smock. Today the humble mannequin wore an evening dress and jacket in a green and black plaid, trimmed with velvet. The skirt had a modest gathering of pleats toward the back, following the latest fashion lines.

"What do you think?" She clasped her hands together. "It's for you, dear."

"Oh, Agnes. This is too wonderful! But you know I don't celebrate my birthday."

"It's just an ordinary gift. The timing's all coincidence."

She refused to let me reimburse her for the materials, on the condition that I wear it this coming Sunday. I wrapped her in a hug, heedless of my rain-dampened clothing.

"But you'll have to tell me why you included bees' wings in my new ensemble, of all things."

She laughed. "I suppose that does seem strange, doesn't it?"

"A bit, yes."

"Well, it was something your mother taught me to do when you were small."

"My mother?" I had once found a crushed dragonfly's wing under the lining of a school jacket when I'd torn a sleeve on a thorn bush.

"Well, she was one of the Mystic Sisterhood, though it went by another name back then."

"Of course." It was a fact of Mother's life I liked to forget. Her faith in the supernatural might have comforted her, but it had not saved her from a withering death.

Agnes sat on the edge of her desk and sighed. "Oh, we miss Helena still, I'll tell you. Your mother had her own special way with the spirits. I always said she had a touch of the psychic too. Now, when she explained this charm of protection to me, I'll grant you I'd never heard of anything quite like it before, but then again, I know little of the old arts from the continent, being born and raised here on the island, you see. And your mother being foreign, I took it to be a custom of her kinfolk. Anyhow, it gave her joy to do that for you when you were a babe. Later on, when she took ill and hired me to help around here, she showed me how to find the feral hives and collect discarded wings. I used to put them in your school clothes until you grew too old to want handmade things. Now, when I started this dress, I just thought it would be nice to do that for her again."

A hall table laden with old photographs stood beside Father's second-floor library. Most of the tintypes and daguerreotypes were of people I'd never met, their faces amber in the gaslight of a flickering wall sconce. Circus performers and acquaintances of my parents from their performing days. No family other than the circus, so Father always said. No doubt most, if not all, were dead.

"Father, may I speak with you for a moment?" My hand rested on the glass doorknob.

"Yes, please come in."

The sound was like the rustle of parchment. Torn and cracked with age. I remembered a time before his health waned when his voice had been hale and robust.

I took a seat across from where he perched in his favorite reading chair, surrounded by stacks of books. Behind him was a framed poster from his past. *Errol the Astounding* read the scrolling caption above a cartoon rendering of Father's long-ago stage persona, an escape artist breaking free of iron chains. As I expected, he finished the page, one finger hovering to guide failing eyes.

I slipped out of my house shoes and rested my feet on the settee. A crackling fire warmed the library. Outside mullioned windows, twilight neared. The rain had cleared, and the remaining clouds refracted dwindling sunlight—each drop of moisture a prism to divide this liminal light into full spectrum, before the heavens faded to blue-black. Venus twinkled above the ocean's dark horizon. In the distance, Seastone's lighthouse beamed. That illuminated pulse brightened and dimmed as its lens turned in a fixed orbit, just as Galileo's moons of Jupiter waxed and waned, revealing their first secrets of motion those centuries ago.

Father set his book aside. He pushed a pair of spectacles up his nose and faced me, shrunken hands folded on a lap blanket. His blue eyes had once been full of fire—another reason he'd drawn the crowds in his circus days. Now his wan features were perpetually shrouded in melancholy.

"Did you deliver my invitation to this Mr. Gale, the *apothecary*?" The disdainful way he spoke the words gave me little hope this meeting might yet be salvaged.

"Yes."

"What was his response?"

"Mr. Gale… didn't read the letter when I was there, but he accepted. He'll be here on Sunday."

A grumble. "It seems he and I have much to discuss. That the man will consort with my daughter before even speaking to me does not bode well for his character."

"There's been no *consorting* of any kind." I swallowed, wondering at how quickly the lie had escaped my lips. "I visit his shop to pick up tea. Mr. Gale and I have only pleasant conversations."

"Of course you do." His sigh became a miserable cough. He covered his mouth with a threadbare handkerchief. "Furthermore, it isn't safe for you to travel alone in town. Have our butler drive you from now on."

"I'm a grown woman, Father. This is a new century. I can choose where I go, or whom I see."

He slipped off his spectacles to rub his temples. I didn't expect my words had reached him. "Something else troubles you today. What is it?"

I couldn't tell him that my world had turned on its axis to face a terrifying new dawn.

"Today, I attempted to ride the trolley."

"And?"

"And… I failed, again. I don't understand why I can't control these phobias of mine. As much as I *choose* to. Why am I full of such contrary foolishness? I know you can't give me an answer, but…"

"Why do you ask? If you think I have no answer?"

"Perhaps I just wanted you to know I tried."

He shifted forward in his chair, hands clasped together. "It's well you tried, my daughter, but one day you'll have to accept your limitations. Some things in this world are simply not within your grasp. To each of us, the cards of fate are dealt at our birth. Yours have been... *difficult* in this life. I'm sorry, but I can't change it."

"I... I understand."

I stared at the floorboards and the Persian rug. As a child, I would imagine grotesque faces in the abstract floral design—would trace the red and black lines with my small fingers. They would infect my nightmares.

With a shaking hand, Father reached for his cane. "Violet, I only want what's best for you. I didn't always make the wisest choices, but I won't be around forever. You must become strong enough to survive on your own. It's a terrible world sometimes. And you will always be... at a disadvantage. I don't want to see you hurt by another man. That is all."

"The world can be beautiful, too." I couldn't smile.

He stood on unsteady legs, leaning on his cane. "How long has it been since we went up to the cupola to view the stars?"

"Far too long." I sprang from the settee and grabbed two coats from a nearby wardrobe. "It may be cold tonight."

"They'll be all the clearer."

CHAPTER 4
WINDOWS THROUGH TIME

hen Sunday arrived, Agnes set me to work sculpting radishes into roses while she tended to her roast and its accoutrement. At length we heard a carriage drive up, and I was rushed away from the kitchen to make myself presentable before I could greet my gentleman caller like the proper lady I was not.

Roger stood in the parlor, sans coat and hat, looking sharp in a white band-collar shirt, blue and yellow patterned cravat, and a slate gray waistcoat. He held a bow-topped basket in his hands. I caught him studying one of my paintings before I descended the stairway.

"I'm a little surprised you came," I said. "Thank you."

His raised eyebrow and playful smirk told me he knew I wasn't, in fact, surprised. "Despite whatever else I may be, I'm a man of my word."

There he went again, hinting at something I wouldn't like about him. Perhaps Father's antagonistic view of Mr. Gale or his family had grounds. A sobering thought.

"Is this Mrs. H's latest order?" I asked, pointing to the basket in his hands.

"No, it's for you. Although he might be the luckiest of the parties involved."

"He?"

I heard an unmistakable mew. I peered inside to find my favorite black kitten from Maggie's litter. The creature stared up at us and mewed before he jumped; I caught the squirming ball of fur in mid-air.

"Don't you recognize me, little one? Your friend from the alley."

30

Green-gold cat's eyes met mine, tiny paws velveted. The cat perched on my forearm against my chest, seemingly more at ease.

"Have you decided upon a name for him yet?"

I tickled behind the kitten's ear. "I can think of only one. Puck."

"Ah. Why not Oberon?"

"This one's a trickster. Definitely Puck."

"Well, Puck, I wish you all the best with your new mistress."

When Roger petted the kitten, I noticed a gold band on his right hand. The ring was set with a round black stone, like onyx; into that were recessed four small diamonds at the stone's perimeter, outlining a square or perhaps the arms of a cross.

"Your ring. I've never seen you wear it before."

"I usually have it with me, though I wear it only for special occasions." He gestured to my new ensemble. "On that note, you look lovely tonight, Miss Morgen."

I knew this charming trick of his. Give an evasive answer and change the topic. I would have pressed him further if Puck hadn't chosen that moment to leap from my arms into a nearby chair. The tiny creature scrambled across the parlor and disappeared behind an old harpsichord. Roger insisted he was just taking in his new surroundings, and I resolved myself to let him explore while I listened for anything crashing.

When I thanked him, Roger said, "Of course I did clear it by your Mrs. Holstead first. She's been so enthusiastic about this plot, I half expected you'd already know the surprise."

I had my doubts as to exactly which part of this scheme Mrs. H favored, given her previous aversion to wharf cats. The curtains along one wall fluttered as in a wave, disturbed by tiny kitten steps.

I gestured to a sofa across the parlor, and we took a seat. What did the distance he placed between us reveal? Not but two hand-spans apart. Even now, his closeness kindled a fire within me like I had never felt before. *Damn it all.* I looked away.

From the side-table, Roger picked up a silver-framed tintype. The likeness etched on the shining metal was of a young woman sitting in an ornate chair in front of some traveling photographer's backdrop. She wore a feathered hat and what I thought of as her favorite dress—far more decent than any of the circus costumes she'd worn for other photos, the ones Father kept on his desk.

"Your mother?"

I nodded. "This was taken before I was born."

"The family resemblance is strong. She is beautiful, like her daughter."

"You were admiring a landscape." I glanced at my artwork on the tangent wall, distracting myself from his proximity, the smell of spice which clung to his hair and clothing, and any more memories.

He set down Mother's photograph. "Truly, the artist was inspired."

"Did you know it was one of mine?"

He smiled again, enjoying himself.

"You could at least be honest. No need to flatter me unnecessarily, Mr. Gale."

"Unnecessarily?" He raised an eyebrow.

Before I could formulate an intelligible retort, he pointed. A feline ear emerged from underneath the skirt wrapped around one of the harpsichord's legs, only to disappear again.

"Come away farther." Roger took my hand, and we stood. "It might give him courage."

We made our way to my painting. Considering his impression carefully, Roger said, "The light intensifies in the center here—reflected in the sky. The artist is fond of this view." His eyes settled on a rowan tree I'd rendered in bright brushstrokes. An impossible mixture of the seasons—chartreuse leaves, red berries, white flowers, and silvery bark against the indigo swirls of imminent storm.

"My mother was never so happy as when we visited the Welterwood. Naturally, I've returned many times, although it's been a while. Do you know this spot?"

He shook his head. "I haven't set foot on Welterwood soil in many years."

"Oh, perhaps I shall take you there. It's such a lovely view from that hill. In spring, violets cover the entire clearing. Mother said she named me after them, in fact." Then I remembered I might not see him again after tonight.

"I'm sorry, but I can't go there with you, not even to see such wonders." Roger pinned me with sorrow-filled eyes. Then he knew it too—that this was the end. "I cannot travel into her forest. It was a punishment given to me long ago."

"*Her* forest?" Not what I expected. Did he mean his sister? I thought of the pressed violet I'd found in his book.

"The Welterwood belongs to the Queen of the Fae."

"The Fae?" I breathed a nervous laugh. "You're joking. But you can tell me the truth, you know."

"I am."

Nonplussed, I rested hands on my corseted hips. "So, you believe in fairies, Mr. Gale?"

"I most certainly do. Don't you?"

"Oh, won't you just be serious for a moment?"

"I *am* serious. They're real as you and I. Your Mrs. H believes in them."

Was he hurt? Or was he avoiding something with this vile distraction? Either way, I didn't like it.

I shook my head. "Agnes believes all sorts of nonsense. For as long as I've known her, she's practiced some odd folk magic or another. When I was a child, she had me believing fairies lived inside every flower and gnomes under every stone. I've since grown up, but if that fantasy still makes her happy, what business is it of mine?"

"Indeed." He frowned, agitated.

Now why did I feel so guilty? Perhaps I was being a touch dismissive of her—of *their*—religion or whatever it was.

"Did she make this?" He pointed to the top of a mullioned bay window. There beside a cracked pane, which we'd never fixed, perched a small wagon wheel Agnes had woven from straw, grapevine, and beads. She placed it there years ago, after a crow flew into the glass one evening as I sat reading. It had fallen to the ground outside the window, flapping horrible black wings and crying, before it found the strength to fly away. She'd called it a bad omen, and the spell she made was to counter it.

"Yes." I sighed, trying to shake my misgivings. "Well, her peculiarities are harmless, anyway. Father tolerates them because Mrs. H does so much for us, and she's so wonderful, it's easy to overlook her flaws. I mean, she even put bees' wings into the hem of this dress." I gave a nervous laugh, slipping my gloved hands along the tartan fabric. "But it's lovely work, and I'm grateful, nonetheless."

Why did I feel terrible? It was my mother's custom, after all.

"Flaws. Is that how you view her beliefs?"

It stung to see the hurt in those gorgeous eyes of his, knowing I was the cause.

"I… didn't mean that." Well, damn. I turned away, feeling like a small-minded idiot.

Roger stared at the floorboards and nudged a loose nail with the tip of his shoe. "Does it bother you that I believe in magic? That I practice it?"

"I… uh… don't know." I couldn't think of anything nice to say. I knew what the man was all along. Some kind of modern-day witch doctor. I'd allowed him to think it didn't matter because I'd held him at such an impossible distance. He was an unattainable dream. Just my friend. My eccentric Muse. Then he'd kissed me, and it felt too good. Now that he was here, in my parlor, I had to face the truth. It mattered what he believed. It bothered me.

I hadn't expected that.

The dinner bell rang from the kitchen, and he beamed a sardonic grin. "Perhaps we can continue this conversation later." Though he didn't sound like he would enjoy it. "Please lead the way."

Like a gentleman, if he wasn't mocking me, he bowed and gestured toward the hall.

As we left the parlor, out of the corner of my eye, I caught a tiny shadow. Puck darted around the base of a pedestal stand, crept along one wall of bookshelves, and followed.

Mrs. H and Travers refused to dine with us, though in our household, we'd long since abandoned the pretense of separating staff from employer at mealtimes. The four of us usually took our meals in the kitchen, when Father was able to move about the house and didn't eat in his room. That evening, with only the two of us seated beside our guest, the display felt dishonest in its representation of who we were, despite adherence to propriety.

Father was kind enough to allow us wine and hors d'oeuvres before the interrogation began with a basic inquiry into Roger's vocation and education, for which Roger was only a little evasive. He had hinted to me before of his studies overseas, though I was surprised to hear he'd studied medicine in London.

"I was sorry to learn of old Eustace's death." My father said.

So, he was on a first-name basis with Roger's father? Why hadn't I ever heard of this?

"I take it the two of you were well-acquainted?" Roger no doubt had similar questions to my own.

"I knew him not as well as some, but better than others, you could say." Father sliced a tomato with a silver knife, his hand noticeably jittering. Gimlet-eyed, he continued. "Only once did he ever mention he had a son. The topic pained him greatly."

Roger nodded and shifted in his seat. "My father and I had never been on good terms. I stayed away from home most of my adult life, at his request. I returned only three years ago to be with him at the end. We made peace, though it could never be enough."

"Hmph," Father stroked his gray goatee. If he understood something, I knew none of it. "What are your intentions with my daughter, Mr. Gale?"

"Sir, I wish to court her if she would like me to do so."

It wasn't lost on me that Roger phrased it that way. That he didn't say, *if you agree to let her* court me. It wasn't lost on Father, either.

"You will do *nothing* with her if I don't allow it, Mr. Gale. You have not yet finished answering my questions."

Surprised at my brashness, I interrupted. "No. I enjoy Mr. Gale's company. If I choose to see him, or *anyone*, that's my business, and mine alone." Blood drummed my temples. My hands trembled. I gripped the linen napkin below the table like a severed lifeline.

"You are not...." Father tried to lower the anger in his voice, but he trembled as he pointed at me. "Violet, you do not understand. There are elements at work here to which you are not privy."

"Such as?" This was madness.

"You will be silent, my daughter!" His hands shook. I could not remember ever seeing him in such a state.

Father held his dinner knife up, like a throwing dagger from one of his old stage acts. "Tell me the truth, Mr. Gale. Are you a member of the Reliqua, like your father?"

Roger took a sip of wine and set the glass down before he answered. "Yes."

"As I suspected. Then your true interest in Violet is not so noble, now, is it?"

"I'm sorry? What are you insinuating, sir?"

"You know exactly what I mean. I'm acquainted well enough with the laws that govern your order to know you have only sorrow to offer her. Your father Eustace did a great service for me and my Helena once, when Violet was young. That's why I'm willing to give you this warning. Stay away. You'll have nothing more to do with my daughter, do you understand? We've broken no laws."

"Father, what in God's name are you talking about? What laws?"

Ignoring me completely, Father continued. "I will not have you or another of your kind sniffing around here like dogs. My daughter may be weak—her mind may be broken. Even so, she is smarter than your lies. Sorcerers and petty conjurers. You feed on fear." He glanced at me, and I wondered how much of this tirade was for my own ears, as punishment for my defiance. All of it, surely. He shook a fist at Roger. "You don't know how to win the love of an audience. I never had to convince them my magic was real. They *wanted* to believe the dream. They knew that's all it was, but for those few moments I set them free. That's the true magic. You lot—have abased it."

"I'll tell you what I can't believe," said Roger, no less shaken than on fire with indignation. "That you would call your daughter *broken* to her face. She is... the most beautiful person I have ever known. Perhaps you should care about her love, as much as you care about your long-gone audience."

Father flinched at that, but I didn't think it was genuine remorse.

Roger continued, "Furthermore, it's unseemly… no, it's downright sinister to keep her so in the dark. To let her believe she's ill. To allow her to suffer so needlessly. *That* is madness. If you don't tell her the truth. I will."

Father grabbed his cane and stood, shaking. "*You* know nothing of what her mother and I sacrificed for her. You will leave, sir, on your father's honor, and never come back. Do you understand? You'll never speak to my daughter again. She won't fall prey to your lies. Violet, I forbid you to see this man again."

"No. You can't simply *forbid* me—" I balled a fist and bit my lip. If I said any more, I would scream.

"What *lies* have I told her, Mr. Morgen? Tell me. Tell us—" He gestured to me. "Why is every nail, hinge, and doorknob in this house—even your housekeeper's keys—made of bronze or tin and not iron? Why do four laurel trees grow at the perfect cardinal points around your home? Why are bees' wings sewn into Violet's clothing? Why are—"

"I'll hear no more of this! Mr. Travers, please escort our guest to the door."

Roger stood and tossed his napkin on the table. "There is no need." Fire raged in his eyes. Yet for me they reserved pity. "Good evening, Miss Morgen." Then he turned and walked toward the vestibule.

Despite the look of stern admonition from my father, I stormed after him.

A staunch-faced Mr. Travers handed our guest his coat and hat and opened the door. Roger met my eyes for an instant but proceeded down our front steps without a word. How callous of him. Anger, as well as despair, saturated my veins.

"Wait!" I caught up with him on the path leading to his waiting carriage, a fine two-horse Brougham.

He stopped when I laid a hand on his coat sleeve. I could feel his body full of sublimated tension. He exhaled a ragged breath.

"You can't just leave," I said. "You owe me an explanation."

"I know, but you won't like to hear it." His eyes were reddened.

"What does it matter if you're leaving?" I blinked back my own tears.

He asked his driver to stand by.

I felt like a wiser Daphne, leading a too-hesitant Apollo into the angled shade of one of those laurel trees he'd mentioned—as though they signified something important. Yet they were just trees.

"Violet, Mr. Morgen is right in one thing. I shouldn't see you again. If it will cause such division in your family, I cannot…" He glanced at the sky, as though hoping the words would come to him. An innocent enough expression, but it gave me chills. "I'm sorry that I ever…"

My thoughts spun. My heart sped. "No, I'm the one who should apologize. I didn't expect tonight would be quite this disastrous." I exhaled, clenching a fist against my fluttering nerves. "Will you tell me what great *Truth* has been hidden from me, which both you and Father know, while I'm left in the dark?"

"It's not that simple."

"Of course not. Nothing worthwhile ever is."

"The truth often hurts."

I couldn't hold back the sarcastic laugh. "Don't you think I know that? I'm not so naïve, Mr. Gale." I gestured toward a path shaded by hemlock branches. "Will you come and sit with me in the garden, if this is to be the last time we speak?"

He nodded, jaw clenched, before he said. "Lead the way."

We entered a wooden arched gate overgrown by Mother's roses. They'd finished blooming, but for a few stubborn holdouts. Soon enough, Agnes would collect the fruit to make rose hip syrup. I led Roger down a path I knew as well as the flow of my favorite sable brush. My mother's dahlia beds I tended in her memory. The lilacs and peonies were now past bloom. Chrysanthemums and bush daisies still held their color. Daffodil and narcissus bulbs slept underground to awaken in spring. A young rowan tree, which my mother planted long ago, still bore clusters of red berries, behind an angel statue Father added after she died. Roger and I walked by a marble and brass sundial—its shadow lengthened. The sun would soon disappear beyond the inland hills.

On a stone bench beside towering sunflowers, now gone to birdseed, we sat, shielded from view of the house. Roger removed his hat and faced me from a closer distance than had existed between us in the parlor. If I wasn't furious, I would have reached for him, because I could sense he longed to do the same.

I steeled my nerves with a deep breath. "Tell me. What is this Reliqua and what does it have to do with Father?"

"I don't know what dealings your father had with mine, but doubtless it involved your mother. The Reliqua is… We are a society of warrior magicians sworn to protect the balance between this human world and the Otherworld—the realm of Faerie, though it has many other names. Our Houses are found in every country, and our generations reach back into the origins of mankind's civilization."

"So, I see." I crossed my arms in front of my chest, wishing it were not so cold, but it was more than the weather which chilled my blood. "You're a group of crazy people, like Mrs. H's Mystical Sisterhood. What does any of this nonsense have to do with me? Or my mother? Was she part of this coven of yours?"

"No. Not exactly. Your father has hidden something important from you. In doing so, he's caused you harm." He faced the ground before he turned to me with pleading eyes. "There's no easy way to tell you this. Nor should I be the one to do so, but I must. Violet, you are only half-human. Your mother was a Fae of the Royal Courts. Some call them the Tuatha de Danan. They call themselves, among other names, the Sídhe."

"A Fae? You mean a *fairy*?" *Oh, merciful heavens... Was he really this cruel?* Maybe Father was right. I wiped a hand over my eyes.

"Yes. This is the truth of your heritage. Your Fae blood is the reason you've always believed you were ill. The reason you fear coming into town. The reason you can't cross certain thresholds. If they have iron above the doorframe—"

"What? *Iron*? You mean like a horseshoe or a nail? That old wives' tale?"

"Precisely. Your body knows cold iron is poisonous and responds with physical warning signs. Because you don't understand what you are, you mis-interpret this as a nervous episode—or an irrational phobia. You believe your-self to be weak, when in fact these are symptoms only of your strength. The tea blends I made for you... they were designed to help you cope with the harmful effects of living near human civilization. I'll wager they've helped, have they not?"

"You're honestly saying I'm not *human*?" I stood and paced. This disgust-ing distraction must not continue. "My mother wasn't a *fairy*. She was just a sickly, sad woman—like me. And she died too young. How could you..."

He stood alongside me. "Violet, I mean no insult to you or your mother."

I wanted to slap that smug, gorgeous face of his, but I balled a fist. "There are far kinder ways of getting rid of me. You don't have to spew such hurtful lies. You don't have to mock me—"

Roger was making fun of my worst qualities—my *mad flights of fancy*, as Father called them, before he'd sent me away to any hospital or doctor who promised a cure—just as Bryce had declared, after he'd charmed me into his bed with false promises, that he would have nothing further to do with a lunatic.

There was no better way to hurt me.

"No, I am not. I would never belittle your suffering. I swear."

"Did Father tell you I was insane, in that blasted letter of his? That I'm ruined? Did he inform you I'd been locked away in a lunatic asylum? That I saw things… in mirrors? In my dreams? That I sometimes hear voices? Aren't you getting rid of a terrible mistake? It wouldn't benefit your reputation, or your business prospects, if you married a lunatic, now would it, Mr. Gale?"

Married. I shouldn't have said that. It was a scar still I bore from years ago. I threw my shaking hands into the air as in defeat, but they fell to the sides of my lovely new skirt, and I clenched a fist around the smooth fabric— as if that were all the comfort I needed.

"No. It's not—" Roger's face looked ashen, eyes pleading, as though he also was in turmoil.

"And think of my children. They'd be crazy as their mother, no doubt. Isn't it fortuitous to have discovered this now, before it's too late?" Those unexpected words of mine sounded like something Bryce might have told me. I couldn't take them back. It was just as well.

Roger reached for me. I pushed him away.

"I promise," he said. "None of this is a lie. This is the truth you wanted." He exhaled a shaky breath. "I'm afraid there's more you must hear."

Tears glossed his cheeks. Did he believe any part of this fantasy to be actual fact, or had his conscience manifested some genuine regret for harming me now?

"The Otherworld magic I serve exacts a heavy toll on humans. We are given much power, but with it comes much responsibility. I am…"

"I don't need to hear any more. You've made your point clear." I drank the cold night into my lungs, as if the pressure might numb the pain.

"Violet, I am one hundred and seven years old. I've seen and done many things in this long life which cause me continual sorrow. Yet, finding you I shall never regret. You have reawakened my heart."

That was it. He was as crazy as me. It cut to the quick. It also repulsed me, hypocritical as the impulse was in the bosom of a fellow lunatic. If he was this out of touch with reality, what hope was there for us? At least I knew my dark visions were only illusion.

I shook my head before I reached to caress his youthful cheek. He leaned into my touch. Because it was our last moment together, I combed the naked fingers of my other hand through sinuous locks of his hair, darker than oiled walnut, from the pulse at his temple, behind his shapely ear. I'd daydreamed the very thing since we'd met. The actual sensation did not disappoint—perverse torture though the memory would soon become. He closed his eyes, tears glistened under thick eyelashes. I almost wanted to believe him, so I would not need to hate him.

"I'm not blind, or so gullible, Mr. Gale. You can't be much more than thirty years old. Anyone with eyes can see that. There is no such thing as magic. Fairies only exist in bedtime stories. The real world is a cruel and terrible place. I know something of this truth, despite my only twenty-seven years. Therefore, you must either have lost your own mind completely, or… you are a heartless liar." I swallowed the kiss I could not plant on his lips. "One or the other. I can't love either. I want you to go."

"Heartless? You called me your Muse once. Is that all I was to you, Violet? Aside from my looks, you hate everything about me, don't you? My magic. My profession. My view of the world. Have we ever been friends, or was I just a pleasant distraction?"

I pulled away. "After what you just said to me, you've no right—"

"Don't I? Do you know how many years it's been since I've kissed someone like that? Do you think it means nothing to me?"

I turned to hide my face. He laid a hand on my shoulder, but I shrugged him off. "Mr. Gale. I think… we should not see each other again."

A cold sea breeze rustled the forested hills. I wiped away tears, but I didn't turn around to look at him again.

Roger remained for a silent moment, before he said, "Goodbye, Violet."

He returned to his waiting carriage. I followed from a distance only to the garden gate, stood and watched him say a word to the driver, board and disappear.

Pulled by two dappled horses, the brougham cast its lantern light down the road into a mournful gloaming.

The sun set. I lingered in my garden as stars appeared before tear-glazed vision. Roger had forgotten his top hat on the bench. I sat beside it and drew a linen handkerchief from the velvet-trimmed jacket Agnes had made for me and dabbed my cheeks. Before I returned inside, I would collect my wits. She didn't need to see how much I'd been unsettled.

A pleasant distraction, he'd said. He was right. This relationship had always been doomed, but I led him on, because I enjoyed his company, flawed and delusional though the man was. I was as cruel to him as Bryce had been to me. Well, perhaps not quite so cruel, but I despised myself for it all the same. At least we ended it now before any more damage was done.

Except my heart was broken.

Fireflies emerged from their diurnal resting places to dance in indigo shadows. Glimmering spirits of the night, they pulsed green and gold. True enough fairies for this world. I followed the worn paths of my sanctuary. Quite a few of these insects gathered around what I thought of as Mother's memorial, though her remains were not here. Those otherworldly lights illuminated the figure of a winged angel nearly life-size. There was surely a scientific explanation for the insects' behavior. Perhaps they favored shelter in the branches of the rowan tree growing behind her lichen-covered wings.

"Father was right." I whispered to the statue. "I need to accept my limitations."

Though I expected no reply, a voice compiled of many sounds, like the rustle of myriad leaves, answered.

Why?

I held my breath, listening to the night. Nothing moved, other than the dance of fireflies. I heard only the wind, cricket songs, the distant shore, and the rush of blood in my ears. The statue's carved eyes seemed to guard secrets, like it had spoken the words from stone lips.

I had not heard a disembodied voice in years. Not since the time I'd sent myself to the hospital.

Violet.

"No." I shook my head, speaking under my breath. "Go away."

I surveyed the garden. I could see no one.

Violet. Remember.

The word *remember* struck a chord. I had heard it spoken that way in a dream. There had been an unusually vivid one six months ago, near Mother's birthday, which refused to retreat from my eyes upon waking. Nightmares had been a regular occurrence since I was small. Always a shadow being. The same Shadow who stalked me in mirrors. Sometimes it crawled like a faceless caterpillar, with a body the size of a horse. But this dream had been different. It was of a city. Somehow, though only an imaginary place, I'd seen it before.

I turned to face the statue. "Remember what?"

Fireflies congregated near its pedestal base. I crouched to investigate. Luminescent insects danced in a tight grouping under the rowan tree's branches.

A glint of metal protruded from the soil. I scraped away decomposing leaves to reveal an old paintbrush. The wooden handle had rotted, but the nickel-alloy banded tip and a few bristles remained. I found a faded maker's mark. This was one of the brushes Mother used.

I remembered…

Mother and I were painting in the garden. It was just before she died, so I must have been seven. We sat under tall pines, beside her dahlias and a new rowan tree I'd helped her transplant earlier that year. From this vantage point, we could view the sea. I, with my smaller canvas, struggled to depict clouds above the trees. Mother painted an imagined vista. She'd added a fanciful castle to the distant sea cliffs.

When evening light waned, she and I packed away the oils and brushes and carried our wet canvases. She spoke to me in the twilight.

"Now we will always remember this day. These paintings are windows through time and space, don't you see?"

What was the memory trying to tell me? I held the rotted brush aloft, like Agnes used a dousing rod, hoping for more inspiration.

"See *what*, Mother? I don't understand."

Nothing. No more voices or visions. Only the night garden, an ocean breeze, and a silent stone angel. Fireflies dispersed into their natural patterns. Mosquitoes pestered me. Exasperated, I headed inside, determined to find that painting.

Agnes had fed my new kitten and kept a plate of food warm for me. We spoke little about tonight's unfortunate events, yet I inquired if she knew what prior dealings Father would've had with Roger's family. She didn't know. Father had retired for the evening. I would have to question him in the morning—if he would answer.

Puck proved quite fond of me and did not mind being confined to my rooms for the night. I gave him dishes of food and water and a tray of sand required for feline hygiene. He explored every inch of my space—sniffing each furniture leg, jumping from chair to desk to bookshelf.

I kept Puck under surveillance while I searched for that old painting of Mother's. Father had framed a few of her oils, but I'd always thought the sight of them brought him too much pain. Most of her canvases were stored in the attic, and a few in my room. I climbed a stepstool beside my armoire to search. I blew away an embarrassing layer of dust. With delight, Puck pounced on a clump of fuzz which floated to the ground. I would have to make him some proper stuffed toys.

By flickering candlelight, I located the correct painting, and brought the loose canvas to my desk.

Mother had depicted vertical cliffs, similar to our real coastline, but she'd cast a night scene while we'd painted in daylight. She'd added a quarter moon, reflected in the horizontal lines of a calm bay. Pinpoint stars shone between moonlit clouds. Instead of a lighthouse, there stood a castle or a fortress—unlike any I'd ever seen in woodcuts or photographs. Billowing smoke rose from chimneys, clinging like fog along the cliffs. Her envious way with detail was a skill I could never replicate. Turrets jutted from the rocky architecture—their dark parapets strung with banners she'd painted in blues, violet, and silver. One or two bore the suggestion of a symbol. Actual letters or simply make-believe? I grabbed a magnifying glass. The banners became clearer the closer I looked. Almost *real*. Incredibly, they appeared to move, as if they blew in a genuine breeze. It was like looking *through a window*. Just as Mother said.

Puck hopped up to the desk beside me. I blinked. The canvas became solid fabric and paint once more—the colors once again indistinct brushstrokes. My exhaustion must have been playing tricks with my mind.

Puck nuzzled my hand and mewed. I held the purring kitten to my chest and kissed his tiny head. His fur smelled of an herbal hair tonic. No doubt Roger had given him a bath. I sighed and placed the wriggling cat on my desk. Then, in a flash, I realized where I'd seen those symbols on the castle's parapets before.

I drew out my crystal pendant, comparing the engravings in the gold band against Mother's painting. Shapes and angles were similar, but I could match none until I tried the lens again... and there... a dot within a rhombus. Another—a swirled figure between parallel bars. There were slight style differences, but several more glyphs looked too alike to be coincidence. Were these letters or hieroglyphs?

What had Roger called it? An *ancient magical language*.

I found more of the symbols; hidden in the foliage shapes she'd painted in the foreground. I sketched them in pencil. At least three more were a match for my pendant. What did they mean?

No. I was looking for imaginary connections. This was nonsense.

I covered the painting with another sheet of loose canvas and went to bed. Puck slept beside me in a contented purring ball.

When sleep finally came, a nightmare lulled me into timeworn terror. My dressing mirror, usually turned toward the wall, faced me like a gaping maw. I stood before it, staring into impossible depths. A figure formed from the blackness of my inverse room. My Shadow. Human-sized, it slithered toward the surface dividing us. Darker than a starless night, faceless as always, it raised an ethereal fist. Paralyzed, I could only watch as its gnarled and writhing limbs struck the mirror again and again, until the glass shattered.

Violet.

I stepped through into a dark forest. The trees, the grass, even the darkling sky exuded blue-brown viscous gloom, as though made of wet oil paint. I walked toward one small, twisted tree crowned in a sickly glow. It... bled. Scarlet fluid oozed from a knothole in its wooden heart. I tried to run, but my legs froze and would not obey. Incorporeal, I sank into the ground and beheld its roots dripping with blood. Red rivulets tunneled through layers of soil and stone, staining the crystalline bedrock with the offal of some terrible sacrifice.

I awoke with a gasp. Puck mewed and purred, sensing I needed comfort. The kitten's presence pushed the remnants of the nightmare away. I lay awake for hours, watching the waning moon through the window, holding my new kitten, thinking about the man who had brought him to my door.

Chapter 5
Tears of the Moon

ather disappeared sometime that night.

In the morning, we could find no trace of him. Our horses weren't missing; no one had heard or seen a carriage drive up after Roger's left.

Travers, Mrs. H, and I checked every inch of the property. No sign of him in the basement, outbuildings, or even the gardens.

We examined Father's rooms and found a letter on his desk. I'd never seen the intricately carved rosewood box that sat empty beside it.

My Dearest Violet,

I've gone on a vital errand. I have waited too long for this important task already and pray it is not too late. It may be months or years before I can return, if I can at all. However, this task is fundamental to my life, and to a far more vital promise, of which I am sworn to secrecy. I regret the unfortunate timing which necessitates my leaving on the same night I discovered the nature of your new friend and his intentions. It was foolish of me to lose my temper in front of him. If it were possible, I would have told you so this morning in person. Even so, for your own good, I warn you to stay away from Mr. Gale.

I have made provisions with our solicitor for ownership of the house and property to be transferred into your name. There is nothing for you to do in this regard; the matter is already settled. I regret I cannot bequeath more to you, but an estate built upon the meager earnings of a retired entertainer, even wisely invested, was sure to dwindle in time. I know in your resourcefulness, my clever daughter, you will find your way.

—Your father, Errol T. Morgen

Stunned, I paced the room. Mrs. H noted how unusual it was that the curtains were open. Father detested drafts.

An old brass spyglass was aimed at the northern horizon. I went to investigate, and my shoe bumped an object on the floor. I bent to pick up a small glass vial, like a perfume bottle with no decoration and a plain metal cap. On the carpet beside it were lines of white powder, nearly disguised in the rug's design. The glass contained remnants of a pale liquid and glistening grains, like a dissolved mineral. I opened it and didn't recognize the off-putting chemical smell.

"Mr. Travers," I stood. "Do you know what this is?" I handed him the vial.

"No. I've seen nothing like it before."

Mrs. H came to inspect. "Neither have I. And have a look here." She pointed to similar marks on the adjacent wall. Someone had sketched something large. The smeared chalk lines marked a pattern all but lost in the floral wallpaper. I did my best to ignore the oval mirror in their midst.

Father usually kept it covered with black fabric, as we had done to all the mirrors in the house for the customary year after Mother died. Out of courtesy for me and my phobia, he'd never taken it down. Until now, it seemed. The drape was laid over a winged-back chair by his fireplace. Mrs. H touched the silvered glass, which appeared dirty when I allowed myself a glance. Her finger came away covered in something black. "It's soot," she said. "Oh, it gives me chills. What was he doing with a candle so close here? But I don't see any spilled wax. And what of these odd markings? I can't make them out."

"I don't know." Averting my eyes, I paced.

"I don't like it," Agnes said. "I can think of only a few things one does with such a combination. None too seemly. I never believed your father would dabble in sorcery, but this sure looks like it. Tsk, tsk." She shook her head. "Never in all my years. But it's the ones who protest the loudest you should worry about, eh? Oh, and today would be a powerful time to work any spell."

"Why do you say that?"

"Because today is the autumnal equinox. When night and day are of equal length. Full of magical power."

I didn't feel like quibbling over her misinterpretation of an astronomical phenomenon, or her assumption that Father had taken up sorcery merely because he'd sketched on the wall.

"Regardless," I said, "I'm afraid I'll have to cancel this morning's appointments. I must pay a visit to Mr. Gale's shop at once. He might know something about this bottle which will help us." I tucked the strange vial into a pocket.

"You don't think your Apothecary had anything to do with this?" Mr. Travers sounded almost too ashamed to ask the question.

"No. I watched Roger enter his carriage and drive away last night, after he and I had been together in the garden. There's no way Father went with him, unless he was already in the carriage. Did either of you speak to Father after dinner?"

Mrs. H nodded. "I brought Mr. Morgen his cup of chamomile at the usual time, around nine o'clock. Saw him with my own two eyes, I did. He was in bad sorts, of course, and eager to cut our conversation short, but seemed otherwise fine. That was at least an hour after Mr. Gale left. Yes, I noticed the brougham drove away, my dear. At sunset. 'Twas only my respect for your privacy that kept me out of the garden after that."

"Thank you," was all I managed. I had to stay focused. "Mr. Travers?"

"No, miss. I'd already retired to my apartment and a good book before then. I can tell you I heard nothing out near the carriage house last night. On foot, maybe he'd be that quiet, but I can't see as how he'd get very far in his condition."

"So, Father had to have left sometime after nine o'clock. And quietly."

I paced, staring at the empty vial in my hand. Was it a different make than the bottles I'd seen in the apothecary shop the other day? I heaved a sigh. "I've got to find out what was in this bottle. That is… if Roger will even speak to me."

"Aye, lass. He will. You've no fear of that." Travers exchanged weighted glances with Agnes. "Because I'm going with you. Come on now, get your coat."

On the drive that rainy morning, I pondered events. Roger's bizarre words last night. Father's letter. Mrs. H's equinox. The ember of a memory flickered in the back of my mind.

I was a girl of no more than ten. From the cupola, Father and I observed a quarter moon—half light and half dark. I'd peered through the old telescope, admiring the sculpted features of Luna's half-lit face. The sea of tranquility. The mysterious canals.

He'd said, "See the line dividing the light half and the dark? It's called the terminator. Right now, it lies perpendicular to the sun's light source, just as happens here on earth at the equinox. The hours of day and night are the same on that day, twice a year. But it's far more. Some believe it's a magical time, when the barrier between the fairy world and the human world is thin; when spirits run up and down the tails of meteor showers. You ask Mrs. H. She'll tell you it's true."

The barrier between worlds. Human and Faerie.

I'd also seen a quarter moon in Mother's painting. Then there were the odd symbols she'd painted. Was it all only coincidence? It had to be.

I was obsessing over nonsense. Roger had drawn me into a new madness.

At 709 E. Harbor Street, we found a locked door and a placard which read 'Come Ye Back Again.' I knocked and pleaded in the rain, my voice echoing off the alley walls, but no one answered. No sign of Maggie or her brood, either. No lights shone through the street level windows of Roger's rat-plagued laboratory.

"Mr. Travers, do you know how to find Mr. Gale's home address?"

"Aye." Travers said from the buggy's driver's seat. "Reckon I should, as I had naught to do but entertain his driver yesterday. Odd sort of fellow, that one. Polite, but wouldn't leave his carriage. Darnedest thing. The place isn't too far from here."

"Wonderful. Let's go." I hopped onto the vehicle's brass step. Strange that I'd never noticed it wasn't iron.

"We can go to the police. If Mr. Gale can't help."

"What good would it do? Father's letter states he intended to leave us. Presumably of his own free will. Especially if he'd arranged everything with the solicitors ahead of time."

"That he did." Travers sighed. "I wondered why the law clerks had come and gone for the past weeks. He'd never say a peep about his business, but your father's always had his quirks."

"Still, it doesn't feel right. Something's wrong. If Mr. Gale has no answers for me, I'll keep searching. I must."

I shook off my umbrella and climbed into the buggy seat beside Travers, glad for at least the partial shelter of its cover.

We drove away from Seastone's merchant district to a portion of our countryside populated by the grand estates of wealthy merchants. Rough cobblestones transitioned to smoother gravel under our horse's shod hooves, though the going was a little slower through the puddles. We passed a posh address on East Sailing Street, one which had hosted a charity function given by the Seastone Society for the Advancement of the Arts once years ago. As a new member, they had invited me to display. It was like a dream. For one candle-lit, gilded evening, my work stood alongside that of other well-known painters, and I sold more than a few. A chance so many of the young women I taught might never have. It had always been my goal to change that inequity somehow, but my own deteriorating health had darkened my hopes for the future. My subsequent hospitalization had all but ruined my social standing in town. Rumors and slander about me had spread like wildfire after that, in no little part thanks to Bryce, whom I had met on that ill-fated night.

We turned onto a side-road and rolled to a stop before a wrought-iron gate. Another headache grabbed my skull. Disturbingly, Roger's fantasies of fairies and their aversion to iron surfaced in my immediate thoughts. Even if the pain wasn't as bad as it could get, it was damned inconvenient.

Travers hopped down and pulled a lever beside the gate, ringing a bell. The gate immediately opened, as though guided by a hidden mechanism. Our horse whinnied and Travers spoke a few words of calming to her before we continued down the drive.

From the road, the Gale estate imposed itself upon a spacious, tree-dotted lawn. It was not among the largest homes in this area, though perhaps one of the oldest. The structure was of brick and stone, darkened by the rain. Fine arched windows graced tall turrets. Topiary of boxwood and privet softened the lines with spirals and spheres. Sculptures of classical nudes, cracked and moss-covered gods and goddesses, stood sentry along a gravel path which paralleled the drive, shaded by larch trees. Though well-tended, the gardens possessed a forgotten and slumbering look under the mist and clouds, as if they yearned to be filled with color, like they must have known long ago.

Hardly the home of a humble apothecary. Perhaps Travers had gotten the wrong address.

Travers drove us under a covered portico lit with the flames of gas-lamps against the gloom of rain. Before our horse came to a stop, a footman descended the wide steps to meet us. Travers conversed with the man briefly before I opened the door and insisted I speak with Mr. Gale. The footman nodded and motioned for me to follow. So, we had the right place.

Up a columned staircase of curving granite, we met a wide set of wood doors with a doorplate cast in bronze. The entry appeared to creak open on its own, facilitated by unseen hands.

Mr. Gale's marble-tiled foyer was a checkerboard of gleaming white and black squares, crowned by a massive cut-crystal chandelier. Antique furniture accented richly paneled walls. Dueling stairways curved to the left and right. Arched doorways opened to spacious rooms on either side. The dim morning light illuminated a room at the opposite end of the hall; perhaps a glass conservatory or courtyard occupied the home's interior.

The footman, a man of such unremarkable appearance that I promptly forgot what he looked like, took my damp coat while the doors closed behind me. Whoever closed them had already disappeared along with the footman.

"Odd folks, these," said Travers. "Don't say much, do they?"

I was too stunned to answer.

A large portrait of two young people drew my attention, and I walked closer to inspect. A boy of perhaps eight or nine and a girl of eleven or twelve; both had raven hair and green eyes. Were they Roger and his sister, or ancestors past? Faces serene and regal, the portraits lacked much expression beyond a thin curl of the lips and blush at the cheeks. Their jewel-toned costumes looked to be from the Regency era unless a later painter had copied that style. At the children's feet sat a pair of hunting dogs, lean and servile. I drew near the canvas and found the oils cracked with seeming age. But we artists were often paid to present an illusion, rather than fact.

Another portrait depicted a lovely woman with indigo eyes and braided sienna hair. She wore an old-fashioned dress in shades of emerald and ochre. I stepped toward that canvas when another servant, perhaps the butler, approached us.

"Miss Morgen, Mr. Travers, greetings." The silver-haired gentleman wore a fine tailored uniform, but, in a strange visual incongruence, the man's features were like an out-of-focus telescope view, though his clothing seemed clear as the rest of the room. It must be the headache playing havoc with my eyesight, as it often did.

"Good morning," I answered, finding it odd the man hadn't given us his name. "We are friends of Mr. Gale's. We must speak with him at once."

The butler nodded. "Mr. Gale is finishing some work, but he will be with you soon. May we offer refreshments while you wait?" His voice was almost monotone.

"No, thank you," I said. "It's rather urgent, I'm afraid. If Mr. Gale is indisposed, may I deliver a note to him? Do you have pen and paper handy?"

The butler seemed to consider the idea for a moment before he said, "Come. We will relay your urgency to the Magister," and turned to lead us down the hall.

Magister? I rubbed the back of my aching head.

"Bear up, my girl. We'll find your father." Travers wrapped an arm around my shoulders as we walked, and I was grateful for his comfort there in the cold, echoing expanse of Mr. Gale's exquisite foyer. One couldn't help but notice the quality rugs we trod were threadbare and worn.

We entered a wood-paneled corridor lined with more antiques and paintings. Landscapes. Hunting scenes. Sculptures. I recognized a few sought-after artists from generations past. Archways into well-appointed but sparse rooms. A large parlor. A drawing room. Bedsheets draped much of the furniture, as though it sat unused for years. We passed an empty ballroom—an expansive floor of diamonds, vines, and florets under a ceiling of fancy medallions and chandeliers. I imagined dancing ghosts in Victorian finery. A grand piano lingered in a far corner—the only thing uncovered in the room.

How had I considered Roger a friend for months and never known he lived like this?

Then again, I may have been left in the dark on many things concerning my life.

I asked Travers, "Do you know what business Father had with this family years ago when I was small? Did he ever mention it?"

"No, lass, I can't say as he did. That was before my time, anyhow. I came on not a year before…"

"I know. Before Mother died."

The butler led us to a large decorative archway surrounding two wood and glass doors. He bowed and opened the doorway, indicating we should walk on ahead. Travers and I stepped into a glass-walled solarium filled to bursting with living plants. The air was warmer and more humid within, smelling of earth and flora. I detected the aroma of citrus under the sharp tang of something like crushed lemon balm. Orchids bloomed in riotous colors, hanging from the branches of tropical trees. Vines leapt toward the high ceiling on wooden trellises. Herbs and flowers crowded pots and barrels on the tiled floor or lined tables in disorderly rows. A mint plant trailed from a repurposed teapot. Small cacti perched on a pyramid shelf near what must have been a south-facing wall. I found it hard to feel anything but joy in this space, despite the dread urgency of our mission.

"Over here." Roger's voice carried through the dense foliage.

We wove through the maze of living things toward the center of the space and found him working at a table over several uprooted plants, sleeves rolled up and his hands in a tray of soil. Behind him, another worktable hosted an antique alchemical apparatus—a series of Bunsen burners, bubbling beakers, alembics, bain maries, and undulating glass tubing. One beaker contained a mixture of crushed herbs and liquid. Roger piled some loose soil over the exposed roots of what appeared to be a clump of mandrake, misted it with a spray bottle, washed his hands at a nearby sink, dried them on his work apron, and slipped the eyeglasses he seldom wore into a waistcoat pocket.

He stepped toward us and bowed. "Good morning, Miss Morgen. Mr. Travers. Welcome to my home. A pleasant surprise. I'll admit…" he gazed at me with what might be sadness or guilt, if not longing. "I hadn't expected to see you again. What brings you here?"

No doubt sensing my tumultuous emotions, Travers answered for us. "We tried your shop first, Mr. Gale, and I hope it's no intrusion, but we have an urgent situation and need your advice."

"Of course. How can I help?" He stepped closer, and I noticed, for a man of usually impeccable appearance, he looked wan and tired. His eyes, that continued to seek mine, a little red. Perhaps he hadn't slept well either.

"It's my father," I said. "He's disappeared."

"What? How?"

"That's just it, sir. We don't know." Travers filled him in on the morning's events and Roger seemed as shocked as we had been. When Travers related the strange markings on the floor and wall, Roger rubbed his chin, staring off in thought.

"Did you find anything else in the room? Anything out of place or unusual?"

"Yes." I swallowed. "This." I pulled the vial from my reticule and clenched it in a fist for courage before I walked toward him. "That's why I'm here. I was hoping you might know what it contained."

He drew near but didn't take it from my outstretched hand. "Where did you find it?"

"On the floor beside those odd smudges."

He nodded. "Well, it's not from my shop, I can tell you that. I don't use that sort of container. Hmm. Just one moment." He walked to a nearby wooden cabinet and retrieved from a drawer a pair of black gloves, which he slipped on before locating a set of goggles from another shelf.

He returned, wearing the strange ocular device. "Spectrocles. Invented by a friend of mine, the special lenses allow us to see certain energy fields invisible to the naked eye."

Loops of glass in multiple colors pivoted on minute hinges over each eye. He rotated them, settling on a dark rose-colored lens for the left and a cerulean one for the right, before he focused an aperture, inspecting the bottle in my hand. The lenses magnified his squinting eyes, and surplus loops fanned out from either side of his face. I might have laughed if my mood were not so dark.

"May I?" He asked me.

I gave him the vial.

Roger opened it, sniffed, and frowned. "I believe I know what it is, though I've not seen it in person before."

"What do you suspect?" Travers asked.

Roger exhaled and rubbed the back of his neck, and I noticed he had not shaved. "Well, it's difficult to explain."

"You mean it's magical?" I didn't care to hide my vexation. "Go on, just tell us what you think. We'll hear you out. I promise."

He grinned, almost hopeful, blinking at me through those absurd lenses. "Everything is magical in a way, but this… this is a concentrated form of aetheric energy. I've heard rumors of such a tincture which allows humans to work Faecraft, that is, fairy magic. It's called Tears of the Moon."

"Fairy magic? Bollocks," Travers exclaimed. "I understand why Mr. Morgen was annoyed with you. Men like you wish to see phantoms where there are only shadows. It's an easy way out of the hard truths of life, isn't it?"

I rolled my eyes. So much for my promise that we would hear him out. I suppose Travers hadn't agreed to that plan anyhow.

Travers continued, "Is it a drug? Poison? Just tell us what you know."

"I understand your hesitation to believe me, sir. Here…" Roger slipped the goggles from his head and handed them to Travers. "See for yourself."

He held the vial aloft for inspection after Travers reluctantly donned the eyewear. My butler gasped and took the vial, holding it up to various angles of light. "What in creation?" His magnified eyes blinked, staring at his other open hand, then around the room. "What sort of trick lenses are these?"

"No trick. They show auras and living energy fields. You and I have them. All living things do. Many objects imbued with magic potency also contain such energy. Like the substance in that vial."

When Travers walked in my direction, he pointed. "What do you have around your neck, Miss Morgen?"

"Oh?" I pulled out the crystal pendant from below my blouse, which, to my eyes, still appeared as a normal stone. "You mean this?"

"Bloody hell!" He took a step backward.

What did he see?

Travers offered the goggles to me, and I glanced at Roger.

"Please have a look. Here, I shall help." He unbuckled the strap, no doubt realizing it would be harder for me to slip them on over my pinned-up hair than it had been for them. I placed the rubber-padded brass on my nose, and he secured them in the back.

The first thing I noticed through the strange lenses was a scintillating glow coming from my pendant. Each face of the mineral—every geometric edge, internal and external—glinted with a spectrum of pearlescent color. The gold setting and chain gleamed like molten metal in a jeweler's crucible, nearly overwhelming to my headache-strained vision.

I glanced up to gauge Roger's reaction, and *he* took my breath away, but not for the usual reasons. The ambient room appeared darker through the tinted lenses—all the colors muted by shade. But an aura of bright golden-yellow light surrounded the man in front of me. The radiating outline was faint, but alive and pulsing, like the corona of a star. Roger's eyes seemed more green than humanly possible. Dumbstruck, I turned to Travers. He also radiated an indigo blue luminescence. Not perhaps as brightly as Roger's, but nonetheless dazzling. I lifted my hand to behold a halo of faintest… violet.

"I would say your mother named you well." Roger smiled.

I'd always thought I'd been named for the color of my eyes, though I considered them gray. Could Mother have seen this? Intent on inspecting that vial, I stepped toward Travers, who handed it to me. Like my pendant, the drops of remaining liquid inside—the entire bottle—exuded a deep red. Different from the living outlines of our bodies, the energy seemed to… ooze. The sight unnerved me, reminding me of last night's nightmare.

I gave the vial back to Travers, wanting to be free of the thing for the moment.

"How does the illusion work?" I scanned the room through the goggles—none of the other inanimate objects gave off similar light, but the plants… I approached a citrus tree. Veins in the young leaves pulsed with life, alive in a vivid green and blue halo; creamy flowers scintillated with every color of the rainbow. Not as defined as the light from us humans, but a peaceful radiance—a vitality I had always sensed from plants but had never seen with my eyes.

Humans. I was starting to doubt everything. That was crazy.

"I can assure you it's very real," said Roger. "No illusion."

Of course, Agnes and her spiritualist friends spoke about auras and the like, enough that I consigned such ideas to the realm of superstitious fancy, but perhaps there was some real-world merit to the concept after all. If these bizarre goggles were some advanced scientific tool, the magical symbols engraved in the brass might merely be theatrical stage-dressing.

"Mr. Gale." I tugged the goggles down to my neck and blinked, adjusting again to natural vision. "If this is not some illusion, then it's a remarkable science—I'll grant you that. No doubt your friend's invention reveals some hidden light spectrum, or the luminous aethers that make up all physical matter, through the clever use of lenses and optics. But that's a far cry from proving magic exists."

"She has a point," said Travers, who seemed otherwise a bit shaken.

"Correct. Even so, ask yourself this: Why does your crystal pendant, and the liquid in the bottle, radiate this visible energy, along with every other living thing in the room, while nothing else does?"

I slipped the goggles up over my eyes again for a moment to ascertain what he said was… indeed, true.

"Well… Hmm." now I was at a loss.

I peered down into a large blooming cactus plant; its clay container was mulched with what appeared to be polished beach rocks, made of quartz, just like my pendant, but these stones did not glow when viewed through the tinted lenses. They only caught the natural light of the rainy morning.

"Ah. I have something else nearby which is magically charged."

Roger, haloed in golden radiance through my dark-tinted view, walked to a wall of cabinets behind his alchemical apparatus, which, when he opened a tall wooden door, appeared to contain rows of dried herbs.

"Miss Morgen, perhaps you'd care to test this theory. Do you see anything unusual in this cabinet?"

I walked to inspect. Through the Spectrocles' lenses, some of the glass containers emanated a little color, as if the life of the dried plants had not yet faded. An eerie glow issued from the third shelf down. I bent and moved several large crocks out of the way to find a flickering light the size of a coin.

"What is it?" I asked, hesitant to pick it up.

Roger drew near and retrieved the small coin marked with peculiar symbols. In his black gloves, the metal pulsed like he held a fallen star. "It's a talisman I charged to keep these herbs fresh in that cabinet. Works well too. Here."

The strange geometric engravings emitted a gold-white brilliance from within. Intriguing, but it made the hair on the back of my neck stand on end. Yet when I slipped the goggles down, it was just a piece of ordinary polished brass in my hands, lifeless as any other coin.

"This once inanimate matter is now a repository of living magic; the source was my own energy along with universal force I drew down into it during the consecration ritual. The substance in your mystery vial would have been similarly charged before your father obtained it."

"All right." I was starting to warm to this bizarre theory more than I wanted to admit. "Let's suppose, for argument's sake, that any of that is true. You say the liquid in that bottle helped him work fairy magic. Do you use something like it when you work magic?"

"No. Well, in a different manner. I don't need to drink anything like this, but I'm able to draw on this same power because I have years of training, and because I myself was consecrated to serve the Queen in her Court. For many people without such a background, shortcuts are tempting. This potion may be one such shortcut."

"Father drank it?"

"A portion. I believe so. The rest he would've used to paint those sigils on the walls and floor, and—"

"Why?" A flustered Travers interrupted. "Mr. Morgen's letter said he was going away on business. Why on earth would he bother with such thing first? He was never one for this sort of... partiality. He never took to omens or divinations either."

"You knew him better than me, sir. Do you think anyone else could have been in the room with him last night?"

"I don't see how someone else would've gotten past us. We found no evidence."

"You must understand, I suspect the ritual Mr. Morgen performed was the very means by which he left on his journey. I believe he literally opened a portal and stepped through it. That's why none of you heard him leave the house. The fact that he did this last night only seals it in my mind. And we have a good idea of where he's gone. For today is—"

"The equinox," I said.

"Yes. Did he mention it?"

"No. At least not recently. Mrs. H thought of it this morning."

"She's right. The day of the equinox, plus three before and three after, mark the strongest link between our worlds. We call this period of seven days the Equinox Bridge. Only during this time twice a year can humans initiate travel to and from Faerie. For someone like your father, today would be the safest day to make an attempt. If Mr. Morgen had wanted to transport anywhere else in the world, he could have done so any other time of year. Considering this, and your marks on the walls and floor..." He paced, rubbing his chin. "But we're missing something. He'd need a traveling relic, as well as a conductive surface, to create such a portal. A bowl of water. A mirror. Even a painting containing the right magic."

"The mirror on the wall was covered in candle soot." said Travers. "Right in the middle of those marks he'd made on the wallpaper, in fact. We couldn't make any sense of it and, ah..."

"In the midst of them? Why didn't you say so before? Then it's precisely what he's done."

Travers shot me an apologetic glance when he must have seen my reaction to the topic.

Roger raised an eyebrow. "Was there something else?"

"It's not that. Travers is aware of my... shall we say, *healthy phobia* of mirrors."

"Ah. I'd forgotten." Roger appraised me with pity, which only made me more embarrassed. "Catoptrophobia, I believe. It's far more common in people who are sensitive to magic. Not without good reason. Mirrors are conductive to transfer between worlds, as your father must have known."

I shivered, because if it were true my Shadow might be real, and right now I couldn't handle the thought.

"Did you make out any of the symbols he'd drawn?"

Travers answered, "No, they were all burned or smudged away."

Roger nodded. "Most spells of this sort seal themselves behind the caster. That means he wouldn't be able to return through that same portal."

This all felt like the skewed logic of a dream. I might be dreaming, if not for this damned headache.

"Now that I think about it," Roger continued, "the letter Mr. Morgen wrote me some days ago mentioned an upcoming journey. I'm afraid if you want to find him, we've no time to lose, for Equinox Bridge closes in three days. If we can't locate him by then, we'll have to wait another six months to try again."

"You mean the letter I brought you on my birthday?" I ignored for a moment what he'd said about Faerie, and Travers was fit to burst. I motioned for him to hold his questions.

"The very one." Roger answered.

"I'd like to read it," Travers insisted.

"Of course. It's in my library. Please follow me."

CHAPTER 6
BELIEVE THE IMPOSSIBLE

oger led us down another grand hallway, past a row of hollow soldiers—empty suits of armor from many cultures and eras. We passed a tall portrait of a dark-haired man who looked much like Roger. The man stood in a night-cast room beside a spherical astrolabe and a skull, wearing a blue cape lined with stars.

Noticing my inspection, Roger said, "My father."

"In the foyer, I saw a portrait of a young boy and girl. Another beside that of a woman with red-gold hair."

"My sister and me. My mother."

"Beautiful family," said Travers.

"Yes, they were." Roger walked ahead of us.

"Were? Tell me you aren't the last, Mr. Gale."

"Indeed, I am."

"Ah, well. I've few relations left myself. Only an uncle and second cousin down in Portstown. Never bothered myself with a wife and family; considered them a burden, I did. Can't say as I have too many regrets in this life, but sometimes I wonder what I missed."

Travers glanced at me, and it surprised me to see a glint of sorrow there. I'd never heard him speak this way.

"Here we are." Roger opened a set of arched double doors.

We entered the library through a pair of decorative pillars. The space opened into a two-story rotunda—filled, from marble floor to frescoed ceiling, with books arranged on labyrinthine shelves. A faceted, stained-glass oculus crowned the room, surrounded by a vivid panorama of neo-classical angels, gods and goddesses, and mythical animals. Behind them, white and gold clouds floated in celestial blue days, interspersed with star-dotted black nights.

Heavy curtains muted tall windows. Gas sconces held back the shadows. An open second floor appeared to house scrolls and larger books around the perimeter of a curving balcony. A wooden staircase spiraled toward that upper level. I thought of Jacob's dream ladder, with angels descending and ascending its rungs between earth and heaven.

Like riding the tails of meteors.

I stepped into an angled beam of light cast by a tall window. "You know, your house doesn't seem this big from the outside." The expansive acoustics echoed my thoughts.

"You're correct. The illusion is intentional." Roger's voice sounded like he was right beside me, although he was meters away.

Travers eyed the room with awe and suspicion.

As we neared the center of the library, black-and-white checkered floor tiles gave way to a large black medallion, which paralleled the zodiacal fresco above. Eight angular symbols on tiles hewn from golden marble formed a ring around a circle of what looked like smooth onyx, or some other darker stone.

He led us to a reading table near a colorful wall of books. On it were a few open volumes and a folded piece of linen paper. I recognized Father's stationary—a wax seal stamped with our Morgen family shield, broken only a few days ago.

Roger handed it to Travers, who sat down to read, pulling his spectacles from a coat pocket. I sat beside him.

Roger snapped his fingers and both lamps on the table lit simultaneously.

"Good grief, sir! No need for the tricks."

"No trick. Just magic." His eyes sparkled with mischief when he glanced at me.

Travers bent to look under the table. "I don't see the cords, but they must run down the legs, right? Electric ignition. Where's the switch?"

"No switch. No electricity." Roger arched an eyebrow. "If I ask you to believe the impossible, I'd better provide a little proof."

Travers laughed. "You forget, I've worked for a retired stage magician for years. I've seen it all."

I rubbed the back of my head. It was all too much. Roger noticed and frowned. "Another headache?"

I nodded.

"I'll send for a tonic. One moment."

Our host disappeared through a different door than the entry we'd come through. While Travers read the letter, I examined the tomes on the table beside us. A large, leather-bound volume contained yellowed pages of hand-written script. Much of it was in English or French. A little Latin. Histories and descriptions of countries with fantastical names. Perhaps it was some antique saga of a mythological land. I turned a page and encountered those same letters as I'd seen on the necklace and in Mother's painting. Though I could not understand a jot or tittle; the symbols seemed so familiar. The hair on the back of my neck stood on end. My cheeks flushed. I closed the book.

Another lay open to a flowing diagram like a family tree, the names artfully penned in more of that obscure language.

"Hmph. So, he did say he was leaving. Might have bothered to tell us, too." Travers shook his head before he handed the letter to me. "You'd better have a look."

> *20 September 1907*
> *1210 West Bay Drive*
> *Seastone, S.K.S.*
>
> *Mr. Gale,*
> *I request the honor of your presence this Sunday evening at my home for a visit. I was a friend of your father. Eustace Gale once performed a great deed of service for me and my wife, Helena, after Violet was born. It is with a spirit of gratitude for your family's aid when I was most in need that I extend this invitation to Eustace's estranged son. Furthermore, although I was not aware of your present dealings with my daughter until now, I will reserve judgment until we have a chance to speak. I may not keep the same company you keep, sir, but I know a little about how the world works, having been here longer than even you. I require some assurances of your intentions before I will allow Violet to see you again.*
> *If you are anything like your father, you will make time for us this Sunday. We have much to discuss. Time is of the essence, as I'm afraid I will be leaving soon, if I can manage the journey. One way or another, I'm not long for this world. Be here at six o'clock.*
> *Sincerely,*
> *Errol T. Morgen*

My cheeks heated. I was angry.

"I promise he never said a thing to me about it, lass. I would have told you, even if he'd asked me not to."

"Oh, I don't doubt you." I sighed and rubbed my eyes. "What can we do? I don't know if what Mr. Gale says about this... magic portal is true or not. Either way, it's clear Father was planning his last disappearing act. And took pains to exclude us from his plans."

"Aye. It's odd. I'm not sure what to make of all this talk of magic spells, either. Gives me the chills, it does."

"You and me both." Though it seemed the evidence was starting to stack in Roger's favor. Could I have been wrong about something so fundamental as the nature of the universe itself? If so, what else had I gotten wrong?

Roger reappeared, followed by one of his servants, who carried a tray of tea, pastries, and fruit. I hadn't realized I was starving. Of course, none of us had eaten in our bewilderment that morning. Our host's kindness distracted me from darker thoughts. The dose of familiar headache tonic went to work in moments.

I brushed off Roger's inquiries about Father's letter. I needed to think, and that was damned difficult in his presence. He unbalanced me in wonderful and terrible ways. We sipped our tea and ate currant scones, pretending he didn't just claim my father disappeared into thin air.

Roger said, "Tell me the truth. When did your headache come on? Perhaps when you approached my front gate?"

I glanced at Travers, who shrugged and gave me an "I'm-innocent-and-he's-crazy" look. I almost laughed, but I wanted to scream.

I smirked and ate a tangerine wedge.

Roger wouldn't give it up. In fact, he seemed a little too smug. "Anyone like you would sense the iron, not to mention the wards, I have in place around my home. In fact, if I had not dropped them, you would not have made it through the gate. Still, they affected you, I'll wager."

"Anyone like me?" I huffed and set down my half-empty teacup. "You're on with that fairy nonsense again, aren't you? And what *wards*? Do you keep them locked in your basement with the rats, huh?"

"What? Oh, not that kind of ward. Stars! Why would you think I... rats?" He shook his head. "Right. I'm sorry. That was indeed a lie. One I must often use around my... uninformed customers. The truth is a goblin had come calling that afternoon—a rather rude one at that."

"A *goblin*?"

"Yes. In my shop's basement there's a magical doorway called a Wayportal, but for most of my Otherworld patrons it's only operational during Equinox Bridge, which began that morning."

I sighed and rolled my eyes.

Undaunted, he continued, "Wards are magical barriers. Spells of protection. I employ them to keep out any unwanted guests."

"Unwanted guests like me?"

"What's he talking about, Miss Morgen?" Travers had the decency to appear incensed.

"Oh, just a persistent delusion of his. A fantasy regarding fairies. And goblins, apparently. It seems I'm part of it. Well, no longer." I stood and pushed my chair away from the table. I threw my hands up in defeat. "Look at this place, Roger. You make your living selling tea. Or so I believed all this time we've been friends. I don't know you at all, do I? How can I possibly trust you?" I was starting to tremble.

"Violet, you know the real me. You always have."

"No. I appreciate your hospitality this morning, Mr. Gale, but it appears I will not find what I'm looking for here, and I must be going. Why did I even come here in the first place?"

Travers stood beside me, a troubled look on his face, but he said nothing.

"Violet," Roger walked to meet me. "You came here because you need answers. I have more to tell you, if you'll allow me. Please let me show you something I found in my records last night when I couldn't sleep. I think it might concern your mother. It may well be connected to where your father has gone."

"My mother?" Could it have to do with what Father hinted at in his letter? Whatever *great deed of service* they had requested of Roger's father when I was born?

"Yes. If you don't want to hear more after that, I'll understand."

I sighed. My hand went to the crystal pendant under my blouse. Had I only imagined Mother had painted words in this same language? My heart was at war with my better sense. Still, the riddle would eat me alive forever if I didn't seek to answer it.

"Very well. Will you excuse us for a moment?"

Travers and I walked out of earshot of our anxious host, down through the library stacks, past shelves of antique volumes. One of Roger's strange servants lurked, stock still, beside a settee and another door, white-gloved hands folded together in front of an impeccable black uniform, as if he intended to be invisible unless called upon. No doubt a custom of propriety, but one I detested.

Beside a globe crafted of semi-precious stones, I spoke quietly to Travers. "I want to hear what he has to say about Mother, but I won't be long. Will you give us a moment of privacy?"

"Aye. I'll see if that chap will show me around for a while." He indicated our silent sentinel by the wall. "You can learn the most about a house like this from the servants, I always say." He winked. "Keep your good sense about you, lass."

"I will."

We hailed Roger, whose servant ushered Travers on a tour of the rest of the house, to meet us later in the front parlor.

Roger and I returned to the table where our half-eaten breakfast sat beside the old books. We inspected the family tree diagram I had noticed earlier.

"This is a biography of the Royal Summer Court families. I began some research into your mother's possible history last night. I discovered who I believe she was. Here." He pointed to a name on one of the tree's elaborately scripted branches. "This row lists the children of the last Queen, Titania. Ariadne, the firstborn. She is the current Summer Queen.

"Wait a minute. The Summer Queen?"

"Queen of all Faerie. She whom my House is sworn to serve."

I shook my head and sighed. "Just go on."

Undeterred, he tapped his finger on another name written in that fanciful language. "Here is Raymond, King of the Autumn Courts. Here is Vaela, who, according to this document, received a high-ranking position in Ariadne's court, along with the Queen's younger sibling, Helena, until—"

"But the last name is struck through."

"Yes. This Helena was exiled."

Exile. It was a word Mother often used to describe herself. I always thought it was some lamentation of the heart she'd expressed, rather than a literal thing.

"I'll fetch another book which may shed more light upon our mystery. One moment."

"Wait." I touched Roger's arm. Even that small action awoke again those butterflies in my stomach. He must have felt it too, evident in his quick intake of breath.

I swallowed, pushing back the sting in my eyes—squelching the tidal wave of emotions which threatened to drown me. "Do you have something I can use to write with?"

Perhaps reluctant to pull away, he walked to a nearby secretary, retrieved a sheet of paper and a fountain pen, which he brought to me before leaving me alone at the reading table.

I sipped my now-cold tea and closed my eyes to recall the symbols I'd sketched from Mother's painting last night.

When the images came to mind, I scribed them in ink as faithfully as possible from memory. I managed a line of seven. There was more I was forgetting. Only after I'd gotten them down, I compared them to the glyphs in Roger's old book. I found a match to five, interspersed among the rest of the strange words. A few others held traits in common with my last two. Then it was some real alphabet; that fact seemed unavoidable.

Latent anger stirred again. Father's duplicity was clear. Mother's secrets might keep themselves, but why had she kept them from *me*? If I was only half-human, my partial humanity had been broken all my life, because of this *half*-ness.

"Ignorance might be less painful than some truths," I said when Roger returned with another opened book. "Perhaps that's why my family kept me in the dark."

Roger set his book down with cautious hope in his eyes, though his brow was knit in concern. "Do you wish you had stayed in the dark?"

"No. I've always sought the truth wherever it led me."

"What do you have?" He glanced at my paper.

"Can you read this?"

"Yes." He sat beside me and donned those gold-rimmed spectacles he sometimes wore. I thought they made him look distinguished. They reminded me of some memory I could never place. Roger traced a finger below my row of letters. "It says, 'Here where my roots grow in... rock *something*, or perhaps *something* rock.' The last symbol is only a partial word. A place name, most likely. This is the pictograph for stone, or rock," he tapped the last symbol, "This surrounding glyph signifies a proper name, but it's missing its closure. Where did this originate? Is there more?" He scanned the book in front of me, to see if I'd perhaps copied something.

"Mother included them in one of her paintings. I always thought it was nonsense until... I realized it matched some of the writing on this." I drew out the pendant. "What does this say, anyway?"

"It's a charm of protection against iron, among other things. Activated by Fae magic. That's why I gave it to you."

Then he cared that much about me. "You're right. I forgot the last few letters she'd painted. Could the word be Seastone?"

"Possibly. What else was in the painting?"

"It was a fanciful landscape. A castle on a cliff by the sea. Like nothing I've ever seen."

"Hmm. Perhaps I can translate the rest of it for you sometime." He slid another crumbling old tome my way. "Have a look at this."

He tapped a parchment page of elegant letters penned in my mystery language. I saw again a few of the ones I had just written. "It's a record of one meeting of the Courts. This portion is in High Fae. On the opposite page is its translation in English. I can only think it concerns your parents."

"The Courts?"

"The four Courts of the Fae. Summer, Autumn, Winter, and Spring. Each is ruled by a royal family."

I read aloud the English portion—slowly, for it was in an antique hand difficult to parse:

> *"Helena, youngest daughter of Titania, for taking a human mate, and for turning her back on her people's traditions, her Queen's decree, and the laws of the Courts, was judged worthy of exile. On the fifth day of Second Bridge in the year twelve thousand, five hundred and twenty-eight, she was forthwith stripped of powers, titles, rank, and all rights as a citizen of the Otherworld; banished along with her mate, Errol, to live out the remainder of her days on Human soil. Henceforth, her name shall be stricken from the record books and shall not be spoken, neither shall she be remembered in our Songs."*

I asked, "What was this date in our years?"

"Time in the Otherworld dates from the Rift, and is rather more fluid than in our realm, but it works out to around 1806 A.D."

"The Rift?" He was about to explain, but I interrupted. "Never mind. Tell me later. It can't be the same Helena. That's too long ago. Mother was born..."

With horror, I realized I didn't know the year. Nor had I ever heard them discuss her age, even when she died—only that she'd been *too young when she left this earth.*

"Your mother was a Fae of the Royal Courts. They're one of the longest-lived species in the two worlds. I've met some who are a thousand years old."

"Well, my father can't have been. So, this isn't them either way."

"Are you so sure? In his letter, Mr. Morgen said he was older than me—an odd thing to mention, if appearances are to be taken at face value."

Roger's proximity and intensity gave me pause, as it often did. I remembered what he'd said about his age last night. I'd dismissed it, along with his other statements that seemed delusional.

"You believe he's like you? Quite... old?"

"I think it likely, though he's not a member of Reliqua. If he married a Fae, no doubt he'd traveled with her into the Otherworld. Any human who has eaten the food or drunk the water of Faerie for long enough will live for centuries. That is the source of my own longevity."

As impossible as it was to think this youthful man in front of me was almost four times my age, I had always felt an unusual depth of experience in his gaze. I'd considered him an *old soul*, as Agnes was wont to call her spiritualist friends. If that were literally true, would it matter?

If any of this was any more than mad fancy. I needed to focus on what was important here—finding my father, who apparently had planned to disappear without a trace and without warning anyone but Roger.

I exhaled in frustration, stood, and paced, rubbing my forehead.

"Is the headache tonic not helping?"

"No. I mean, yes. That's not it. I just need a moment." I folded my arms; boots pacing checkered tile floors, my footfalls echoed through the maze of books. Roger stayed behind, giving me space, which I appreciated.

Arms crossed, I stared up at the domed glass oculus, holding the sky in its lotus blossom pattern, and tried to banish anxiety with rhythmic steps.

The letters in Mother's painting. Father's disappearance. That he told Roger he was leaving, but not us. The odd markings in Father's room around the mirror. Roger's Equinox Bridge. My own… aversion to iron—I had to admit, it seemed to be true. If this was real… What did it mean if I was half-fairy? Father knew about this Reliqua. He made a show of condemning sorcery, but then used it himself. Could he have wanted Roger to find out where he'd gone? No doubt he knew I'd tell the man what happened, despite his warning that I should not see Roger again.

Misdirection. That fundamental principle of stage magic, as Father had taught me.

And Mother. She had been his assistant. A fellow illusionist. A member of Mrs. H's coven.

The woman in those old photos, wearing outlandish circus costumes, was someone I never knew. She and Father had once led a nomadic and adventurous life. Before I was born. Before she became ill. I always thought I had stolen her joy away, which caused her to die. It was only logical Father would resent me for it.

Could she really have been some mythical creature? A fairy? It was all so ridiculous it made my stomach turn—because I almost believed it.

And why? Because it might mean I was special. That there was a reason for my suffering. *That I wasn't simply ill.*

Before I'd realized it, I'd lost sight of our reading table, and Roger. I paced along a side wall, lined with more artwork. A landscape in oil depicted a morning view of sea cliffs. A marble sculpture of the god Mercury, crowned with wings, lithe body poised as in perpetual motion, carried a caduceus staff. I passed a portrait of a nun; another of a couple clad in fine Elizabethan clothing, with dark hair and features like Roger's.

A thread of melody ran through my thoughts. An old song Mother used to sing. I always thought she had learned it from the circus. The words were nonsense, she had told me, but I remembered them because they had a sort of rhyme and rolled off the tongue.

Nonsense words like the fanciful symbols she painted.

I sang a few lines. The song came back to me like I'd heard her sing it yesterday.

My crystal pendant hummed against my skin. I drew it out from behind my blouse, and it... glowed. A beautiful greenish blue-white, like a tiny star within the clear mineral.

I gasped. Blinked.

The light faded when my voice silenced. I sang another few lines of what I now understood was High Fae. The glow intensified again—brighter the longer I held the notes.

My voice echoed through the expansive library, amplified by the acoustics, lending my music a resonance that gave me gooseflesh. My pendant brightened. More disturbing, another light issued from my reticule. The vial.

I drew it out. The residue in the bottom emitted a reddish light. Visible to my naked eye this time, just as my pendant still shone. I sang the verse again, and the glow intensified.

I heard Roger's approaching footsteps and walked to meet him in an open central aisle.

He stood some paces away, gazing at me with awe.

When I'd sung the last note, tears sprang to my eyes, but I held them in check.

"It's a song my mother taught me. What does it mean?"

"Tell me the words again?"

I only spoke them, but the glowing pendant hummed against my chest. Roger translated after each line:

> *Round about me the ever-day*
> *Bright the morn and bright the night*
> *My love, my life, my radiant heart*
> *Keep the flame of life alight*

"It sounds like an illumination spell. Perhaps that's why it's caused your pendant to emit Faelight."

He saw it too. *It was real.*

"And this as well?" With a trembling hand, I held the vial aloft to show him, but when I looked at the glowing residue within, I heard an inaudible whisper. A sickly susurrus itched the back of my brain. The tone somewhere between laughter and obsessive chant. I gasped and clenched my eyes shut. It had been years since I'd endured this torment. Not since I'd last checked myself into the asylum. "No." I demanded, trying not to feel helpless as the child who had too long borne this burden alone.

The glass slipped from my fingers and shattered on the marble tile.

"Violet, what's wrong—" Roger quickened his pace to meet me. "God! What's that?"

I opened my eyes to see his wide with alarm, trained on something… behind me.

Swiftly, he moved to place his body between me and what I beheld, to my horror, was a tall mirror on the wall at the end of this aisle, hung alongside the paintings I had admired. I had not noticed it as I'd approached, framed in gold the same as the other large canvases.

Inside the mirror loomed my Shadow.

CHAPTER 7
TERRIBLE COST

enacing taller than life, the disproportioned silhouette obscured our reflections in the inverse library. It wavered and flickered, oozing over the silvered glass surface like a nightmare of oil on water.

"You… see it too?" Ice coursed through my veins.

"Of course. I don't know how it got past my wards. Unless it came in when I dropped them for you."

Not just in my head. It had been *real* all these years.

Violet. Come to me.

The hissing voice was not the same kind one from the garden last night. No, but I'd heard its sickening tones before. Too many times.

"Did you hear it speak?" I asked Roger.

Standing between me and the mirror we both faced, he took my hand. "No. What did it say?"

"It wants me to come to it."

Jaw clenched, he squeezed my hand in reassurance. "Stay here."

He strode toward the fiend, right hand raised in front of him, palm open. He chanted, quietly at first, but his voice rose into a commanding vibrato—a song of one sonorous note, full of resonance that reverberated through the wide expanse. The onyx ring he wore glowed a dark blue. The shadow quivered. Agitated. When Roger neared the mirror, he traced a large shape—a five-pointed star. The lines hung in the air like trails of luminescent smoke. I could not decipher the surrounding symbols he drew. With fingers outstretched, he punched through the center. My ears popped as the pressure in the room changed in an instant. With a crack like breaking glass, blue-white crystals formed in the middle of the mirror's surface. He made a fist and the ice spread like jagged tendrils of lightning, veiling the horrible silhouette of my enemy in a layer of frost.

Cautiously, I approached. The temperature of the ambient air dropped near the frozen mirror. Small icicles dripped from the gilded frame.

Roger turned to me. "The Shade won't be able to use this portal. At least not for a while. But there are other mirrors in my house. I'll need to reinforce the wards. If it addressed you, then it's fixated upon you somehow. Have you ever seen it before?"

"I… uh. Don't think so." My entire world had been toppled, and my mind was grasping at anything to keep from sliding into the abyss.

Roger knit his brow, as though he knew I was lying.

"You called it a Shade?" I asked, changing the subject. "Like a ghost?"

"Possibly. I don't yet have enough information. But there's no time for research. If I'm to find your father, I must leave right away. However, I must ensure your safety first. I fear this attack is no coincidence."

"What? You're leaving without me?" I ignored for the moment his inappropriate presumptions concerning my safety.

"Violet, you have no idea how dangerous it is where I intend to go. I can't put you in harm's way without good reason. Please, let me help. That's why you came here. If Mr. Morgen has crossed through to Faerie only last night, he can't have gotten too far. You have my word I won't rest until I find him or news of him."

"Why would you even help me, Roger? After how I treated you last night?"

An unspoken battle warred in those eyes—between honor, restraint, and reckless desire. He took my hand. "We're still friends, are we not?"

I swallowed, my heart heavy. "Yes. We are."

"I won't let you down. I promise."

I exhaled, closing my eyes to shut out the distraction of his. I thought of my father, my mother. I couldn't let this mystery pass me by, regardless of the danger. I had to follow it.

I met his passionate gaze and said, "I'm grateful for your help, Roger, but you're not doing this alone. If my father—my elderly, infirm father—journeyed into this Otherworld like you say, then I can survive it too. Besides, this is *my* quest. I'm not about to let you ride off to finish it for me. I understand there are risks, but don't you see? I must learn the truth of what I am—experience it firsthand. There's no way I can settle for less."

His eyes glimmered with what might have been pride, before they retreated to the somber aspect he often wore. "Very well. But there's more you must know. The Otherworld itself changes living matter. Infuses it with magic. It will transform you in many ways, both visible and invisible."

I sighed. Of course, it wouldn't be so simple. "Such as?"

"You will sense magic and other magical beings far more strongly than you do now. Your hearing and eyesight will be altered. Possibly your physiology. Your very thoughts may change. You may live for centuries. The Otherworld has given me longevity, as well as stronger magic. And my blood is mostly human."

"Mostly?"

"A distant ancestor of mine was a prince from the Winter Courts. Even so, just a season spent in Faerie, as every Reliqua warrior must do upon their thirteenth year, altered me forever. I've long ago forgotten what it was like to be only human."

"You make immortality sound so unappealing."

"I'm not immortal. I can be killed like anyone else. I do age, however slowly, which itself becomes a burden."

I breathed a frustrated laugh. He would make eternal youth sound like a curse.

"I'm serious. Do you want to see loved ones grow old and die while you remain unchanged? It's more difficult than you know. Not only that... I'm not sure what will happen if your family—I mean your mother's relations—discover you. They may force you to stay in Faerie. From what I read last night, that's Treaty law and custom regarding human hybrids who are born to the Royal families—the firstborn children, at least."

"Hybrids?" I might have been incensed at the label, if not for more pressing concerns.

"Yes. Our laws are quite specific. Because your mother was exiled, however, I'm not sure how they'll be interpreted. It's far from my expertise. One thing seems clear; your father must have wanted to keep your existence a secret. If you stay in this world and never cross through the Divide, your magic will diminish, and you'll become fully mortal. I can only think he wanted you to live what he considered a normal life."

I shook my head—an undercurrent of anger roiled within me. "Fade away? Diminish? No, thank you. I cannot forgive Father for hiding the truth of who I am from me. All my life. For such a theft of my heritage—of my *power*. He should've given me this choice, as you have. I have my difficulties in life, but I'm no coward."

"I know." He smiled. By God, he was charming when he smiled.

"We'll just have to keep my identity a secret."

"It might not be so easy. You're sure about this?"

"I am." I thought so. How long did one need to contemplate immortality? "Though I'm not exactly prepared for a journey. Do we have time to stop by my house so that I can pack some luggage?"

"I'm afraid we must leave right away. Every hour during Equinox Bridge is critical, but if you'll give me a few moments, I have… some of Felicity's clothing which should fit you. And I need to prepare a few other things." As always, when he spoke of his sister, sorrow tinged his voice. He walked toward a nearby shelf and drew out a book bound in blue leather. "In the meantime, here's some information about Faerie which may be of interest."

I took it and sat in a nearby reading chair. He snapped his fingers and the lamp on the table beside me flickered to life.

"Travers was right, you know. My father used to do that trick all the time."

He grinned. "I hope I have the chance to get to know him better."

To that, I had no answer.

"I won't be long. I'll find your Mr. Travers and bring him here. He can see us off."

"From here? How do we… Is there another mirror?"

"Not in the library." He scanned the room. "You'll be safe here until I can return. We shall open a doorway of light—over there in my circle." He pointed to the large black medallion in the center of the library. And why not? It made about as much sense as anything else this morning.

The book was part atlas and part bestiary, with woodcut illustrations of many creatures, both known and unknown to human mythology. The continents of Faerie appeared analogous to this world, though with many fascinating deviations—islands and mountain ranges unknown. Sections of Earth's familiar topography missing or moved to other places, like a hypothetical pre-history I'd seen of the primordial Earth, dreamed up by some zealous geologist. I shut the book closed after only a quick perusal.

What was I doing? I stood and paced until I was within sight of that awful ice-frosted mirror. It showed no signs of melting and oozed a genuine-enough bone-chilling cold. If Roger's magic was mere illusion, like my father's old stage acts, then his bluff would be called if he could not produce his *doorway of light* as promised.

And if it were true… what did that mean for my life? How could I live with myself if I *didn't* learn the truth of what I was? My birthright.

He's hiding something.

The thought was a dagger to my mind. Not from a disembodied voice like before. Not exactly. It was more of a whisper from my intuition, but it triggered physical anxiety I couldn't shake.

My headache, which had been dulled by the tonic, flared up with a vengeance, piercing the back of my eyeballs. I moaned and rubbed my temples.

I blinked. When I opened my eyes, I *was not in the library.*

Roger stood within a landscape of impossible green under a scarlet sky—but he was so young—somewhere between boy and man. His face twisted in torment, yet resolute. He raised a hand, gripping a silver dagger. The jewel in its pommel glowed dark red. He lunged toward me.

With a breath the vision vanished. My heart raced like a fleeing animal.

Now I was imagining dangerous things.

I navigated the maze of bookshelves and exited the room in the opposite direction as I'd seen Roger leave. Of course, I'd not gone ten meters before I ran into one of his servants. Again, I found it difficult to focus on the man's face, though I saw everything else in the corridor well enough.

"Can I help you, miss?" came the monotone inquiry.

"Ah... yes. Will you show me to a water closet? I'm afraid I need to freshen up." That wasn't a bad idea. After all, we were leaving on a journey, and I'd just drunk too much tea.

"Right this way." The man gave a half-bow and motioned for me to follow.

We passed through a smaller corridor toward what must have been the kitchen and servants' areas.

"Tell me about yourself," I asked as we walked. "You're not exactly human, are you?"

"Pardon me, miss?" The gruff voice sounded as though he were speaking through a thick mask. His gait was rather stiff and clumsy for an able man of middle age.

"You're a fairy, right?"

"No."

Look closer.

The thought was almost intrusive. It compelled my attention.

I blinked, determined to see his face clearly. The man's skin now appeared to be burlap. I willed my vision to focus and beheld... an animated doll. Behind two black buttons for eyes were glimmering pools of blue liquid light, as if the doll were stuffed with some macabre sorcery instead of sawdust. His mouth was a straight line, stitched in thick black thread. He had no nose or ears. Bald but for one small lock of real hair, the same color as Roger's, sewn into the seam at the crown of the dolls' head.

My hands shook. Reality didn't function this way.

If I ran, how quickly would I find the exit?

"Don't be alarmed." The thing stopped alongside me; stitched mouth curved into a mimicry of a smile. When it spoke, its lips didn't move.

"Are all Mr. Gale's staff… like you?"

The question puzzled the doll. It bent its canvas head, creasing a stuffed neck. "We need the poppets to work." It took another jolting step, gesturing for me to follow.

Reluctantly, I trod after it. "Poppets?"

"The bodies Magister made for us."

Another servant approached us in the corridor. Now that my mind had solved the enigma, I could see blazing orange eyes in a similar doll's head. Rough stitches pulled gaps in the sawdust-stuffed burlap of an eldritch smile.

"Do you require anything, miss?" The other one asked.

"No. I'm afraid I'm not feeling well." An understatement. "Just a wash-room to freshen up."

"Here we are." The first poppet bowed and opened a door to a vacant guest room. How did those mitten hands even manage the glass doorknob? They showed me the en-suite water-closet before they left to allow me privacy. But I sensed one or more lingered nearby.

I closed the door. Gasping in shock. *What on earth was going on here?*

The old Victorian plumbing fixtures in the Gale estate's guest water-closets were immaculately preserved. Here again, the house was lost in the past, as if everything had stopped on some eventful day long ago.

I couldn't trust Roger until I knew what else he was hiding. I exited through a different door leading into a deserted, linen-draped study, then into a sitting room; this one hosted more cloth-draped furniture and a partially revealed harpsichord. On a wall hung another portrait of Roger's sister Felicity, wearing an empire gown in white and celadon. The girl's wistful eyes peered right through me.

Voices in the rooms to my left sounded as though they had bodies of some sort, so I took a doorway to the right. Perhaps I'd find a stairway. People with secrets might well keep them underground.

I found the house's main turret, hoping no one would hear my footfalls on the tile. The surrounding gardens filled large windows. Light from an overcast sky illuminated a swirling pattern in the mosaic floor. I followed a sickening taste of iron toward a curving staircase.

An *iron* staircase. This must discourage Fae from approaching here. What was in that tower?

Not surprising, my headache returned. Pain and dread warned as I neared the abhorrent metal.

If I were Fae, I was only half so. My human blood had allowed me to climb those trolley steps just days ago. I failed to conquer that steam-breathing dragon, but I was always able to enter the belly of the beast before I ran away in terror. This time I wouldn't run.

I leapt forward. Momentum carried me the first few meters. Ice crawled my spine. Pain like hot needles accosted my heels with each ringing thud of my boots, but I did not grip the forbidden railing.

On the wooden second floor landing, I gasped for breath, gathering strength for the second flight. Roger's voice echoed from below. He called my name, but I did not answer. I had only one more flight to go. Puffing from exertion, I couldn't slow down.

At the top of the stairs, I found a circular landing. Tall windows framed a view of the grounds. From tiled roof peaks, stone gargoyles gazed at a darkling sky. A storm was moving in, stirring somber evergreens from their slumber.

An arched door stood before me. Amber burl-wood grains lay opposite one another in a butterfly effect. The mottled ink-blot pattern formed a fearsome face. The door itself inflamed my senses, more than the iron doorplate.

"Violet." Footfalls shook the stairwell. "Wait for me, please. It's not safe for you!"

I grabbed the iron latch, searing my skin like ice and fire. I cried out in pain and frustration and swung the door open, clenching a throbbing fist as I stepped forward.

At the sight which greeted me, I stood frozen, numb with shock, even when Roger's steps approached behind me.

He touched my shoulder. "I would have shown this to you, if you'd only given me time."

Shafts of light poured from high skylights into a dark, wood-paneled room. A collection of hunting trophies appeared to cover the walls—the sort wealthy gentlemen will plunder from foreign continents. But of course, it was only illusion.

The camouflage lifted before my newly determined discernment. I witnessed an ordinary bison head dissolve into a monstrosity full of reptilian teeth, with glass eyes the size of cricket balls. Curved horns crowned metallic scales gleaming against the trophy's ebony-wood mounting. Dragon. I'd never believed in their literal existence.

There beside a velvet chase was a rearing beast—eagle-like claws spread in a taxidermist's recreation of a predator's lunge. Golden feathers, a mane of fur, and a cruel-looking beak. Griffon. Frozen in a silent lament, it might once have possessed a frightful voice.

I shrugged off Roger's touch and strode into the center of the room. Horrors accosted my vision. The heads of so many unearthly creatures, frozen in death with expressions they may never have worn in life, gaped back at me. Skin, feathers, tentacles. Even some faces covered in bark and antler-like branching. Above a stone hearth was an oil painting of a hunt on horseback, in much the classic style, but these rifle-bearing riders chased a centaur.

I approached a wall of shelves. A tiny creature with miniature, human-looking hands and feet floated in a liquid-filled jar of formaldehyde (if fairies didn't require some unique chemical preservative). I turned away when I spotted a lifeless head, though it was no bigger than a bean. Row after row of specimens sat in multi-colored jars. Cloches covered stuffed oddities mounted to driftwood or stones.

What did he mean to do *with me?*

"How many of these did you kill?"

"Violet." Roger's voice was nearly as cracked with strain as my own.

An ornate set of brass scales dominated one marble-backed countertop. Beside it marched crocks and jars of powders, mixtures, and dried bones.

Labeled. As though they contained ingredients for sale.

"How many?" I demanded, finding the courage to meet his eyes, this man who must have made his comfortable living by selling literal pieces of creatures like me.

"Many." His shoulders slumped. "This room contains trophies collected by seven generations of my family. I've added many prizes to this room. Please understand, all these creatures violated the Queen's Treaty, becoming threats to humanity. This is part of our duty as knights of the Reliqua."

"Prizes… Threats."

I had no desire to run. Preserving my own life seemed less critical than knowing the truth. A wave of nausea swept me. I braced myself on a nearby leather chair.

"None of us can decide the circumstances of our birth in this life." An edge of desperation in his voice.

"Am I another prize to you, Mr. Gale? Will you keep me prisoner here like those horrid dolls you call servants? Or will you harvest me for profit?"

"What? No. I could never harm you. *Never*, I swear. Violet, I… I'm in lo—"

"No! Don't you dare…" With a trembling hand, still stinging from the burn of the iron doorknob, I pushed his words away.

I turned to walk along a macabre apothecary shelf, wincing at each label. A jar marked troll dung sat next to one filled with glittering sea-serpent scales. Arrayed on a framed cork board were what should have been butterfly wings, yet they were some unknown, beautiful shape. The sight pulled on me from within, like a primeval memory.

Fairy wings. Plucked. Dried. Pinned like bugs.

At the tread of his step, I retreated farther away.

"Violet," he pleaded. "These were lawful kills. Each of these Fae crossed into the human realm intending to do harm. The Reliqua protects the balance between worlds, as I told you before. Sometimes we must do so… at terrible cost."

"Intending to do harm?" I wiped my face with a shaking hand. "Do you kill them before they act on such intention? What if they don't even know what they are? Like me?"

I backed away, willing my breathing to slow, asking my heart to calm. I needed to think rationally, but in my current state, that was impossible.

Violet.

The voice was not Roger's. I clapped hands over my ears.

A long glass box, bordered and hinged in gleaming gold, caught my eye. Inside was a horn. White, pearlescent, and spiraled, it tapered to a beautiful point. Beside it lay a silver knife. Bits of the horn had been shaved away from its base.

"Tell me that's not what I think it is." But my heart knew the truth. It called to me with a siren song, underneath the awful silence of the room.

Roger did not answer.

"Did you do this?" I wiped my face with trembling fingers.

"Yes." Tears pooled in Roger's eyes before they rolled down those sculpted cheeks.

"Why?"

"The horn of a unicorn is full of healing properties. With it I have saved many human lives. Many more will be." Roger's voice took on a hollow timber, nearly void of emotion, yet his face couldn't hide the shame, even behind practiced words.

"How can you weigh one life against another?"

A flash of light blinded me. A vision of gleaming fur and mane against green—an animal of ethereal light. Old sorrow overcame me, from a source not my own.

Violet.

A compulsion overwhelmed my rational impulses. The vision wanted—needed—to impart some hidden truth. Before Roger could stop me, I lifted the box's glass lid and touched the horn.

The floor disappeared below my feet.

"No!" Roger's voice faded into echoing distance.

I fell. Gravity. Air. Blue-violet sky.

Tree limbs and thorns tore at my clothing before all went black.

CHAPTER 8
GUARDIAN OF THE FOREST

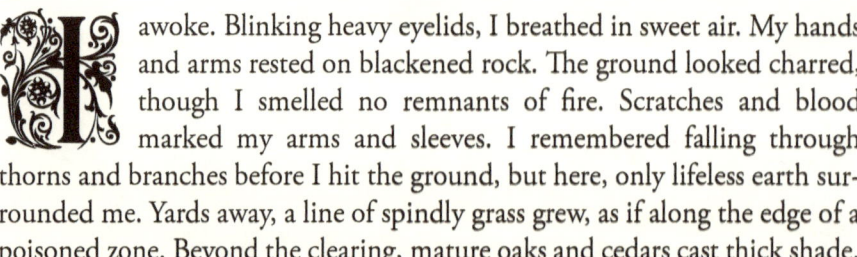

awoke. Blinking heavy eyelids, I breathed in sweet air. My hands and arms rested on blackened rock. The ground looked charred, though I smelled no remnants of fire. Scratches and blood marked my arms and sleeves. I remembered falling through thorns and branches before I hit the ground, but here, only lifeless earth surrounded me. Yards away, a line of spindly grass grew, as if along the edge of a poisoned zone. Beyond the clearing, mature oaks and cedars cast thick shade.

I stretched my limbs. Nothing seemed broken, but my arms and cheek were scratched from my fall through thorns and treetops, though none of the cuts looked bad. What vegetation? When there was nothing around me now? Perhaps I had been moved. I stood and dusted off my torn sleeves and skirts.

What happened? I'd discovered Roger's macabre trophy room at the top of that tower. I'd touched the unicorn horn and seen a flash of... terrible vision. I remembered the fall. A sensation like being pulled along a beam of light.

Then I awoke here. But where was here?

The sky was ablaze with color. Either sunrise or sunset. The sun must be just below the horizon, and... I could not define a singular light source for the scene. The sky was equally illuminated in all directions. I'd painted many a morning or evening view—scrutinized all manner of heavenly lighting schemes. Nothing natural ever looked like this.

This had to be the Otherworld.

The view of the Atlantic seemed familiar. A rocky creek angled downhill toward the sea cliffs, dropping away to the ocean's indigo line. I was facing east, if I correctly read the southern coastline, but the countryside was devoid of all human alteration. No lighthouse perched on Gull Peak. No dynamite-blasted rock made room for roadways. No fishing docks or steam-breathing ships. Yet, far more colorful architecture lined the distant shore. Was there a Fae village here, in place of the Seastone I knew?

From this elevation, I could just glimpse the Atlantic through inland hills. I must be in the Welterwood. If our worlds were indeed mirrors of each other, how had I arrived at this geographical location from Roger's house?

Roger. Damn him and his secrets. I pushed away the memory of his gorgeous, shocked face in that horrific room.

Overcome with thirst, I needed to find water. Through the sea breeze, I heard the rush of rapids. I limped in that direction until my legs found their strength.

Rocky land sloped into a fern-covered ravine. I picked my way down to a wider stream. Along the pebbled shores, where moldering leaves blanketed fallen logs, clusters of blue-green bioluminescent fungus lit the flowing water. Ferns and moss clung to any patch of soil between massive boulders. No doubt this waterway hosted rapids when spring thaws melted winter ice and snow.

Once, long ago, I'd seen foxfire. Mrs. H had called it *will-o'-the-wisp* when we spotted it from our carriage. She didn't want us to stop, for fear of bad luck, but my father insisted upon investigating. We'd walked into the swampy woodlands together, in search of that mysterious light, and found what he told me to expect. A patch of glowing fungus sprung from the side of a fallen log.

Bioluminescence, Father had said. *There's always a rational explanation for whims of fancy. No higher magic than the science of the natural world.*

After following the rocks upstream, I located a still pool of water. I knelt and drank my fill, not much caring if I muddied my skirts. I remembered Roger's warning about drinking the water or eating the food of Faerie, but it was impossible to turn back now.

The water tasted wonderful. Sweeter than honey wine; so said the bards of yore. They must have been here.

I splashed my face, washed my scratched arms and hands. The blood ran away with the current. My skin was clean and healed. No injury remained.

Before I could wonder why, a powerful drowsiness overtook me. I yawned and lay on the pebbled ground. The air tasted of living forest, earth, stone, and sea salt. Clouds veiled fading stars like flowing layers of silk.

There was something important I must do, but I was so... tired...

I heard music on the breeze. Enchanting notes like bells accompanied an invisible piper's flute. Eerie lights twinkled at my vision's hazy edges. Bigger than fireflies, they encroached upon me. I was near powerless to move, like that paralyzed state between sleep and waking wherein my Shadow appeared.

The music was so fine; I closed my eyes. I wanted to dance—if I were not so tired. I could listen to it forever...

Something crashed through the trees. The noise jarred my senses. My heart sped, startling me back to consciousness.

The pixie lights scattered—retreating into the forest, along with their music. Only the sound of the wind remained. Even the birds had silenced.

A hideous screech pummeled my ears. From upstream—made by a *large* creature.

Exposed as I was, I saw no easy access to higher ground. I crouched in the shadow of a large rock.

The beast tramped through water, moving in my direction. I could not outrun it, and I had no weapon.

Splash. Splash. Heavy steps grew closer, followed by a rasping growl.

A hand on my shoulder made me gasp in fright.

A woman crouched beside me. She was dressed in trousers like a man, her blonde hair pulled back in coils of braid. She wore a leather cap and coat, and a kind of aviator goggles, with one lens turquoise and the other a dull red. Like Roger's Spectrocles.

She placed a finger over her mouth to indicate silence.

"Basilisk," she whispered, "Its eyes are deadly. Don't look directly at them, or you'll turn to stone."

She carried a large handgun, augmented by a tube of luminous gas above the barrel. I sensed iron. In her other hand, she held a silver-framed mirror, one a lady might keep on her dressing table. She slumped alongside me and tipped her mirror just past our boulder's edge, spying on the approaching creature's reflection.

Forcing myself to watch the mirror, I caught a glimpse.

The creature's head resembled a dragon's, but with the beak and wings of a bird—talons and stance like a rooster's, and a serpent's belly and tail. Its plumage was turquoise and silver. Scales tipped with gold. The reflected face held two red orbs for eyes. Atmosphere around the beast appeared to shimmer in heat mirage.

It stomped through the rushing stream, sniffing the air, its heat creating steam. It screeched again, snake's tail rattling. This close, I feared my eardrums would burst.

The woman flipped a switch on the side of her pistol, and some miniscule dynamo cranked up a high-pitched whine. Gas-filled chambers above the stock glowed. She watched the mirror, aiming behind her back, and fired.

The bullet left a tracer of green luminescence. She'd only grazed the beast's wing.

"Shit! Run!"

I dashed one way and she another, shouting to draw its attention. I crouched behind a different boulder. The basilisk screeched. She shot again, blind-sighted as before. This time, her bullet connected somewhere near a leg, but it didn't slow it down.

I remembered reading about basilisks in an old book of fairy stories. Shiny things mesmerized them, so the legend said.

What did I have to lose? I grabbed the crystal necklace and sang Mother's song. The spell of Illumination, Roger had called it.

In this world, those syllables awoke a store of energy I never knew I possessed. Power pulsed through my body—at once alien and familiar, like I'd flexed a forgotten muscle. I tasted a charge in the air, like ozone after a storm. My hair follicles stood on end. I was a conduit for some unknown force as natural as my quickened pulse.

The pendant glowed almost too brightly. The beast turned and hesitated—flummoxed. I only risked a glance before I averted my eyes.

The basilisk paced toward me, mesmerized by the light. The grass withered and died where it stepped. It radiated heat like a furnace blast.

The woman took this chance and shot. This time, she connected. The beast reared and roared, turning its fury on her. She fired again and missed.

Twisting, the massive bird-like beast whipped its snake's tail to strike. The woman staggered backward. The foe raised a claw. I shouted, but it struck her arm. She dropped her mirror and cried out in pain.

I ran to stand in front of her, chanting my spell. The basilisk faltered when it contemplated my aura of magical light.

My new companion arose and drew a sword from over her injured shoulder. In one quick move, she severed the basilisk's head from its neck. I heard a dull thud hit the grass, seconds before the rest of the body slammed into the ground.

"It's safe to look now," she said. "Thank you, Lady." She knelt and wiped her blade on a patch of charred and smoking grass. "Whoever you are, I owe you. I've not seen one of those in ages." She pointed to my crystal.

I clasped the pendant. "A gift from a friend."

Friend. How could I overlook what Roger was? A hunter of Otherworld trophies.

Like this woman, it seemed.

She checked a bleeding shoulder. Blood darkened the black sleeve of her coat. Wet fabric clung to a limp arm.

"Are you all right? Your arm… I mean."

"It looks worse than it is."

"There's a healing pool nearby. I can show you."

"No time. Help me gather as many feathers as possible. Quickly—before it petrifies. You can keep them. I'm only after the eyes."

She parted a section of bluish-green feathers and pulled them out by the root. She offered me the first handful, and halfway bowed. "Dr. Evelyn Crane. I don't believe we've met." Her manner of speaking, and her commanding demeanor, were at odds with her delicate-looking, youthful face. She seemed to contain far more experience in her goggle-framed gaze than a woman of her age should. Not unlike someone else I knew.

"Violet Morgen, pleased to meet you." I could think of no reason to hide my name, but little reason to trust her, either. I pulled feathers while she inspected the severed head. When she drew a knife and set to work extracting the eyes, I turned away in disgust. The brilliant color of the plumage in my hand nearly made me sick.

What had I done? I helped her destroy this thing. A creature of Faerie. Like me.

Had the Basilisk only charged us in defense? Perhaps it would have tried to kill me, but I had no way of knowing what would have happened if she hadn't taken the first shot.

I set down the bag of feathers and walked again toward the stream. I found a large leaf and fashioned it into a cup, filling it as well as possible. I brought some back to Evelyn, who placed two bloody orbs on top of the hand-held mirror.

"I'm no expert," I said, "but you really should tend to that wound. This is water from the spring that healed me moments ago. You should use it on your shoulder. If it's not enough, I'll go back for more."

"Thank you, but it won't work for me."

"It does. I promise."

"You're Fae. Don't you see that I'm human, thus, the magic won't work on me?" To my baffled expression, she added. "But you've saved me a trip. Would you pour that on the mirror here? I need it to preserve these."

"You're a Reliqua warrior, then?" I hadn't meant for it to sound exactly like a question.

"I am." She shifted to sit cross-legged.

"How old are you? If you don't mind me asking."

She laughed. "I'm one hundred and eleven."

"Is this some sort of spell?" I pointed to the mirror.

"More like a chemical reaction. The water in the Spring Courts is charged with a property which reacts to silver, and in turn on the magic of the basilisk."

I poured water over the extracted eyes, as large as two bloody boiled eggs. The hand mirror's silver frame was just tall enough to contain a thin puddle. The water bubbled as if boiling, turned dark green, then black. Within seconds, the tissue absorbed all the liquid.

Evelyn wiped her gory hands with a rag, drew a symbol in the air over the mirror, then picked up one petrified orb. It shone like polished marble. Black, veined with traces of gold, scarlet, and umber.

"Priceless," she said. "A shame I'll need to destroy it."

"Why?"

"Now, there's a question I can't answer until you've answered a few of mine, Lady of the Summer Courts with a human name."

"Oh?" I didn't know how she even recognized me as Fae, let alone the rest. Perhaps Roger had told her.

Evelyn pointed at me with a bloody knife. "First, why are you wearing human clothing out here—an inappropriate ensemble at that?" She pocketed the two petrified eyes.

"Inappropriate? I beg your pardon."

She wiped her knife on the dead grass. "Evasive too, I see."

"Look who's talking. And for your information, I'm not exactly certain how I was transported to this location. I might have worn different clothing if I'd properly planned."

"Which brings me to the next point. Just whom are you working for?"

"No one. I'm here on my own quest. That's a direct enough answer, I presume?" I crossed my arms, wishing she didn't have me on the defensive.

The sky still hadn't changed, though hours must have passed since I arrived. The basilisk's body had lost color. All the vibrant feathers had turned gray, save the ones I'd pulled from the corpse. She could keep her blasted feathers.

"Why exactly did we kill this creature? It didn't seem to be a threat until we provoked it. Was it only for those *priceless* eyes?"

Far from offended, her response was guarded, cautious. "I've been tracking this beast for a day. It'd crossed through to the human realm and burned down a warehouse before I was dispatched to kill it. It evaded me by slipping through the Divide, so I pursued. I intend to make a full report for the Courts."

Did she think I was someone else? Someone important? She called me a Lady of the Summer Courts. This presumption might work to my advantage.

Best to only nod and not say much. She'd slipped her arm and shoulder out of her jacket and blouse to check her wound.

"You need a few stitches."

"I don't have a med kit with me. I'll have to wrap it tight until I can find a healer. It's not bad."

I began tearing strips from the hem of my skirt, the unmuddied portions anyway, enough for a new rag and bandages. She thanked me. I suggested we locate the patch of yarrow I'd noticed not far back to make a poultice.

"Yarrow? Did Roger teach you that?" She pressed the fabric against her shoulder. She wore a ring like Roger's on her right hand.

I almost answered before I caught what she'd done. "You must mean Mr. Gale." No use in denying it at this point.

Evelyn sighed. "It was the crystal. Took me a moment, but I remembered it. She sometimes wore it—his sister."

"Felicity."

"Yes." She slid the goggles down to hang around her neck, revealing steel-blue eyes. Her gaze swept to the far horizon. "She was… dear to me." Evelyn still held the loss close. I saw it in the creases of her eyes and the stern set of her lips.

"I'm sorry. He misses her too."

Her exasperated sigh signaled contempt. "Gale's actions are the reason Felicity killed herself. Whoever you are, Miss Violet Morgen, be warned. House Gale caused the Welterwood's curse. He killed the sacred guardian of this forest. Over a century ago. Not far from this very spot." She gestured in the direction from which I'd come.

"Was it a… unicorn?"

"Then you know."

"Not exactly."

She shook her head, pressing the bandage to her wound.

"No time for yarrow. The bleeding has almost stopped." I wanted to help her tie another strip of cloth around her shoulder to hold it in place, but she insisted upon doing it herself.

"You should understand," she added. "Gale broke one of our most ancient laws. By killing its guardian, this forest was left vulnerable to all manner of corrupting evil. This basilisk—it never would have ventured here before. Not so near the Queen's Circle."

"You mean… the old ring of standing stones?" I surveyed the surrounding landscape, but I had been so many years since I'd visited that ancient monument, and the woods on this side were different from home. "They're not far from here?"

"Yes, just a few miles that way to the east." She pointed.

"It's hard to gauge one's direction in this world with no visible sun," I said. "When will it ever rise?"

"How is it you understand so little about your own world?" She allowed me to help her stand, at least.

"My father is human. I didn't know about the Otherworld until only a short time ago. How is it you can tell I'm Fae?"

She tapped her goggles.

"Right. Spectrocles. Roger showed me those too."

"I invented the things, you know." She grinned in evident pride at her work, then she sighed. "To answer your earlier question, since it seems Gale hasn't told you much at all... We're in the Spring Courts—the world of perpetual dawn, where Seastone's double exists. The Otherworld is divided into four seasons and four portions of the day. In the Queen's Summer Court, it is always daylight. In the Autumn Court, the sky is forever twilight. And in the Winter Court—"

"It's eternal night?" I thought of Mother's painting with the castle under a moonlit sky.

"Yes."

"Why are you here?" she asked.

It was a good question. "I'm searching for my father. I believe he's here in Faerie. He's unwell and needs my help."

"Ah. Well, I've not seen another human since I arrived. However, I've been in pursuit of this basilisk all day, and haven't spoken to many others."

So, what was my next step? "The village by the coast. I think I'll go and ask around myself."

"It just so happens," she said, "I'm headed to a road which will take you there." Evelyn looked upstream and added, "Tonight, I will observe an equinox ritual at the Queen's Circle. I'll speak with others of my Order about your missing father. If anyone has seen or heard anything, we shall send word to House Gale. No doubt he can relay information to you?"

"Roger won't be there? At the ritual?" It wasn't exactly a question, but it avoided her last one.

"No. Gale is banned from the Welterwood and cannot partake of our ceremonies in that sacred place. Much to his detriment—and ours. Despite our longevity, our numbers in Reliqua are dwindling. Many of the lights of our Houses are extinguished."

Roger spoke about his duties to this mysterious order of knights, but he'd not mentioned he was on the outs with them. I wasn't sure if that was good or bad.

He was *cursed*. I'd seen enough already to know she was right, but what did it mean? I didn't want to ask. It made my heart sick.

We walked upstream and climbed the opposite bank, leaving behind a new boulder not far from the healing water. If one looked closely at those rocks, one might think them a weathered old monument, its purpose long lost to time and erosion. In its smooth shape, little evidence remained of the basilisk, or the role I'd played in the creature's demise.

CHAPTER 9
HEART'S COMPASS

We walked toward what Evelyn called the Fae Roads.

Our path meandered into a glade lined by maples, their dew-laden leaves like stars in the morning light. A pond in the distance reflected colorful sky. The landscape bore no evidence of human habitation or roads of any kind, other than the thin footpath we followed.

A shimmering mist floated through the air just above the treetops. The farther we ventured into the meadow, the more I noticed threads of iridescent-gold winding through the atmosphere. The clouds appeared like the lining of an abalone shell.

Dr. Crane explained that a kind of magic charge was concentrated near ley lines, such as along the Fae Roads, which had long ago been marked by the old standing stones, which she called Waystones. According to her, Fae could use these roads instinctively, while humans relied on relics to detect and use them.

"Such as this map." She drew from her vest-pocket a velvet pouch containing a crystal ball the size of a small apple. We stopped, and she held the orb aloft. The sphere refracted the surrounding landscape, capturing miniature hills and valleys upside down. She hummed a string of syllables and threads of light appeared inside. When she moved the map, it showed a menhir beyond the next hill. Its fallen twin lay beside it. I'd sketched those stones before. Remnants of a forgotten epoch.

"Here." She handed me the orb. "The Road can take us almost anywhere on the island. Even across the sea, although a trans-oceanic path is extremely risky. Avoid it unless you have no other choice."

"How does it work?" I held the sphere aloft, catching the inverse horizon.

"Wait," she said. "Look there."

One of the many threads of light within vibrated like a plucked harp string. A bead of brilliance pulsed along its length, traveling in our direction.

"Someone is coming." Evelyn pocketed the sphere and drew her pistol. "We have the advantage; they'll be momentarily disoriented."

Though I'd never in my life fired a gun, I wished I had a weapon.

Evelyn and I faced the Waystones. The corona around the granite brightened. A ball of light coalesced in the air between the two monoliths.

With a flash like silent lightning, a figure appeared. A man, wearing a black fedora and longcoat I recognized. Roger caught his breath for a moment before he took a wobbling step, and rested a hand on the stone.

"Is that you, Gale?" Evelyn shouted. She lowered her gun but didn't holster it.

"Evelyn Crane?" Roger turned toward us. "Violet! Thank God!" He hurried in our direction.

Evelyn aimed her weapon at him. "Come no closer, House Gale. You are forbidden to set foot on this sacred ground."

Roger raised his hands in mock surrender. "House Crane, there's no need for this. The forest is a mile away." He pointed to the woods from which we'd traveled.

"Nevertheless, this Waystone marks the proper border of the Welterwood. I cannot let you pass. You know what the Queen said would happen if you transgressed her ruling."

"The ground will swallow me whole." Roger couldn't hide the bitterness and near desperation in his voice. "Hyperbole… ceremonial hogwash. I respect my boundaries."

"Do you?"

Roger peered across the moor to the distant tree line. His expression fell into familiar sorrow. "Right now, I only need to know my friend is safe." Roger turned to me. "May I speak with you, Violet?"

I could read in his face a genuine concern for my safety. My heart fluttered, but my mind wanted to evaluate him with caution. How foolish this contradiction of will and desire.

Evelyn answered for me, with her gun still trained on him. "You can see well enough from there. Your friend is fine. No thanks to you."

"If you've come to her aid, House Crane, I'm in your debt once again. I never would have sent Miss Morgen through without a guide, but we were… unexpectedly separated."

Roger took another step toward us, but Evelyn raised her hand in warning. He halted, shoulders slumped, entreating eyes meet mine. "Violet, I am so relieved to find you. I've been searching for you these last few hours. What happened?" He looked at my torn sleeves. "Are you injured?"

"I'm fine."

"I promise I won't leave you out here alone again."

"What if I asked you to? Let me go on alone, that is?"

I didn't expect to see genuine remorse—even defeat—in his eyes.

"It's not safe. I can't allow you to put yourself in such danger. At least travel with Dr. Crane if you don't trust me."

Evelyn moved to stand in front of me, blocking Roger's view. She furrowed her brow, whispering. "What has he done to you?"

What had my father said to me a few nights ago? *To each of us, the cards of fate are dealt.* But Father had known my phobias controlled my life, and he'd known the reason for them all along, but had kept me in the dark.

"Roger only told me the truth," I answered her, "when no one else would. I hated him for it, but now I know he was right."

"Perhaps." Evelyn holstered her weapon. "Accepting truth is never easy. Finding it can only be done alone. Don't exchange new lies for old ones, regardless of who tells them."

I walked to Roger, sensing his palpable relief. Were it not for the iron in the weapons he wore, enough to keep me at a comfortable distance, I might have been tempted to walk into his arms.

"Mr. Gale," I addressed him. "What gives you the right to decide how I conduct my life? If I choose to put myself in danger, that's my business. Do you not put yourself in danger every time you go on one of your horrible trophy hunts? Besides, now that we are out of the forest, *which you cursed*, I think I shall encounter fewer obstacles."

"That's not true," Evelyn interjected. "There are dangers everywhere. Gale is right in that much. Traveling through this realm is too hazardous for the uninitiated. You need a trained guide."

"Understood." I turned to Roger. "If you still wish to accompany me, Mr. Gale, I have one condition."

"Yes?"

"You follow my lead. I'm going to the village to see if my father left any clues. I'm doing this one way or the other, should you choose to come along or not."

"Agreed," he nodded, with not-so-subtle relief written on his face.

Roger pulled from his coat pocket a glass orb like the one Evelyn used moments ago, along with a small brass compass. While he set about searching the horizon for a point on the compass, Evelyn approached us.

"Here." She handed me the leather bag full of basilisk feathers. "In the village, these are worth a good deal in trade. You'll need them if you stay here for any length of time."

"I can't take this. Didn't you need them?"

She shook her head. "It's our tradition. You helped make the kill, so you've earned part of the spoils. Besides, I only wanted the eyes."

"You killed a basilisk?" Shocked, Roger looked from me to Evelyn. "What was it doing in the Spring Courts?"

"Exactly. This was a Winter Court sub-species, no less." Evelyn scrutinized him, as though watching for some tell of guilt. "Have you heard nothing of the shipyard fires it caused this morning?"

"No. What was it doing by the shipyards? Could someone have been transporting it?"

"So the Council wants to know. They dispatched me to neutralize the threat, but the basilisk fled to the Queen's Circle and opened a portal to the Otherworld. I crossed through, followed its tracks for half a day before I located it a few miles to the southwest." She pointed in the direction we'd come. "And found Miss Morgen, who helped me trounce it."

"Dr. Crane," I offered a hand. "Thank you. I hope we shall meet again."

To my surprise, Evelyn hugged me in return. "As do I. Be safe. Remember, appearances in this world are deceiving—the rule rather than the exception."

She nodded to Roger. "Fare thee well, House Gale."

Evelyn waited some paces away, perhaps for her turn to use this ancient transportation device.

The upright menhir loomed twice as tall as me, unnaturally bright, weathered and dotted with lichens and moss, like the fallen stone at its side. When we drew near enough, I sensed a low, inaudible tone emanating from the stone. When I laid a hand on the cold surface, energy like a struck tuning fork resonated through my bones.

I pulled my hand away. "I fear I'm connected to the magic of this world in ways I don't understand. Earlier, I sang Mother's song and felt..." I couldn't put it into words.

Roger came to stand closer beside me. I'd missed his ardent voice, the way his greater height always made me look up into those green eyes, the way he smelled like spice and open air and seasoned old books. Yet I couldn't ignore the gnawing sense of the iron weapons he wore, or the knowledge of what he was. What he'd done.

"Your link to this world's power is real, but you mustn't fear. You can learn to use this power for great good or great evil. Above all else, you must trust your heart, for thoughts alone often deceive and confuse us." He held the brass compass out in front of us. "Let it be your guide. If you listen, it will pull you in the right direction." He pointed to a spot on the horizon to the southwest. "There's an exit point not far from your house. Do you know the Waystone by... our orchard?"

"Our orchard?" Remembering our kiss, I attempted, despite the resulting rush of emotion, to raise an eyebrow at him.

He grinned in return, distracting me from my burning questions. I almost didn't care.

"We can walk to the village from there. It might do to check the area around your home first."

"Right."

Roger placed the crystal ball in my hands. I held it up to better catch the vibrant horizon.

So much for my own internal compass. Roger himself was a powerful magnet; his fields of force skewed all my other means of perception. I don't doubt he had an inkling that was so. Furthermore, it seemed, in the way he looked at me, I might do the same to him.

"Here..." He patted his jacket, searching for something in a pocket, and drew out a ring. "You'll need this too. It's a traveling relic."

He placed on my right index finger a gold filigree band containing an oval stone, one side black and the other white.

I moved my hand into shadow and detected a faint light from the stone. If it seemed my hand also glowed, it might only have been the stone's halo.

"How do I use this to open a doorway?" Inside the glass orb, threads of illumination ran to and from the reflected Waystones.

"If you'll forgive my intrusion, we must be in physical contact, as you shall be the one to transport us. May I?"

I nodded, and Roger slipped an arm around my waist. I held the stone out in front, while he searched for our destination with his compass.

"Trace the path we should go, like this." He demonstrated. "You will speak these Words of power." He whispered the sounds beside my ear, enticing a frisson along my spine. The language of my ancestors took on shape and substance in my mind, settled into place like lost puzzle pieces of my soul.

He continued, his voice an embrace. "Visualize the destination in your mind. With your speech and intention, move us from here to there."

As though my finger were a brush, I traced the path of the road across the smooth glass surface. I spoke the Words. Their shapes and sounds awoke within me a vibration akin to the energy of the standing stones.

The Waysphere's light intensified. The world brightened until I had to close my eyes.

My feet left the ground. We clung to one another, weightless. If we were falling, it was sideways. The motion held no unpleasant jolt, for it was no ordinary force which propelled us. Our limbs remained stationary, yet we flew, as though we stood on a transient beam of light. I winced at an approaching bank of clouds. Roger braced me. Incorporeal, my fingers might just pass through his surface. As soon as my mind had made peace with that thought, the earth rushed up, and gravity connected us with solid earth once more.

I landed partially on top of my companion, in a meadow of green grass. Dizzy, we gasped for breath. Racing hearts beat side by side. I was in no hurry to move, even though the iron he wore gave me chills. He let me brush a wayward lock of hair from his face; his satisfied grin all the more bewitching. Even as the disorientation passed, my pulse sped, having nothing to do with exertion. I wanted answers, but I also wanted to kiss him again.

I moved away to break the spell and immediately missed his warmth.

The magic ring on my finger dulled. From the ground beside us, I retrieved the orb, which now appeared as nothing more than ordinary glass. If we were in the orchard near my home, no cultivated fruit trees grew on these hills. The view to the sea was identical, albeit sans any manmade structures. The same Waystone I'd sketched on many an afternoon loomed beside us— our Fairy Road exit point.

Roger sat up and took the orb when I offered it, returning it to a waistcoat pocket.

I tried to stand and walk, but my legs were jelly. I plopped back down and braced a spinning head.

"The aftereffects of traveling via the Fae Roads. It will pass in a moment." Roger took my hand. "Breathe."

I drank in the sweet air. The trees here grew wild—not the pruned and orderly orchard rows I knew. Here among evergreens bloomed crabapples, dogwoods, cherries, and myrtles. Earthly jewels to mirror the brilliant sky. Bees drifted among fragrant blossoms, adding their music to the crash of the not-too-distant sea.

Roger didn't speak until I turned to him. He'd been gazing at me.

"Violet, back at my home, I was terrified when you disappeared before my eyes. I don't know how that happened. I tried to stop it, but the powers at work were greater than mine. Please believe me when I say I'd never allow any harm to come to you. I would die to protect you."

"Why?" The word surprised me, but it also emboldened me. "Why, Roger? Because you say you're in love with me? You've only known me for a few months."

He looked stung. "Do you feel nothing for me?"

"Nothing?" I threw up my hands in despair. "No. I feel *many* things for you, Mr. Gale. Difficult and complicated things. Why should I believe you? Now that I know what you have done? Evelyn told me about the unicorn. She said Felicity's death is your fault. Is it true?"

I hoped more than anything that he would say no, but of course, he swallowed, rubbed the back of his neck and said, "Yes."

Chapter 10
An Impossible Dream

hy did you do it? Why did you kill the unicorn?"

His exhale was full of sorrow—eyes reflecting the morning sky. "Felicity was... sensitive and brilliant. Her magic was just coming into its own, but she was already stronger than many of the most experienced Reliqua warriors. She was a gifted psychic and... she shunned society because the emotions of everyone near her were, as she told me once, like an open wound. Being in crowds gave her pain. She rarely left the house."

"Oh." I could understand that much of her torment. It made me wonder what Roger saw when he looked at me.

"Father was so distant—from us all. She and I were both attached to Mother, but my sister more so. One spring, when I was fifteen years of age and Felicity was eighteen, our mother became gravely ill. None of the doctors or healers could do anything. Father refused to do *enough*." Roger's jaw clenched, and I saw this was at the root of their division. "I foolishly vowed to make it right if he would not. My magic had not yet fully awakened, but I was already training to become a sorcerer, consecrated to the Queen's service two years prior. I read every book of spells I could find, combed through our ancestral grimoires, determined to find the remedy to Mother's illness. Eventually, I came upon a spell involving the freshly harvested horn of a unicorn. A spell to save anyone from death, no matter the cause. I knew it was forbidden to kill a creature of pure light. This was dark magic I'd sworn never to touch, but in my grief and anger I didn't care, or understand the weight of these sins I intended to commit.

"I set out to hunt the unicorn that dwelt in the Welterwood. I'd never seen it, but knew when and where to find it. I needed help, so I asked Evelyn if she would go with me. She and Felicity were closer than sisters. Evelyn knew how desperate we were, but she, in her wisdom, could not condone my plan and refused. Despite the danger, I was determined to finish it alone, but Felicity discovered my intentions and followed me that first night of Equinox Bridge. I couldn't convince her to return home. I should have prevented her from following me, but I did not. For this, I will never forgive myself."

Roger paused and sat up, rubbing his eyes. I waited until, with a heavy breath, he continued.

"We found the unicorn. Felicity lulled it to sleep, and I slit its throat. I took the horn, along with the carbuncle stone I needed. I returned to Father's laboratory and prepared the spell in secret. To make sure it was safe, I tested it on myself. I carried the cup to my mother's room, but she was already dead. She had breathed her last while I worked my dark magic. I tried to force the potion past her cold lips, but soul had been separated from body long enough that even the unicorn's life could not bring her back. I'd committed this unforgivable sin for nothing.

"I didn't resist when Father took me to face Reliqua Council. In turn, they brought me to the Queen's Court for judgment. I didn't care if my life should be forfeit, but she spared me because I am the only male heir of House Gale. Even though I'd already been disowned by the same.

"After they escorted me home, I learned Felicity was gone. She had returned to the field where we killed the unicorn and... she jumped to her death from the sea cliffs not far from that accursed place. Her body was discovered by fishermen the next day."

I sat up and hugged my knees to my chest.

"I've not told many people that story." He wiped tears from his cheeks with the back of a hand. "But I wanted to tell you, Violet. Now that I have, I know you can never think of me the same way again. For that, I also grieve."

"You did it for love of your mother and your sister," I said.

He shook his head. "I knew it was wrong. Love would have accepted my mother's time had come, like she told us. No, it was fear. Fear and selfish defiance. But there is no way to outsmart the Fates. All I did was compound our suffering and damn myself and my House. Yet my sister was the one who paid the ultimate price for my sin."

"Roger, I do not believe you are damned."

"You said it yourself. The Welterwood is cursed because of me. Felicity's death is a black mark on my soul. I answer for it every day in this life, and I will do so in the next."

"Don't you believe in redemption?" I laid a hand on his arm, and he stared at it for a time, as though my touch were some inexplicable, foreign thing. He took my hand in his.

"There is none for me. What's done I can never undo. Violet, I cannot let my sins burden your heart. I should never have allowed us to become this close. I am more the fool…"

"Allowed? Do you think you have authority over my will… or my heart? That's not how this works, you know."

"This?" He blinked tear-glossed eyes, but I saw a glimmer of hope when he looked at me.

"Life." I sighed. "Love."

I crept closer, pulled a handkerchief from his waistcoat pocket, and blotted the moisture from his cheeks. He didn't react more than a widening of his eyes. When I stroked his dark hair, he leaned into my touch and kissed my wrist. "Love?"

"Isn't that what you tried to tell me? In that awful tower of yours?"

"Yes." He breathed a ragged exhale. "Can you love such a monster as me?"

"You're not a monster."

"Violet, I am *cursed*. As surely as I cursed the Welterwood."

"I know." The thought alone was a quagmire. I would be forever lost in his sadness if I roamed through it without a guide. Was my heart enough of a compass? I had no doubt it pointed me to him.

Yet, I also understood something of this weight, and I needed to tell him. What was love if not to risk everything?

"I've always felt… cursed too."

Roger's brow knit in concern. "What do you mean?"

Nervous, I held his hands while I considered what to say. "That Shade. In your library mirror."

"Yes?"

"I lied to you. I said I'd never seen it before, but I have. Many times. In mirrors. Puddles. Dreams. Nightmares. It takes different shapes. I'd always thought it was a hallucination—a plague of my illness—until you saw it too."

He squeezed my hands in reassurance. "Your mind is not unwell. You've always been able to see what others cannot, because of your heritage, but what you saw was real. I'm uncertain what kind of shadow being we're dealing with, but we'll find out what to do. I promise. Can you tell me anything more?"

"It… often says my name. It's said more to me in dreams, but I can't remember."

I didn't think I'd let any emotion show on my face. I was so accustomed to this horror of my life, I'd become inured. *Not unwell.* Roger saw through my act and pulled me into a hug. The comfort he offered was too needed for me to protest.

"How old were you when it first appeared?"

"I was… nine. About a year after Mother died. I saw it in a rain puddle. It… tried to pull me underground. I fled into the woods and hid for a night."

"Did you ever tell anyone what you saw? Your father, or Mrs. H? A physician?"

"No. I only told them of my nightmares." *Because I didn't want to go back to the hospitals.*

"I'm sorry you've had to bear this alone. You never need to again. I will teach you ways to protect yourself. Your magic is more powerful than anything a mere human can command. Only allow it to awaken within."

I exhaled. "That terrifies me too."

"Trust in yourself. You were born for this."

He almost made me laugh but succeeded in making me smile.

We clung to each other. Seeking only the comfort of human touch, we made no demands of our pasts or future. Friends, lovers, or enemies, I need not define us. For one silent moment, he was my harbor in a sea of despair. Cursed or not, his heartbeat, his breath alongside mine were true. Both wounded, yet together our pain seemed lessened, our darkness a little brighter, my purpose clearer, even if I could not frame it in words.

Holding Roger, I also detected his magic, and mine. Our auras embraced, along with our physical bodies. Magnetic fields of astral current entwined us in ways unknown, but which felt natural as my connection to the life in my garden. Hadn't I always known the thoughts of the birds, the insects, the plants—on a subconscious level?

His gentle laughter, all-too rare a sound, brought me back from reverie.

"I think we've discovered another of your powers."

The grass surrounding us had grown at least a foot. New ferns unfurled. Wildflowers bloomed where before there were none. Delicate vines entwined our legs. Fragrant, pea-like flowers burst open as tendrils reached skyward, our two bodies for their trellis.

I wasn't alarmed, for somehow I sensed the plant-life was friendly. I whispered, "Slow down."

The vines obeyed. When I focused my attention, the link was so sure—like these green shoots were my own veins.

"Release us, please." I'd always talked to plants, but never quite expected a response.

They loosened from our limbs and slithered through the grass in the opposite direction. Had I been the one to summon them when my thoughts strayed to my garden? No doubt the proximity of the ley line and Waystone magnified the effect.

"You're amazing, My Violet," Roger whispered. His eyes, still reddened from tears, now shone with pride and astonishment.

"Oh, I am." I smirked.

Before he could reply, I kissed him. Not so hesitantly—not so timidly as I'd returned our first.

He responded with a low moan, which sent shivers down my spine. He drew me closer. My hands slipped under his coat to caress his back, my fingers traced his solid lines, longed to touch the warm skin below his layers of clothing. *My Violet.*

Beating alongside his, the energy of my heart unfurled into radiant new bloom. I yearned for more—a dawning of our love. As much as my heart might wither in the sun's heat.

All too soon, I broke away. Startled, I gasped. What I'd first taken for more bees were the creatures I had seen before. Like a swarm of multi-hued fireflies, they cast shifting lights on the surrounding foliage. Iridescent wings and tiny bodies like indistinct porcelain dolls, they were no bigger than wasps, with bulging eyes reminiscent of the same.

"What are they?"

"A species of meadow pixie," he whispered. "No doubt they're curious about us. Magic draws them. If we keep alert, we should be safe from attack."

"Attack? But they're so tiny."

"In large enough numbers, they can be deadly. Let's get moving."

He grabbed his fedora from where it lay almost buried in the grass and offered me a hand as we stood. An ache of physical longing passed between us, plucking my nerves like a harp. I'd never experienced such a thing. Perplexing, vulnerable, delicious. Was this love or lust, or some divine admixture of both? Our eyes promised a return to this moment, though neither of us spoke a word. He squeezed my hand.

We continued southwest, toward the direction of my house if it had existed in this world.

The pixies' numbers appeared to be growing. They filled the woods, drawing nearer. Like sparks of sap crackling in a bonfire, they radiated an auric heat which bespoke warning.

Roger said, "The crystal you wear can call forth a magic shield. It's not foolproof, but useful in times like this. Visualize a circle of light protecting you and intone these words, as you did your mother's illumination spell.

They are the symbols written on the gold setting." He gave me the magic words, and I repeated them back to him, letting the sounds settle into my mind and memory. I sang them again louder and visualized a protective shell of light. Threads of light issued from within the crystal and encompassed us, forming an iridescent wall, like an ethereal soap bubble.

The pixies distanced themselves from our center.

As we walked, the shield faded. By the time it was gone, the pixies had lost interest and dispersed.

I would not have recognized my garden, were it not for the lay of the land, the oldest ash and laurel trees, and the rowan. None of my other shrubs existed in this mirror of reality. No human structures or earthworks. We searched for clues as to my father's arrival on this side of the world, but found only a few boot prints. The size and the tread seemed to fit what Father might have worn. Alongside them were the marks his cane made on the soft ground. As we'd already guessed, the tracks led in the village's direction.

We followed, nearing Mother's rowan tree. I remembered the fireflies which had shown me the buried brush; the vision which had brought to mind her painting of that fortress by the sea.

"*Where my roots grow in…* something *Stone or Rock.*" I quoted from his translation of what she'd painted. "Could it have been an actual place in the Winter Courts?" I asked. "Since she painted a night sky?"

"A night scene, you say? Hmm. I suppose the word could have been Wyvern's Rock. The capital city, where the Winter King rules. Indeed. The fortress you described might very well be a match." Roger stared at the ocean, where the sun just crested the horizon, unchanged since I had arrived here. "Why would her roots be in the Winter Courts if your mother was a Summer Court Fae?"

"Maybe she had an ancestor from the Winter Courts. Or maybe the Helena in your records was a different person."

"No. That must be her. The other facts all fit. It's possible she had such an ancestor, yes. The royal families of different nations intermarry often, much like their human counterparts. I'm afraid I haven't studied her history enough to know offhand. Aside from that, your own resemblance to the Queen is uncanny. There's no doubt you're her niece. I'm amazed I didn't see it before." Roger touched a rowan branch beside us, laden with both fruit and flowers, an impossible combination of seasons. "You say your mother planted this tree?"

"Yes. It was… a cutting she'd taken once when I was ill. She brought a vase of flowers into my room and placed them beside my bed. The others faded, but a rowan branch remained and grew roots in the water. We planted it together when I recovered enough to go outside."

"Rowan is sacred to Fae of the Summer Courts. Perhaps your mother knew its energy would help you heal."

"How does this tree exist in both worlds? We planted others in this garden, but only a few are here."

"I'm uncertain. The magic between Fae and their sacred trees is largely unknown, even to the Reliqua. But I've heard many of them grow in a special garden under the Winter King's care…" he snapped his fingers. "Of course, that could be it."

"What?"

"What your mother meant by *where her roots grow*. Something to do with her family's sacred trees. Perhaps they grow in Wyvern's Rock."

I reached for a cluster of berries, red ripe alongside white spring blossoms. Tiny buds of green erupted from twig tips, pulsing into new leaves around my fingers. A faint corona of light surrounded its branches, as if viewed through Roger's Spectrocles.

"I think she must've wanted me to remember that place one way or another. That's why she painted it. Why the dream helped me recall it. Could it be connected to why Father is here?"

"I don't know. Perhaps we'll discover more in the village."

"Agreed. Let's go."

We followed the tracks most likely left by Father and made our way down the hill toward what would be West Ridge Drive. Here it was only a thin path near the rocky cliff line, likely made by deer but used by the occasional biped. Roger explained that Fae who looked like my mother, nearly human, were the rarest kind. All, in fact, were members of the Royal Court families, though not all held positions of power. Royal Fae was more of a general species term.

As a half-human, the only thing I lacked, it seemed, was wings, but he assured me they might appear as my physiology changed.

"You did warn me, I suppose."

"You… would have the power to make them appear and disappear at will. Perhaps it won't be so bad."

"Easy for you to say. You're not at risk of sprouting new appendages."

He grinned. "Regardless, I plan for us to return before any of that happens. For if you become a full-blood Fae, you cannot return home. At least not permanently. You could visit only at equinox, midsummer, and a few other special days throughout the year."

"No. I can't stay here. My home is in Seastone. The human version, that is."

"We'll make it back in time. I don't know how long the process takes for someone like you, but for an average human, a year in Faerie is enough to transform us beyond the point of no return. As every Reliqua warrior must, I've already spent half a year in this world, though it felt like an age. I must return with you before the next equinox, or my body will become dependent upon this realm to survive. As a Changeling, I might, in fact, *sprout new appendages*, as you say. The magic of Faerie alone decides what physical form to grant such hapless souls."

"Changelings. I remember an old nursery-story—one told to frighten children. About fairies who abducted infants from their beds at night, only to replace them with dolls made of straw."

"Legends are often based on truth. There are many such people here. Most of them have forgotten what it means to be a member of the human race. Some lead good lives, but most become servants, slaves, or pets."

"That's appalling! Surely that cannot be lawful in your so-called Treaty."

"It's not. The Faerie High Courts punish their own when convicted of this crime. But it happens, nonetheless. There are not enough knights of my order to stop the practice."

"Knights." I huffed. "Trophy hunters more like it. Your people may claim to protect humanity from monsters like us, yet you seem to profit from a lucrative trade in our remains."

He stopped and pulled me beside him, a tortured look on his face. Here in the brighter light of the open meadow, his eyes shone an almost unearthly green.

"We have protected humanity for millennia. Since we owe allegiance to no one kingdom or country, we must finance our independent operation. The legal sale of relics from our practice is conducted with the highest ethics."

"All those dead creatures in your tower." I clenched a fist at the memory. I thought of Evelyn harvesting those bloody priceless eyes.

"All crossed into our realm and threatened humanity. All broke the Accords. All except one. Now you know that tragic story."

Threatened. I sighed. "Yes."

"I understand if you can't forgive me for what I've done. But you must understand the Reliqua serves the Queen of the Fae. We are necessary. We work to protect both our worlds. I'll do anything to protect *you* most of all, Violet Morgen. No matter what the cost. Trust in that alone, if you can."

101

I had no answer. His haughty and pretentious ethics nettled me. Before I said anything I might regret, I turned to walk. He followed.

Then I remembered a burning question I should have asked sooner.

"What about your servants? In your house. Are they some kind of Fae slaves?"

"What? No. They're... not even alive."

"Are they dead?"

"They never possessed life. They're just projections of my will. Echoes of my thoughts, infused with Elemental magic. Like... machines I've designed for different functions. They possess no motive power outside my grounds—or my carriage, in my driver's case."

"Have you no living servants?"

"No. Father kept on a small staff until he died. Afterward, they retired, not wanting to work for the son who destroyed the family legacy. I had no reason to keep up appearances. It's a rare day when I entertain guests. My own needs I could well manage alone, but the house itself takes more effort than one person can provide. My enchantments serve in that regard."

I shook my head. "I saw one of them... change. Into a hideous doll."

"The spell I used to give them human appearance only fools the willing. The illusion is like Fae glamour, though not as powerful. If you've not yet discovered how to use your natural camouflage, no doubt you will."

Of course, he'd changed the subject, but I looked at my hand, curious. "Glamour? How does it work?"

"Unfortunately, I understand little about it. Human magic relies on a blend of intuition and precise science, while Faecraft is as natural to your kind as breathing. Nevertheless, it might be wise to try and master the skill. A glamour disguise would be useful in the capitol of the Winter Courts. Someone who looks suspiciously like the Queen might draw undue attention."

Despite my doubts, I needed his help. With my life or my father's life at stake, I could suspend my reservations and walk beside him. Nor could I deny my emotions, or the passion he returned. I would decide what to think about it all soon enough.

We would have been near Crestfield Park in the human world. I stepped over an abandoned albatross nest. Down feathers lodged between the heather branches upwind. Broken eggshells littered the ground where pebbles and twigs had been scratched into rough circles.

Our path met a sharp incline. We ascended a foreign slope—one which the dynamite of human progress must have leveled on our side of the world. More than once, Roger helped me negotiate a hazardous step. We found a narrow wagon road, paved with crushed shell and gravel like many on the island I knew.

Ahead in the distance, the Fae village came into misty view. Architecture of many colors gleamed in morning light. Sky-hued towers and roofs spiraled like the peaks of giant shells. Shops and dwellings appeared to have grown organically, like fungus or structures in a coral reef. Floating ships were moored in the sky—elegant shapes like seafaring vessels dangling from colorful balloons, not boxy like human dirigibles. Made of brightly painted wood and metals, some of their hulls glittered with scaley tiles. They hung in the air, weightless as kites.

We determined to check the airship docks and shipyards first, in case Father might have gone there in search of travel to another location in Faerie. He might even still be waiting for a ship to depart, though I doubted my luck would be that good.

A donkey cart approached on the road ahead, and Roger questioned the driver, a fellow with the legs and horns of a goat. Anxious, I folded my arms, attempting to hide the rips and bloodstains on my ruined sleeves and skirt.

In a quivering voice not unlike a goat's, he said, "I've seen no humans besides yourself. Thank the Powers. What are you doing with this royal lady, eh?" Addressing me, the satyr said, "And what are *you* doing with this disgusting creature? Eh? An Iron-Bearer no less."

"Excuse me?" seemed a more than generous reply.

The satyr laughed and urged his donkey to trot faster, leaving us in the dust.

When it was far enough behind us, I said, "Terribly rude."

"Satyrs are quite the unpleasant lot. But I do think he was telling the truth. We'll keep trying. Someone will have seen your father. Are you cold?"

"No, I'm just in a sorry state."

"Oh? Right. Your clothes. My apologies." Roger fumbled in his coat pockets. "I forgot." He drew out what looked like a doll's traveling valise and pointed to a thick stand of lilacs and willows not far from the road. "If you wish a change of wardrobe, now's your chance." He handed me the miniature bag.

"I don't think anything in here will fit." I smirked.

"Just set it on the ground and it will return to normal size until you pick it up again. I'll keep guard nearby, and I won't look. I promise."

"Well, I suppose I'll take the risk." The prospect of clean clothing had me acting the fool.

We descended a slope toward a streambed, supporting a lush grove of lilacs. Soon, we were far enough from the road to be assured of at least tenuous privacy.

Sure enough, the valise morphed to life-size as soon as I set it on the ground. Handy trick.

Felicity's old clothing proved a decent fit. I opted for a pair of wide-legged trousers and a ruffled blue blouse. I'd never worn such a fashion, but they would no doubt prove practical. My bundle of soiled clothes tucked inside the valise, it shrunk back to miniature size.

"You all right back there?" True to his word, Roger never looked—not that I would have minded if he did.

I pushed past the lilac branches and twirled, earning a whistle. He tucked a lilac flower in my hat band and helped me re-pin it in place.

"A little worse for wear, we're still quite the pair." I added a matching sprig of lilac to his waistcoat pocket.

He beamed a smile.

After we returned to the road, I said, "Evelyn's warned me about trans-oceanic travel via the Waystones. Does that mean we'll need to take a ship, if Father has gone to the Winter Courts, that is?"

"Or an airship. It would still take several days." He took my hand. "There's a faster way, but I can't help you. Through the Old Gate—the Queen's Circle in the Welterwood."

"You can't help me because you are banned from that place."

He nodded, eyes cast to the ground. "Unfortunately, yes, but if we find Evelyn in town, she can help you open a portal to the Winter Courts. Or I can summon another of the Reliqua to meet us here. It might take some hours, but it will be faster than the days it would take to travel there physically."

"But we'd be separated again." I sighed. "No, I'd rather take the airship with you. Assuming we can find proof that's where Father has even gone."

"The journey will take longer than Equinox Bridge lasts. We might be stuck in this realm for another six months."

"I don't mind. If we're together."

Pensive, he added. "I won't leave you, but I'm not sure what staying here that long would do to your physiology. I don't want you to transform beyond the ability to return home. As for me, I'll be safe if I return by the next Bridge." He rubbed his chin. "Ah. Perhaps someone in the Winter Courts, someone with influence and the right Faestone, can open a portal and send you home sooner. Yes, that will work. We'll need to avoid the King's attention, but I've a few favors still owed me. Your Royal Fae blood makes you strong enough to survive a crossing outside of Equinox Bridge, but I cannot go with you. I'll stay here with your father after we find him, and he and I will return next March."

"Sounds like a good plan. In the meantime, this is my chance to learn who I am. Explore places I never dreamed existed. I wouldn't miss this for the world."

He squeezed my hand. "That's more like it."

"You wanted a little enthusiasm, perhaps?"

He nodded.

"A little passion, even?"

"We needn't go that far." His playful grin was infectious.

"I assure you I'm quite capable of passion, Mr. Gale. I'm not always such a dour person." Nor was my insinuation unintended, improper as the notion might be.

"Dour? Oh, dear." He laughed. The sound wrapped my heart with unexpected joy. "You know, when it's discovered that we've absconded from town together, people will talk."

"Let them. My reputation is rather a lost cause, anyway." I sighed, and it hit me. "Travers and Mrs. H!"

"All is well. Mr. Travers watched me open the portal to Faerie. Perhaps it was a bit much for him to process, but I assured him I'd find you and keep you safe. And so I shall."

The road widened, paved with pebbles as we neared the village. We passed outlying dwellings built of patchwork stone, a hotel so covered in blooming vines they obscured the walls, a house with diminutive doorway and windows. A walking tree lumbered by. Wasn't there a similar taxidermy on Roger's wall? I shuddered.

We encountered no vehicles other than an occasional goat or horse cart, but the villagers all eyed us cautiously. They walked on foot—or hoof, or paw, or wing, or tentacle.

Nothing human.

Roger spoke to a Fae with greenish skin and feathers, but the creature shook their head and crossed two wing-bearing arms, like they wouldn't listen to a human. Roger hailed another resident who had the antlers and hooves of a deer, but she didn't have any useful information, either. I understood a few words in English, but the rest of her reply was a series of grunts and clicks in a brusque tone.

After we'd gone out of earshot of anything aside from a long-necked bird, I said, "They don't seem to like us."

"I'm afraid it's only me. They sense the iron I wear."

Roger slipped an arm around my waist and guided us across the street. A man approached who looked human in nearly every respect but for his bright scarlet skin and metallic-looking hair, worn in long locks like cords of copper or brass. The Fae was tall and muscular. He wore a black tunic embroidered in flame red, a loose cut of black trousers with a wide gold sash, and boots; a rather more ordinary human ensemble than what I'd yet seen worn by other citizens of Faerie.

The man stopped and stared at both of us, addressing Roger. "What business have you with this Fae, human?"

Roger turned around, placing himself in front of me. "Good morning, sir. We're just traveling through."

He pointed at Roger. "I know you. The cursed Apothecary."

"Roger Gale. At your service." He tipped his hat. "Have we met?"

Bright yellow eyes met mine. "Do I know you, Lady?"

"I don't believe so."

He bowed. "Forgive me, but I see you are of the Summer Courts. I am the Changeling called Septimus. Seventh son of a seventh son. I serve the Queen."

By now, a few other passers-by drew closer.

"My name is Violet. We also serve the Queen." Had he known my family on sight alone? Perhaps Roger had not been exaggerating.

When the man furrowed his brow at my answer, I cleared my throat and added, "I'm searching for an older human gentleman. He has gray hair and walks with a cane. Have you seen anyone like this?"

"No, but a human male came through on this road from that direction." He pointed toward the southwest, from which we'd come. "He was older than you, but his hair was brown. Pale skin. No cane. I heard he left on an airship. The docks are that way."

"I thank you, sir."

He glanced from Roger's lilac to the one in my hat. "Lady Violet, this is your mate? This Reliqua Human?" He spoke the words with contempt.

"That's none of your concern."

"Don't you know such a creature may not consort with a Fae? This is against all our codes. And theirs."

I took a step forward, keeping eye contact. "With whom I choose to travel is my business."

The Changeling grunted his discontent. "This Iron-Bearer is a liar and a murderer. If he's using you, let me end him for you now." Septimus clenched a fist, cracking knuckles. His fingernails more closely resembled golden claws.

"Caution." Roger stepped between us, staring up at the taller Changeling. "You should not make idle threats."

I had no wish to see blood spilled in front of me. For the size difference between them, I was not a little concerned it might be Roger's. I raised a hand and said, "No one is threatening anyone. Both of you, please remain calm."

Roger relaxed but didn't take his eyes away from Septimus. "As you wish, Violet."

"Ha! So, it's love. How unfortunate for you both."

"We must be on our way." Roger took my hand and lead us forward.

The sullen Changeling sidestepped our path, glaring at us.

I turned back to see him duck into a turquoise shop's door half his size.

"Do you think the human he saw was my father? Could he have used a glamour?"

"Possibly. If Errol ate food from this realm, his health would recover. Perhaps even his youth. More quickly if he'd spent any length of time here before. We should keep sharp. He may not be easily recognizable now, even to you."

We proceeded toward the harbor. Trees canopying the lanes became sparser as we neared the rocky shore. On my side of the world, warehouses and dockyards would be the bleak counterpoint for these colorful structures. We passed cheerful paddocks of goats and sheep. Fishing nets drying in the wind.

A woman with lavender hair and glittering silver wings shaped like a bat's walked beside a blue boy with gills. A weasel-like creature with a headdress of birch bark closed a curio shop window from the inside before Roger and I could get any interior view.

I shivered in the sea breeze. Roger put his arm around me—his body warm and solid against the cold.

"It's true, what he said, isn't it? A Reliqua warrior cannot... consort with a Fae? Even a half-breed like me. I read it in your eyes."

"Yes. Intermarriage between our worlds is usually forbidden. Except in rare circumstances."

"Usually? You said all Reliqua families have Fae blood." I had no right to be so presumptuous, but perhaps I should guard my expectations.

"Our Houses must intermarry with Fae once every seven generations, to ensure magic runs strong in our lines. The Queen and the leaders of the Council arrange these unions. All other such liaisons are forbidden, but..." He squeezed my hand. "That doesn't matter, because I would give it all up to be with you."

"What do you mean?" I stopped beside a sand-colored brick wall, covered in vines with daisy-like flowers. Their fragrance might have been a lovely distraction, if I were not so focused on that rare fire in his eyes.

"I would leave the Reliqua. This burden was never a life I chose. I was born into it. But *you*, Violet—you I would choose regardless of the costs."

My heart wanted to burst with joy before a weight crashed down on my chest. How foolish was I? This love was an impossible dream. We were impossible.

"I can't allow you to throw your life away for me. You are the last of your House. How can I ask you to turn your back on your family? Your heritage?"

"I have no family, Violet. I had no purpose left. Until I met you."

"That's just not true. You have a power I don't understand. A purpose that goes beyond us both. To discard such a precious thing… would mean destroying who you are. You would only come to resent me for it."

"No." He faced the ground.

"You know I'm right."

"Violet, I will never resent loving you." A tremor in his hands as they reached for me and held me close. "What do you believe we should do?"

"We should go look for clues. Find our ship." I pulled away before I lost the will to speak.

CHAPTER 11
LOVE NOTWITHSTANDING

e walked a road the color of lapis lazuli, past a haphazard block of shops, and turned toward shore. A wooden pier connected to an upper level of docks where dozens of colorful airships glimmered against a periwinkle sky.

As we climbed the stairs toward an upper level, a Fae who looked human other than his pointed ears, his too-dark eyes, and his youthful too-pale face, passed us on the first landing. He wore long white hair in a topknot and a flowing indigo cloak. He frowned at Roger but nodded to me. I shivered as he passed.

When we reached the upper boardwalk, a clock tower constructed of rosy stone came into view out of the mist. In the clock's face, silver emblems marked the moon's eight phases.

We entered an airship station. Windows in the plastered walls contained no glass, shutters were thrown open to the lofty sea breeze. Tree-sized columns supported a ceiling like intertwined branches. Clusters of gemstones or glass, carved to resemble leaves and flowers, cast illumination in myriad hues. Colorful banners and a large shield design—a gray wolf on a field of black—decorated interior walls.

Many species of Fae gathered around an undulating countertop made of a split tree trunk. On the wall behind them hung wide strips of vibrant ribbon, bearing embroidered letters in High Fae.

"Those are the names of ships, I presume."

"Yes." Roger pointed at a cluster of banners in gold, red, and orange. "Do you see the falcon? That's the emblem for the Queen's family. These ships are sailing to and from the Summer Courts." He pointed to another group in dark blue. "There's a dragon—symbol for the Winter Courts. One of those ships may take us near Wyvern's Rock if we can arrange passage. Assuming that's where we want to go."

"Perhaps they will tell you if a human passenger came through here recently."

"Humans are generally mistrusted. Reliqua warriors more so. But *you* should have no trouble getting answers."

"But I can't even speak my mother's language." As embarrassing a revelation as that was.

"There's no reason I can't speak on your behalf, Your Ladyship. I am, after all, your most loyal bodyguard and personal thrall, one whom you spellbound to do your every bidding." He bowed and kissed the back of my hand.

"That's our cover story, is it?"

He smirked. "Haven't you read any good fairy tales? Your women are celebrated for capturing human males for their amusement. We may be less conspicuous if we play those roles. At least in public."

"Very well, my captive man." I curled a beckoning finger. "Follow me."

At our inquiry, the managers of the air-station summoned a rat-like shipman who had earlier attended the boarding of passengers to another vessel. The language they spoke was foreign to my ears, yet a few words I understood. Roger explained many Fae used a translation glamour in this multi-species crowd, or used the human vernacular of the land. The shipman described a human male who sounded much like my father, down to the make of his favorite coat; though, like Septimus had said, this man did not walk with a cane. The airship he'd boarded was indeed bound for Wyvern's Rock. My theory seemed to have borne out.

Within half an hour we'd traded the basilisk's feathers for passage aboard the *Minerva*, bound for a city near the Winter Court capitol. My legs shook on the gangplank leading up to the magnificent carrack-style vessel with sails and a balloon the color of marigolds. There was no accursed iron here, but I always had difficulty with heights. A flock of gulls passed under our feet. I pulled my gaze up from the rocky shore far below.

The boat rocked in the breeze. Another two steps and the sails above us caught a powerful gust of wind. I grabbed for Roger's coat.

On the busy ship's deck, a wide diversity of Fae busied about their tasks. Another luggage-bearing passenger had skin and fur like a seal. I recalled the legends I'd read of selkies. I didn't notice the approach of a stately woman until she spoke.

"Your Ladyship." She bowed and doffed a feathered bicorn hat. I was unused to being addressed in such a manner, but at least she spoke in English.

"Captain Meadowgrass." I greeted her with as much confidence in this charade as I could muster.

Our captain was taller than Roger. Nearly human-looking, her gold eyes beamed catlike and too large, yet in balanced proportion to her elongated ears. Freckled skin the color of starfish complemented her braided magenta hair and aqua tunic. At her waist, an old blunderbuss-style pistol emitted no sense of iron.

She clasped my hand with both of hers. "We are honored to have a Lady of the Summer Courts flying with us. And her human consort. What was the name again? Gale?" She asked the latter without looking at my companion.

"Indeed, Captain." Roger tipped his fedora and bowed, but Meadowgrass ignored him.

"Lady Morgen. Welcome aboard the *Minerva*. We have but a few small rooms for occasional passengers. Not the luxury you are accustomed to, but I shall see you're assigned one of our best. You may join the crew in the mess for meals and entertainment."

"Thank you."

"I'm afraid I shall have to ask your human to remove his iron weapons. I don't allow the metal on board my ship." Her tone suggested she didn't much enjoy ferrying humans around either.

A tall bipedal creature with a face resembling a dragonfly approached, barbed blue arms akimbo.

"You must understand," I said, "he's my bodyguard. He won't act without my orders, Captain. I trust him implicitly."

"Understandable, Milady, but rules are rules. I cannot let him board if he won't relinquish the iron."

"Do as she says," I commanded, though the thought of us losing one measure of protection against unknown odds was disquieting.

Without a word of protest, Roger handed his pistol along with a knife he'd hidden in his boot to the insect-like crewmember—a Changeling. For they can touch iron, I learned.

Another rat-like steward, the height of a young child, led us to our quarters, which proved to be in the forecastle below main deck. Cozy would be a generous description. The space was just a large enough for a tiny cot, a diminutive desk, and a washbasin outfitted with a giant abalone shell for a bowl. Communal bathing facilities were down the hall to the port side. An unsettling prospect, but perhaps my bravery would continue to grow once I got the feel of the ship and her crew.

After the steward showed us the call-bell switches and departed, I inspected the small built-in bed. It looked clean and serviceable, but there was hardly room enough for one human-sized occupant. I might have to bend my knees to fit. The two of us? There would be no room for any privacy to say the least.

"I plan on spending the night out topside," said Roger. "You'll have the room to yourself, *Milady*. I doubt I'll sleep, anyway."

"Just don't wander too far off, my thrall. In case I can't sleep either. I might need you close by."

Roger raised an eyebrow. "Duly noted." He tossed his hat on the desk. Now he looked anxious.

I drew closer to him and touched the lilac in his waistcoat pocket. It still smelled sweet, though a few of the petals had wilted. He clasped my hand.

"You were going to tell me about some history of this place," I said, for we both needed a distraction. "You said time here dates from the Rift?"

"Right." He turned to gaze through the porthole window, perhaps searching for a memory. "I'll give you the story as it was told to me. Once, many thousands of years ago, there was no barrier between our Fae and Human worlds. We kept separate strongholds, yet in many cities we walked and lived together. There are legends, but the true cause of the war is lost. All we know for certain is that the peace which existed for millennia erupted into hostility.

"For a hundred years, much blood was shed before the Fae lost ground. Mankind discovered their newly wrought iron weapons killed these enemies. Armies of iron-bearing soldiers advanced into Fae lands and captured their cities.

"The Fae countered with a way to quell the violence—and their losses. Their councils voted to remove every soul from danger. They waited until the planets and stars aligned and performed a powerful rite, separating our universe into parallel dimensions. The Rift tore our two realities asunder."

He raised both open palms, facing one another, to illustrate his next point. "I think of our two dimensions as parallel waves, moving through time and space like this." His hands snaked in mirrored curves, until he rested the side of one hand on the other to form an X. "They cross at the equinoxes. That is why we say the barrier is thin today. The literal space between our dimensions is smaller. The bridge we can open with our human magic functions only at those times of year. Although there are other days when our worlds interact in fascinating ways. Beltane and Midsummer, for example."

"And Halloween, I imagine?"

"Yes. Samhain has more to do with the realm of the dead, however."

"Oh, my…" I hadn't considered it, but if fairies were real, perhaps ghosts were too. My skin crawled. I thought of Mrs. H's Mystical Sisterhood, and their now not-so-ridiculous seances.

"After the Rift, the leaders of humanity and Faerie formed a Treaty and the Reliqua, established to oversee the remaining Faerie magic which still connects our worlds. The Summer Queen charged us with her Accords."

"The word means *remainder*. I'd wondered about that."

"Indeed. The Waystones stand as such a remainder on both sides of the Divide, many carved by Fae hands. Relics of Faecraft were discovered on Earth for millennia after the Rift—enchanted objects used by heroes of myth or folklore. Many of these are now in Reliqua possession. The Eye of the Graiae. The chariot of Apollo. The Golden Fleece. Sleeping Beauty's Spindle. The real thing is rarely like the legends; nevertheless, we must ensure they are not used for evil, or in such a way that disrupts normal physics of this reality. The constant battle raged long before I was born. It will continue long after I die."

He turned to gaze out the window.

"Evelyn said your ranks were dwindling."

Another silent pause before he answered. "It's true. One day, the Queen will remedy that deficit. It's within her power to create new Houses, but others in Faerie wish to see an end to the Treaty and the Reliqua. I know not what the future holds. I've yielded everything to that cause. My duty to my Queen has been my only love in this life. Until now."

"You've loved no one else? In all the years of your life?"

"How could I allow myself any happiness when I'd failed everyone I loved? No, I never allowed myself to get close to anyone before. I didn't deserve it."

"Then why me? Why now?"

"You won't like my answer."

"You say that too much, Roger. Just tell me."

"Very well." He rubbed a hand over his face. "I had a dream once, many years ago—as strong as a vision. A beautiful woman called me by name, when I was lost in deepest despair. In the dream she needed my help, and when I awoke, I was convinced I must find her, but… the truth was she saved me. The will to find her gave me renewed purpose when I had no reason left to live."

"Who was she?" Although I suspected, in the way he gazed at me, what he would say.

"You must understand, I was never the clairvoyant my sister was, or my mother, but I can sometimes glimpse the future. This was one of those visions, and it came to me more than once over the years. That's why I had to find you, although I had no idea who you were, or where you might be. I searched for you everywhere my journeys took me, though I knew not if

113

you were a real person or only some unknown angel who graced my dreams. Eventually, the dreams stopped, and I began to think you'd only ever been a mirage.

"Not too many years ago, I thought I glimpsed you in the eyes of a troubled young woman I met only briefly, but your face was too young, so I reasoned it couldn't be you. Our paths diverged, and many years passed. I lost hope of discovering the truth of my mystery. When you walked into my shop this summer, I recognized you without a doubt. I'm surprised you didn't see my heart stop when I shook your hand. For then I knew the vision had always been real, and I'd found the woman I'd been searching for all my life."

"Oh."

How could I judge this confession? Was he telling the truth? It might explain why Roger had warmed to me so easily in those first weeks of our friendship. Though I found his attention flattering and welcome, it might have been odd. But then again, what did I know about love?

"I'm sorry. That's a bit much to hear. Listen." He took my hands. "I don't expect anything from you, Violet. I never have. You owe me nothing, but I always knew you would ask something of me one day. You needed—would need—my help. And so..." He gestured around the cabin, out the porthole window at the mist-shrouded Fae village. "Here we are. Because you need my help to find your father and discover your heritage. I tell you this not to burden you, but so you understand why I'll do anything you ask of me. Love notwithstanding."

I touched his cheek and brushed aside strands of his dark, glossy hair, sparking cascades of awareness through my body. He drew me closer. I yielded to this delicious new gravity, yet caution held me at enough distance to draw a steadying breath.

"You said you saw me when I was younger? When?" I didn't like that he'd called me *troubled*, although the description of my youth was apt enough.

"I hoped you might remember in time, but I must explain that as well. It was about... ten years ago. My face has not changed, but in those days my appearance was different. I wore my hair shorter. Had a moustache. And spectacles, I think."

"What do you—"

A sharp rap at our cabin door.

Roger crossed the room and stood by the door, but did not open it. "Yes, what is it?"

"The Captain needs to speak with you, human." The gruff voice of that steward. "It's urgent."

I shrugged, before Roger answered, "I'll be there presently, thank you."

"My orders are to take you there at once. You'll come with me now." A pause. "Please."

Roger whispered to me. "Stay here. Keep the door locked."

"No. I'll go with you. Whatever she has to say, I need to hear it, too."

He frowned.

"Remember our agreement, my thrall." I lifted my chin.

"Indeed, *Milady*." He donned his hat. "Just stay close."

Our steward, and another hulking shipman with scales, escorted us to the hold. From a cable-railed catwalk, we had a good view of the ship's clockwork heart, which, for all its size and complexity, made no more noise than a room full of sewing machines. No vulgar gasoline or coal smoke, only steam hissed through vents glowing with a cold green light.

Rotating on long wooden axles, bronze propeller blades churned at open sky through the ship's underside. What might have been the mainmast protruded like a pipe-laden tree trunk from near the engine's core, disappearing into the decking above.

We climbed to an upper level and neared the captain's quarters at the stern. Three more shipmen joined our party, followed by another two dressed in warriors' uniforms of black and purple. A familiar sense of physical unease gripped me. What I'd always thought was mere panic. *Ironfear.*

In the cover of the mechanical hum, I whispered to Roger. "I sense iron. From inside the room ahead."

Roger drew me close and whispered in my ear. "You're sure?"

I smiled and nodded, pretending for the guards that he'd only whispered sweet nothings.

"I fear something is awry." He took my hand in his left. "Be ready to close your eyes."

Under his breath, he began to chant. The wind stirred around us, and my skin rose into gooseflesh. The ring on his right hand glowed. Swifter than the guards' reaction, Roger traced a symbol in the air. With a word of command, everything cracked like thunder. My ears popped. I remembered to close my eyes just as the magic flashed hot as a reflected sun. He tugged my hand, and we dashed through a wall of indigo smoke into a side corridor.

We sprinted up a wooden stairway leading top-side and wove past crates and startled shipmen. Our pursuers grew closer, boots pounding the deck behind us. We ascended another narrow stair when an unforgettable voice shouted.

"House Gale! Surrender the Fae woman to Her Majesty's Courts. This is our Council's missive. I am here to ensure your compliance."

I spun around. Evelyn stood below, her pistol trained on us, accompanied by five crossbow-bearing soldiers who looked Fae.

Roger grabbed something from a coat pocket, so quickly I almost missed it. He whispered, "Be ready," and placed his body between me and the line of fire. He turned and presented what appeared to be empty hands to our pursuers.

"House Crane. What's the meaning of this?"

She flipped a lever on the side of her pistol with a finger, and a tube above the barrel flared bright red. "Don't try anything, Gale."

"You have no grounds to arrest—"

"You hid who she was from us. Now I know to what purpose."

"Dr. Crane, what are you talking about?" I demanded, backing up another step.

"My *purpose* is to ensure she remains free." Roger did the same.

"Your only choice is to yield." Evelyn demanded. "You will both be taken into Her Majesty's custody."

"I think not."

With a flick of his wrist, Roger turned to me. "Run."

A blue-tinged flame exploded on the stairway below us. There was only one direction to flee, toward the safety of shore, but when we reached the gunwales, the gangplanks were gone.

In a few short meters, we found a rope ladder leading down the side of the ship toward open sea. When Roger set his hand on the wooden railing, I noticed what looked like ink on his fingers. Where the liquid touched the wood, the surface smoldered, but his hand appeared unharmed.

Noticing my inspection, he said, "Iron gall ink. Here, it corrodes anything made from Otherworld vegetation, like that stairway." He pointed over the side of the ship. "Hope it buys us a few seconds. Can you climb?"

The end of the wind-rattled rope dangled far above the ocean's surface. Nope. "I don't think so."

"Then we'll jump. I'll open a gateway, and I need a reflective surface. Water will do."

"What?"

"Don't worry, we'll cross back through where they can't find us."

He'd already closed his eyes and began to chant, holding his hand toward the sea. The ring on his finger glowed, seeming to draw light from the sky, transmuting it into shapes drawn by the words of his spell.

Jump? I peered over the deck and nearly lost my footing. My stomach flipped. "Oh no, I don't think—" But the surface of the bay directly below us had formed a small whirlpool. So far down. "Roger, I can't do it."

"Violet, we can't be captured here. If they take you to the Summer Courts, you may never return home. I won't see you become a prisoner. Even in so fair a prison." He leaned out to face the bay, tracing symbols in light which hung in the air like mist. They swirled on currents of wind toward the churning water below, illuminating symbols of liquid fire atop the ocean's frothy waves. He hummed a note of power. For a moment, I was mesmerized.

A scuffle behind us. Four soldiers wearing uniforms of silver, black and blue approached with swords drawn.

Roger took my trembling hand. "Hurry. I'll make sure you land safely, and I'll be right behind you."

I climbed up to sit on the railing. Wind whipped my hat away. Gone before I could snatch it. I inhaled sharply at the yawning height below my dangling feet.

"Ah. We found ourselves a prize."

A tall, white-haired Fae, with eyes as solid black as onyx spheres, strode toward with uncanny grace, laughing. His expression froze my blood. It was the man we passed earlier on the pier.

"Go!" Roger shouted.

I held my breath, fixed my eyes on the gateway below, and leapt.

The ring on my hand shone as I clawed open air.

I could not turn to look behind me for the cold snap of the wind around my hair and clothing. Roger shouted. A commotion.

The turbulent circle of sea, bordered by glowing symbols, rose to meet me.

A gentle cross-current softened my fall in those last seconds. Roger's magic.

Arms flailing, I lacked any grace when I struck the surface. Sinking fast, my lungs compressed. Frigid pressure. I fought the urge to suck in lungsful of seawater. Something big swam beside me. Scales in hues of green and purple glimmered through seaweed. A diaphanous golden fin. Human faces with dolphin-gray skin held doe's eyes; gills under their jawlines. Fishlike tails flashed through murky depths.

Mermaids? Had the gateway failed?

A hand grasped my arm in the liquid darkness.

Come with us.

The being who stared at me set the words inside the forefront of my brain.

The mermaids pulled me downward.

A stream of silver bubbles escaped my mouth. Pressure surrounded me, squeezed me from all sides. My lungs burned for lack of air.

Indigo faded to blackness as we sank. I kicked, fighting their slippery grasp with as much effort as my pressured limbs could muster.

A golden-green light enveloped me—my crystal necklace grew brighter. Scaly mermaid fingers released their hold on my limbs, groping for the light's source. In the frigid water, I could not feel them break the chain. A water-muffled shriek when the radiance grew bright enough to burn an after-image behind my eyelids.

I swam upward as quickly as panic propelled me. My limbs burned from more than cold when I reached the surface. I gulped air, treading water.

It was night.

I scrambled toward a shoreline of algae-slicked rocks.

Hands too numb to feel much pain, I heaved myself out of the water onto a jetty. Coughing up seawater, the foul-smelling air of the fishing docks never tasted so good. A ship's bell rang out not far away. Seastone's lighthouse beamed from its rocky peninsula, where it had not stood in the Otherworld. I must be home.

I shook from fatigue. "Roger," I whispered. "Why didn't you follow me through?"

Perhaps he did, or he would soon enough. Either way, I couldn't stay here.

My numb feet slipped on the slanted rocks. A wave crested my tenuous hold on the jetty. I grabbed a rusty section of discarded pipe and pulled myself up onto a flat rock.

A splash disturbed the water's surface, like a jumping fish or the slap of an oar. I turned, hoping to see Roger.

Instead, aqua-gold eyes shone above the rippling tide.

Slithering shapes with long gray arms and hair like knotted seaweed emerged from the water and advanced up the slope toward me. Three—no—four. Another head crested the murky bay. If these were the same mermaids, they had lost their tails in favor of scaly legs.

A feline howl echoed down the rocks.

The creatures halted their macabre advance and stared to my right.

I turned to see a striped tabby cat. She perched beside me and issued another fierce growl and hiss.

The mermaids scattered, retreating to the water. They dove, spindly legs transformed once more. Tails slapped the surface before they disappeared.

The cat nuzzled my cheek. She had elongated teats, as if she'd recently born a litter of kittens.

"Maggie," I whispered. "Is that you?"

She meowed and purred.

"Oh, dear Maggie, bless you." I scratched behind her ear with my freezing fingers. "Who knew you could frighten away monsters?"

She enjoyed my attention at first, then pawed at the rock beside where I sat.

"We need to get out of here, don't we?"

Footsteps crunched on the slope above.

"What's this? Who's there?" A man's voice.

Sand and pebbles cascaded into my face. Did I hear laughter?

I didn't see the falling rock before it struck my head.

CHAPTER 12
ABYSMAL MIRROR

Monday, 30 September 1907
(Six days later)

ood morning, Miss Morgen. I am Dr. Porter. Do you remember the last time we spoke?"

The stout, red-moustached man ground the remains of a cigar into a cut-crystal ashtray, which held half a dozen other stinking butts. He hadn't looked at me once since the orderlies had rolled my wheelchair into this opulent office, a stark contrast to the bleak hospital wards below us. He shuffled through paperwork strewn across his expansive ebony desk. I wanted to stare him in the eye, but on the wall behind him hung a massive gilt-framed mirror. I had to keep my swimming gaze averted from the pull of that inverse void.

"No. How long have I been here?" The medication the nurses forced down my throat just minutes ago had left my words sluggish, my voice parched. My heartbeat seemed both elevated and labored. I shifted in my wheelchair but found no relief to the pain. The thin, worn fabric of my patient's uniform could not keep off the cold. Still chilled from my brusque wash in the women's communal facilities, my damp hair had been piled atop my aching and bandaged head. On my forearms, near the elbows, tight bandages itched. My skin was sore below the cotton wrappings. I could not remember what wounded me. The notion made my stomach turn.

I wanted to scream, but my drugged body could only muster the will to sigh.

"Three days. We've had this discussion before, Miss Morgen. Can you recall anything?"

"No."

"Amnesia often occurs in patients with similar head trauma." Porter spoke to a police officer sitting beside a fireplace a few feet away.

"You're the expert, doc." A younger man, the police sergeant sipped a porcelain cup of coffee, staring at me like a hungry wolf.

"Philips, we want to record this session."

"Yes, sir."

From a nearby shelf, one of the two orderlies who had been my personal escort this morning, a ruddy-faced man whose gray-eyed leers made me shudder, drew out a wooden box festooned with brass knobs and exposed wires. He set that on Porter's desk, along with an object like a phonograph horn elevated on a short pole. A cloth-covered wire joined the machine with an electrical outlet. We didn't have electricity at home. Its use was still much of a mystery to me, although in a long-ago science exposition, I'd once seen Tesla coils arc with generated lightning, and considered it nothing short of wizardry.

"An improved audio recording device of my own invention." Dr. Porter opened the box and set a wax cylinder into place, adjusting a needle. "You see, Miss Morgen," he continued, still without gracing me with a glance, "This is the first time you have been lucid enough for a proper interrogation. We must take every advantage of this opportunity to discover the truth. Wouldn't you agree?"

"I don't understand. For what am I being interrogated?"

Porter flipped a brass switch, and a high-pitched whine stung my ears before it subsided. The needle hissed, etching copies of our voices into wax. Porter's accent bore with a touch of Eastern Europe perhaps, though I'd never been to the Old World, or even the Americas.

"Ah, but you do. Everything we need to know is buried in that pretty head of yours. We shall work diligently to extract it all. I must record your progress for posterity. This is how you will be healed, and will help others to do the same."

The bitter remnant of sedatives cloyed my throat, and I coughed on lingering cigar smoke. My headache pounded with renewed force. Pity they hadn't given me a painkiller. I missed Roger's miraculous headache tonic. *I missed Roger.* What had happened to him?

Porter deigned to look at me. "Someone bring my patient some tea. Would you like that, my dear?"

The too-personal appellation felt like an unwanted touch. Being parched, and with little other recourse, I answered, "Yes."

Porter gestured to an orderly named Ace, who had been kind to me that morning upon my dazed awakening to the horrors of my captivity. The umber-skinned man with striking features and long black locks seemed so familiar, though I could not place him. He nodded and straightaway quit the room.

"Very well, let us begin." Dr. Porter opened a folder of yellowing documents. He donned a pair of brass-rimmed spectacles and stroked his goatee, as though pondering words chosen for the wax cylinder's benefit, and his *posterity*. He said, "It is eight o'clock in the morning on the thirtieth of September, nineteen hundred and seven. I am Dr. Archibald Porter, chief alienist at St. Ivy's Asylum for the Mentally Infirm. My female patient's name is Violet Morgen. A *painter*." He grinned, as if dismissing my profession as a vain hobby. "Twenty-seven years of age. I see you've just had a birthday this month. Belated congratulations are in order."

He looked at me for some response, which I did not give.

Porter rifled through more papers and handed one to the officer. "I would be remiss if I didn't introduce Sergeant Smith. He has been assigned to your case and may also have a few questions for us."

"My case? Am I accused of a crime?"

"Not at this time. Perhaps the good Sergeant can explain."

The police sergeant shifted in his chair and sighed, as if he was disinclined to speak to a lunatic. "Miss Morgen, a week ago, you were reported missing by your household staff. We've been investigating your kidnapping at the hands of a suspect, Roger Gale. We need you to tell us what occurred on the afternoon of Monday, September the twenty-third. Seven days ago."

"Kidnapping? No. I wasn't kidnapped. I..." They wouldn't understand the truth, but I couldn't allow them to think Roger was guilty of anything. "I left town of my own free will. What's happened to Mr. Gale? Where is he?"

"Dr. Gale is still missing," said Sgt. Smith. "His whereabouts are an ongoing concern of this investigation."

"But you can't possibly think he's done anything wrong. He—" Then it hit me. I blinked. I willed my mind to stay alert, but the drug's undertow was so strong. "What do you mean, *Doctor* Gale? Do you mean Roger Gale, the Apothecary?"

"Let us hold those questions for a moment. Now..." Porter drew a fresh cigar from the box on his desk and clipped the end with a device shaped to resemble a miniature guillotine. "You say you left town of your own free will? Where did you go?"

"I… We…" I prepared to make the lie sound convincing. "We went to the Welterwood forest. I wanted to go camping."

"For what reason?" Porter's clinical monotone held a note of questioning. He struck a match and puffed to get the fire going, all the while the wax cylinder recorded our awkward silence. Soon enough, a haze of sharp-smelling tobacco smoke pooled at the ceiling.

"Surely you see the obvious." I endeavored to seem incensed. "My father forbade our acquaintance. Roger and I wanted to… spend some time alone together."

Let them think me an immoral fallen woman for all I cared. Most already did. If word of this supposed kidnapping had spread in town… My heart sank. I would lose all my students—my only income. No respectable families would allow their daughters to visit my home for painting lessons now. And what of Roger's reputation? Was his shop ruined as well? Somehow, I would have to set it all to rights.

"Why didn't you just stay at Gale's house?" The police sergeant inquired. "Or go to some hotel for your tryst?"

It was a valid question. "I… wanted to be in the Welterwood. I go there often when I need respite from the world. The forest is… soothing to my nerves."

The sergeant laughed. Porter smoked his cigar, reading my file.

"Miss Morgen, I have here your patient record going back…" Porter shuffled through several folders. "Ten years. I suspect there is more pathology at work, but you have already been diagnosed with… Agoraphobia. Anxiety neurosis. Neurasthenia. Hysteria. We have documentation concerning night terrors and somnambulism." He pointed to another page in my file. "Ah, here are a few don't see too often. Fascinating. You have a fear of doorways, and… reflections?" He chewed his cigar, glancing at the massive mirror behind him. "We must be nervous? Hmm?" He chuckled.

"Are you ridiculing me?"

He set down his cigar and reclined in his leather chair, resting fingertips against each other in a mockery of supplication. "No, dear child. Our job at St. Ivy's Asylum for the Mentally Infirm is to cure. This, I assure you, is our primary goal."

Child. I would have laughed if I weren't in such a miserable state. "Primary goal?"

"We are also a research hospital. Our work together will help advance the modern science of psychology. Now… Tell me. When did you first make Dr. Gale's acquaintance? That is, when is your first recollection of meeting him? We'll remind you this is a police matter. Your truthfulness is not only expected, it is required."

"I… met Mr. Gale on a visit to his apothecary shop several months ago. I've been there many times since. Yet you insist on calling him Dr. Gale? Perhaps we are not speaking of the same person."

"I assure you we are. In point of fact, Miss Morgen, Dr. Gale was once *your* physician." His scrutiny seemed to focus on my hands, where they rested on my knees.

"No." I shook my aching head. "That can't be right."

Could it be? Did I remember each face of the myriad doctors I'd seen throughout my sickly life?

"Indeed, it is. Dr. Roger Gale was once an alienist at this very institution. Until ten years ago, when his employment was terminated, and his medical license revoked." Porter stared once more at my file on his desk.

Revoked? Why wouldn't Roger have told me any of this?

"I was never a patient at St. Ivy's until five years ago, when I… self-admitted. I wasn't here ten years ago. You're mistaken."

"Hmm." Porter exchanged knowing glances with the smug-faced sergeant. "I do not believe her prevarication is intentional. You can plainly see my patient's memory is not sound, but as often with these cases, there are still ways of ascertaining the truth. If she does not soon remember on her own, my machine will suss it out."

"What kind of machine?"

"You will see soon enough, my dear."

If I were a bird, I would fly away! There were no iron bars covering the windows in this elegant room.

The door opened, and Ace reappeared, this time leading a white-capped nurse. She pushed a cart evidently bearing my tea. The service was of fine porcelain and silver—not the dented tin plates and chipped cups which served the hospital's scant patient meals.

It wasn't until the blonde-haired woman drew near enough that I recognized her. *Evelyn.*

"You!" I reacted before I quashed the impulse. I balled weak fists. Even through the sedatives, my heartbeat sped, aggravating my headache. I swallowed the rest of my outburst, lest I reveal too much unawares.

"Now, now." Porter shook a finger and clicked his tongue, scolding. "Nurse Crane's patience with your incessant tirades is truly admirable. You should be more kind to the hands who feed you, hmm?"

Evelyn said nothing, but I swore some vapor of guilt shrouded her proud Valkyrie's face as she poured my tea and mixed in the cream. Evelyn knew she was hiding something. Just *who* in this room knew *what* exactly—was the real question.

Not to mention the fact I couldn't remember seeing her in this hospital before, despite Porter's assertion that I'd subjected his nurse to prior *tirades*.

Evelyn bowed and turned to leave. She shot a sidelong glance at Ace before she exited.

Ace, in turn, met my eyes for an instant. Did I only imagine an unspoken word of caution in his expression?

With shaky grip on the cup, I sipped my tea, which proved to be a robust earl gray. For such a comfort in this sorrowful place, I was more than a little grateful.

"Now," continued Dr. Porter. "On the subject of teas. Your housekeeper, Mrs. Agnes Holstead, has cooperated with the police. After all, the whole town has been searching for you since you disappeared. We are aware of the special herbal concoctions you have been drinking for some months. As we speak, these formulae are being analyzed by my laboratory assistants. We may yet discover what hallucinogens Gale used to control you. I can only speculate as to what other ways he dosed you, for I can find no evidence of injections in your skin unless you took his drugs willingly. Hmm?"

Injections? I looked at the bandages on my arms. A few other women in my ward had similar wounds, but my nurses would not tell me what had happened.

"No. He's done nothing of the sort. The only drugs I've taken are the ones your staff forced on me. No, I assure you, Mr. Gale's teas only eased my headaches and sleeplessness. That is all."

Having retrieved and revived his cigar, Porter blew a ring of smoke. "You see, Miss Morgen, ten years ago, not long after your first stay at St. Ivy's, we discovered that the good doctor Gale was involved in, shall we say, *unsanctioned* experiments which led to the death of a patient here. I was his devoted understudy. It was a blow to us all, especially myself. The ordeal would have been quite the scandal in town, if the hospital's board had not seen fit to shield public eyes from certain inconvenient facts. The matter was resolved quietly before Gale left the country to hide from his sins. Not so, this time, it appears."

"This time?"

"Tell us where Dr. Gale is hiding," said Sgt. Smith.

"I've already told you. I don't know where he is. And he did *not* kidnap me. Do my statements even matter to you?" I clenched my fists. My headache throbbed.

"They do indeed," Porter answered for him. "Your statements have already proven your memory, and thus your mental competency, is not sound. I have right here—" He drew another paper from my file. "The record of your first stay at St. Ivy's in the fall of '97, over ten years ago, which I assure you, did in fact occur. It seems you had suffered a psychotic episode and had gone missing for two days before you were found in the woods near your school and brought here thereafter. Remarkable coincidence, wouldn't you agree? Since this was, in fact, the first time you met the good Dr. Gale. He is listed as your attending physician."

"No. That simply can't be right."

But was it possible? Could I have forgotten my first stay at this place? When I came here five years ago, parts of the grounds had almost seemed familiar, but... No. He had to be lying. Why?

Porter handed a document to Sgt. Smith, who skimmed it before he said, "The good Dr. Porter is right, miss. I'm holding the police report of the incident right here. Including your photograph. If you aren't lying to us, then your memory is unreliable. Either way, it nullifies your testimony."

My cheeks flushed hot. My hands trembling. I set down a half-empty teacup. "You mean you intend to just disregard—"

"Furthermore," he interrupted. "I'm agreeing with the hospital's recommendation to make you a ward of the Commonwealth." He held up a folded piece of paper, embossed with a round seal. "You are hereby assigned to the legal protection and provision of this institution for as long as necessary. Since you're unmarried and have no living relatives aside from your father, who, oddly enough, is also missing, all your assets will be held in trust under the administration of Dr. Porter, until he deems you fit to reenter society."

"Please. My housekeeper can manage everything while I—"

"You no longer have any such need," said Porter. "Your house will be boarded up. Your servants dismissed."

"You... can't just take my property. You can't fire Mrs. H and Travers."

"I am afraid it is a necessary step. You're a very ill woman, Miss Morgen. You are not fit to function in society. This is for your own protection."

"How can you revoke my citizen's rights without a trial?"

"I assure you it's all well and legal under the law, miss," the police sergeant answered. "All we need is a signature from a judge friend of mine, and you aren't going anywhere."

"Please. You can't do this!" Outrage flared under my drowsy haze. I struggled against the weight of the sedatives, like a nightmare.

I rubbed my aching head and noted, with less terror than warranted, that the policeman's shadow on the rug was... *wrong*.

The dark void of light fell at odds with the room's proper lighting sources. Even more disturbing, when the man shifted in his chair, his shadow didn't move along with him. Rather, it lagged or predicted another slide of the foot by a fraction of a second.

My eyes must have been playing tricks. Or it was the drugs. No. I wasn't insane. I was *Fae*.

"I think we shall not get any more out of her without proper hypnosis." Porter spoke to the sergeant. "We shall record a session now. You are welcome to stay and observe. My methods have been called nothing short of revolutionary." He set about loading a fresh wax cylinder into the machine.

"I'm not feeling up to any more questions. I've a headache. I can't—"

"Nonsense. This will be a refreshing experience, my dear. You can awaken from the trance whenever you choose. I shall not tax you overmuch." Porter stood from his desk and snapped his fingers. "Assist her, please."

Ace pushed my wheelchair toward a velvet chaise lounge along one wall of books. He helped me stand, and I, being no invalid, refused any further aid to take my new position, as humiliating as it was to recline in front of these men.

I did my best to ignore that abysmal mirror into which I now directly gazed. The ashen face of a prone woman in patient's garb stared back at me before I turned away. She looked sick and vulnerable—out of place in this lavish room.

The other orderly Philips brought over a pair of clunky spectacles attached to a cloth-covered cord. He set the cold metal on the bridge of my nose and slid the ear wires through my hair, his indelicate fingers managing little care for comfort. I didn't react to his lecherous leer. Through the haze of the thick lenses, Porter approached, carrying the phonograph listening device. He perched the thing on a side table and took a stool beside my chaise.

"Are you testing my eyesight?" I asked.

"No. Only your memories." He rotated the round lens frames, one at a time, counterclockwise, until I heard a metallic click. An uncomfortable heat emanated from the cord, followed by another high-pitched whine. My vision of the room warped and transformed. A shimmering light coalesced before me, though it must only be contained within the lenses. Scintillating and greenish-gold, this was some electric mirage. It entranced me.

Soon enough, I could look nowhere else, nor did I want to. A deep breath tasted of Porter's obnoxious cologne, mixed with an odor I assumed to be laboratory chemicals. I caught an undertone of rot.

"Now, watch the light. Relax. You are safe here. As difficult and traumatic as our memories may be, they cannot hurt us if we do not allow them. Do you understand?"

I nodded, but I couldn't let them discover the truth. How could I protect my own memories—my words—from this? I clenched a fist, my drugged muscles barely able to form the movement.

"I want you to imagine this is your mind's spotlight. We will shine it into your past. Even into the places you cannot see. Remember, you are safe here in my laboratory. Hmm?"

"Yes." A trapped part of me wanted to scream.

Porter adjusted the left lens on my glasses. With a click, the mid-ground light in my altered vision slowly pulsed. It dimmed and brightened. Like a breath.

My own breathing echoed the pattern. Transfixed, all other sense of the room faded. There was only the pulse and my mimicking breath. My eyes stung from contact with air. A shimmering tear glazed my spotlight.

"Now we travel backward in time. Your eyes have become heavy. Close them."

I did.

"Miss Morgen." Porter's voice echoed from far away. Was it all a dream? "Tell me where you are."

I drifted out to sea. In the air above the waves. A bird, with wings like ship's sails.

CHAPTER 13
MEDICAL MIRACLE

Monday, 30 September 1907
Mid-afternoon

My eyelids were heavy as stones. A nasty antiseptic smell hung in the air. Or was this a taste in my mouth? I stirred but couldn't move. Starched linens covered me from neck to toe.

At least I wasn't shackled, like I had been when I'd awoken in the women's communal ward this morning—if that was this morning. Three days here. That didn't seem right. Had I forgotten my first two days in this terrible place?

Had I forgotten the entire first time I'd been admitted here, as Porter claimed? Had I forgotten *Dr. Gale*?

The last thing I recalled was... Porter's bizarre hypnosis machine. A lingering odor of rot.

What did I tell him and the police sergeant? I couldn't remember. Afterward, they might have wheeled me somewhere else. I fell asleep in another hospital bed.

This was not the same women's ward as this morning—the same one where I'd stayed before, five years ago, when I self-admitted. No, I didn't think I'd ever seen these rooms. They must have been kept for well-to-do patients. Faded blue roses papered the walls. Rusty iron bars, shedding strata of ancient paint, covered the sole window. I glimpsed the sea beyond a stretch of green and autumn gold, from a higher elevation; perhaps this was an upper floor. Aside from my cot, the room held only a washstand, wall mirror, and two wooden chairs.

Within the mirror's oval expanse at the periphery of my vision, a shape stirred. My blood ran cold until I realized it reflected the room's door.

"She's up, is she now? Good."

I turned to see a familiar nurse. Maggie Wilkes, with her sunken cheeks, stern demeanor, and false smile, crafted to disarm the insane. I hated it more than callousness.

Yes, I remembered her from this morning—when I'd awoken bewildered and chained to my cot in one of the women's wards, with no knowledge of how I'd gotten to this hospital, nurse Maggie had told me her name, and had laughed at me for not remembering it from the day before. She and the other nurses bathed me and the other women, herding us through our morning ablutions like cattle, before she'd handed my wheelchair to two male order-lies, Ace and Philips, who in turn had carted me off to the upper floors to see Porter and the policeman. I recalled that much.

But wasn't Roger's cat named Maggie? It was a common enough name, I supposed.

Maggie pushed a tray of food toward my cot.

I tried to sit up, but was too dizzy, or drugged, to move. "When was I brought to this room?"

"Some hours ago. After your session this morning, Dr. Porter wanted you kept for private observation."

I didn't know what that meant but didn't like the sound of it. "When will I be able to return home, Mrs. Wilkes?"

"She remembers my name today, does she?" She smiled at me as though I were a fragile child. "Here now. I've got your supper. Later we'll go down to Commons."

She disappeared, leaving me a tin tray of burned potatoes, and a cup of broth just this side of rancid. I didn't know how anyone could maintain sanity on such a diet. I didn't once turn to look at that mirror.

I had to get out of here. How did I even get here?

What had happened to Roger?

Why did my head hurt so horribly? The bandage! I reached up to touch a small row of stitches just under my hairline. The sutures didn't hurt too much, which seemed a good sign. I felt for any other injuries and sucked in a breath when I discovered a small patch of hair had been shaved away just behind each ear.

The bandages on my forearms—I could not remember what had caused them. I pulled at them, but, weak as my grip was at the moment, the fabric would not tear.

After some time passed, and I'd managed to eat a little food, Maggie returned and loaded me into another wheelchair. I offered no protest.

We took an elevator down two floors. I couldn't sense the iron. At all. Just as the bars on the window had offended nothing but my aesthetic senses.

It was all I could do to keep from weeping at such an inconvenient fact, but I maintained my calm. I didn't want to give Maggie a reason to force any more drugs down my throat.

Past another hallway we entered Commons, where many of St. Ivy's inmates congregated on dilapidated sofas and conjoined wooden chairs, which looked to be castoffs from some condemned theatre. The bleak room had once been a hotel lounge when St. Ivy's was young. One old woman smiled at me, displaying a mouth of missing teeth. Several individuals carried on brusque conversations with the walls or empty chairs. Two older women played chess. One younger man with a bandage on his forehead pinned me with an unwavering, predatory look. I could still feel his gaze on the back of my neck from the next hall.

Maggie rolled me outside. I drank in the salty island air. We passed a vine-covered portico, making our way toward a crushed shell path. Hedged evergreens lined one side, a row of lanky, bug-bitten roses the other.

A wide lawn on a hill gave us a view of the distant bay. An impromptu croquet game was in progress in one field, overseen by uniformed attendants. I wondered that the patients were allowed to swing those wooden mallets. The ball was struck with a resounding crack.

"May I try and walk a little?" I asked. A grouping of beech trees some meters away told me a water source must be nearby. The grounds of the Institute, this far north of town, lay not too many miles from the edge of the Welterwood.

"No, you have an appointment to keep, lass. We're headed to the research wing."

We approached the next stone building, nearly identical to the last, and continued through an open-air breezeway. An ugly sort of turret loomed over us like a prison guard tower. It would not have surprised me if gunmen patrolled that crenelated roof. We entered through an unknown set of doors.

"I remember painting lessons for the patients. Years ago." My voice echoed off worn marble-tiled halls.

"Yes," said Maggie. "Art on every Tuesday. That'll be tomorrow. They start around two o'clock. You can join in if you like."

"I would, yes."

Maggie led me down a corridor to another dreaded iron elevator. We traveled up several floors, exiting into a dim hallway. Through one open doorway, a patient lay strapped to a bed, partially hidden behind a curtain. I heard a muffled moan before the door shut.

"What kind of research happens here?"

Another wail, from behind a closed door, punctuated by a scream.

Maggie didn't answer.

We approached a wider set of doors at the end of the corridor. More bootsteps behind us. Maggie moved aside, and the orderly Philips took my wheelchair.

I faced forward again and read the room number of our destination. 709. No!

A sudden sense of dread. The worst ironfear.

"I don't want to go in there." Every nerve was aflame with warning.

"Relax," said Maggie, who now walked beside my chair. "It'll all be fine."

Philips laughed.

They shoved me into a brightly lit space. On the opposite wall behind an operating table was the most dreadful-looking machine I'd ever beheld, yet it must have seen it before. Made of wood and brass and iron, I knew, by the glass domed dials and the multitude of cloth-wrapped wires and steel probes, it was a thing designed to meter out electric current.

"What is this?"

"Electrical therapy, Miss Morgen." Porter spoke, hidden as he was by a room divider. "Yet, this technology is so much more."

"I…" I stammered. "I was never a… severe enough case. My other physicians always said so…"

Dr. Porter moved aside the curtain with a swish of metal rings on a steel traverse rod. He picked up a helmet-shaped device, made of riveted semi-circles of brass, which connected to the machine by multiple wires and hoses. It had two leather muffs to cover the ears. I shuddered.

"Electricity is a medical miracle. We are only beginning to unlock its manifold secrets." His smile turned my stomach.

Philips rolled me in front of Porter and took the helmet.

The doctor adjusted a row of small dials. "The efficacy of such therapy is well documented. But none can compare to the new science I employ here."

Maggie and Philips directed me out of the wheelchair and into a reclining seat beside Porter's machine. I was in no shape to put up any fight.

The doctor gestured, and Maggie shoved the helmet over my head.

"Your contributions to my research are invaluable, Miss Morgen," Porter continued. "You are ensuring your own place in history and helping future patients. Few lunatics can boast such an accomplishment."

"Lunatic. I'm no physician, Dr. Porter, but I would wager 'lunatic' is not a real diagnosis." My blood burned like fire, but I could no more stand and run than overpower that massive orderly.

Porter sighed, staring at a panel of dials, switches, and gauges. "Give her something stronger this time. I hate it when they scream."

Philips approached me with a syringe. Maggie fastened the helmet's strap below my chin and shoved a bite-guard into my mouth. I mumbled a useless protest when the needle stung my arm. A drowsy heat surged through my veins.

The doctor threw a lever on his iron machine. Motors turned in high-pitched precision as the dynamo's revolutions sped. A glass panel arced with dancing light. Somewhere inside me, another person cried, but I was far away. The drug melted my conscious awareness of this misery. The world went blank.

CHAPTER 14
KEEP YOUR EYES OPEN

I said, it's Tuesday. Remember, girl? Art on a Tuesday. Did you want to go down today? They'll be startin' soon."

I blinked. "Maggie?"

I sat up in my hospital bed, staring through those iron bars on my window. I'd previously determined my bed on this floor was fashioned of steel, not iron. Albeit one was merely an alloy of the other, could they be different enough? Magically? Roger told me the iron in my blood was not the same Cold Iron hated by the Fae.

Maggie snorted. "Forget I asked."

"No." I grabbed for her arm, wrapped in a black uniform sleeve like a stovepipe. "I want to paint. I'm sorry. Please, will you still take me?"

"In the wheelchair you go."

I made no fuss about the chair, though I was certain I could walk. Well, perhaps my legs were a little uncertain.

Where had this morning gone? I'd picked at a foul porridge breakfast. They'd given me more pills.

What about the previous night? I had no memory of dinner. What had happened that afternoon? I dimly recalled an unfamiliar wing of the building. A long hallway, a bright flash of light, but everything else was hazy. Did I speak with Dr. Porter?

The bandages on my arm looked fresh. And the skin below them itched terribly.

The nurse rolled me past the gathering of sad souls in Commons, toward the illusion of freedom outdoors. Soon, I espied our volunteer painting instructor. The same elderly woman as I recalled from five years ago. Maggie assisted me with set-up of the dilapidated field easel assigned to me, lowering the height so I could paint from a seated position.

She left me with the other bedraggled art students, of which there were ten. The class perched in the shade of a cedar hedgerow, our vantage point overlooking a grassy meadow which rolled toward the sea cliffs. Distance shrouded the ocean's blue horizon in a misty haze. St. Ivy's croquet devotees were gone this afternoon, leaving the scene unpeopled. On the other side of our view, forested hills rose to an outer edge of the Welterwood, kindled by the first embers of fall.

I set about filling my palette with colors. Most of the oils were lumpy and dried solid in their cracked tubes. I had to mix the ultramarine with rancid linseed oil, or I would not get a sky. The brushes were as destroyed as one might expect.

Afternoon wore on. Our class grew quiet. Before long, I was lost in the fragrance of sun-warmed cedars and the chatter of sparrows—entranced by the play of the wind and light on a grassy meadow.

The perspective I'd rendered wasn't right. Colors too jarring. My coarse brushstrokes inelegant. Surely it was the drugs.

"There you are, my dear Violet."

I turned to see Mrs. H walking toward me. I swished the dilapidated brush through turpentine and wiped it with a multi-colored rag.

"They told me it was fine to come out here." Mrs. H spoke to the orderly who walked to meet her, handing him a folded piece of paper. "Dr. Porter said it was good she'd have a visitor."

The tall man in a greenish khaki uniform read the note and nodded.

I stood from my chair and hugged her. "Agnes, it's wonderful to see you. Any word of Father?"

She shook her head. "I'm sorry, nothing yet. You can be sure Travers or I will tell you as soon as we hear anything."

"Thank you. What a fancy hat. Are those peacock feathers?"

She touched it, blushing. "A gift from dear Mrs. Tremble. We've become fast friends since that day… when she found you and came to your aid. Our family is forever grateful for her courage."

"Thus, she gave *you* the hat?" I smiled, pushing aside the terror of not remembering one minute my so-called rescue.

"You see, I may have already purchased several others and asked a few sisters to patronize her shop as well. She's become somewhat of a local hero, after the newspapers."

"Right," I slumped in my wheelchair as dread realization dawned. "Of course. All Seastone must believe I was kidnapped, but it's not true. How

135

will I ever face anyone again? Even the families of my students? But I've lost them, haven't I?"

Agnes dragged a folding chair across the lawn to take a seat beside me.

"It's all right. We'll make do."

We wouldn't. There would be no home left for us to keep up. But I couldn't tell her here—too many ears.

"Roger's reputation is ruined as well. He only wanted to help me. It's not fair, Agnes. I've got to set it right. I've got to tell the papers he's innocent. Would they listen to me, since I'm such a scandal? Would they print my story, in my words?"

"Ah… I don't know." She laid a hand on mine and sighed. "Don't you think it'd be wise to wait until you can remember everything first? Before you go telling your tale to the papers?"

Not to mention the testimony of a lunatic female was worth little to reporters or police.

Lunatic, why did the word insert itself in my mind? I remembered it spoken by Dr. Porter, but… when? Was that last night?

"Listen," I whispered. "We need to talk in private."

She glanced around the group. "Maybe they'll let us go for a stroll. What do you say?" She raised her voice for the benefit of our nearby overseers.

"Yes. That would be lovely." I clapped my hands. Hoping to make the idea look innocent enough to take a mad-woman's fancy. I abhorred pretense, but I could act the part when needed.

A few other patients stared, but quickly lost interest.

Mrs. H signaled an orderly, and he approached. It was Ace. He reluctantly agreed to let us go, but warned us not to be gone long.

When Mrs. H rolled me and my wheelchair to a path yards away, I asked, "How is Puck doing? He must be so frightened and confused. Would they allow you to bring him for a visit?"

"I'm afraid that's not possible. He's run off. Been gone nearly as long as you have. We were so preoccupied with searching for you, we didn't notice he was missing for some time."

"Oh, no."

"I'm so sorry, dear."

A part of me went numb. How could I have caused such a fate for the poor creature? The little soul who trusted me? He would have lived happily down by the fishing docks if I'd not interfered in the natural course of his life.

I scrubbed a hand over my face. "No, he must be all right. Puck will come home. Keep looking for him, will you please?"

I glanced to see my housekeeper dab away tears with an embroidered handkerchief. The path thinned, becoming a trampled pair of lines through sparse lawn. Vehicles must drive this way. We headed toward a stream I'd just attempted to paint. I smelled living earth and water. River polished stones rich with moss.

"Don't you hear a waterfall?" I asked.

The compound was not thirty acres, and I estimated we neared the perimeter.

I shifted in my chair and noticed a paintbrush in the folds of my dress. Before I questioned the impulse, I'd tucked it alongside my thigh. The metal-capped tip might prove a useful bit of contraband. I wasn't certain Mrs. H would be complicit in such a scheme.

"What did you need to tell me, dear?"

I exhaled. Where to even begin? "Have you spoken to Dr. Porter?"

"Several days ago. He's a fine physician. Folks talk highly of him."

"I think he's a monster." Nor could I exactly say why. He hadn't harmed me, that I recalled. I just *knew*.

"Now, Violet."

"He declared me a ward of the Commonwealth. Did he tell you?"

"What? How do you mean?"

"They've revoked my citizens' rights. I spoke to a police sergeant yesterday. He took my testimony but assured me it's invalid. Together, they have judged me mentally incompetent. My property has been placed under the authority of this institute and Porter. He told me… that you and Travers were to be dismissed. The house is to be boarded up, since it's now his."

"This can't be right, Violet. I… I have a meeting with Porter this afternoon. I'm sure it's some misunderstanding."

"It's not, Agnes. I was there. I heard everything they said."

She pushed my chair down a path which became a service road. We followed the wheel ruts alongside the quickening brook. Our level embankment rose, while the stream tumbled into a ravine.

The institute's perimeter wall loomed ahead through the trees. A tangle of rusted, vine-entangled barbed wire crowned the ivy-covered bricks. Toward the front of the institute, the wall boasted decorative ironwork to serve the same purpose.

"There it goes under the grate, just beyond the bridge," said Mrs. H. "I hear your waterfall. It would be nice to see it on the cliffs from the other side. Like Eagle Point farther down the bay. You remember going there to picnic when you were a girl? You used to sketch the falls."

The smell of water and iron hung in the air. She rolled me alongside the rocky edge of the path, overlooking the stream.

"I remember."

Father would go out among the rocks and collect sea urchins and shells at low tide. I'd sketch them later, and he'd help me learn their scientific names.

I got as good a look at the grate through which the water escaped as possible from that distance. Slick with algae, the iron bars looked too close together for any person to swim through.

Dappled shade from the beech trees made me shiver. Mrs. H gave me her shawl and sat on a mossy rock beside my chair.

"Will you tell me what really happened that morning you disappeared? Travers said he saw Mr. Gale perform some sort of disappearing stage act. Said he was off to find you in Fairyland, of all blame things, but Travers didn't believe it. The police couldn't find hide nor hair of either of you. Turned that fancy house upside down. They took one of his servants downtown for questioning, but somehow the man got away under their noses and left a horrible mannequin in his place. It's all in the newspapers." She shook her head.

"Oh, Agnes. It's true! Roger did come to find me in Faerie. It's too wonderful! You always believed in magic, and I never did, all those years. I was wrong."

"I wouldn't say so. Your painting is magic."

"No, I mean literal magic. Your folk-charms and potions and stories of the Fair Folk, the Sídhe—you do believe them, don't you?"

"Well, I do—"

"So, you *must* understand. It's all real. The Otherworld is like our own, but a mirror image. Some things are the same and some are so very different. Mythical creatures of every sort you can imagine live there. I have seen wonders! I've worked magic, Agnes! Real magic. I have that power because of Mother."

"What do you mean?"

"Mother was a fairy. In fact, she was the sister of the Queen of the Fae. I'm only half-human. That's why I've always shunned iron. It's why I'm anxious in town near so many iron machines…" But her distressed look silenced me.

"Did that Mr. Gale tell you all this?" She spoke his name like it was cursed. *Ironic.*

"Yes, but Agnes, I've seen the proof with my own eyes!"

"Violet…" Sorrow passed over her face, if it was not shame.

"Of all the people in the world, I thought you would understand."

"I didn't say that. I want to believe you, Violet. It's simply…" she sighed.

"Why do you insist on attending those séances of yours if you don't believe in the supernatural? Whom are you trying to impress?" It was perhaps a cruel thing to say, but she might have deserved it.

"I do believe in that." She heaved a sigh. "I thought I saw her once… I've been chasing that ghost ever since."

"Who?"

"My daughter."

"Oh. I'm so sorry. I never knew."

She drew out a handkerchief to dab her eyes. "Gertie was almost eight. She was learning to help me with the laundry and the alterations for our shop when she got sick…. I wish I'd understood the protective arts back then, like I do now."

"Why haven't you ever told me?"

"I didn't want to burden you."

I had only known Mrs. H was married long ago for a short time, but that it had ended badly. She spoke little about it.

"I'm sorry."

"Don't be. It can't be changed, and it set me on the course I followed. Studying the healing herbs and the old ways, finding my strength and the teachers my path brought to me. Joining the Sisterhood. When I came to work for your mother, it made me happy to help her through her illness, and to help you. You reminded me of Gertie when you were small. But now… you're here again, and I hate to see you so."

"I won't stay here. They have no reason to keep me. I've done nothing wrong, but they won't listen to me. Perhaps you can talk some sense into Porter this afternoon."

She shook her head. "I'm afraid I tried already. They say it's a police matter and you can't go home until they finish their investigation."

I turned toward the rushing stream. "Something's not right. Porter is lying. I just don't know about what."

After a moment, she broke the strained silence. "We should head back, or they'll come looking for us. This road must connect with the main grounds. We'll follow it on around."

In about twenty yards, we espied another structure ahead through the trees. Smaller than the central buildings, this appeared to be a residence, perhaps an old caretaker's cottage, from the asylum's hotel days. The landscaping was overgrown. A few of the windows in the ivy-covered brick house contained broken panes of glass. An engine, like an automobile, rumbled to life.

"We should turn back," I said.

"I second that notion."

She pushed my chair as fast as she could in the direction we'd come. Though I doubted I could muster the strength, I'd almost got out to try and walk, before a motorized truck rattled over a rickety wooden bridge, heading our way.

With Mrs. H distracted by the man hailing us from the open window, I drew forth that paintbrush. The car's engine sputtered a smoky staccato. I snapped the metal tip away from the brush's wooden handle before the motor idled. I pretended to adjust a button on my blouse, tucking that into the minimal corset I was allowed to wear.

Splintered wood stung my skin, but with any luck I'd avoid a search. Remembering I had it in my possession tonight? That was an entirely different matter.

Mrs. H and the man in the car conversed yards away. I made out the words *garden* and *stream*, and Mrs. H pointed in the direction from which we'd come. The stench of burning fuel was enough to make me want to flee in pursuit of breathable air.

Presently, Mrs. H turned around, frowning. "I'm afraid we have to go with him."

Philips hopped out of the idling vehicle. "No one's allowed out here. Don't you know monsters live in those woods?" He pointed to the wall. "Do you think that wall's only to keep you loonies in?" He laughed.

Mrs. H muttered under her breath.

The orderly lifted my wheelchair into the back of the motor-truck.

Mrs. H took my arm. We both squeezed into the vehicle's only passenger seat.

Philips sat behind the wheel. I caught the odor of harsh chemicals on him.

"Don't wander this far away again." He shifted a gear, and the shadow below his arm moved in the opposite—impossible—direction. "If you know what's good for you."

I held my tongue.

When the truck approached the institute, I witnessed the remainder of my fellow art students marching inside, carrying their easels and canvases. I didn't care about my abandoned, half-finished painting. The thing was only fit for a dustbin. I hoped it was just the stress of my situation, and the sedatives, which had stolen my spark, but it felt like more. What had happened to me? I couldn't even walk on my own for more than a few paces. Something had drained my strength, other than whatever had caused this bandage on my head.

Beside a portico leading to the main wing of Commons, several orderlies, along with Maggie, made a fuss over returning me to my wheelchair. She and Agnes exchanged a few words I couldn't hear.

"I'll come back tomorrow after my rounds, Violet." Mrs. H kissed my forehead. "Rest until then."

I nodded. It was easier to say nothing.

Maggie came to take the handles of my chair. "I understand you had quite the adventure. Whatever gave you the notion to stray that far from the group?"

"I heard the waterfall down the creek and wanted to see it."

We passed the entrance to Commons, headed toward a wing of the compound about which I remembered little more than a general foreboding.

"I shouldn't have to tell you it's dangerous in those woods." She huffed. "Common sense is rare enough around here. We can't have our patients getting in trouble where we can't find them."

We entered through those double doors again. Bad things happened in this place. I just couldn't remember what. My fingers strayed to my side, touching the spot under my clothing where I'd tucked that broken paintbrush tip.

"Where are we going? I need to rest. Please take me to my room."

Maggie laughed. "Listen to this one, won't you? Thinks she's giving the orders."

She motioned to an orderly folding a stack of hospital gowns. The sturdy woman left off her task to help escort us through that dim, marble-floored hall toward the elevator.

"We're late, thanks to you," Maggie said. "Dr. Porter is not a man to string along. He has many patients to see."

"All the more reason not to trouble him now. Really. I don't need treatment today, only rest."

Ensconced in brass at either side of the corridor, electric lights dimmed, flickered to embers, and quickened again with a dull hum of a hidden dynamo cranking back to life.

When we reached the end of the hall, our escort pulled a lever on the wall. Ironwork doors opened. My heart clawed at my ribcage like a trapped animal as they rolled me inside the tiny elevator car. I gasped for air. My limbs tingled, like waking again after a terrible sleep.

"She's hyperventilating," said Maggie, sounding far, far away. "We need a sedative."

I sensed we'd traveled upward, though the control dials were not designed for laypersons to read. When the elevator doors opened, the female orderly disappeared down another hallway.

Now was my chance.

I sprung up from the wheelchair and shoved it backward. Maggie shouted when it slammed into her. A wave of dizziness tested my brashness, but I leapt into a sprint.

I ducked into an open doorway. A miasma of chemicals and sickness assaulted my nose as I caught my breath. A patient inside that room moaned. I had not the courage to look long at the figure under those stained blankets. I only sought the barred window. Daylight. Blue sky. We must be above ground.

Was this the seventh floor? Why did that seem correct?

Stairwell. I didn't know where it was, but I ran. Behind me, Maggie yelled.

An orderly darted from inside another room and lunged for me.

I twisted out of his grasp. This proved sufficient incentive to increase my speed. My hospital-issue slippers gave tenuous purchase on slick tile. In frenetic seconds, I reached another set of double doors and flung them open. Pursuers behind me. I yanked the sash from my robe and slid it through both handles, tying a knot. It might only buy me an extra minute.

I dashed down a flight of stairs, thankful the way appeared deserted. Cold and damp as a cave, it seemed abandoned. Past the first landing, I turned a corner into darkness. The electric bulbs dimmed and hummed before they went out. I could not see the concrete steps. One false move and I would fall and injure myself.

Fists pounded the doors I'd tied closed. Muffled shouts and threats echoed through this hollow passageway.

I gripped the railing. Because it didn't hurt my hand, I stifled a sob. It had to be iron, but it was only dead, rough metal under my skin. Nothing poisonous. Nothing magical of any kind.

"No."

I would not accept this. I must escape.

I kicked off my miserable slippers and found the edge of the step with bare toes. Fingers wrapped around that hideous railing for balance. One cold step after another, I descended the dusty stone steps through pitch black, until a dim light appeared below. A small window on a lower landing.

A clank of metal and shouts from above; they'd broken through my hasty knot.

I leapt two and three stairs at a time. If I fell, it might injure me enough to require transportation to a different sort of hospital. One in which the treatments didn't cause me to forget whole days.

"Violet," Maggie shouted.

At least two other voices alongside hers. Male orderlies. Shouting for me to stop.

I reached the ground floor. The grimy window shed sufficient light to reveal portions of the service corridor I'd descended. Another door, this one chained and padlocked.

"Where's Houdini when you need him?" I pulled out my metal paintbrush tip, bit it to flatten the cylinder, and set to work on the lock. A skill I'd learned from Father, who, in his stage acts long ago, used to brag no chains could hold him.

In seconds, the padlock sprung open. I wrestled with the iron chain. It only just stung my fingers.

The chain dropped with a clank, and I shoved. The heavy door budged. I released a cry of determination and broke through. Tendrils of ivy showered me with dirt and debris as I parted tangled vines.

I flattened myself against the foliage-covered brick and inched along the west-facing exterior wall.

Fresh air. How rare and precious a thing after the stench of that place. I drank it in before I readied my trembling legs to run.

I would crouch behind any cover, making my way to the woods. The waterfall. There must be an exit through that grate, or perhaps the one upstream.

I only had to reach the forest…

A tendril of ivy twined around a lock of my hair. I blinked and touched the silken leaves—alive and vibrant. Tiny spirals unfurled below my weary fingertips, but it was quite possible I'd simply brushed up against that spiral. Probable even.

Down the alleyway I sprinted, bare feet numb to the stony ground, one direction as good as any to get me clear of the compound. Before I reached the building's corner, shouts echoed from in front of me. I hesitated, legs trembling.

I took a weedy side path. I might find cover, but a tall fence stood between me and the forest.

"She's this way!"

I ducked behind a stack of dingy mattresses, which leaned against clapboard siding. They smelled of mold and sorrow.

Bootsteps on gravel. This was no good. I'd be trapped. I ran to the other side of the structure, hoping speed and sheer will might carry me to safety.

"She can't be far." Was it Evelyn's voice?

Four orderlies approached. Evelyn accompanied them.

I shrank against the wall beside a hedge. More ubiquitous ivy covered the brick here. My olive-colored patient's robe draped open without my sash. I pulled it around my white nightgown, hoping to hide that bright contrast of color.

Short of breath, I mouthed the silent words. "Pass on by. You don't see me."

They drew near. If I ran now, they would spot me for sure. My heart thudded in my ears.

I might give up. Plead for mercy. Or laugh and call it a fun game. After all, I was a lunatic.

Close enough now, I could see their breath in the cold air. They scanned the horizon as if still searching, but they were only yards away. The hedge no longer blocked their view. Frozen in terror, I couldn't move.

Why didn't they notice me?

"Stop. She's nearby. I know it." Evelyn stared at an object cupped in her hands.

"We fan out," said one orderly. "Alert the perimeter guards."

"No, wait!" Evelyn raised her left hand. "There." She pointed in my direction before she took a step.

"There's nothing here. Just trash." The orderly snickered. "Are you daft? These nutters rubbing off on you, Ev?" The others laughed.

Terror clamped me like a vice. Evelyn calmly approached my ivy-covered hiding place and grabbed me by the arm. I made not a sound.

The orderlies gasped in astonishment. "Saints almighty! She was there the whole time? How?"

"You must always keep your eyes open, gentlemen," said Evelyn. "If you're not careful, they can deceive you."

Before I could twist away, Evelyn stabbed the needle of a syringe into my arm.

CHAPTER 15
WONDERFUL LIES

y sore eyes fluttered open to harsh electric light. It took a moment to recognize my surroundings. A dark window.

Night. I had no memory of any nights here at St. Ivy's.

I shifted in bed. Straps held my wrists and bandaged arms.

Just breathe.

I felt powerless.

Were it not for Evelyn, my escape attempt might have succeeded. Somehow, I'd hidden myself against that wall, vanished in plain sight of the men. My glamour. Was it that simple? Evelyn must have used magic to discover me.

"Hide," I whispered. I concentrated on the olive color of my blanket. The wrinkled ecru of my linens. The dull steel of the bedframe.

My hand shimmered and disappeared.

I blinked. No, my skin was painted to match the background. Like I possessed a chameleon's scales—a perfect camouflage, but for the bandages.

Little good my Fae blood did me for strength. My glamoured arms could no more break the restraints than mere human limbs.

I gasped in frustration. My arm returned to its normal pale color.

A knock at my door. "You up, lass?" Maggie's voice. "Dr. Porter's here to see you."

Her chipper tone unsettled me. Maggie, complicit and nonchalant about this atrocity as ever, straightened my bedsheets and nightgown into their proper places.

"Maggie, please. Unlock me. I'm no threat. I only ask for a little dignity."

Her fake smile flattened.

"I'm afraid that's not possible, Miss Morgen." Dr. Porter spoke from the doorway. "You proved your untrustworthiness. We must treat you accordingly."

The doctor, holding a folio of documents, crossed the room, followed by a larger orderly. Maggie left us, slamming the door shut.

Porter sat in a chair beside the bed and drew a pair of spectacles from his vest pocket. He slid those up his nose and opened the file.

"Here is something for you to consider." He rustled through several yellowed papers, hand-written and typed. "This is your complete medical record."

The doctor stroked his reddish goatee, shifting forward in his chair. A silver and black medallion suspended from a rope chain slipped past his collar before he tucked it back under his shirt. It exuded a sense of evil, but straightaway I dismissed the idea as foolish—another distraction from the true dangers in this place.

He held a page for my inspection, printed with the hospital's letterhead and written in longhand of elegant penmanship. At the top was my name.

"You see here the record of your first visit. We have no reason to falsify such a thing. Shall I read it to you?"

I said nothing.

Dr. Porter cleared his throat and began,

> *Patient: Violet Morgen (M-) Female*
> *Location: Seastone, St. Ivy's Sanatorium, Female Ward C*
> *Date: 23 September 1897*

> *Patient M-, a young woman of seventeen years, was admitted to this hospital on the 21*[st] *of September, two days ago. According to the school nursing staff, M- suffered what witnesses described as a paroxysmal manifestation, before she fled into the nearby woods. She was not found until the following evening, when she was admitted to General. After ruling out any physical cause for such symptoms, her physicians ordered a psychiatric course of evaluation. My initial diagnosis after reviewing all notes and speaking with M-, is dissociative fugue precipitated by anxiety neurosis.*

> *Patient M- has exhibited no acute symptoms since her arrival at General. She understood the nature of her stay at this hospital, although she did not remember the events which transpired prior to her arrival here. M- appears to have made a full recovery in only a few days, a fact confirmed by my understudy, Dr. Porter, and staff. It is my opinion that*

for patient M-, any prolonged stay in such an institution as this would be detrimental. I believe she will recover fully under self-care and have hereby signed this patient's discharge order. In addition, a copy of this record is to be provided to the aforementioned Dr. Porter to add to her existing medical records at General.

"This document is signed, Dr. Roger Albert Gale, Minister of Psychiatrics." Porter allowed me a moment of silence before he said, "You accused me of lying to you on this subject. I thought hard evidence might help you see reason."

"What do you want me to say?" I shut my eyes. "I can't remember any of that."

"Nevertheless, I wish you to ask yourself why Gale chose to associate himself with you now, given this history. What did he stand to gain, aside from the obvious benefits of a beautiful woman's company?"

"If you have something to tell me, doctor, please do so."

He wheezed a laugh. "Very well, I will present my theory. You'll not want to hear it, as is so often the case with delusionals. Facing the truth of reality is too much of a shock, so the ego goes into hiding—inventing alternate truths. These fantasies can become so convincing to us that we revel in them. In a prior session, you described how you and Dr. Gale entered another dimension and experienced grand adventures."

"I said no such thing." Could I have? It was possible, considering the gaps in my memory, but Porter had to be lying. He certainly knew more than he let on.

"You have told us many remarkable things in our sessions. Oh, I know Gale has convinced you he has magical powers. All the more easily because he is gifted in sleight-of-hand trickery. I've witnessed him do amazing things myself. That is beside the point. I want you to consider how Gale took advantage of this weakness of yours. He has been experimenting on your mind with various psychoactive drugs. These left you vulnerable to his hypnotic suggestions. He has led you through a fabricated fantasy world and your pliable mind has taken it for truth. My staff finished their analysis of the tea blended for you by Dr. Gale, and given to us by your housekeeper. Would you care to know what we found?"

I didn't answer.

Porter continued, "The poisonous herb belladonna, as well as traces of another chemical compound which we have yet to classify, but which resembles a mind-altering substance extracted from blue lotus. Therefore, I theorize..." he licked his lips. "Just before your disappearance, he may have given

147

you a dose of something too strong for you to handle. Perhaps you slipped into a coma from which he couldn't resuscitate you. He may even have believed he killed you. It wouldn't be unthinkable for Gale to have dumped your body into the ocean before he departed Seastone."

"No." I strained at the leather straps. "That's all a lie. Roger would never do such a thing."

"My dear," he said. I hated him for the condescension. "I have followed your new beau's research for some years. At one time, Gale was lauded by our profession for his ground-breaking discoveries in the fields of Mesmerism and therapeutic hypnosis. Even I considered him brilliant." He opened the second folder and pulled out what looked to be an old paper-bound medical journal, but he did not open it. "Gale's research was only hampered by his lack of volunteer test subjects. It seems he's found a way around this obstacle. Ours is a competitive business, seeking the esteem of the Royal Medical Academy. Many a physician will bend the rules in favor of accolades. Gale's license was revoked years ago, following an unexplained death here at St. Ivy's. He is on Academy probation, indefinitely. Although perhaps he might yet salvage his reputation if he were to publish a groundbreaking new study, featuring new... field research."

I said nothing. My mind was numb. I stared at the ugly tin ceiling; my arms and feet strapped to the bed.

"I know he told you that you're special, Miss Morgen. That you're not meant for this common life, but for something better. Who among us doesn't want to hear such things? Oh, how easy it is to believe such wonderful lies. That we are the chosen ones." He laughed and stroked his beard. "I'm sorry, but the truth is you're just a very ordinary, albeit very ill woman, one that fell prey to a dastardly scheme." He sighed, resting his hands on the edge of my bed.

"It will require work, but we will help you remember the truth. Then you shall be free. Meanwhile, you must trust us. Take your medicine and report for your treatments without incident. If you continue to be uncooperative, I'll be forced to make it increasingly uncomfortable for you. Hmm?" He smiled.

I turned away and faced the wall.

At Porter's cue, the orderly forced me to swallow two pills with a paper cup of water. I showed him my empty mouth before he backed away.

"Accept the real world, Miss Morgen. It hurts, but it's where you live."

They left my room. The lights went out, and I spit out the bitter pills I'd tucked under my tongue.

Movement in the corner of the dark room froze my blood. I blinked. Was it the shadow of a figure cast by my moonlit window? I turned to look, but no one was there.

My heart thudded. I held my breath to listen for the slightest sound.

Nothing. The shadow was gone—if it had ever been there at all.

I exhaled and slumped back into the cot.

Why would Roger hide such a thing from me? He told me he practiced many forms of medicine. Before we were separated, he'd tried to tell me where we had met years ago.

Why couldn't I remember?

I'd had my doubts about trusting him at first, but Roger had never done me harm. Nor had he given me experimental drugs. Tea. My special blend. I'd experienced nothing unusual after drinking Roger's tea. No, it only quelled my anxiety and headaches. Gave me welcome relief. Helped me sleep without nightmares.

Not until that morning at his house. I'd drank more tea—and taken a headache tonic.

But that wasn't the reason I'd seen all I did. The Otherworld was real.

Despite my will to stay awake, I drifted into sleep.

A noise. A hand over my mouth. Evelyn's face. Pale blonde hair pinned underneath a nurse's hat.

"Shh." She placed a finger over her lips. "I'm here to help you escape." She set to work freeing me from my restraints.

"Escape?" I whispered, too harshly. "I'd already be out of here if not for you this afternoon." I rubbed a sore wrist.

She frowned. "It's possible you would've made it to the gate, but your odds were not good. Even with your glamour." My hands free, she moved to my ankles. "The gates are always guarded. Aside from that, you can't leave just yet. You're the only one who can help us now."

"What? Are you making fun of me? Is this a test? Tell Dr. Porter this joke is too cruel." I raised my voice, not caring if I was overheard. "If my memories are in fact true, you were the one who betrayed us on that airship. You were going to turn me over to the Summer Courts, as I recall."

"And there you must still go." She spoke just above a whisper. "Listen. I know you don't trust me, but I saved your neck earlier today. The sedative I used was strong enough to knock you out for the duration of the afternoon, thus you missed your scheduled treatment. Precisely why you're awake at this moment. If you care anything for Gale, you'll hear me out."

"What happened to Roger?"

"He is in custody in the Winter Courts. Awaiting execution."

"What? No. How can that be?" My heart might have frozen.

"I will explain more later. Right now, I need your assistance to locate a Fae relic hidden in Dr. Porter's collections. With it, you may be able to travel into the Otherworld and help Gale. I cannot do so myself until the next Equinox Bridge."

If this was some kind of trick, I didn't care. If she offered me any chance of helping Roger, I was willing to try, to say nothing of escape from this prison. It was still worth the gamble.

"What do I have to lose?"

"Everything. Like us all. However, if you stay here, Porter will kill you anyway."

"Don't you work for him?"

"No. I'm investigating him."

"Is he a part of the Reliqua?"

"*Gods*, no." She opened a satchel and pulled out a folded stack of clothing. "Put this on. Not the hat yet. We haven't much time. I'll return shortly."

I dressed in the pair of men's trousers, green uniform shirt, and jacket, thankful for boots in nearly my correct size. A vast improvement over institute-issued slippers.

I tore at the itchy bandages on my arms. The first layer came away, only to reveal a series of smaller cotton wraps. Before I could remove those, Evelyn reappeared, pushing a gurney.

"You'll lie in this until we're past the main floors. Safer disguise. I don't think you have too strong a control yet on the use of your glamour."

I lay on the stretcher. She covered my non-patient attire, collar to boots, in hospital sheets. I concealed the hat under the blanket.

Traveling through the corridor, I affected the look of a sedated patient. Few of the night-shift nurses spoke a word to Evelyn other than greeting.

She rolled my gurney into an open elevator. Iron mechanisms clanked and whirred overhead. Their presence jarred even my numbed senses, which was a comforting relief. My sensitivity was starting to come back. What had dulled it so terribly?

We descended several floors, perhaps below ground.

"Pretend to be asleep," she said before the doors opened again.

Through nearly closed eyes, I saw an orderly down the corridor, standing with arms crossed.

"Who are we transporting tonight?" He leered at me. The same orderly who earlier called me a piece of trash.

"One of Porter's trial subjects."

"Doc's out. Didn't you get the schedule, Ev?"

"Porter's coming in shortly. He asked me to prep this one for sample collection. It takes time. He doesn't have time to waste."

"In the middle of the night?"

"You're still new here, aren't you?"

"Nope. Doc always goes by the schedule." The man touched my face, stroking my cheek. It was all I could do not to scream. "I'm sorry. Can't let you take this one back. I'll have to escort you both upstairs." He pulled the bedsheet down around my neck, no doubt expecting to find skin instead of a man's jacket.

My eyes opened. Evelyn grabbed for something by my boots.

"What the?"

Evelyn swung at him so fast her movements blurred in the dim light. She struck again. A dull crack to the back of his skull.

The man yelped and staggered, slamming the gurney, with me still on it, into the side of the corridor.

Evelyn tossed aside her wooden baton and shoved his torso onto the gurney. I helped her shift the hulking dead weight into the place my smaller body had just occupied. Evelyn retrieved a loaded syringe from her medical bag and dosed our new patient.

"With luck, he won't remember anything come morning."

"Is that what's happened to me for the past five nights?"

"Not quite. Here, help me secure him." She pulled a leather strap from underneath the stretcher's frame and threw it over the man's torso. "Porter's electro-shock treatments also produce that side effect. Which means you lose hours before and after the procedure each day. Sometimes whole days. Your reactions to the device have been more severe than normal, but then again, I suspect he adjusted your treatment regimen because of what you are. I'm sorry I couldn't stop it."

I pinned my hair back and donned the man's uniform cap, ignoring for the moment the thought of being subjected to electro-shock treatments. I touched the spot behind my ear where a patch of hair had been shaved away.

"He knows I'm Fae?"

"I believe so." She pushed the stretcher, and I walked alongside. "There are many patients here with Otherworld ancestry, albeit far more distant than yours. No doubt you're the purest specimen Porter's ever seen."

"He accused Roger of experimenting on me, when all the while he's the culpable one." I stopped and rested with a hand against a wall, exposing the white cotton of my bandage beyond the jacket cuff. I could not remember a time when I had been this exhausted. "What in God's name is he doing to us—his patients?"

"He is collecting Faerie magic, from your blood and others like you. He turns it into a drug he sells for profit. And I believe he may be involved in much worse. Let's hide this one, and I'll explain."

Chapter 16
Path to the Greater Light

e rolled the now much heavier gurney into a supply closet, closing the unconscious orderly inside. When he woke up, he'd probably make enough noise to be heard by someone. Not that I should feel sorry for the bastard.

At the end of the corridor, Evelyn unlocked another door and lit a hand-held electric torch. We entered a storeroom for medical records, containers of specimens, jars of chemicals, and crates of old equipment. I walked through a maze of file cabinets, stacked with journals and books, toward a reddish haze in a far corner.

"The Reliqua has been investigating the illegal trade of a substance called Tears of the Moon," she said. "With it, ordinary humans can work Faecraft. On the black market, the extract commands a high price. We learned the drug is produced here at the institute, which gave us two suspects. Both men had the medical knowledge needed as well as the connections to profit from its export."

"Roger," I said. "And Dr. Porter."

"Gale and Porter were once colleagues. Magic is used in the drug's manufacture, so that's why we suspected Gale's involvement. I've discovered much in these previous months of my assignment here, but I haven't found evidence to link Gale to any of this until now."

We maneuvered past wooden crates to another locked door. A dim red light issued from around the doorframe.

"This key was difficult to procure." She unlocked the door and gestured for me to wait. "There are magic wards on this room. One moment."

She moved both of her hands in a counterclockwise circle and hummed a low note before speaking three words. Her ring glowed just as Roger's had when he cast a spell. She clapped on the last syllable. The pressure in the air shifted. My ears popped.

"Now, it's safe to enter."

By electric torchlight, we entered a smaller storeroom. Crates of cast-offs—many stamped *Fragile* and *Antiques*. Yellowed volumes of records lined rows of dusty steel shelves. I followed a mysterious glow to the back of the room and opened a wooden crate to find it packed with small glass vials of phosphorescent liquid.

"Did you think I was involved in all this?" I lifted a bottle—identical to the one found in my father's room that morning he disappeared, except this was filled with a substance like shimmering paint. "Why did you try to capture us before, on the airship?" I returned the bottle to the crate, alongside thousands of others.

"Gale was only to face a formal inquiry. Unless he was guilty, he had nothing to fear. You would have gone to the Summer Courts to meet your long-lost family. Gale complicated matters by getting himself captured by Winter Court soldiers. I crossed through the Divide to search for you. I found this, but I could not locate you." She drew something from an apron pocket and gave it to me—my crystal necklace.

"Oh! I lost it in the bay." I wondered more than once in the last days if that had all been a dream. "The chain was broken."

"I bargained with mermaids to get it back. They must have fixed it."

"Then they were real. But in the human-world's ocean?"

"Yes. We have warned that pod before to stay on their side of the Divide. Troublesome creatures. But at least their theft kept it out of Porter's hands. They only told me you'd washed ashore. Can you remember how you got here?"

I fastened on the necklace and tucked it under my borrowed uniform shirt.

"I came ashore and… I think someone found me, but it must have been that a rock hit my head." I touched the stitches at my hairline. "Afterward… I woke up here."

"Another day or two is unaccounted for—before you were officially admitted to St. Ivy's. That much I can offer. I know it's no comfort to hear. I'm sorry."

All I had were questions. How was my father connected to this? At least I'd learned the origin of the substance he ingested to cross through to the Otherworld. How many times had he done such a thing before? Did he know where it came from? Roger denied knowing anything about the bottle's origin when I showed it to him. But I wasn't sure what to believe now. My heart was sinking, but my mind tried to keep me afloat.

"You said you found evidence indicating Roger's involvement?"

"Over here." Evelyn directed the electric torchlight into another corner of the room.

I followed her toward the displaced contents of an abandoned laboratory. On a dusty desk sat beakers containing dried residue. Torchlight revealed yellowed papers of typed and hand-written notes. Photographs of what appeared to be journal pages, some bearing Roger's name. Charts of numbers, with logs of dates and symptoms. One or two diagrams contained geometric shapes and letter-like symbols, hastily drawn.

"I'll want to have this analyzed by my fellow scientists, but I believe these notes detail the formula for making the drug, along with a method for extracting it from living patients."

I picked up another document. The handwriting looked different from what I had seen of Roger's, though it bore his name and a date of over twelve years ago. The page appeared to contain algebraic formulae alongside notations in Greek and Latin. A rough sketch depicted some kind of helmet-like apparatus worn by a faceless man seated in a chair. Above it was the symbol for a crescent moon, along with an indication of moonlight striking the device. The man's hand rested upon an unknown circular object, perhaps a bowl. The lower edge of the paper had blackened and flaked away, either by fire or mold, but I made out the edges of several large glyphs such as I'd seen in Roger's books. Not the fluid lines of Fae Royal Script, but some other cryptic language known to sorcery.

Horrified, I set the page on the desk and turned away.

Evelyn said, "All that I've found dates to the time when Gale was employed at this institute a decade ago. He may or may not be aware of this current operation."

"Is this why Roger is to be executed?" I asked.

"No. I've yet to inform the Courts of this evidence. I'm afraid I don't know what charges the King has leveled against Gale, but Winter is notorious for his cruelty and capriciousness."

"How can I help him?"

"You must go to the Summer Courts and petition the Queen. She alone can intervene. She is the supreme ruler of the Fae. Even the Winter King obeys her. If Roger is innocent, you can plead his case to her. You have only two days before his trial; there is no time to waste."

"How can I travel there alone? Outside of an Equinox Bridge?"

"Your royal blood allows you to open a portal at the Queen's Circle any time of year, with the right relics. You already know how perilous the journey will be. I cannot go with you. You must decide if you can risk it alone. No one will fault you if you wish to stay." She walked farther into the crowded room.

"I have no desire to stay a prisoner here, one way or the other." I brushed aside a dusty cobweb and followed. Did I see her jaw clench? Like she knew something she didn't say. Doubtless they would keep me prisoner in the Summer Courts, as Roger warned might happen. Would I do it anyway, to save his life?

"If you don't decide to travel into the Otherworld, you must leave town. Many of the police are working for Porter. They're still looking for Gale. If you return home, I'm afraid you'll be recaptured."

"Wait." I spoke in a harsh whisper. "Someone's here…" I glimpsed movement across the far wall, as though a person had been watching us.

The figure fled her searching torchlight.

"Where?"

"Didn't you see a shadow?" I pointed, but the silhouette was gone, and I heard nothing else in the room.

"No." Evelyn drew what looked like a small brass compass from her uniform pocket. She held it aloft, taking readings from watch-like hands and dials. "You likely sense the magic flooding this room. It's difficult to read specifics with this portable magitrometer, but… I think we're still alone. This way."

We approached an antique secretary bookcase. Decorative keyholes graced each of the wooden drawers, most of which had been broken open. Inlaid in a lighter marquetry were elegant Fae letters, disguised as part of the design.

"Porter somehow acquired this from another Reliqua House. Just one of the many magical artifacts he's collected of late. See." She shined her lantern at a stack of those odd crates I had noticed. "In his quest to find *what* exactly, I'm not sure. I've witnessed Porter receive many such shipments since I arrived here a few months ago. Most are old books. Grimoires. Scrying mirrors. Relics of sorcery from various cultures and eras. Few of the staff know this stuff is even down here. Look." Evelyn held the magitrometer near the antique cabinet's wood and glass doors. She lifted the torchlight for me to read the device. One of the tiny gold hands moved to the upper edge of a gauge, while another silver hand pointed at the cabinet. "Do you see? There is a powerful source of magic inside this cabinet. Porter must think he's removed from it anything of value, but I believe he's overlooked something important. That's where you come in."

Evelyn opened a drawer in the center of an upper shelf and touched a hidden lever. A clicking sound repeated from other sections of the cabinet. Another door swung ajar at the mechanism. Empty inside. Our dim reflections stared back at us from the mirrored interior.

"That's not an ordinary mirror," I said.

"Good. You can sense it."

I touched the glass-coated silver speckled with age, amazed at how easy that simple action had been, considering my usual reaction to mirrors. "What must I do?"

Before Evelyn answered, a ring of illuminated symbols surrounded my hand, followed by another two rows. On and on they appeared; rings of script faded from vivid candle-flame gold beside my fingers to whispers at the glass' edge. I raised my other hand to touch the cool surface. Concealed letters flickered to life, brightest close to my skin. They revealed only hints of a vast arcane design.

"Beautiful." Evelyn's voice betrayed wonder. "The wood is Otherworld oak. The mirror is made with enchanted glass. Your blood brings it to life. There's a hidden chamber we must find. I only hope it still contains what I believe it should."

My crystal pendant shimmered, casting the reflected image of my face in eerie blue against the darkness of the storage room.

Evelyn traced a line of glowing script with an index finger. "It says... 'Harken ye Fae of Royal blood. By the lesser light, the path to the greater light will be revealed. Heed the watchers.'"

I repeated it under my breath. "What does it mean?"

"Lesser light and greater might refer to the moon and the sun. Yet, it could have many meanings."

"Perhaps the watchers are the stars," I said. The illuminated letters, connected by curves and lines, were like constellations. I didn't recognize any configurations from my human understanding of astrology, but underneath the foreign groupings, I recognized earth constellations.

"By the lesser light, the path," Evelyn repeated. "How shall we get moonlight in here, if that's what it means?"

"You said the words could have multiple meanings." I removed one hand from the mirror and grasped my crystal pendant. "Could it mean Faelight?"

"Yes," Evelyn said. "Of course. Can you control yours yet?"

"You mean this necklace?"

"No, your own Faelight." She turned to me. "Violet, how did you summon your glamour before? Do the same, but imagine you are luminous. Uncover the light within you."

I took a deep breath of air that smelled like mildew and old paper, wishing I saw the sky. I envisioned moonlight casting graceful shadows from the trees. The Milky Way on a clear night.

Nothing happened. My hand remained as dull as usual. The glowing script started to fade. From the adjacent corridor, I heard the scuffling of boots. Someone bumped into something, causing it to fall. Distant voices.

"We're running out of time. If you want to save Gale, you must do this, Violet."

Mother's illumination spell.

As quietly as possible, I sang the words. My hand began faintly to radiate. So did my necklace.

Incredibly, the cabinet's interior reflected a faint light cast by my own skin. In the mirror, I beheld my glowing face. This was not imagination, nor hallucination. I truly saw it, and so did Evelyn.

"There," she said. "That new circle of script."

I bent to inspect. A hidden chamber, large enough to contain a small object, had appeared between the glass and the silver backing.

"Can you sense how to open it?" she asked. "Try."

Shouts echoed from the adjacent corridor. I recalled the soldiers Evelyn brought to bear on Roger and me.

I shut my eyes. My hand passed through the glass as if it weren't there. Freezing air met my fingers. I grabbed something both solid and yielding—a mixture of surfaces. I drew back and opened my still-glowing hand to find a silver medallion set with a jewel—pale blue veined with rainbow iridescence. It was attached to an old silken cord.

"Brilliant," she said. "House Zuria's insignia, as I suspected. Take this to the Queen in the Sumer Courts. Tell her where we found it. It should be proof enough of Porter's involvement in more than just illegal exports."

I slipped the medallion's cord around my neck and tucked it under my shirt alongside my crystal.

She added, "The medallion contains a powerful Faestone, which you will need to open a portal outside of Equinox Bridge. Think of it as an amplified traveling relic, accessible only to Royal Fae. You must get to the Queen's Circle in the Welterwood. Do you know the way?"

"Yes. How do I use this Faestone?"

"I'm afraid I cannot tell you much; only that moonlight activates this stone's power. I believe your doorway to the Summer Courts should appear in the Southwest, but the secrets of these gate stones are guarded by a select few of your kindred. If you trust your instincts, you may find the knowledge of how to use it hidden in your blood."

The shouts from the next room grew louder. A man's laugh.

"I can't be seen with you," she whispered. "Come on."

We ran to another door. Evelyn unlocked it and pointed down a dark passageway. "Go. Take the next corridor to the left and follow it to the main hall. You will come to the laundry. Someone is waiting there who'll help you escape the grounds. An orderly named Ace. Use your glamour; he'll still recognize you. You can trust him." She hugged me. "Fare thee well, Lady of the Summer Courts."

"Thank you, Dr. Crane," I whispered before the sound of rattling iron keys silenced us.

Evelyn extinguished the torchlight before the door opened.

I sprang into motion, navigating the dark maze, only faintly lit by my fading necklace. An old tray of surgical scalpels caught my eye. I grabbed one and tucked it into my boot. No time to ponder why I could see so well in the dark.

Before I saw the laundry, I smelled it. I leaned against the concrete wall to catch my breath, pulling in the acrid stench of bleach. Voices ahead sounded unalarmed—the normal banter of people at work.

The man's clothing I wore was a hospital service uniform. Would they notice I was female, even with my hair covered, and my hat slung low?

Glamour. Now was as good a time as any to give it another try.

As I walked, I started with a simple task. My hand. I tried to visualize a man's hands, and of course Roger's came to mind. His face I could paint from memory, but such a disguise might not go well if someone recognized the good Dr. Gale. I settled for a mental image of Travers—his expressions, his posture. How I once sketched him while he tended our horses. His smile when he sipped his after-dinner whiskey or played his accordion.

When I opened my eyes, my hands appeared to be that of a middle-aged man. I blinked in stunned amazement. Would it hold out when I entered the main laundry?

I turned the corner and strode into the space like I knew where I was going, making no eye-contact. Other men dressed in uniforms like mine—and women in matching dresses—gave me only a passing glance as I walked by. Not until one of them hollered at me.

"Hey, you." It was Ace. "We need another warm body outside. Come on." He pointed toward me, and there was no one else in my general area to suspect was the target of his summons. Could he truly be trusted? Could

Evelyn, for that matter? Yet the promise of the word 'outside' meant this might be a legitimate means of escape.

"M—" I cleared my throat, trying to sound a bit more masculine. "Me?"

"Yeah," said a second man, laughing. It was Philips. "Are you daft, old man?"

Old man. My glamour must have worked. I was not insane. A sobering thought.

"Right away," I said, in the lowest voice I could muster. Pity I didn't know how to glamour my vocal cords.

They enlisted two others. I followed the group past a boiler and massive tubs for the soaking of hospital linens. The stench of ammonia and other chemicals assaulted my nose. The odors of this commercial laundry were nothing like what issued from our own washroom when I helped Mrs. H on laundry day. The workers boxed me in as we walked, fore and aft. We entered a smaller chamber. An iron-grated service elevator dominated one end of the room. I tried not to cringe. Could I hold my glamour disguise caged within so much iron?

Gurneys lined one wall. Two held what looked to be patient-sized lumps under rumpled blankets. Unattended and unmoving, held in this dimly lit service area, if those were bodies, they were dead. My stomach turned and my face flushed cold.

Philips ordered us to grab two gurneys, and our cohort rolled them onto the elevator. I focused all my will on holding the Travers disguise, like my life depended on it. Luckily, the elevator car was only dimly lit, pocked with shadows from the grated iron cage. I tilted the brim of my hat, hoping to keep my face shrouded.

The machine ground to a stop, and our grim procession exited, pushing two gurneys loaded with dead bodies, myself steering one of them down another dim corridor. Ace hummed a tune with such energy I half expected him to break into dance, but he kept his soldierly stride.

I dared not pull back the blanket and look, but I risked a question. "Who were they?"

"Don't know." Another orderly yanked at the fabric covering one cadaver, revealing a pale face, the head bandaged. "Ah, that little rat." The others laughed. "Guess he won't be bitin' anymore." More laughter.

I recognized the dead man's face—a patient who'd glared at me in the Commons room just days prior. The man's physical health had looked fine. How had he perished so quickly?

"Who we got up there, Philips?" said a man with rotten teeth.

"Two Knocks." He opened a set of doors, and we proceeded outside into the cool, early morning air.

"Might miss the old fart," said Ace.

The other replied. "Nah."

"What killed them?" I asked. Perhaps it was the illusion of liberation, which gave me the foolhardiness to press my luck.

"Crazy," answered Philips. More laughter from the others.

Ace shot me what might have been a warning glance before he returned his focus to his song and the path ahead.

Under cover of pre-dawn darkness, we rolled the gurneys toward the garages. Our procession found another of those work trucks which had yesterday shuttled Mrs. H and me back from the edge of the grounds.

Without ceremony or dignity, we loaded the two bodies into the vehicle's rear bed. One man hopped in to drag them along. Bone thudded against iron. I was nearly sick.

If I ran now, I might find places to hide, but this near the institute, there were too many workers—guards—to take the gamble. I'd been able to hold my disguise this long. Chances were good our party was headed toward more seclusion.

I sat in the backseat next to Ace, keeping my hat slung low. Philips drove. The terrible iron contraption rattled over a road of crushed oyster shells, past another bleak wing of the institute.

The man in the front passenger seat pointed at me. "How long you been here?" His rotten teeth matched his pungent breath.

"A… week."

Ace said, "Pay's good. That's to keep us quiet in town. But you know that already, don't you, Kid?"

"Yes…" Wait a minute… did he call me Kid?

"You look too young to have any sense," said Bad Teeth. "You'll learn to keep your mouth shut about what goes on 'round here. We're all for one. Take my meaning?"

All the blood seemed to drain from my face. My disguise must have worn off. But how? It would do no good to bring it back now.

"What's gotten into you, dimwits?" said Philips. "You lot been sampling the meds again?"

I eyed the door handle. We weren't traveling too fast…

"You ought to know. You're the one selling them on the side." When Ace turned to me this time, there was no question those brown eyes held a warning.

"Watch your mouth, Ace," said Philips.

Bad Teeth laughed. His eyes widened before he grabbed my hat, spilling my loosely trussed hair.

"That ain't no kid. That's a girl!"

Chapter 17
Barrier Between Worlds

girl?" Philips barked. "Shit! I recognize this little Houdini."

He threw on the brakes, jolting me off balance. But I caught myself, levered open the door, and tumbled to the ground, the brunt of my weight on one knee and arm. No chance to check for wounds. I ran for the thicker woods. The morning sky darkened under threat of an approaching storm.

Shouts behind me. The vehicle's engine revved. Gravel crunched under rubber tires as the truck roared toward me. If I reached the tree line, they would have to follow on foot. My knee screamed in protest.

The vehicle sputtered over grass and underbrush, gaining on me. I darted to one side, but the truck was too nimble off-road. They were beside me in seconds, then out in front. I changed trajectory. The man who had ridden in the back with the bodies leapt toward me.

Arms around my torso. We both toppled over in a kicking, clawing tangle. I grabbed the scalpel from my belt and slashed at the hand gripping my forearm. The man screamed. I broke free, scrambling to my feet. Not two paces later, Bad Teeth caught me and wrenched the knife from my wrist.

Blood rushed behind my ears. I elbowed one in the gut. My skin flickered a shade of summer-worn green, the same color and texture as the grass below us, whether or not I had willed it.

"Did you see that?" hollered the man still on the ground.

"I got the knife," said Ace, who held both my wrists behind my back.

"But she—"

"Yeah, I saw it. She barely scratched you. Quit your whining!"

"Evil little bitch!" He spat. Red seeped through the man's fingers where they pressed his other forearm. "She's gonna pay!"

Philips sauntered toward us, carrying a coil of rope. "Ain't she the one's in trouble with the Police? How'd you suppose she got this uniform?" He clicked his tongue in mock reprimand.

"Oh, I can think of a few ways," said Ace.

"It's been what, at least a year since another of you lot managed the uniform scheme? I salute you!"

They laughed. I coughed, swallowing bile.

Philips said, "But what I can't figure is how she traded places with that old man back there. Right under our noses." His thin lips formed an evil, knowing grin.

Ace shook his head. "What are you talking about? What old man?"

"Uh huh." Philips wound the rope around my bandaged arms, yanking my injured shoulder.

I stared at the place where the man's boots met the ground. His shadow was *wrong*. Just as the police sergeant's had been before, and the old blind beggar's. Ace's shadow and my own were diffused in the low light of that cloudy morning. But Philips' looked darker. With sharp edges. How did the others not notice such an incongruence? Perhaps only a Fae would see.

There—the shadow twitched, shifted, when Philips did not.

My skin crawled in revulsion.

"She tried to escape yesterday too," said the one I had cut. "Reckon she needs a lesson or two in respect."

"There's four of us," said Philips. "That'll be at least four lessons. Won't it, sweetheart? Shame you won't remember any of it tomorrow."

More laughter.

"Now, you all know she's one of Porter's favorites," said Ace. "For that pet project of his. If she turns up injured, there'll be hell to pay."

"We'll be gentle." More laughter.

"Or we make sure she don't turn up."

"Let me go!" I demanded, but they snickered.

"You idiots are missing the point." Ace said, still holding my ropes. "This one's worth a lot more to Porter. Whole lot more. We need to think bigger here."

"How much you talking?"

"Can't say, but he's not been this obsessed with an intake in a while. And you know well as I do, he's a jealous god."

Philips heaved a sigh, staring at me. He licked his lips, winced, and shivered, as if something pained him. None of the others reacted to his bizarre display, which was odd in itself.

Philips sighed, calm again. "Yeah, okay. Load her up. In the back with the bodies this time."

If they took me outside the gate, would I have the chance to get away? Ace had my knife on him somewhere. I could still wiggle my bound hands.

He hefted me up to standing and leaned in to whisper beside my ear. "It's all right, Lady of the Summer Courts. I'm here to help you escape."

Could I trust him? With the holes in my memory, it was possible I'd told the nurses and orderlies of my adventures in the Otherworld while under Porter's hypnosis. It was likely they'd gotten a few good laughs at my expense. Was it sarcasm or deference I heard in his voice?

They dragged me away from the forest, toward the waiting truck. The gray morning clotted with clouds. Thunder crashed in the distance. Wind stirred nearby trees. I twisted my arms, straining at the ropes over my bandaged arms. That loose padding gave me a chance. I took an erratic stance, pretending to have trouble with my balance. Being the daughter of an escape artist might count for something, after all.

I shook the rope from one wrist. In the time it took Ace to curse under his breath, I kneed his groin. He shouted in pain, but I didn't look back as I ran.

I crashed into a stand of thick underbrush, still dragging rope. Fast as fear and willpower could carry me, I followed an animal trail through brambles and thorny vines. The path led down a slope to the west. Soon enough, I heard rushing water.

I leapt over a fallen tree. On the other side of that obstacle, my boot heel met a patch of slick clay. I slid, catching myself in mud and rocks, slashing open my palm.

The mossy trunk gave little cover. In those few seconds, I listened, and wrapped a loose strand of fabric bandage around my injured hand, tying it tight. The men must have spread out. Up the slope behind me, boots crashed through the shaded woods.

"I can't see nothing." Philips' voice. Electric torchlight beamed across the trees and rocks, avoiding my location.

"She's this way." Ace shouted from upstream. Could he be trying to lead the others away? Or had he spotted me?

Silently, I dashed in the opposite direction. I took cover behind river grass when I spied movement through the woods.

Boots splashed, heading toward me. Too close.

I crouched beside a rock outcropping and slipped behind a veil of fine roots.

Hide. I summoned my glamour.

I painted my skin's canvas with the rippling stream, the lichen-covered rocks at my back, the lines of living tree roots.

It began to rain. Thunder rolled over the sea.

The men approached. I held my breath and became one with the surrounding scene.

The man I'd cut staggered by, still holding his injury. Then came Ace. He stopped. I sensed he knew where I was, yet something compelled me to stay put. Energy surrounded him, foreign yet familiar to my developing Fae senses.

Of course. Ace must be Fae. How had I not seen it before?

He glanced at me, and his face shifted. Brown skin became impossibly red. His locks shone metallic bronze—eyes golden and reflective, like a cat's. He said nothing. The effect was over before I'd blinked. I recognized Septimus.

He lifted a finger to his lips to silence me before he splashed across the rocky stream. He shouted in another direction, pointing through the rain. "That way!"

"I saw it too," Philips shouted, footfalls sloshed away from my location.

Ace, or rather Septimus, paced over river rocks toward me.

I'd already picked up a stone and prepared to lob it at the man, when his face reverted to that unmistakable likeness of the Changeling I'd met only days ago in the Otherworld version of our village. The one who claimed fealty to the Queen, like Roger. Could this be a hallucination, as the nurses told me was possible with my medications, or was this real?

Septimus hesitated, as if waiting to make sure the others had run far enough away. He crouched beside me, held out a hand, offering me my knife, handle first.

I took it. My fingers brushed his palm. He felt solid. Fairly convincing for a hallucination.

"How well can you swim?"

"I'm good enough." I moved aside that curtain of tree roots and faced him.

"I thought so, Lady." His smile was rather charming. "You can make it under the north water grate. That way." He pointed. "I'll keep them distracted long enough for you to get to the Welterwood. If you'd stuck with me, I would've gotten you out of here another way, but this must be the path fate chose for you."

I took his hand as I stood. "Sorry I kicked you in the—"

He shook his head. "I'm fine. Do you still have the medallion?"

"Yes."

"It once belonged to my family."

I drew out the jewel I wore below my clothing and handed it to Septimus. His eyes widened, reflecting sadness.

"Are you part of the Reliqua?"

He held it close to his heart for a moment with his eyes closed. "No. My family was Reliqua—ten generations of my ancestors. But all are now lost. I search for answers still. That's what led me to Porter. I followed the artifacts he'd stolen from my family's old estate."

"They're lost? What happened?"

"A story for another day." He gave the medallion back to me. "For now, you must hurry. Be careful. I've heard rumors of unnatural things hiding in the Welterwood. Hostile creatures. Keep alert." He glanced at the sky, his crimson face beaded with rain. "When you reach the Queen's Circle, wait for moonlight to awaken the stone. That's all I know. I would go with you, but other Fae and Changelings are held prisoner here. Their lives are at stake, and I must help them. I can't afford to return to the Otherworld now."

"I understand. Good luck." I squeezed his hand, and he nodded.

"There's a legend which tells of the heart of Seastone, a powerful rock as old as Atlantis, deep underground below the Welterwood. They say it's why the Fae love this country. May it watch over your journey tonight."

He shielded his eyes from the rain and scanned our surroundings. "Now's your chance. I'll distract them for you."

"How?"

But he'd already dashed behind a large fallen tree. A stifled moan. What emerged afterward was not a man, but a massive lion with reddish-golden fur. Golden eyes met mine in silent recognition.

Not knowing what else to do or say, I bowed.

The lion sprinted in the direction the men had traveled and loosed an echoing roar. Behind the log, I glimpsed his discarded clothing.

The rain became a torrent. I ran upstream. In the distance, the men shouted, followed by another roar and several gunshots. I prayed Septimus was unharmed.

The creek bank's slope provided scant cover as I ran toward the perimeter wall. A siren alarm cut through the rain and thunder. The institute was on alert.

Elbows on sodden knees, I paused to catch my breath. With my scalpel, I sliced away the remaining rope from my wrist and threw it into the rushing water. Beside a distant outbuilding, headlights of at least two work trucks flickered through the trees, leading in opposite directions. I pushed ahead with renewed urgency.

At the wall, a wooden bridge connected a service road on either side of the creek. A grated brick arch allowed the water to flow through.

I waded in. Frigid water up to my shoulders, I fought the shock and grabbed an algae-slick bridge pylon to keep from flowing downstream. Lightning flashed in the distance, illuminating the underwater metal bars of my goal. A deafening thunderclap. I took a deep breath and dove.

I glided through liquid swirling gloom, struggling against the current. With the last of my strength, I gripped an iron bar on the grate. Even veiled with algae, the metal burned like fire. Groping my way in the darkness, I found an opening and scrambled through a space just wide enough for my body.

On the other side, I kicked against the iron and surfaced, gasping. My fingers, toes, and ears were numb, but my crystal necklace and medallion were safe. I sloshed from the water as quietly as possible.

Teeth chattering, I followed a footpath alongside the creek and kept to the tree shadows. Dogs bayed in the distance, like a pack of hunting hounds. Would the rain help hide my scent?

The creek. I'd read that in a book once. I slogged ahead through the shallow side, glad for the sound cover provided by the rain. Estimating I'd traveled far enough to confuse a pack of dogs, I emerged from the opposite bank.

Thicker and wilder grew these woods. When I passed the first century oak, I'd reached the outskirts of the Welterwood. Shivering, I strained to hear a distant howl, farther away than the pack had been before.

I dashed ahead. Thorny vines ripped at my numb hands and clothing before I reached a deeper section of woods. Trees old and full of memory, as Mother used to say. My muddy boots trod a carpet of Autumn's red-gold leaves.

I had to keep my weary limbs moving lest my muscles cramp from exhaustion and cold. Soon I spotted another creek and trekked through ankle-deep water for the better part of a mile before I emerged into a new grove. It had been many years, but I found the ruts of a familiar wagon road and followed it for miles, the chill fading as exertion warmed my body. I veered off toward the clearing where my family used to picnic. All the violets that grew here now lay dormant in the rocky ground. Grasses and sedges ran along a thin brook. There was the lone rowan tree I'd often sketched and painted, laden with red berries and foliage turned gold. I drank in the perfume of this special place and swallowed back tears.

My trail curved northwest, rounding through a beech-shaded ravine and a spruce grove toward a grassy clearing. Morning light gleamed over the rain-soaked granite monoliths of the Welterwood's stone circle.

I ran until I came to within paces of the ancient monument. The rain thinned to a mist, driven in gusts by sea wind. The stones shone too brightly. I sensed the old power here, like never before.

This was my portal to the Otherworld, but I must wait until moonrise. If I could last until nightfall without being found by the dogs and taken back to the institute—or worse—I would attempt to use the medallion. There was nothing else to do until then, besides get warm. I couldn't risk a fire.

At the eastern edge of the clearing, a fallen tree's upturned roots sheltered a patch of relatively dry soil. I ducked underneath and buried my soggy clothing in a mound of moldering leaves. The insulation and warmth from composting organic material would help. I had learned this trick before, when I once spent the night in the woods behind the elementary school when I was nine. But now I remembered flashes of another night alone in another woods when I was older. Had it been the Welterwood? No. Was Porter telling the truth about my first stay at St. Ivy's? I'd seen the hospital record—written by Dr. Gale himself.

If it were true, why couldn't I remember? Had I jumbled the two memories into one? My childhood hospitalizations had been frequent. At seventeen, I must have been an upperclassman. I recalled being out of school due to illness for several months the year I graduated. The date on that report was interesting. Whatever had happened occurred on or near my birthday. Had it been another vision of my Shadow which had caused me to flee? Around that age it had escaped my nightmares and began to show itself more often in the real world—in reflections, or in that liminal state between sleep and waking.

The flash of some lurid shape, born in a shard of glass and pool of blood, flickered behind my closed eyes. I shuddered.

The repressed memory flooded me—stole my breath with its returning force.

It was my seventeenth birthday. The thing with no face, the shadow demon from my nightmares, had appeared in a mirror in the school gymnasium. It had... spoken to me, which it had only ever done in dreams. Never in the light of day.

Come to me. Step through.

No!

I threw a cricket ball at the glass, and one panel had shattered. How had I forgotten? Shards of glass lay scattered over lacquered wood floorboards.

Come to me.

In the unbroken sections of mirror, the Shadow showed me what to do. My reflection, free from reality's constraints, walked toward the glass dividing us from the other side.

Spellbound. I watched her pick up a jagged piece of the shattered mirror, then some dread force compelled me to mimic the same. My mirror image cut her finger and drew a symbol on the glass in blood. The outline of a doorway, glowing like embers, appeared in the glass.

Horrified, I pulled my eyes away long enough to remember my own will, drop the shard of glass, and run.

I ran past befuddled fellow schoolmates before I escaped into the woods. I hid. Slept in a hollow by an old ash tree, where I knew evil could not follow me. Until I heard the baying of dogs and far away voices shouting. Kind strangers drove me to a terrifying hospital, when all I needed was my home.

What happened after that? The hospital. There had been more than one. They brought me to St. Ivy's after the first doctors decided I was insane.

Had Roger been one of my alienists? There were so many over the years. Had there ever been a kind face among those jumbled memories?

Yes. I found a vaporous image of someone who had spoken to me like I was a real person. Not a thing to be pitied or shunned. The man in my memory had short hair, graying at the temples, though his attractive eyes looked young. He wore gold-rimmed glasses and most often faced the notepad in his hands as he took down my story. I told him I'd seen something that frightened me, and I accidentally broke the glass, just like I'd told the doctors at the first hospital.

Just remember to breathe. Here's a technique you can use when you become afraid. Like a magic spell. Close your eyes and imagine a shield of light surrounds and protects you. Repeat these words to yourself, It's only fear. My mind will clear.

Another thread of memory. It must have been days later. I was terrified of this room. Strapped to a gurney beside a nightmare machine of brass and wood, my headache throbbed. Dials and diodes cracked with electric light in the dim space.

I remember two men arguing. Voices raised.

I could hear some of it through the half-open door, but pinned as I was, I couldn't turn to look.

"Why is she even here? For God's sake! I already signed her discharge papers."

"Your diagnosis was sloppy and incomplete. I made necessary adjustments to ensure this institute's reputation for scientific thoroughness remains dependable."

"And the others? Were they necessary too?"

"All scientific progress must weigh acceptable risks. You of all men know this."

"No, this is unacceptable. Unconscionable. I have no choice but to report your methods to the board. And the Academy. I cannot allow this barbaric treatment to continue."

"If you do that, mark my words, Roger. It will be a mistake you'll long regret."

"No. Your career is finished, Archibald."

Then he burst through the door, followed by a nurse, and they freed me from the machine.

"Miss Morgen, can you move? Good. We're getting out of here. Right now. You're going home this time."

To the nurse he said, "Have someone send for her family. Immediately."

Why had I never connected any of this before? Never remembered it?

My shivering stopped. Sensation returned to my limbs, bringing pain in equal measure.

I fought exhaustion, but my eyes refused to stay open. Before consciousness drifted away, I thought about the date on that report. Equinox. My birthday had always been during Equinox Bridge. A time when the barrier between worlds was thin.

Chapter 18
The Standing Stones

I dreamed of a gleaming unicorn on a field of green. A glint of silver. The dread of iron. A pool of blood. Red so dark it was almost black.

A thunderclap woke me.

I blinked at a sapphire sky through amber treetops. The Welterwood. Another flash of lightning in the distance. No rain yet, but the sky loomed ominous over the bay.

Still protected by the base of this fallen tree, I was warm and comfortable. Dry.

I sat up, scattering leaves. My clothes felt heavy. Something coated my trousers. I brushed a clot of mud from my ruined sleeve, but it clung stubbornly. A tuft of moss, cool, moist and alive, broke away in my hand. I pulled another clump from my shirt. Underneath tiny fibrous roots, the fabric was now dry.

Every inch of my stolen maintenance worker's uniform was covered in green moss.

Whether by my will or another's, this moss had both dried my clothing and kept me warm. But how long had it taken to grow so thick? How much time had passed since I fell asleep?

I grabbed the remains of a tree root. At once, the slick bark turned green. Luminous moss fibers reached from my shirt cuff and netted over the wood's surface, as if I watched natural growth in accelerated time.

When I let go, the moss dulled to an ordinary hue—no longer growing. It was still daylight, but the sun was lower. I rested in the leaves, cocooned and dry in a suit of moss, and waited for nightfall.

I drew out the silver medallion. The polished blue-gray mineral in its center reflected trees and sky. In veins like living nerves, a spectrum glimmered. I'd never seen such a stone. A compass rose covered the medallion's oval base. Perhaps marking ordinal directions, four engraved sigils marked the quadrants, beside four wings which might have represented the four winds. Four animals graced equal points between the wings. One image depicted a wolf, rendered in heraldic style—forearms raised to strike, exposed tongue like flame. Mirroring the wolf, a serpentine, winged dragon reached toward the central stone. Below them were a flying falcon and a rearing stag, each facing the center. The medallion's silken cord appeared timeworn.

Artfully made though it was, I could see no way to activate its magic. I only hoped when the moon showed her face, my intuition would guide me, like Evelyn said.

Wasting a day in hiding, when Roger awaited execution even at this moment, was torture. And where was my father? Was he even still alive?

"I'll find you both." I whispered. "Just hang on for me a little longer."

By evening, my stomach growled. Hunger might be ignored, but not the powerful thirst which overcame me. I left my hiding spot in search of water.

The little tributary wasn't far. I knelt beside one pool and cupped handfuls to drink.

A twig snapped. The rustle of an animal's body against leaves. Movement. I sensed eyes on me and drew my stolen knife.

The creature walked on four legs—the size of a large dog. A wolf, maybe? Or a deer. The skin on my arms rose into gooseflesh. The animal oozed an energy of sorrow… dissolution. Chaos.

I stood. Showing no fear might be the best strategy. Without taking my attention from where it lurked, I proceeded toward the stone circle.

It paced behind me on the opposite bank until a bend in the stream, then it continued into deeper shadow.

When twilight finally neared, I leaned against an old oak in my moss-covered clothing. Why couldn't I remember what happened to me those days before I was found? In that treatment room? Room number 709. The same number as the street address for Roger's shop.

None of that made sense. Porter seemed not a little obsessed with his former colleague, Dr. Gale. Had he chosen that very room in which to conduct his experiments as a kind of sick joke? Or was it something more?

At last, the rain clouds passed. Venus shone clear and bright. The moon would be up soon.

A barking howl stretched over the cold distance, followed by a longer series of calls. Was it a feral pack? It didn't sound like the same hunting hounds from this morning.

I stood and walked toward the circle. The granite monoliths, emanating timeless power, shone like whitened bones against the gloaming.

When I passed the outermost stones, the night grew silent. Wind rushed through treetops, but the sound was muffled, as if I'd already stepped one foot out of this world into another. The center pulled me onward.

Light trickled from underneath my moss-covered jacket—the necklace. I drew it out; only a pinprick of light glimmered within the crystal, smaller than a firefly. It refracted through every facet of those natural geometric lines—an arrangement of silica so far elevated above ordinary beach sand, yet composed of the same element.

Like steel and cold iron. And blood.

I trod a path worn by many visitors, both human and animal. I passed another row of stones, these capped with lintels, one having fallen off its supports centuries ago. If this place was a magic machine designed for transport between realms, did the broken parts matter?

A howling yelp pierced the silence. Too close this time.

Clutching the medallion, I entered the centermost ring. When I crossed an invisible threshold, the hair on the back of my neck stood on end. I laid a hand on one cool stone.

Lightning flashed in the sky to the south. A jagged arc illuminated the curtain of velvet clouds. I paused, entranced by the show, even if the storm meant doom for my quest. The moon had not yet risen. A few stars peeked through breaks in the weather.

I whispered the words Evelyn had translated from the cabinet's glass.

"By the lesser light, the path to the greater will be revealed. Heed the watchers."

Half shrouded by the uncooperative weather, I identified constellations of an autumn sky. Ursa Major, the Pleiades, Orion. There was Pegasus, the valiant helper to Perseus, dancing to the east. Draco to the northeast. Cassiopeia, the queen.

Waiting for moonrise, I sat on the grass and studied the medallion again. On the back, letters in High Fae marked the convex silver surface. The piece was thick, like a casing for a large pocket watch. I found no means of opening it. I brought the stone closer to the light of my pendant, hoping to locate any trigger or catch or hinge.

In that fairy glow, the embossed metal symbols took on new shapes. They cast a line of shadows as recognizable words: *Between House Zuria and the sign of the Red Lion, this bridge is made. May her memory unite our generations.*

In whose memory? Septimus said this had once belonged to his family. More mysteries.

I walked from one standing stone to the next, searching for a recess that might fit the medallion. Any markings at all. I raised my crystal pendant aloft. Its cool blue light revealed nothing unexpected.

The moon should have risen. I searched the forested horizon, but I could not see her.

A howl cut through the night, answered by a chorus of barks and bays. Had they found my scent?

Not yet. I paced toward the center, medallion resting in my open palm. I watched for any change—in the sky or in the talisman. Dark clouds parted, revealing open stars. At last, the crescent moon appeared.

I caught the moon's reflection on the jewel's polished surface. Lines of light veined those inclusions. Fae script illuminated from within the medallion's silver, just the mirror cabinet had done. I gasped in wonder, before the sight of movement along the distant tree line froze my blood.

Dark shapes, too large for dogs, darted in and out of the forest. They must be wolves, but they kept their distance—for now. Perhaps they'd not yet spotted me among the standing stones. Should they turn on me, I could not run fast enough to get away.

The face of the medallion glowed, but I could not decipher the directional glyphs. I'd watched sunset, so I knew which stone marked west, but how did that align with these symbols? Evelyn said my doorway to the Summer Courts was in the southwest. The falcon was the Queen's emblem, according to Roger. I pointed her to the southwest. Lines of color in the jewel sparkled like distant nebulae, as though brought into focus through a telescope lens.

I held my breath as the wolves drew closer. Nothing happened. What was missing? Perhaps I stood in the wrong place.

Taking in my position relative to the massive stones, I tried to find true center. The light in my hand grew brighter.

"This must be right," I whispered. "Please."

Under what I took for a natural rise in the ground, my boot heel trod something hard. I knelt to inspect and found buried stone. With my knife,

I tore away clumps of dirt and grass, revealing a flat granite surface, like an old millstone.

There. In its center—a round indentation.

By Faelight, I detected faint traces of ancient petroglyphs. I could only trace a few continuous lines in the age-pocked stone, but they pointed in the four ordinal directions.

Carefully, I laid the medallion in the center.

Through the carved channels, the jewel's light seeped—impossibly tangible—like a liquid or luminescent gas.

Northeast and southeast, the fluid light hit obstacles of dirt and matted grass roots. I dug with cold-numbed fingers, freeing pathways. Light expanded to fill every revealed line. Swirls and spirals connected the quadrants of this ancient design. I witnessed the true art of this place, hidden for unknown ages, as it was meant to be seen.

Dust stung my eyes. I wiped them and looked again. Only bare rock, with a lifeless piece of jewelry in the center. My crystal pendant was now the only light.

I gazed up at a cloud covered sky. A hidden moon.

Another gust of wind swept over me, tasting of more rain. Had that been my only chance? Was it now gone?

The mournful cry of a wolf. Not far away.

Answering barks. The glint of reflective eyes. The pack encircled the monument. Pacing, but not drawing near.

One of them stood at least a foot taller than the others. It sniffed the air and howled again, a deeper sound than the responding cries.

I drew my knife, but the wolves had yet to approach.

They sang out another chorus. Muzzles turned to the sky.

The clouds parted, and the lunar crescent reappeared. My medallion returned to life. Blue liquid light seeped through the stonework designs once more.

With my knife, I cleared away grass and soil from the stone lines. Cresting the edge, luminescent beams traveled just above the ground until they reached the eight main upright stones.

An arched doorway appeared on each monolith, crowned in illuminated script. Though I could not read the words, never in my life had I beheld such a wonder.

My skin began faintly to glow.

At once, the wolves silenced. From the center of this clearing, I looked to the revealed stars.

Which doorway to choose?

"If I go to the Queen," I whispered, "will I ever be able to return home?"

Evelyn insisted I travel to the Summer Courts, though Roger was being held in the Winter Courts. She once tried to force me there against my will, lest I forget.

Roger was in the Winter Courts, because he traveled there in search of my father, who was likely in the same country. Mother had painted her vision of Wyvern's Rock. The telescope in Father's room was pointed north. Polaris. On the medallion, the symbol marking northeast, was the Dragon.

Evelyn said my instincts would guide me, but my time had run out.

I knelt to retrieve the relic. The medallion's magic had done its work, and the jewel dimmed. I slipped the cord once again around my neck. Like my luminous skin, the doorways remained aglow, but likely not for long.

With steadfastness, I approached the northeast standing stone. Not yards away, the large wolf turned to face me but did not approach. Intelligence reflected through those eyes, so did my own glowing form.

"Thank you," I whispered to them.

At the menhir, I stretched forth a hand haloed in violet light and touched the granite. My hand passed through, disappearing up to my wrist.

"Land of eternal night, here I come."

I inhaled the cold night and walked forward.

Darkness enclosed me. A space without up or down, left or right.

Was there any ground below my feet? I urged them onward. Pressure squeezed all breath from my lungs.

I was trapped inside the stone. No air to breathe. No way to move.

Then I flew through the vastness of space.

Like a shooting star.

PART 2

THE LIGHT

CHAPTER 19
CHANGELINGS

Cold wet pressed against my cheek. Snow.

I coughed and sucked in icy air. My eyes opened to a night sky bright with stars—the Milky Way flowed like a heavenly river. A sliver of moon crowned a glittering expanse of white-dusted forest. If this was the Otherworld, I had to be in the Winter Courts.

A blue glow emanated from my hands, but it was not my own Faelight. With sudden horror, I beheld a tiny creature gnawing on my knuckle. It resembled a hairless doll with elongated limbs, fishlike eyes, an over-large mouth, and transparent wings like moonlight on frost. Claws gripped my finger. Needle teeth sunk in for another bite—my red blood turned black inside its translucent gullet.

"Ahh!" I slung the scuffling predator yards away into a snowbank, ripping a small chunk of skin from my knuckle.

I hauled myself up to sitting and wrapped the bleeding digit with my other numb hand—as though grasping a corpse's frozen digits, yet my spilled blood was warm.

Frostbite? I wanted to laugh.

In fact, the hideous creature resembled one of the uglier jarred specimens I'd seen in Roger's trophy room. He'd insisted his Reliqua only killed Fae who posed a danger to our world. *His* world, I had to remember.

I didn't believe him back then. I did now.

That nasty sprite, blood still covering its disproportioned mouth, came at me again. It emitted a high-pitched buzz like a squadron of mosquitoes.

With my crystal pendant, I called my shield of light, as Roger had taught me, as fast as I could sing the magic words on chill-numbed lips.

The creature backed away before I finished the incantation. More of the things flew toward me, but they kept a distance from the ethereal barrier I'd summoned.

I stood and dusted snow from my frozen suit of moss. I tore a piece of my undershirt and tied it around the injured knuckle. Red soaked through the white cotton. I could not feel it, but at least my blood still flowed. With each breath, the icy air hollowed me out and stole my dwindling warmth. Without shelter, I would soon perish.

Around me were equally spaced lumps in the snow. If I had come through another stone circle, these standing stones were much smaller, or buried by time and ice.

Only a few stunted conifers and sedges interrupted endless white. If this Otherworld ground was parallel with any human realm, as was true back home in Seastone, the portal might have transported me to some distant tundra. I wished I'd paid better attention to that atlas of Roger's.

The evil sprites kept their distance while my shield remained. I clutched the crystal and held the shape of the sphere in my mind, but it was fading. If I called upon the magic again, how long would my strength last against this cold?

Dragging my numb feet, I left the circle, searching for cover.

Like a school of fish, the pixies fled in unison.

A hidden rope tripped my next step. The trap sprung before I hit the ground. A whooshing sound. The crash of a flexible weight on my back. I collapsed in the snow. My shield dimmed to a dull haze.

I struggled to escape, but the net cinched tighter with each movement. I rolled to my side, drawing the scalpel from my belt. Footsteps crunched in my direction. Snowshoes. Someone yanked on the net.

My blade sliced through two sections of rope and was into a third, when a figure knelt beside me and grabbed my wrist. A large male, I guessed. A fur-lined hood hid most of his face. Hands covered in rough leather gloves, he twisted my arm until I dropped the knife.

Another set of footsteps. Voices muffled by the wind. Dogs barked.

"It's female," shouted the man holding me. "Smells human." This was not a language I knew, but nonetheless, I understood the meaning. A translation glamour.

"I'm half Fae," I said. "A daughter of the Summer Courts. Please. I need your help." It might be worth mentioning if I had any status in this world. As much as I loathed the idea of captivity, if these people had shelter nearby, perhaps I wouldn't freeze to death.

"Did you come through the Old Gate?" The man asked in a gruff voice. In English this time.

"If you mean the stone circle, yes."

A glint of blue light reflected in his eyes, hidden still by a parka hood. His gloved fingers reached for the glowing crystal at my chest.

I reacted too late to use the crystal's magic. He snapped the chain from my neck and cupped the pendant in his large hand, growling.

"Where did you get this?"

"A gift."

He grunted in disapproval. Thankfully, he'd not seen the medallion.

"If you take me to shelter, I'll tell you what I know."

The man stood easily seven feet tall. He growled again—an animal's roar combined with a hunter's shout. The sound echoed through the sparse winter forest, sending chills through my bones. "We found her!" He shouted into the snowy night. "Arimos will be pleased. Bring the sled."

Someone was looking for me. Was that good or bad?

An answering shout from behind. I could not turn to see what approached, but the bark and whine of a team of canines was enough to indicate a dogsled.

The hooded man grabbed up my net and dragged me along the ground.

"Let me out of here, please! I won't run."

I reached one arm through the net, combing numb fingers through the snow where the knife had fallen. I found nothing. My forearm scraped a rock.

My captor hauled me into the air and tossed me onto a pile of snow-dusted firs. Irregular shapes below might have been supplies they carried. I shifted my weight. No. Not supplies. An antler pressed into my back. A hoof and leg grazed my cheek. These were fresh kills. I smelled the iron of blood. They tied me to the pile.

Exhausted as I was, this present situation didn't fill me with as much horror as it should. Still warm, the animals' bodies gave some respite from the cold. If the men took me to their camp, I might at least be kept from freezing. If this Arimos wanted me, I only prayed he or she wanted me alive.

If their faces looked anything human, I could not yet tell. One shouted a command, and the dogsled team burst, barking and yelping, into motion. We sluiced over snowdrifts, traveling through an endless night. The landscape gleamed, reflecting moonlight and the starry sky.

We reached a cave entrance and slowed to a halt. Another hooded figure met my captors. They exchanged words I could not make out. Breath hung like steam in the frigid air. From inside the cavern's mouth drifted the smell of cooking fires and charred meat. My stomach growled.

They dragged me from the pile of kills, removed the net, and tied my arms with more rope. Depleted as I was, I offered no fight. I mustered strength to walk unaided as we traveled deeper into the cave. We found an encampment; more dogsleds, crates of supplies, tents, people of diverse shapes and sizes wrapped in fur-lined parkas. Dogs ran free or barked from within wicker cages. A curious animal like an ostrich with scales instead of feathers wore a saddle and tack; it was docile enough to be led by a child. Farther inside, the light of burning torches revealed wide tunnels.

They hauled me toward a mechanized vehicle on a railroad track. I had not gotten a good look before I was face down in a bin of coal.

"Try to jump and it will kill you, understand?"

I said nothing.

An engine roared to life. The men hopped into the front seat of the machine as it rumbled and jolted us forward. When our speed steadied, I shuffled until I could turn sideways and cough away the coal dust. Lights beamed and faded through the tunnel as our transport rattled down the tracks, toward a destination deep inside this underground cavern, if it was not a mountain.

The air grew warmer. The vehicle bounced over each junction of track. Once, my bound hands hit a sharp edge of metal. If I drug my ropes across with enough effort, they might cut.

We exited the narrow tunnel. Industrial lanterns revealed cave formations, stalagmites, and stalactites. Soon I heard the rush and rumble of an underground river. We reached another passageway, wide enough to accommodate several rows of tracks, and passed a small multitude of steam and smoke-chuffing machines. Folded canvas sails and wooden propellers meant a few were designed for water, if not air. I sensed no pure iron anywhere.

At this bizarre subterranean station, we came to a stop. Above, stars shone through a circular exhaust port. An artificial breeze smelled of rubber, as though hoses piped in warmed air.

One man jumped from the vehicle. The hood of his parka was thrown back to reveal a human-like face. Large and of sharp bone structure, his features resembled a bear's. The man's tawny skin bore the lines of age. His long hair was the color of straw.

Several new figures, dressed differently and of more human stature, strode to meet him.

"Get the Captain. Now! I have something he'll buy," spoke the bear-man.

I could not hear the station attendants' reply, but I didn't miss the answering growl.

184

"You tell him we have a human female who came through the Old Gate. Arimos will pay whatever I ask."

The second of my two escorts approached the cart.

I pictured the blocks of surrounding coal, willing my glamour to conceal me, just as I severed the last rope fibers.

"What the!" A snarl. "She's gone. We lost her."

The other spun around. "That can't be. I tied her good."

The big man sniffed the air. "She's not far." He knelt to inspect the wheels and undercarriage, but of course I was not there.

My heart thudded so loudly in my own ears, I feared they might hear it.

The leader stood and shouted. "Listen! There's a human on the loose. Find her and bring her to me. You'll be rewarded."

Whistles and answering shouts echoed throughout the cavern. My captors dispersed. Unless my glamour confused scent along with vision, this ruse would not last. When they'd walked far enough away, I slunk from the bin, boots crunching on gravel. The cart's hissing boiler masked the sound.

I needed a disguise. From behind the vehicle, I observed the other Fae in the station. They were of many shapes and sizes, as I'd seen in the Spring Courts, which gave me an idea. I recalled the elegant face of Captain Meadowgrass well enough to sketch it from memory. I concentrated; my hands and fingers shimmered for an instant before they elongated, turning shell pink, yet to the touch, they remained normal underneath. Glamour must be only a trick of light and color, like a hologram. Faelight wrapped my suit of moss with an illusionary tunic and trousers like Meadowgrass had worn.

I kept to the shadows and proceeded through a nearby tunnel, appearing, I hoped, like one of a dozen others who had scattered, searching for the runaway human. I made my way toward a large, well-lit gathering place for these cavern-dwelling Fae.

Farther in were the first of many merchant stalls. I passed unusual wares for sale; roasted insects on skewers, tufts of dried moss and lichen, bowls of spices, baskets of crushed minerals, bottles of colorful gases. A hedgerow of glowing fungus proved nearly as bright a light source as the lanterns strung on electrical wires. Smoke and steam swirled from food carts and odd conveyances.

The crowd grew louder as I ventured into the underground city, wearing my Meadowgrass disguise. The tunnel's ceiling disappeared into the distant darkness of a natural cavern's dome. A colonnade of stalagmites rippled with a texture like waves upon a sandy shore, revealing their ancient underwater formation. They rose to unseen heights. At least four or five species of

bioluminescent fungus cast different hues, refracted and reflected from ge-
ode-like cavern walls. Giant crystalline formations shone with their own inner light.

Fae and what must have been Changelings milled about the thorough-
fare. Many had scales, or shells, or porpoise skin. I recognized no ordinary
earth species. One shark-like creature ambled beside me in the throng, wearing a tank on their back with water pipes to an apparatus over their nose and
mouth. An octopus rattled by, tentacles working a multi-pedaled cart.

A ramshackle building made of weathered boards and canvas lay ahead,
like an old carnival castoff. Its placard depicted a tankard of ale. If my disguise held out, such a public house might be as good a place as any to gain information. On a wide-planked wooden bridge, I stopped mid-way to watch
the river. Flowing deep and slow below where I stood, it was bracketed by
docks and landing platforms. Lights beamed from underwater—lanterns in
wire-mesh cages along the banks. Schools of bioluminescent fish. A submers-
ible passed below. I could make out glass portholes in the front. Was there a
crab-like operator inside?

Fascinated by the spectacle, I didn't see the man with long white hair
approach until he'd appeared just feet from me. It was the same Fae I'd seen
on the airship. The soldier who might have captured Roger.

My hand grabbed for my necklace, but it was gone.

"Captain Meadowgrass." His eyes gleamed like onyx in a colorless face.
"Imagine my surprise to find you here. When I am certain you are aboard
your ship, leagues away. You have grown shorter."

"You must be mistaken, sir." I took a wide step, but he matched my
stride.

"Do you not know, half-breed, that it is the height of rudeness to use
glamour in the King's city? Even if it fooled the Changelings." He turned and
shouted. "Over here."

I dropped into a sprint, but he was too fast. We went down at the edge of
the bridge, mercifully, in a patch of moss. He pinned my arms, immobilizing
me with a forearm to my neck and a knee pressing into mine.

I couldn't breathe. The skin of his arm was like ice.

He grinned at the shock on my face as he throttled me. When he finally
removed the arm, I gasped for air.

Two more soldiers arrived. They bound me tighter than before and led
me back toward the underground station.

I coughed, throat still raw. "I recognize you from Seastone. The airship.
What happened to my friend?"

He didn't answer.

"Where are you taking me?"

"To my Master." Great devotion weighted those words, but he would not turn my way.

"And your Master is…" This earned me only a sidelong glance. His eerie eyes reflected like black mirrors.

"Lord Arimos, King of the Winter Courts."

Chapter 20
Wyvern's Rock

ae soldiers led me across the station room, amidst jeers and cat-calls from onlookers. Someone growled.

"Cynbel, you double-dealing bastard! Son of a banshee. You owe me at least three hundred."

"She escaped your custody, Druk. I owe you nothing."

Another snarl. "You found her because my pack brought her right to you." The tall man with the bear-like features lunged for Cynbel, whose attendants rushed to block the attack, which must not have been in earnest for how quickly Druk backed down.

Cynbel spoke to his men. "Pay him one hundred. We do not want the Changeling rabble to go hungry."

Druk scowled but took the offered coin-purse.

They hauled me inside a larger vehicle, which I refused to correlate to a trolley despite the similarities. Like a train's passenger car, it was furnished with wood and bronze benches, tables and lanterns. One man led me to the opposite wall, bade me to sit on the carpeted floor, and began tying my rope to a handrail when Cynbel ordered him to remove my bonds. I tried with little hope of success to appear ladylike, shivering in my coal-dusted, moss-covered man's uniform—my face, hair, and hands filthy and scratched and bruised.

Cynbel took a seat across from mine. The vehicle's engine grumbled to life, and we rolled forward.

The pale Fae with the topknot of long white hair stared at me with those chilling, too-black eyes. His arms were crossed over a dark breastplate. He wore loose black trousers, a silver sash at his waist, and a long indigo cloak. If he carried any weapons, he hid them.

I braced myself against a spasm of shivering. The rest of them hardly seemed to notice the temperature.

"On the airship," I asked, "What did you want with us? Where is my friend?"

He laughed, though I couldn't guess what he found so amusing. "We took him into custody. He escaped, but not for long. Your *friend* is once again under our watchful eye, awaiting the fate he has earned."

"If King Arimos wants to speak with me, I'll petition him directly. I must ask him to spare Mr. Gale's life."

"What makes you think he will listen to you?" The question was not mocking, only calculating.

"If he's waited for someone to come through the Old Gate, he'll know what I am—a royal daughter of the Summer Courts. I am the Queen's niece. He must listen to me." I wasn't sure if I believed that myself, but it was worth the mention.

"The traitor Gale will be executed in two days, on the orders of my Master. You will not change his mind."

The tunnel grew brighter as we neared a moonlit night. The engine strained as we gained altitude. Outside, temperature dropped, seeping in through the contraption's metal hull and glass windows.

"Why? What did Mr. Gale do?"

"He stole from His Majesty."

"You would kill him for theft? What did he steal?"

"We will speak no more of this. Give me the Faestone medallion you carry on your person."

"What?"

Cynbel's smile made me shiver. "You have two choices. You can either give it to me, or I will take it by force."

I had nowhere to run. Even if I escaped, I would meet miles of dark tunnels, or frigid tundra. I did not want to freeze to death before I had the chance to speak with the King. I reached under my shirt for the medallion, and with a trembling hand, gave it to Cynbel. His icy fingers stung mine.

The pale warrior traced the edge of the jewel, which now appeared charcoal gray. Strange.

"It responds to energy." He answered my unspoken question. "As you have seen. Mine is… unique."

"How so?"

"Look to the stars." Cynbel directed his gaze toward the window. The vehicle emerged out of the tunnel into the frozen night of the Otherworld tundra.

I'd never witnessed the Milky Way like this. A river of light traversed celestial spheres. The planets were heavenly jewels. Mars so red. Jupiter blue. Venus clear and bright. I spotted nebulae with my naked eye. A sight lifted from my dreams.

When I glanced at Cynbel, I gasped.

His face had become clear as glass. The dark of night and the brilliance of the stars shone through him.

He turned that eldritch gaze on me.

Goosebumps rose on my arms. "What kind of Fae are you?"

"Have you never seen a ghost?"

"You mean you're... dead?"

"No. I was born in the rift between realities, so I belong to neither. I am never truly in one place. Even on this plane."

"Why do you serve the King, if you belong to neither world?"

Cynbel laughed and turned his transparent gaze to the view. We approached a cliff face and a mountain range shrouded in night mist. "What compels any of us... to do what we do? How do you reconcile your own life's contradictions, half-breed? What do you see in your own reflection?"

"I..." I thought only of my private nightmare in the looking-glass. "I don't know what you mean."

With a bitter smile, he slipped my medallion into his cloak, his clothing having remained as substantial as the rest of the trolley, while his body was an indistinct mirage.

"We have reached our destination." He stood and walked to the front of the car.

The vehicle entered a tunnel, and Cynbel became solid once more. Another guard took his place, keeping watch over me.

Our conveyance slowed, approaching another city station. The subterranean architecture in this cavern appeared more decorative and less industrial than I'd seen in the last village. Heavy timber beams supported glistening stucco walls and thatched roofs. Stonework edifices held lofty gargoyles so lifelike they might have been living Fae, their toothy visages and immobile wings gleaming in starlight. A cave mouth wide enough for airships to sail through connected this cavern to the tundra's expanse. Smokestacks and exhaust pipes snaked up the rock face, venting steam into the night sky. The only bright colors were a few dragon-emblazoned banners in indigo and blue, which draped from docked airships or fluttered from turrets and balconies.

I was in that strange mountain-side city Mother had painted. Wyvern's Rock.

Cynbel's guards led me up a stone staircase, through a series of lantern-lit passageways. When we exited into another cave, three more soldiers met us, wearing uniforms of black, silver, and indigo. Helmets of leather and bronze covered their faces, and they carried scimitars.

If I warranted an escort, perhaps Arimos would listen to my requests. I doubted they considered me any threat, so the guards must have been here for my protection. The king wanted me alive.

My convoy traveled through an expanse of cave formations, lit with multiple hues of bioluminescent fungus. On the far ceiling, those clusters of life appeared like distant galaxies. On the floor, they were a surreal garden. We approached one wing of a vast underground palace hewn from living rock. Many Fae populated an expansive arcade. Dressed in finer clothing, they might have been wealthy merchants, nobles or politicians. More guards stood at either side of an arched doorway. Through a servant's entrance, uniformed Fae carried trays or pushed carts along an unadorned hallway. My armed escort drew much attention. One young woman with lavender skin gaped and dropped her vase of orchid-like flowers. One of my guards chided her in rough words I couldn't understand.

In a room which appeared to be a laundry, we met a woman who at once reminded me of Mrs. H, though her skin was emerald green, a Changeling no doubt. She smiled and took my filthy and bandaged hand in her human-shaped one, and bid me come with her.

They led me to a washroom. At my protest, the male guards waited outside while the green woman and two other females, one with feathers for hair and another with eyes and skin like a porpoise, saw to my bath and a change of clothing. When they stripped me of the tattered uniform and the remaining hospital bandages, the feathered girl blanched at the sight of my bruises and scrapes—the ravages of escaping the asylum.

Bronze pipes filled a tub made from a giant abalone shell; hot water swirled inside the iridescent oval. Gladly, I submerged my weary body; the water tasted of salt and burned each cut and abrasion on my skin. The green woman poured several bottles of colored liquids into the brew, turning the bath a dark green.

"This will help you heal." She added the powdered contents of a black envelope to the bath. "Soak for as long as you can stand it."

The liquid fizzed, setting my nerves afire before it dulled to bearable heat, bubbling around each of my wounds. I scrubbed with a sea sponge. Under the dirt, my skin had become almost new. All but the worst bruises had faded. The cut on my forehead looked better; the stitches might come out soon. Even the fingers damaged by the frostbite fairy appeared to be on the mend.

Inside both elbows, I found healing puncture wounds. They itched, but small scars remained.

A flash of memory—liquid light draining out through rubber tubes attached to my arms. It made little sense. No, it must have been blood they'd taken. Small wonder I had felt so drained during those days at St. Ivy's.

After my bath, the women dressed me in an amber-colored gown which was cut far too low in the back—an impractical detail for such a cold environment. At least it was warmer inside the palace. They gave me well-crafted lace-up boots of a sort that almost reminded me of home, and a swath of gold silk to drape my shoulders. My hair dried and combed, it fell into natural waves, a contrast to the human fashion for public modesty.

My three remaining palace guards led me next to a kitchen and bade me eat. At the servant's table, I finished one bowl of fish stew, a cup of spiced cider, and a purple fruit which tasted like strawberries. The guards watched my every move while I observed the cooks. Several human-shaped workers had skin in hues of green, red, or blue—horns, feathers, or some other peculiar feature. Roger had said Changelings often became servants in the Otherworld. Had they all been stolen away from their world as children?

When I'd finished, my escort led me down a long corridor. Bordered on one side by a high wall of glass, what I'd first taken for a view of the exterior cavern was a glimpse into the ocean's depths. Glowing schools of fish darted through ropes of seaweed, pursued by larger fish with fearsome visages.

"The palace is underwater," I said.

"Partially, yes," spoke the guard nearest to me, In English.

I could not get a good look at his face under the helmet's visor, but that voice seemed familiar... like I'd heard it long ago.

A shark, so colossal at first I took it for a ship on the sea's surface, blocked out the bright starlight. Light from the palace window shone in the creature's enormous eye.

To hear the guard speak again, I asked, "What does the king want with me?"

"I can't say, Lady."

We climbed a staircase and passed through a massive gathering room, like a salon, as dimly lit as every other place in this night realm. The furnishings were of indigo and black, flocked with silver, and of that same heavy yet flamboyant style I took for Winter Court artistry.

Circles of light pooled below stained-glass windows in the high ceiling. Polygons in shades of blue and purple alternated with clear glass, so the night sky shone through facets of the jewel.

"Have you ever seen the stars so beautiful?" The voice of the guard beside me was now so recognizable, but I had not heard it spoken that way in years.

I whispered the word under my breath. "Father?"

He lifted a finger to his lips to indicate silence and raised the glass visor of his helmet, smiling at me. He appeared younger than the old man I had last seen—a man of early middle age.

One of the other two guards turned to us. Father lowered his visor. I watched my path.

I still wished to speak with Arimos, but this changed the equation. We were now two against many. I didn't have the uncertainty of not knowing Father's fate. Still, I had yet to determine if he was himself, and not Faerie illusion. Was someone here cruel enough to torture me so? Anything was possible.

Through a mirror-lined hallway we approached tall, black-lacquered double-doors. Two attendants, wearing mirrored masks, bowed and pulled braided blue ropes at either side. When the doors creaked open, an icy breeze ruffled my hair. I trod an indigo carpet into a space so wide I could not see the opposite ends. The exterior walls were made of marble, mirror, and dark wood. The floor tiles were of polished black stone.

In the domed ceiling high above, an oculus let in a breeze that tasted of tundra flora and winter sea. Starlight of an eternal night crowned the open expanse, framed by an unknown zodiac carved in stone. It reminded me of the ceiling in Roger's library, but on a massive scale.

My entourage halted when we reached the end of the carpet, taking silent positions at either side. They gestured for me to go on alone.

I passed two guards and cast a hesitant glance at the third, who might be my father. The latter gave away nothing, but said, "Wait. You are half-human." He marched toward me.

Ice ran through my veins, having little to do with the drop in ambient temperature.

"You will not tolerate the cold. Here." He shrugged off his uniform cloak and draped it over my shoulders, whispering beside my ear. "Make him no promises, my girl. No matter what."

"Thank you." I nodded, hoping to show no emotion.

He turned to join the others.

I trod black tiles, soon dusted with white. Clouds misted the starry sky, and snow flurries glittered in the air. After many meters, the oculus above still appeared so far away. Optical illusion, or had I misread the scale of the architecture?

I shivered, glad for the cloak. No promises? They knew I must be here to bargain for Roger. What kind of promise would they ask of me? I would do almost anything to save the life of the man I loved. The thought surprised me because it was true.

Icy mist hung in the atmosphere, lit only by starlight. An empty throne perched on a raised dais in the distance, but no living soul stirred in the massive room, at least none I could see.

The polished floor gave way to rougher granite, encircled by a wide ring of standing stones, as though the King's palace had been built around this ancient place, one imbued with magic I sensed to my core.

Cut into the stone floor were concentric rings radiating from the central sculpture. Medallions filled circular recesses, each unique in size and color, like planets orbiting the sun. I walked from one to the next, but the jewels inside were dim as pebbles.

Approaching the center of the vast room, I shivered. A waist-high block of stone, roughly three feet cubed, formed the base of an array of metal and glass attachments, reminiscent of an astrolabe or an armillary sphere. I grabbed one of the outermost bronze rings and it swiveled on fine axels. At its apex, an enormous silver-framed lens gathered starlight and focused it into a shining orb within. Shadows, reflections, and refractions scattered across bronze, silver, and stone.

All now seemed a puzzle I should crack.

Set into the top of the machine's base was a polished blue stone, like lapis lazuli, flecked with star-like mineral inclusions. A copper vein blazed down the center, suggestive of the Milky Way. Into that a series of eight holes, like the ones which held jewels in the floor, formed a straight line.

The moon peeked over the oculus's edge. She would be in full view soon, though veiled by clouds. The snow magnified the moonlight in that wonderful way I remembered from winters as a child.

I swiveled the giant rings, aligning lenses until a crystal sphere reflected me and my surroundings in reverse, gathering heavenly brilliance into a focused pool. I rotated the next brass ring to align a horizontal prism, dividing the light into a vivid spectrum.

The eight holes were now interspersed within each of the seven rays of color, with one just below, in what might have been the ultraviolet band. Spheres, or perhaps rods, were meant to be placed there. I circled the device but found nothing of the proper sort which might fit. I began a wider search, but was startled by the approach of a tall man. He wore a black cloak; moonlight revealed a deep blue sheen on the rippling fabric as he neared, like an approaching storm cloud on the wind.

"I do not possess all the pieces to this puzzle, Lady Violet, daughter of Helena." The voice sounded human, but when the man drew close enough, I guessed he might be seven feet tall. "You will soon see why."

CHAPTER 21
A ROSE

he Fae appeared to be a youthful man, but his icy gaze held centuries. He looked human, but for his elongated ears and tall stature. His mane of platinum hair was braided with blue and black strands of silk. He wore black trousers and boots, and a shining breastplate inlaid with a pattern like dragon scales. Pauldrons jutted from broad shoulders. His cloak shimmered with tiny jewels, like a mist of ice crystals floating above a dark sea.

"Lord Arimos." I curtseyed, for, though he wore no crown, this could be none other than the Winter King. Nervous, I brushed a wayward tendril of hair behind my own somewhat pointed ear, which I had only considered a variation of normal until now. "You have taken a prisoner. Someone dear to me. I am here, as the queen's niece, to petition you for his release."

"I know why you have come. And Ariadne knows you are here. My prisoner stands accused of breaking sacred law once again. He must stand trial. I can do nothing to stop it, even if I wished to."

Arimos crossed the remaining distance between us. I held my ground, despite his looming presence. He radiated a palpable energy, like an electric current. The hair on my forearms stood on end. "The Queen wishes only to see justice done. This time, she will not grant your human any clemency. He will be executed after his trial tomorrow."

"Why? What can Roger possibly have stolen that demands his life?"

Arimos grasped the outermost ring of the giant armillary sphere and studied the refracted light. The spectrum of color had faded, because snow-laden clouds obscured the sky, yet the Winter King's glacier-blue eyes shone with inner light. His face possessed unearthly beauty, but the lines of his features masked what might have been cruelty.

"Daughter of the Summer Courts, it pains me you know so little of our ways. So little of the truth. If you knew the real Roger of House Gale, you would not rush to his defense."

"You have no right to judge me." I forgot I shouldn't address a king in such a fashion. "If Your Majesty condemns theft, I demand the return of the relics your men stole from me."

He flashed perfect, human-looking teeth, in either a grin or a threat. "Those relics were never your property. I have stolen nothing from you." He turned and walked a few paces away. I was relieved when that powerful gaze left off its scrutiny. "As for my right to judge, you will attend tomorrow's trial and hear the evidence presented against my prisoner."

"If you plan to execute him, why bother with a trial?"

"He is guilty of theft from my garden. This is enough to warrant his punishment. However, I wish to bring to light his other crimes." He turned to me again, and I was a dove pinned by a serpent's gaze. "It is difficult, even for me, to challenge the leadership of the Reliqua. We would force the humans to acknowledge their guilt if evidence presented against one of their own is written into our records."

"Will you allow me to testify on Mr. Gale's behalf?"

"You ask this before you hear our accusations?"

The spectrum vanished. Snowfall increased. I could no longer see the distant walls. The King himself, and the ancient stone monuments, cast our only light.

"Take me to him."

Arimos studied my face before he said, "Come with me."

He gestured to someone hidden in the mists. The sound of bootsteps on polished stone echoed through the snowy expanse. Cynbel approached. How long had he lurked in silence?

"See that our prisoner is ready to receive guests."

"Yes, my Lord." Cynbel bowed and left.

Arimos turned to me. "You are as lovely as your mother, Lady of the Summer Courts." He placed a hand on my cheek.

I froze. His touch was warmer than I expected. My heart raced, as though I'd been touched by a dream or a memory—some part of my past I couldn't forget, even if it wasn't mine.

"Violet." The King's hand dropped, breaking the spell. "I dislike this human name. You have another. Your true Fae name. You must be the first to speak it aloud, before I or the Queen can address you thus. Only then will you be accepted into your place at Court."

"My true name?" The question wasn't for him. It reminded me of a fairy-tale my mother might have read to me long ago.

I walked with King Arimos through a doorway on the opposite side of the throne room from where I'd entered. Three guards accompanied us. Since their helmets' glass visors covered their eyes, I couldn't tell if my father was among them. We proceeded outside through another arcade. In the cold distance, I heard the ocean. We must have been near the shore.

We trod a path of snow-dusted pebbles toward a high stone wall. More guards stood at either side of the gate and bowed to their King's approach. Brass hinges gleamed with reflected moonlight as massive wooden doors creaked open. Inside, snow-draped evergreens towered above shrubs glistening with frost. Trees in leaf, berry, and vivid flower glimmered with icicles. More bioluminescent fungus clung to rocks or the bases of trees, casting eerie lights on the bizarre winter spectacle.

"How do they grow without sunlight?" It was a whispered question I'd not meant to speak aloud.

"Each of these trees is more than it appears." Arimos reached for a white-flocked hawthorn branch. "When a Fae is born, a tree or plant is also. These two are linked for life. One of my sacred duties as King is to guard the trees of the Royal Courts. Here in starlight they grow slowly, therefore their counterparts will live just as long. Their roots are fed by the peculiar minerals of this mountain, which kindle powerful magic within all life here."

"Does every Fae have a tree… or a plant?" *Mrs. H's absurd stories had not been wrong.*

"Yes. Even you."

He faced the snowy path with a wistful smile and began to sing.

> *In Winter's garden, ever night*
> *Long live thee, Trees of Aes Sídhe*
> *Reaching for her wise moonlight*
> *Tall grow thee, Trees of Aes Sídhe*
>
> *Silver branches, bear our centuries.*
> *Hidden roots, drink the mountain's prayers.*
> *Starlight crowned, thy verdant leaves*
> *Guard us from life's trials and fears.*

Through us shield the Earth's great heart
Upon which mankind once, in foolish pride,
With willful mage and warring art,
Faerie House from Human did divide.

Give us Dreams, Trees of Aes Sídhe
Of ancient days, when all was One.
And through our union blessed with thee,
Yield fruit in our last seasons.

"That was beautiful," was all I could think to say. The tune, and his voice, had stirred a primal instinct in my Fae blood. I shivered.

"My translation of an old Winter Court song."

"I… don't know where my own tree grows."

The King frowned. "Your mother would have planted it in the world of your birth, which should have been this one. Since you were born in the mortal realm, there your tree must also grow."

"What happens if it's harmed?"

"You would feel it. If it dies, you will perish as well. Your two lives are no less connected, even if your blood is half human."

"How can I protect it?" *If I could find it.*

"You cannot while it grows on human soil, though your mother most likely set wards of protection over it, even without the use of her own magic. Thus you must keep secret its location. Trust no humans. Especially ones capable of using your magic for evil."

"What do you mean?"

"You have much to learn. We will teach you. Once you take your place at Court."

"No. I have no wish to stay in this world."

Arimos ignored my last statement, turning toward the sound of his captain's approach. Cynbel, transparent as glass in the starlight, bowed to his master. They exchanged a few hushed words before Cynbel returned to his point in formation with our retinue.

"Now you must understand," Cynbel said as he passed by me, "why a theft from His Majesty's garden demands a life." His wraithlike form still left boot-prints in the snow. Perhaps his extravagant display in starlight was merely a powerful glamour, yet that didn't explain his ice-cold touch.

Our path wound through acres of trees of many species. We rounded a bend beside a massive oak, and my heart became heavy as stone. A man's body lay on the ground ahead, unmoving—a mass of dark clothing against white.

I couldn't breathe until I heard the rattle of chains. Behind him was a felled tree, one of smooth silver bark, dark waxy leaves, and drying red berries. A rowan, like the one in my mother's garden back home.

The man turned to me. Through a mess of black hair, I recognized a face I loved, bruised and streaked with dried blood.

"Roger!" I ran to him and knelt in the snow at his side.

"Violet," he whispered.

I cradled his damaged face in my hands.

"My love, forgive me." Roger's voice sounded far too weak. "I'm such a fool." He pulled against his chains but could not throw his arms around me. I encircled him with my own.

"I'm here to save you," I whispered. "I'll find a way."

"Impossible. I'm guilty. I felled this tree. You shouldn't have come here. You only put yourself in danger."

"Why did you do this?"

"It doesn't matter now. I didn't dream… to say goodbye." The verdant fire in his eyes had dulled to an ember.

"No. I won't accept that." I covered his bruised lips with my own. His stubble brushed my cold cheeks.

When he returned the kiss, my own tears ran hot.

I whispered, "I love you." Those inadequate words couldn't express my agony and yearning. I trembled. My skin radiated with Faelight. Roger's eyes widened as I caressed his face.

The snow around us bubbled up from the ground and burst into green. Sweet-smelling vines entwined us. Their life connected to mine, like veins in my body. Luminescent lines trailed from my fingertips into Roger's skin, radiating healing light through the insults to his flesh. My heart had become a conduit for love greater than both of us.

Writhing vines snapped the chains on Roger's wrists, as if they were nothing but ice. He threw an arm around me. Flowers bloomed, surrounding us with color and perfume. Summer in the midst of snow.

Though reluctant to break the spell, I pulled away from my love's embrace. The cocoon of new foliage gave way. His face was healed—the bruises faded. The cuts were gone, leaving only the remnants of dried blood.

I turned and addressed Arimos. "You must release him!"

"House Gale has yet again broken one of our most sacred laws. Punishment is required." Far from anger at my insolence, the king's ice-blue eyes held sadness.

"You can't leave him out here to freeze! How will he stand trial if he's dead?"

"The human is in no danger of freezing to death." Cynbel answered for his master.

"If you won't take him inside, I'll stay here with him."

"No." Arimos gestured to his guards, and they advanced on us.

"You would treat me as another prisoner? Please, Your Majesty, grant us these last hours together."

Cynbel laughed. The king's soldiers surrounded Roger, grabbed me, and dragged me away from his trembling arms. "No!" I screamed and resisted, but I was no match for their strength.

Arimos turned to Cynbel. "Go prepare a room for our new guest."

The captain bowed and left, followed by several other guards. If he should think it necessary to send soldiers instead of chambermaids to ready a guest room, no doubt they were leading me to a dungeon.

The King approached me and touched my chin, turning my tear-streaked face up to his. His icy eyes narrowed at the fire met in mine. "You are not my prisoner, Lady. Come. I will prove it to you." He offered his arm in escort, face cold as the snow, radiating the raw energy of a gathering storm. I would not have taken it, but his armed guards marched closer, ready to enforce the King's every whim.

As they led me back toward the palace, I turned enough to glimpse Roger, lying in the patch of green I had coaxed from the snow. His eyes sought mine before Arimos' soldiers shackled him with new chains.

The King and his retinue led me through the palace to what might have been a vast ballroom. We trod a polished black stone floor. Mirrors covered every vertical surface. A vast colonnade supported an elaborate gothic ceiling. Ornate mirrored plinths and crystal capitals reflected ambient starlight like diamonds. Tapestries of blue and violet, gold and indigo, draped the outer walls, yielding their shaded colors to the kaleidoscope.

Arimos snapped his fingers. High above, chandeliers flashed to golden-red brilliance, casting the jewel-box scene with the illusion of warmth.

"Are you an artist like your mother? A painter?" His tone was level and void of emotion, calculating perhaps. The sound took on an echo of timelessness in that expanse.

"Yes." My own reverberating response.

"As I surmised."

He gestured to servants lingering along one wall. I hadn't noticed them. One approached, casting multiple reflections of a blue and green robe across the mirrored room. When she crossed into the light, I caught the glint of transparent wings, edged in radiant blue-white.

Arimos turned to me. "Your mother's magic flows through your veins. I see her power in you. Yet you are so different."

"Did you know her?"

His clipped laugh sounded like stifled anger. Not what I expected.

"I'll forgive you, if you do not know your mother's history, but I warn you this once. Do not mock me again." He moved closer, eyes flashing a blue blaze.

"I did not mock you." My hair nearly stood on end. Yet, I held my ground.

Indifferent to my fury, he turned to the servant girl, who waited some distance away. At his nod, she approached, curtseyed, and offered Arimos an oblong black box, all the while keeping her eyes averted from the King's. Was her submissiveness simple protocol, or did she know a thing I didn't? I thought of the basilisk's deadly gaze.

When she turned to leave, I saw her wings were shaped somewhat like a butterfly's. She wore a robe cut low in the back to accommodate these appendages, like my dress. Now I understood the purpose of that seemingly impractical fashion detail.

Arimos stared at the box in his hands. "Helena of the Summer Courts was betrothed to me when we were both children. Yet, she rejected our traditions, spurned her duty to her family and her people, and chose instead a miserable mortal existence."

Oh. I didn't see that coming, but it might explain a few things. "And my father," I added.

"Do you think Winter can harbor jealousy? After these centuries?"

His voice betrayed little emotion, though he distanced himself from the events with his choice of words.

Arimos opened the cloth-covered box. Inside, on a bed of black silk, lay a thin rod of what looked to be finely crafted silver, perhaps twelve inches long. I thought it was a wand until he lifted it up, and I beheld a tuft of white bristles. A paintbrush.

"A test." He said, offering the brush to me. "Of your magic."

I grabbed the handle. It felt icy and... exhilarating. A static charge energized my fingers. "What happens if I pass? Or if I fail?"

"You will not fail." The King gestured to the room in a wide sweep. "These colors are your canvas. Paint with your mind and heart. The magic will follow."

I held the silver brush aloft and took a steadying breath. I sensed only the looming aura of the Faerie King, as though I stood next to a powerful magnet. Underneath my trepidation boiled rage.

"How can you speak of my heart? When you've imprisoned the man I love? When even now he is freezing in the snow, awaiting execution?"

Silent, Arimos scrutinized me with eyes austere and unknowable, like a glacial ocean. He said, "Perhaps I was wrong. You *will* fail if you cannot transcend the limits of time and space. You have been too long confined in human flesh. Does the butterfly weep for the death of the caterpillar self? I call you now to awaken."

He stepped behind me. I trembled with fear and fury, trying not to let it show. He reached out an arm to parallel mine. Touching my hand with surprisingly warm fingers, he completed an electrical circuit. I gasped. Power surged through my veins.

The nerves in my hand prickled with both fire and ice, strongest where I cradled the silver between fingers and palm. This close, he smelled like snow on a pine mountain.

"What do I do?" The words distracted me a little from his nearness and my body's desire to fight or flee. Despite my emotions, what he had to show me might prove useful.

No, it was more than that. A primal energy stirred within my Fae blood, inciting a hunger for power, filling me with trepidation.

The King spoke beside my ear. "Close your eyes. Imagine that which you desire to summon. Like a rose."

I did, imagining a single stemmed rose, red petals unfolding to a summer sun.

"Good," he whispered. "Now let it come alive before you. Paint it."

"How?" I hated how much I wanted to know. I yearned to see if I could wield this fairy magic. If it was truly part of me.

Arimos guided our hands to the reflected colors on the nearest mirrored column. "There, the shade of green."

"Yes."

In a thousand broken reflections, the two of us were the only dancers in this vast ballroom.

"You are painting with light. Take it with the brush. You will see."

Suspending disbelief for the moment, I closed one eye, aligned my brush tip with a color like underwater seaweed and pretended to scoop an impossible dollop of paint from the view.

It worked. The white bristles took on ethereal green paint. I gasped.

"Good. Now…" He guided our hands in a sweeping motion through the air. Amid the room's dark expanse, the brilliant image of a floral stem emerged. Feeling a surge of power and purpose, I added leaves, thorns. Shapes glimmered into being with only the briefest thought.

Arimos dropped his guiding hand as I gathered colors from the surrounding light. Deepest vermillion for the soft petals. Fiery gold for the fragrant center. Inky shadows became depths of dimension. Sparks of reflected starlight formed glittering dewdrops.

When I discerned no discrepancy between my inner vision and the image I'd painted, I let fall the hand holding the brush, exhausted as it was. My eyelids grew heavy.

Like he knew what to expect, Arimos caught me before my knees gave way. Warm arms encircled my waist; his silver breastplate had become a wall, yet I didn't resist the support.

The rose, solid and real as the two of us, fell to the ground at my feet.

"This will pass," he said, still bracing me. "Magic can drain us, but it also renews us with time. Breathe. That is most important."

I drank in the ocean-tasting night air, which poured from an unseen window. Steady again, I pushed away from the King's unbidden embrace. "I'm fine."

"Excellent." He bent to pick up the rose and handed it to me. Luminescent red petals cast a glimmer of fire over his pale, chiseled cheeks.

I took the rose. "Did I pass?" I raised an eyebrow.

His smile was an arctic sunrise on some forgotten shore.

"Is it real?" The stem felt as natural as any I'd ever held.

"The illusion will fade when forgotten."

His answer made about as much sense as any other riddle spoken in this world. A thorn pricked my finger. I pressed away a small drop of blood. That much was no illusion.

"It is yours." Arimos closed my fingers around the silver handle. "I want you to keep it. It was meant for your mother. I commissioned it to be made for her long ago. It was to be a wedding gift. The bristles are of unicorn mane. The unicorn was the Court Banner of my own mother's people. She was a princess of the Spring Courts." Sadness pooled in his eyes.

"Court Banners. Are those the eight symbols in… your throne room?" On the medallion I had used to open a portal to the Otherworld, only four were depicted, but eight directions were marked.

"Yes. They have many meanings and powers, which you must learn. Foremost, they represent the eight Otherworld nations. Nine Reliqua Houses once served each, though our human allies have dwindled in number. When the heir of House Gale killed a unicorn, an animal sacred to Faerie, the Queen granted him mercy, against my council. I knew one day I would live to see justice, and House Gale would pay for its sacrilege. However, I did not expect Helena's half-breed daughter to complicate matters a century later."

Half-breed. That was enough to throw much-needed cold water on my thoughts.

"So, you admit this is not justice. This is simply revenge. There's no way Roger will receive a fair trial. And what will you do with me? The half-breed complication?"

His gaze widened, and he stepped closer. Had I pushed him too far? I couldn't afford to show fear.

"For a start, I will teach you how to use your powers."

"I can't accept this." I handed Arimos the brush.

He shook his head. "You must. Do not think of using it to escape. I have reinforced this palace against all forms of unsanctioned magic. It will not work unless I allow it, as I did here. Do you understand?"

I couldn't say I understood the workings of this power I'd only just tasted; or that I read the King's intentions toward me, the daughter of the woman he must have once loved, whom he'd just admonished not to attempt *escape.* I answered only with a cautious bow.

At a snap of his fingers, four guards emerged from their stations and approached. Gone were the winged servant girls; these men carried swords, their faces concealed by helmets. They wore silver bars on the collars of their black uniform cloaks, which I took for some mark of rank.

"She must rest. Take her to her room. See that she has whatever she needs, but do not allow her to leave until I summon her again."

The guards gave a salute in unison, stomping their boots.

They led me from the ballroom, where Arimos lingered alone.

I lifted the rose and inhaled the sweet fragrance. So lifelike. I smelled the heat of an unseen sun. A memory of painting in the garden with my mother surged through my mental canvas. I thought of Roger suffering even now in the snow, bringing the sting of tears to my eyes. If I escaped, how could I save him?

I tucked the silver brush into the wide sash at my waist. Arimos said it wouldn't work inside the palace, but what about outside? It was worth the longshot.

"Excuse me," I said to the soldier next to me. "I'm afraid I need fresh air. Will you please take me outside? Above sea level, that is."

"I'm afraid we can't." This was more or less the answer I expected.

"I'm a prisoner, aren't I?"

No reply.

I needed a distraction. I had nothing with me but the brush and the rose. No, the rose had *disappeared*. I turned to see if I'd dropped it, but I saw nothing in the crowded hall. It will *fade when forgotten*, the king had said.

A chill ran down my spine, but it was a relief. I didn't want to have the power to conjure real things from thin air. Yet the thorn's puncture wound remained.

My entourage turned into a narrow, dimly lit corridor. In unison, the two guards next to me subdued the other two leading the way; each with a cloth-covered hand over the mouth of their victim, containing whatever analogue of chloroform existed in the Otherworld. They helped the unconscious men slump against a wall. It happened so swiftly—I was preparing to scream when one of them laid a finger on his lips, and I recognized the wry smile.

"Father?"

"It's me, Violet." He removed his helmet. There was the same younger version of his face I remembered from childhood. His blue eyes shone brighter than they had in years. His hair was not silver, but gold, the opposite of my own dark tresses, a gift from my mother.

When I hugged him, he said, "I'm glad to see you, but I wish you had not followed me here. I told you in my letter to stay away. It is too dangerous."

"You had no right to hide any of this from me." I stepped back and eyed the both of them. "Let alone keep me from following you, or the truth."

Father sighed. "You may be right, but at the moment, we have more pressing concerns. We'll have to table this discussion. And keep our voices down."

I turned to ask the taller guard in a harsh whisper, "Who are you?"

"Don't you know my scent, little half-breed?" Druk raised the eye-guard of his helmet long enough for me to recognize the broadly chiseled face, pronounced nose, and scraggly white beard.

"Hey," my father elbowed Druk in the side.

"I meant nothing by it. She *is* half-human."

"Is that Druk? Father, this man is not to be trusted. He tried to sell me to Cynbel."

"That was before he knew you were a friend of Septimus. Or my daughter."

"True. I only heard Arimos wanted any humans who came through the Old Gate. He is our king, after all. Would you forgive me, Lady?" He bowed his head.

I had no reason to refuse any aid at this point. "There was no harm done. I'm fine, but we must help Roger. He's going to be executed."

206

"I know. I had a plan in motion to extract him, but it's not without peril." Father shook his head. "And now that you're here, Violet. My priorities have changed. I won't put you in danger to save him. We've got to get you out of here."

"No, I won't leave Roger. Or you." I stopped in protest. "That's why I came here. And that's final."

"Do you truly love Mr. Gale so much?"

"Yes."

It was a difficult thing to say, because this love bore a cost in pain, just as it had done for my parents.

He exchanged a heavy look with Druk, who nodded his head in silent agreement. "Then you must disguise yourself. Quickly now."

They removed the helmet and uniform cloak from one of the unconscious guards and bade me put them on. The black cloak covered my dress. It had a white lining and trailed the floor. I pulled my hair into a knot and slipped on the helmet. The purpose of the visor became apparent. Lines of Faelight crisscrossed the walls. Pulsing, living veins of magic curved around every door and archway.

"I see. I wondered what these visors were for." The altered view reminded me of Roger's Spectrocles. Evelyn's Spectrocles, rather.

"There are several useful settings. They can help us see through glamour." Father pointed to his ear. "The dial on the side—yes, that one. There's a color for moon glare in snow. Others reveal all manner of magic."

I approached a nearby wall and laid a hand on one of the lines. Faelight swirled around my fingers, like blue-green luminescent smoke. My skin nearly itched. "These must be the magic wards Arimos had mentioned."

"Something of that nature. I'm afraid I'm no expert. For that, I had the help of your Mr. Gale for a short time until they captured him. If we want to save him, we'd best hurry."

"Will they be all right?" I asked, motioning to the unconscious guards, both of whom must have been Changelings, for the human appearance of their features, though their skin was green. One snored.

"They'll wake in an hour with a headache." Druk pointed down the corridor. "Let's go."

CHAPTER 22
HEART'S MEDICINE

e descended a spiral stairway. Worn steps emerged from the bedrock like the inner workings of a nautilus shell. Lantern light revealed mineral veins and crystal protrusions in the stone strata.

I asked my father, "Is Mother still alive? Is that why you're here?"

"No, she's not, but I returned here to see to her last wishes, for your own sake. Mr. Gale found me and lent his assistance; thus he faces execution now."

"Tell me what happened."

We reached a lower landing. Druk surveyed a new corridor before he signaled us to follow. Our tall companion led the way through what felt like a mineshaft. Father and I lagged behind.

"Before your mother died, she made me promise to stay with you until you were grown. She knew I must eventually return here, but in so doing, I could never go home again."

"What do you mean?" Although I had a good idea.

"I've already lived in this realm for too long. And such a wonderful year it was, with my Helena, I shall never forget. But now I've returned, I am losing my humanity and transforming into something else. I'll admit the thought scares me, yet I can't help but feel some excitement. From death's grim threshold, I was not far. Had I stayed any longer in Seastone, I wouldn't have been able to make the trip come next equinox."

"So you've become a Changeling. You knew this before you left."

"I'm sorry, Violet."

"Well, you don't have to stay here. I've met Changelings… in our world."

"For short amounts of time we can cross through the Divide, yes, but how can I return to our village looking like this? I don't want to start life

208

anew as someone else. I've done that enough times already. I want to remain in your mother's homeland. Discover what I will become."

We passed through an outgrowth of clear crystals, geometric points erupting into the corridor like arrow shafts, as though the excavators of this place had interrupted a giant, living geode.

Distant lights and the sounds of an underground encampment echoed from ahead.

"Was it Mother's tree you and Roger felled?"

"Yes. Gale arrived here in Wyvern's Rock not long after I did. Evidently, he'd escaped Winter Court custody and was looking for me. He was rather poorly after his treatment, I'm afraid..." Father shook his head. "Luckily, I had made allies in my weeks here and could offer shelter while he recovered."

Weeks? Then I remembered Roger had said time could pass at a different rate here in Faerie. To know Roger had endured torture... It was all too much.

Father continued, "I explained my mission, and Gale agreed to help me steal the tree. We gave them a run for their money indeed, but our plan failed. I'm afraid I escaped, but he didn't."

"Why did you do it? Surely mother wouldn't ask you to do something forbidden. Why did she want you to cut down her tree?"

"Did you see those jewels in the floor of the great hall?

"Yes."

"They're Faestones. The remains of such trees, charged with the magic of the being once linked to them. When a Fae dies, the ashes of those trees are processed into jewels, in the way nature produces diamonds from coal."

"Like the medallion I used to open the Old Gate."

"Yes. It's customary for a Fae to bequeath this stone to their descendants, sometimes their human descendants, in the case of Reliqua families. Your mother's tree should rightfully be ours. Yours and mine." Father lifted his visor so he could look me in the eye. "She wanted us to make such a Faestone so that its magic would help her daughter most of all. But King Arimos owes nothing to the widower of a royal exile. I am not Reliqua, so I have no claim. That's why I had to steal it for myself. Your mother knew this too. She told me of a sorceress here in the Winter Courts who could help when the time came. I needed someone skilled in the alchemy of crafting Faestones, for the magic required is strong and the knowledge is kept secret from all but a few. When I arrived here, I learned the sorceress had died years ago. However, I obtained her grimoire, which detailed the process. My own knowledge of Faecraft was too limited even to read the book, so I searched for a new ally when your Mr. Gale arrived at Wyvern's Rock. He put his life on the line to help us, but I got away in the scuffle and left him there to be captured. I even lost the grimoire."

"We must explain to Arimos that we claim the tree as ours. He will listen to me. I will beg for leniency."

"No. It can't work. King Arimos wants to humiliate the Reliqua. He won't be denied this trial."

"Why?"

"Many Fae, especially in the Winter Courts, resent the Treaty their Queen made with humans long ago. Many of those Faestones in the great hall represent a pact between a Reliqua House and a Fae royal family. If Mr. Gale is killed, the Reliqua will lose another jewel on the map, weakening their power. That's what Arimos wants. And if *we* go to him with such a petition, I fear we'll also be killed. No, we stick to the plan and steal Mr. Gale back."

I touched the silver brush the Winter King had given me, still tucked into my sash. A gift once intended for Mother. No doubt Father had more personal reasons for wanting to avoid Arimos.

"I never knew you practiced magic. I mean sorcery, that is." *You never told me anything.*

"Ah." He smiled. "You just didn't see it, my girl. Well, a year spent in Faerie will do that to a man, you know. Made my act more popular than it should have been, I always thought. Then again, your Mother drew the crowds with or without me."

What grand adventures the two of them must have shared so long ago. Then I remembered why I still resented him.

"Quiet," Druk spoke in a harsh whisper. "We are near the barracks."

I adjusted my cloak, covering my gown, and followed Druk into what appeared to be an underground village for the king's armies. Father walked behind us.

We approached a marketplace made of tents. The smell of cooking fires and coal smoke greeted us—the murmur of a crowd. I lowered my helmet's visor, setting the dial to detect glamour disguises.

A group of five soldiers walked by, dressed identically to us. One of them nodded to Druk and began conversing in an unknown language. I froze in near panic, until they exchanged gruff laughs, and Druk patted the man on the back. They turned to leave, as we did the same.

"What was that about?" I whispered, difficult as it was wearing a helmet.

"We Changelings." Druk placed a hand over his heart. "We stick together. Even down here."

Perhaps the prejudice which existed between full blood Fae and once-human Changelings had stratified Arimos' kingdom in complicated ways.

Past a row of tents, we entered a large building through a doorway draped in weighted canvas. Inside, an audience of Fae and Changelings sat on crates and immobile steam equipment, shouting as they placed bets on violent sparring matches. One tall creature with insect eyes and a reddish exoskeleton snapped pincer-like claws against a mace-wielding centaur. Another match drew a larger crowd; a green-skinned woman sliced a tree-like Fae with her scimitar, and it howled like a bear's growl amidst a swarm of bees. The creature stomped the ground so the building shook. The crowd roared.

If this is what the Winter King's army did for fun, I would hate to see their torture rooms, let alone be subjected to them, as Roger had been. My thoughts continually strayed to the memory of his bruised face and the way his injuries had healed under my touch. That very moment, he lay chained in the snow. The thought was enough to tear me apart, so I pushed it aside.

"Wait here." Druk disappeared into the noisy mob.

Father grabbed my arm, and we made our way to an open bit of floor beside the perimeter wall, giving us privacy. Difficult as it was to hear above the tumultuous crowd.

Father lifted his visor, and I did the same.

"You must have used a portal stone to get here. Do you still have it?"

"No. The king's soldiers took it from me."

"That's unfortunate. We need one to send you home, or you'll be stuck here until next equinox. Where did you find it in the first place?"

"A woman named Evelyn of Reliqua House Crane helped me procure it before I escaped St. Ivy's and hid in the Welterwood."

"What? St. Ivy's? That dreadful hospital?"

"Yes."

Another group of laughing men approached. We lowered our visors until they moved out of earshot.

"Gale told me he'd sent you home to protect your safety. That incompetent, pompous… Or did he lie to me?"

"No. He did send me back to protect me from capture, but when I arrived in our world, I… must have blacked out. I was found and taken to St. Ivy's, no doubt because of my *past medical history* with that place. I can't remember much of what happened. They gave me electro-shock therapy, and it erases your memory."

"I…. I'm so sorry, Violet." There was the look he often wore when I spoke of the asylum. A cold detachment like pity and revulsion.

I took a step backward. "What's worse is knowing I should never have gone to that awful asylum in the first place! You knew what was wrong with me my whole life. I was half-Fae. That's why I feared iron… and reflections.

Why I sometimes heard voices. All those years, you simply allowed me to think I was unwell. Why in God's name didn't you just tell me the truth, Father?"

"I've told you the truth your whole life, just not *all* of it." He heaved a sigh. "I didn't realize… you would suffer so much, or so long. I'd always thought one day your Fae… *tendencies* might disappear." The way he said the word, he meant *weaknesses*. "I believed in time you would lose your phobias. I only wanted you to live a normal *human* life."

"No. I could never be normal. You knew that was impossible. My only choice was to believe I was insane."

"I never wanted any of that for you. Your mother and I wanted you to be happy…" He exhaled in frustration. "We needed to keep your existence a secret. Wanted you to remain free."

"You wanted to hide me from the Queen."

"Yes. If Ariadne learned she had a niece, even a half-human one, she would have demanded you return to this world. That is their law. She would have taken away your choice in the matter. Your mother and I… We never thought we would even have children. You came to us after a hundred years. How could we let you go?"

"You still could have told me what I was. Helped me understand what was happening to me." *Those nightmares…* "Instead, you told me my *cards were bad*. You condemned me to a life controlled by fear. With no knowledge of my true identity. Or my power. You never gave me that choice, either."

"You must understand. We always thought, if you never questioned your humanity, the faster your magic would fade, and the more quickly your phobias would dissipate. If you had known what you were, your powers would have grown, and they would have found you. We would have lost you long ago." He looked crestfallen. "Can you forgive me, my daughter?"

I couldn't answer. "How old are you? When we last celebrated your birthday, Mrs. H and I decorated your favorite cake with 63 stars."

"I'm one-hundred and…" he tapped a few fingers in midair, counting, "thirty-two. I fell in love with your mother in the summer of 1805."

"Does Mrs. H know?" I glanced at our flickering shadows on the wall, cast by torchlight.

"She does not. She suspects you are touched by magic, in whatever way she sees it, but I don't believe she knows anything more. We've never discussed it."

I threw my hands into the air, well beyond exasperated with him—with everything.

He pulled me into a hug, as awkward as it was wearing a helmet, but I was too furious to be patronized and backed away.

My hand shook. I balled a fist. "Did you know where that magic potion was manufactured when you bought it?"

"The Tears of the Moon?" He seemed taken aback, if not embarrassed. "No, but the blasted stuff was outrageously expensive. If I hadn't been so desperate, I'd never have used it. You see, I'd lived away from Faerie for so long, my magic had dwindled to the point where I thought I could never return. Then I heard about that potion... It was an answer to my prayers. The man who sold it to me said it came from the Otherworld, but I didn't have the luxury of asking too many questions." He shook his head. "Why?"

"It came from St. Ivy's. Porter makes the drug from the blood of mental patients under his control—ones with Fae ancestry like me."

"But that can't be true. How is it even *possible*?" At least now he looked shocked.

"I don't know how they make it, but I've seen the evidence firsthand. I think he... extracted Faelight from my own blood." On reflex, my fingers worried the healing puncture marks on my forearms. "But I can't remember everything, thanks to my... amnesia."

Father's face darkened with anger, but he could not speak, for Druk returned with another two guards. Changelings, no doubt. I lowered my visor, glad for the break in conversation.

As a cohort of five, with Druk in the lead and my father beside me, we exited the supply warehouse. We marched through the underground camp into vast training grounds, past shooting ranges with glowing targets painted on stalagmites. The sides and ceiling of the cavern proved elusive—shrouded in blackness beyond the reach of lantern light. The air grew colder, and the campfire smoke thinner, the farther away we ventured, with only bioluminescent fungus-oil torches to guide our feet, and the occasional colony of cave-dwelling glow-worms. Eventually, we found and boarded a small vehicle not unlike the one in which I'd ridden with Cynbel. The steam engine hissed to life, and we jolted forward on a rickety track. It spanned several wide fissures with little to call a proper bridge. We rounded a corner and the vehicle's headlights reflected at last off a perimeter wall. A smaller tunnel gaped at us like a widening mouth with snaggle stalactite teeth, swallowing our track. Were it not for our feeble lights, I would have felt buried alive.

"Old mining tunnels." Father said, like he could sense my worries.

I gripped the side-rail and tried not to watch the uneven rock formations skimming by so close to our open windows.

Starlight peeked through the darkness ahead. We slowed to a halt, left the vehicle, and proceeded on foot until we came to an old bronze gate. Druk and his kinfolk worked at the frozen-shut lock for several minutes until they cracked it open. We exited the cave to find an icy slope alongside the mountain into which Arimos' palace was fused. We trudged through thick snow until we found a well-trod path leading to the garden where Roger was held.

The night sky shone brighter, tipped gray at the horizon, as if before dawn. Even here in the Winter Courts, there was a subtle rhythm to the hours, but the orb of the sun would not appear in the realm of perpetual night.

The garden wall loomed ahead—a glimmering slate-gray vertical. The colossal stones fit together like an ancient puzzle, encircling scores, if not hundreds, of acres.

Our group approached the same gate Arimos had taken me through. Torchlight reflected off the breastplates of another four guards, wearing uniforms of the King's Elites, like Cynbel wore. Praying he was not one of these, I painted a glamour on my face—green skin like many of the Changelings here. I held my breath as a soldier lifted a lantern and shone it in our faces, seeming to linger in his inspection of me. Was his helmet's visor set to detect glamour? I had no way to tell.

Druk spoke a few words to the leader and saluted. At last, one of the guards cleared us to proceed.

"Allies?" I whispered to Father when we were far enough away.

"No."

Inside the walled garden, we followed a trail of footprints through snow. Wide trunks evenly spaced, were like an old forest where the underbrush had long ago yielded to the canopy's competition for light. Green leaves glittered under ice, bejeweled by reflected starlight.

When we lost the path under new snowfall, Druk sniffed the air and gestured in a different direction. We found another trail, no doubt worn by guards working in shifts around Roger's outdoor prison.

I gripped the silver handle of my new weapon, though I missed my crystal necklace. I still wasn't sure what I could do with this brush, only that using it drained my strength.

Soon we met five guards dressed in the same uniforms we wore. They stood at even intervals around the fallen tree and Roger, who lay motionless on the ground. I had to bite my lip to keep silent.

Father stood close beside me while Druk walked to the lead and saluted. They exchanged a few words and a set of keys. Afterward, the others turned and marched away.

Could it be so simple? "Shift change?" I whispered when we were out of earshot.

"Looks like it worked," Father said, with relief in his voice.

That meant the others must trust Druk. He was hanging himself here, for whose sake I couldn't understand. If our actions were discovered, he would be put at fault.

The men stationed themselves where the other guards had stood. I took my cue to do the same, just long enough to watch the first cohort disappear. When Druk determined it was safe, he gave the signal. Father and I approached Roger. My heart thudded with trepidation.

The vines and flowers I had summoned before were now darkened and snapped by ice. I knelt beside the prone figure in chains. Skin almost blue from the cold, his hair was covered in snow; even his eyebrows were frosted.

He didn't react until I touched his chilled face. At first he recoiled, rattling frozen chains. Blinking, his eyes searched through snow-laden lashes.

"Roger. I'm here." I removed my helmet.

"Violet." He strained to roll to one side, chest heaving with the strain of that simple movement. "Are you… a dream?"

"It's me. I'm real." I kissed his chapped lips, brushing snow from his hair and face. "We're here to rescue you."

Druk brought a flask of water, which Roger drank to the last drop, gazing at me from far away. He sat up and leaned on the fallen tree trunk, gasping for breath. Blood, darkened from contact with air, stained his clothing.

"Mr. Morgen," Roger said after a time, his voice too weak. "There is still life in this tree, but it's fading fast. If you want to perform the ritual, it must be done here and now. Or you'll lose your chance."

"So, I feared. Did you study the grimoire? I'm afraid they took it from us."

"Yes. I remember what to do."

One of Druk's men produced the keys and set to work on his chains. Soon they had his arms free. Roger assisted with his ankles.

"It's more important we get him to safety," I said.

Roger took my hand with his freezing one. "I wouldn't have risked my life if I didn't believe this was important. For you. We must try."

I looked from him to the others. "What do we have to do?"

"First, we sever one branch and dig one root. The rest must be burned with a ritual fire. Help me stand. I have not moved for days."

I offered an arm. Druk came to our assistance.

"Are you strong enough?" asked Father.

"I will be." Roger took a step and his knees buckled.

I caught him before he fell.

"I'm sorry you have to see me like this," he whispered to me.

"You're alive. That's all that matters." I kissed his cold cheek. "Besides, I like the stubble."

He smirked. The corner of those perfect lips was split and encrusted with dried blood, and he could use a bath, but he was no less a beautiful sight.

One of Druk's kinfolk approached, holding an ax. "Tell us which ones to cut."

Arm in arm, Roger and I walked to where the branches of my mother's Rowan lay in the snow.

"Go where you feel the tree lead you." Roger gestured to tree limbs laden with ice. "Choose a branch."

Reluctantly, I left him to stand on his own and climbed through the scattered and broken limbs. I spied one which had berries of stronger red color, its leaves still green with life. I gripped the icy bark and sensed a living pulse within the wood. The guard with the ax made short work of retrieving the branch for me. We removed its leaves and berries and placed them in a black cotton sack brought for this purpose, then trimmed the wood to a portion just longer than my forearm.

Father scraped away the snow from around the fallen tree's stump with a small spade, while Druk and his men kept watch. He brushed away dirt to reveal a large root and severed it from the trunk.

Roger took the new wand we'd fashioned and knelt in the snow facing the tree. We watched as he began to whisper in his magic language, words that might have been a prayer. His voice sounded weaker than I remembered, yet no less focused.

With some effort, he stood and held the wand against his forehead, perpendicular to the ground. The branch tip shone above his tangled locks, casting his face in angelic blue-white light.

The tree herself glimmered with green luminescence. Roger took a step and nearly stumbled. I ran to his side and slipped an arm around his waist.

He smiled at me before facing the sky. "We must always mind the position of the stars. Here they move so slowly compared to our side of the universe."

"I'm afraid my instincts are off when it comes to that mystery," I said. "I only guessed the dragon on my compass meant the Winter Courts."

"Yet you opened a portal all the same. Without ever having witnessed it done? Or reading a ritual book?"

"I just… went with my best guess."

"I'm sorry I missed that." He squeezed my hand. "You amaze me, my love."

"Says the man holding a glowing magic wand."

"Trust me," he whispered beside my ear, eliciting goosebumps along my spine. "You haven't seen anything yet."

Nearby, my father coughed, and I turned to meet his disapproving glare.

Roger cleared his throat. "I'm able to stand on my own now, Miss Morgen. Thank you."

I pulled away and missed his warmth.

Roger walked a few paces and looked at the bright stars. "In the Southwest I shall begin the ritual, for your mother was of the Queen's family. You will need to move back."

Druk growled. My father walked alongside me, and we stood facing the fallen tree in this captive forest. I hoped our distant firelight would not be visible to the palace.

Roger raised the wand high. Its light intensified as he sang the first word of a spell in his resonant voice. He touched the base of the wand to his forehead and lowered it to his heart. With the rowan wand, he drew a symbol in the air, knelt and traced another in the snow with his other hand, all the while holding the blazing wand upright. I could not see what he wrote, but the snow at his feet shone. He walked clockwise to each of eight points around the tree. Each time, he repeated what he had done before, though the words were different. I could not understand the meaning of his song, so much as *feel* it stir within my newly hatched magical senses.

Such cruelty, what Arimos had done. The place where Roger had lain without hope. His blood drying on the ground—the frozen flowers I had called—was now the center point of this ritual. The King knew that would be the case should anyone finish what they started here.

Those eight airborne sigils glowed in an unearthly ring, reminding me of the stone circle in the Welterwood, or the lines cut into the great Winter Court hall.

Standing between us and the tree, Roger lifted the wand once more toward heaven. The tree burst into blue and green flames. The energy grew brighter until it stung my eyes, yet it emitted little heat. Like natural fire, the enchanted blaze consumed the tree, yet at an accelerated speed, seemingly without smoke. In minutes, there was nothing left but a silhouette of ash along the ground. A void in the snow.

The circle of sigils faded. The snow at each of those points had melted, leaving only a concave impression, as if a candle-flame had pooled a fresh surface of wax.

Roger fell to his knees. Father and I rushed to his side.

He said, "Quickly... gather as much of the ash as you can. At the tree's heart, you should find a lump of coal harder than the rest. Cover that with snow until cool enough to handle."

Father nodded. He and two of the others left us to gather ash.

"Are you all right?" I asked.

"Yes. I will regain my strength." He laced his fingers through mine. "Especially when I'm near you."

I kissed his wrist, where the chains had bruised his skin. "And why is that?"

"Because your love is my heart's medicine."

I looked away, ashamed of unbidden tears.

Roger gently turned my face back toward his, wiping away a tear with his thumb. "Did you not tell me you loved me? Or did I dream you spoke those words?"

"I love you. But I see this magic of yours—what it must mean to you. I could never ask you to give up such a gift. How can you turn away from what you are?"

"For you, I'd give up anything. Even my life, if it were mine to give."

"I... What do you mean?"

"I know how important this task is to your family, so I will help see it done, but this escape will only delay my execution. I can't hide from the Courts. Not for long."

The heartache in his voice caused my eyes to sting anew. I kissed his cheek, cradling his face in my hands. "We won't hide. We'll petition the Queen. She must listen to me, her sister's daughter. You can't be killed for taking what's mine, on my behalf. Will you go with me to the Summer Courts?"

"I'll follow you anywhere, my Violet."

I wanted to ask him about the notes Evelyn showed me—his time at the Institute. I wanted to know what other secrets he held from me, but my heart couldn't bear it now.

"I think I found it," Father said from a distance. "Come have a look."

Roger and I joined in the inspection of the rowan's ashes.

My father pointed at a still-hot coal amongst smaller faded fragments of ash. "Doesn't that look like the heart?"

"I believe so."

Druk collected snow in a fold of his cloak. He approached and, with a nod of approval from Roger, dumped that on the coals. We all moved back as it steamed. When it cooled enough to handle, they wrapped the heart in fabric.

I asked Father, "How do we plan to get out of here now? Past those guards?"

"There's a second gate, a few miles that way." Father pointed in the direction opposite from where we'd come. "I'm told it may be less guarded than the main entrance."

"The human will wear this uniform. And my helmet." Druk opened a satchel he carried and pulled out another cloak, like the one I wore. "I'll claim I lost mine in a snowdrift."

"I don't think that will work," said Roger.

"It's risky, but we have little choice. After all, Violet got through."

"My glamour was what did it. And dumb luck." Which gave me an idea. "What if there was an easier way?" I untied the silver-handled paintbrush from my sash and lifted it up—white bristles luminous in the starlight.

"Oh? Where did you get that?" Roger turned to me with an inquisitive gleam in those eyes.

"A gift from the King."

He arched an eyebrow.

"Later." I waved away his jealous questions. "I think I could paint a doorway. In that wall."

"A summoning brush then. Can it do such a thing?"

"It's worth a try, at least. Let me get closer."

We trekked through the snow toward the garden wall. Once or twice I sensed—more than heard—a whisper or a word from tree branches, as if an invisible someone sat underneath and called out to us. I didn't have time to investigate. These trees must be capable of such magic if they were all linked to Fae somewhere in the world. No one else seemed to notice.

When we came within twenty yards from the wall, I raised the silver brush aloft. Snow glimmered in the moonlight, illuminating the wall from below. I observed my view's perspective. If there were an opening in this stone masonry, it might be shaped as an arch to support the massive weight above.

My view became a canvas. I pulled from living colors, sketching a rough outline in midair. I gasped as the stones melted under the illusory touch of my brush. The wall groaned in its shifting weight. I painted the depth of shade within the archway. I painted the white of snow through the opening—a glimpse of exterior space. I drew a keystone, strong enough to take the architecture's mass, highlighted with starlight.

"By Fenrir's Fur!" Druk exclaimed.

I dropped my trembling arm and beheld a real opening in the wall—large enough for us to walk through.

Another of our companions growled and uttered something in their language. Beside me, Roger gasped in amazement. Father whistled as he walked toward the archway.

Heaviness pressed in on me, and I sank to the ground on one knee. Hands braced in the snow, the world spun.

Roger knelt and wrapped an arm around me. "How do you feel?"

"I'm afraid. Of… this power."

"Don't be. Remember, you were born for this." He gave me his other hand and I took it. "Let's walk through your doorway before it fades."

We stood, and I, breathless and dizzy, relied on his balance more than I wanted to admit. My vision nearly went dark.

Roger didn't let go of my hands. "Breathe. This too shall pass."

I filled my lungs with the frigid air, held it for a stretch, and exhaled breath like steam. Roger had to be even more exhausted than I. Oh, I would have stayed there to rest beside him in the tree-filtered starlight of this beautiful garden, if we only had the time. We approached the archway I'd summoned into reality, where my father stood inspecting the impossible stone blocks. Druk and his kinfolk had already gone through.

Roger and I crossed that new threshold, and I touched the smooth, ice-cold stone. Polished granite blocks. Just what I'd imagined might line such an opening. I shivered when I realized that was precisely why.

CHAPTER 23
WEIGHT OF AN OATH

e buried our helmets in a snowdrift, which, according to Father, contained a way for Arimos to track his soldiers. We traveled into tundra wilderness toward a silver horizon below the inkwell of sky. Soon, we found a narrow road cut through snowdrifts. Parallel wagon wheel ruts, or more likely made by sleighs.

"Where are we headed?" I asked my father, who walked beside me, cloaked now in white—the reversed, snow-camouflage side of our black uniform cloaks, which included hoods to take the edge off the frigid wind.

"There's a city near here. Druk's kinfolk live there. We should find food and shelter, a chance to rest and regroup." Ice clung to his eyebrows.

"What's the plan afterward?"

"I wish we had a way to send you home before equinox, Violet, but portal stones are rare indeed. If we can finish your mother's Faestone, it might be strong enough. Gale can help us, but we need a laboratory with the proper equipment, and… we lost the grimoire. I know of a wizard in the Autumn Courts who might have another, but it will all take time."

I glanced at Roger, who walked paces behind us. It took everything he had just to keep moving. No doubt they had starved him for the days he was bound in the snow. I hoped we would soon find time to rest.

"Is that why you told Roger you were leaving, in that letter you gave me to deliver, but you didn't tell us? Did you think he'd figure it out and come after you?"

"I wasn't counting on it, but I had a feeling he would, if he was anything like his father. Truth is, I didn't know his intentions toward you at first. I thought he might try to deport you to Faerie, as is their law. Then I saw how upset he was about your situation, and it was obvious he had genuine feelings for you, and, well... I was so angry because he was right. I shouldn't have hidden what you were from you, but I couldn't turn back at that point. I had to go through with this, and believe it or not, I knew you would be fine, Violet, with or without him. With or without your... magic." He wiped his eyes. "And now... for what it's worth, all I want is to see you both safely home."

Fine. I was never fine. And how could he think I'd go back to normal after experiencing *this*? Shivering, I crossed my arms, focusing on what was important now.

"I must take Roger to see the Queen. I will petition her to spare his life. King Arimos won't give him a fair trial, and Roger believes he can't hide forever. Surely Mother's sister will listen to me and won't condemn a member of her Reliqua for helping us claim what's ours by right."

The real problem was, if Roger thought he deserved to die, what chance did we have? This guilt he carried was for sins committed long ago. I wasn't sure I knew the whole of it, either.

Father said, "A journey to the Summer Courts will be hazardous. I don't know how the Queen will receive you. She may listen to your petition or not. She might demand you stay in her kingdom."

"I know, but if I don't try, Roger will be executed. I can't let that happen."

We walked in silence for a moment, snow drifting past us, toward a cluster of distant trees. Though I heard little over the wind, I sensed running water ahead and smelled a hint of campfire smoke. We must be nearing the village.

"Did you know Mother was once betrothed to Lord Arimos, the Winter King?" I asked.

He sighed. "Not at first. One day she told me an arrangement had been made when she was a child for her future marriage, but she'd rejected the suitor when she grew old enough to understand. She wouldn't let anyone control her destiny in such a way. By then we were so in love I would've done anything for her. We ran away together, despite the costs."

"What happened?" I asked him. "How did she become an Exile?"

"It's a long story." Father gazed at the snow-covered road, but he was looking into a memory.

"We have time."

"Did I ever tell you when we first met?" He smiled.

"In a midsummer night's dream."

"I was outside, alone but for the company of the best telescope I could afford. Which was not much." An old stage flourish had crept into the tone of his voice—one I had not heard in years.

"You fell asleep and dreamed of a beautiful girl, and you saw her at your circus act the next night. I remember." I smiled.

"In the dream, she had wings. And when I opened my eyes… Behold!" He opened his hands wide. "There she was. A real fairy with two golden wings sat beside me. You can imagine how I must have felt."

"You never told me that part." If he had, would I have believed him? Maybe. It might have changed how I saw myself all these years.

"She was the most gorgeous woman I'd ever seen. She had wings of light, like a halo. And long, dark hair, like the night. She wore a dress woven from spun dew. She didn't know I'd awoken… herself stargazing, with my telescope. When she heard me stir, her wings flickered away to nothing. Her gossamer dress became plain cloth, like I'd only dreamed the whole thing.

"Somehow I'd seen her before. She said she had no time to stay and turned to run. I chased after her, calling for her to stop—to at least tell me her name, but she was gone. She'd led me through the forest by a stream, toward a hill dotted by old stone ruins. I found no trace of her and feared I'd never see her again."

"But she came to your performance the next night," I added. "Mother said you were both the best and worst actor she'd ever seen."

He laughed. "True, I was a poor Hamlet, but she must have loved me for my other talents." Father gazed at the horizon, smiling at the memory. "She stayed. She joined the circus that very night, and we were inseparable. I taught her part of my act, and she took to it like second nature. The crowds loved her almost as much as I did. I could not believe my good fortune. I saw her wings again one night, but I feared it was only a dream. Then, after three weeks, she vanished. I looked everywhere, eventually searching the stone ruins where I had lost her before. I don't know what power it was, but something in that place drew me through to Faerie, and I found her. She told me what she was, and that even though she wanted to stay with me, it was against their laws. So instead, I stayed with her, here, for a year in paradise, before the Courts found us and brought us to the Queen for judgement. I was willing to do anything to keep Helena safe, even though it meant giving her up. Instead, she gave everything up for me and became human. I cherished her, but love wasn't enough to keep her from dying in my arms, far younger, even in her third century, than a Fae should have been at the end."

We walked in the direction of one bright cluster of stars—the Pleiades. The sky turned so slowly in this realm, as if time stood still.

Up ahead, Druk stopped and sniffed the air. He raised a hand. "It's all right. Don't move."

Four figures materialized from the shadows of scrubby tundra trees. They wore uniforms of the King's Elites, and their ringleader was among them.

"You're all under arrest! By order of His Majesty, Lord Arimos, King of the Winter Courts."

Cynbel's men drew swords and advanced.

Father pulled me behind him.

"It's me you're looking for." Roger strode forward with his hands in the air. "Leave the others alone. I won't resist."

"I want the woman and the Reliqua human." Cynbel gestured toward our escort. "Kill these dogs."

One of Druk's men brandished an obsidian dagger. The black stone burned amber gold, like a hot coal, when he charged forward to meet our attackers.

I held my paintbrush, wishing it were a knife—which sparked an idea. From the shadows and reflected moonlight, I swiftly painted a similar dagger. In seconds, a solid object dropped to the snow. I grabbed the leather-wrapped hilt.

One of our companions cast aside his coat. His roar morphed into a growl. A gray-pelted wolf leaped from the Changeling's torn clothing. Another two of our companions also transformed. The first lunged for the throat of one of Cynbel's men, who didn't move more than a leg as the others fell upon him. Disemboweled.

The stench of gore hit me. I nearly retched.

A wolf yelped in pain. Another howl silenced when Cynbel's men countered, severing a werewolf head. A sword caught another of our cohort under the breast, and the creature tore at the guard's arm before it, too, went still.

I looked up in time to see the captain looming translucent in the starlight. Cold calculation in his onyx eyes.

Roger attacked, but his fists passed through the ethereal Fae, as if he grappled with a ghost. Cynbel retaliated by sweeping Roger's knees, dropping him to the ground, and throttling him with a vaporous hand. Roger tore at the crystalline fingers below his jaw, but he could grip nothing.

"You're lucky my King respects the Treaties, human," he hissed.

I leapt toward them, but Father grabbed me and held me back.

"Let him go!" I shouted with all my will. I didn't expect Cynbel to listen, but he did. Roger gasped. Two soldiers tied his arms behind his back.

Druk screamed. "A thousand curses on you, Cynbel! This was not our deal. None were to be harmed."

"I am already cursed." At his gesture, two more men emerged, training weapons on us.

"What treachery is this?" Father shouted. "I trusted you, Druk of clan Frostrock."

"They have my mate and my sons," Druk pleaded. "He will kill them if I don't cooperate. I had no choice."

One of the soldiers approached their captain, holding our ashes from Mother's tree.

"Excellent. You have the remains of the ritual." Cynbel opened the leather bag and emptied the contents onto the snow. A gust of wind scattered ashes across the winter landscape, out into the night.

"No!" Father cried.

Druk snarled, staring at the spilled ashes. "You go too far."

"One too many warnings from you, my Changeling friend, unless you want to see your family skinned for pelts." Cynbel pointed at my father. "This human is of no use to me. Kill him."

Roger, arms tied behind his back, began to cast a spell. Druk buckled forward with a horrible growl and transformed into a huge white bear, tearing his clothing. A guard raised a sword and swung at my father, but a pattern of radiant symbols materialized in the air, and a resounding note rang out as the weapon struck an invisible barrier. Roger's magic. Cynbel lunged toward where he sat, chanting. I screamed and leapt forward with my conjured knife, plunging the obsidian blade into Cynbel's gut.

My hand came back covered in blood so dark it was almost black.

Cynbel gripped the hilt of my summoned knife, clutching his midsection with the other hand. "Not... possible." The weapon crumbled into black dust. The Fae's obsidian eyes went wide in shock and disbelief. "What sorcery is this?"

"You will take all three of us alive!" I shouted. "I am a royal daughter of the Summer Courts. If your king wishes to bargain with me, I will not speak a word to him if you harm my father or Roger. This much I will swear."

With a bloody hand, I grabbed my paintbrush.

Cynbel sheathed his blade. "Lady, I do not think you understand the weight of an oath sworn in the realm of the Fae. It binds you in more ways than you intend. So be it. I will let His Majesty kill them for you."

Roger's eyes fluttered shut. He slumped to the ground.

Cynbel turned to Druk's bear form and, without preamble, reached into the Changeling's chest with his transparent hand. The bear screamed as the Fae pulled Druk's still-beating heart through skin and fur. He tossed the pulsing muscle into the snow, where it yielded up blood in steaming red rivulets.

The bear slumped to the ground beside the other two slain members of his pack.

I gasped in shock.

The big golden eyes closed, and the Changeling's lifeless body shrunk to once-human proportions, face down in a pool of his own blood.

"If you had given me the Changeling's name, I would have spared him too. Witness now the power of a word. Even unspoken."

The blood on Cynbel's transparent fingers blackened, smoked and blew away on the frigid wind, even as the wound in his gut oozed.

I could not speak.

He stretched his pale hand toward me. I had just witnessed what sort of weapon it was. "Give me the paintbrush, Lady. It does not belong to you."

The power I'd flexed with my earlier demands had proven to be illusion. I gave him the brush.

CHAPTER 24
LAST WORDS

A hospital bed. I blinked, but I didn't know where I was or why. I heard the droning of an engine, the crack of an electric diode. I smelled burning hair and flesh. Two rubber tubes were connected to my forearms, draining away my glowing life's blood.

A rag wet with sharp-smelling ether covered my nose.

I awoke to the sound of my door being unlocked. Startled from the dream, my heart pounded, and I gasped for breath. How long had I slept?

They'd brought us back to the palace on a sled pulled by wyverns—beautiful beasts with clipped wings and broken spirits. Cynbel's men had taken me to this posh, subterranean guest room for a prison cell, but they would not say where they took my father or Roger. I'd spent the first few hours fruitlessly looking for a means of escape, but I'd given in to exhaustion and watched through my room's submarine-like windows as an anglerfish lured unsuspecting prey. I fell asleep and dreamed of torture at Porter's hands.

Had it been a lost memory?

Two sword-wielding guards and two Changeling women entered the room. They answered none of my questions, and I had little recourse but to do as they commanded. The women bathed me in the adjacent washroom and dressed me in another impractical gown, but at least the boots were sturdy. Afterward, the guards blindfolded me and led us out through a maze of corridors until open space swallowed the echo of our footfalls. The air grew colder, and the stone floor too polished for this to be an exterior courtyard. It might have been the king's circular hall.

They bade me sit on the floor, my back against an outcropping of stone. My manacled hands were fastened to another chain. It was impossible for me to stand, though my legs were free. In this much, my captors were kinder than the nurses at St. Ivy's had been.

My eyes remained blindfolded, but I heard the guards march away.

"What is the meaning of this?"

No reply. I strained but could not break free. In the silence, more chains clanked against stone, a sound from only feet away. I froze to listen.

A moan of pain. "Where am I? Violet, are you there?"

I gasped in relief. "I'm here. Roger, are you hurt?"

"I'm fine. Now that you're with me."

"Is Father here?"

"No. They took him somewhere else."

I pulled at my chains, knowing they would not give any more than the stone at my back. "Do you think they mean to kill us?"

"They'll kill me. But you are too valuable. I know not why Arimos holds you here. Perhaps he means to intimidate you into doing his will."

"I am not so easily moved from my will." The words surprised me, but they were true. "If I'm so valuable to them, I will bargain for your life."

"No. I've lived long enough. Your life has only begun. Do not give away anything else for me, Violet."

"Roger, I've given you nothing I didn't want to give. Only my heart."

"You gave me your innocence. Something I had no right to take. I should've let you live out your days as a human, like your father intended. If you'd never set foot in the Otherworld, you would still be at home now. Safe. Mr. Morgen might have completed his quest. You'd never have been the wiser, if I had not interfered, out of my selfishness."

"Roger, that is nonsense. You opened my eyes to the truth of what I am. Helped me understand my fears so that I could conquer them. You showed me I have a power I never dreamed possible."

Roger didn't answer. Even in this vast space, I could hear snowfall. Icy wetness covered my arms. My manacled hands became numb. Tears filled my eyes.

"Is that not what we all do?" A low voice, coming from another direction. I recognized Arimos. "Trade innocence for power?"

A group approached us. My blindfold was pulled away. The Winter King stood before me wearing polished silver armor under a cloak of blue and black. Guards stood beside him dressed as Cynbel's men had been, though the captain was not among them. I couldn't see Roger, but now I knew where we were—chained to either side of the central stone in the throne room of the Winter Court hall.

"That is not the sum of his sins, dear Lady," said Arimos. "He will soon unburden the causes of his guilt. For he will be made to speak the truth at his trial."

"Let her go," said Roger. "She does not deserve such treatment."

"You presume to give me orders, human?"

"I only beg Your Majesty. She has done nothing wrong."

"Even in that, we cannot agree." Arimos stepped closer, ice-blue eyes gleaming under his frost-like eyebrows. I could now see what he held in his hand—my paintbrush. "Lady Violet is now an accomplice to your theft. Moreover, she used this stolen relic—*my gift*—to attack one of my most loyal servants."

"Your *loyal servant* killed three of our friends in cold blood!" I strained at my chains. "Roger had already given himself up before they attacked us."

Arimos looked toward his guards, as though he'd forgotten Cynbel was not among them. He said to me, "If this is true, my captain will answer for it, but I have reason enough to mistrust you."

"How dare you speak of trust when you have tortured us." I rattled my chains, sitting up as straight as possible in that painful position. "What have you done with my father?"

"He is alive, for the moment. It is not my wish to cause you distress, Lady of the Summer Courts. I am bound by the commandments of this universe, just as you are. The Courts mete out punishment for laws broken. Winter must always be an instrument of justice." Arimos turned his gaze up to the brilliant canopy of stars, revealing his elongated ears, usually hidden by his platinum braids. Not human, though so human-like; that same alien blood coursed through my own veins. "Your trial will begin when the moon is in view. Until then, contemplate your actions. You will drink the wine of truth to loosen your lips and your thoughts. Another gift to you, Lady."

I shivered. "Tell me what laws we have broken when my mother's tree belongs to me? Father and I asked Roger to help us. He did not act on his own accord. I cannot steal what is rightfully mine. You must release us!"

He snapped his fingers. Two guards approached, each holding a silver cup. One knelt before me and pulled my hair so that my head tilted upward. I tried to turn away, but I had no room to fight. They forced my jaw open and poured black liquid down my throat. Both bitter and sweet, its flavor was like wine laced with powerful herbs. When I didn't swallow, the guard shoved my mouth closed, covering my nose until I was forced to do so in order to draw air.

The King and his men left us alone.

"The Wine of Truth." I coughed on the sharp taste. "I suppose it must loosen our tongues."

"Yes." Roger heaved an exhale. "They made me drink the beastly stuff once before, when I was fifteen and brought before the Courts to be judged for my crimes. Though I had no reason to lie, then or now."

An arc of light illuminated one side of the massive oculus above the king's court hall, bringing into relief the zodiac symbols carved around the opening. From my vantage point, the rings of the armillary sphere drew a dark silhouette against stars beyond, veiled as they were by wisps of snow-bearing clouds.

"Violet, if these are to be my last words to you, I must unburden something."

"These are not our last words. Not by a longshot." Silence. I could sense his turmoil, even though I could not see his face. I had my own burning questions, but I wanted to hear what he said first. "All right, I'm listening."

"I was once an alienist, employed at St. Ivy's Institute for not many years, in the span of my long life. I had spoken to you so briefly; I didn't expect you'd recognize me when we met again. Moreover, my appearance was different back then—older—not a thing I could easily explain at first. Later, when I revealed to you what I am and what the Reliqua does, I should have been more forthright concerning this. Please forgive me."

"You tried to tell me on the airship."

"Yes."

"I recall some of it now. You were kind to me, after... I saw that apparition at my school." The Shadow which had risen from my blood on the broken glass—that voice which had beckoned me to walk through the mirror before I ran, but was taken to the hospital. The memory stung, because I couldn't recall enough of what Porter had done that time ten years ago—only that he'd used me for one of his experiments. But I remember now, someone had quite literally carried me out of that darkness into the light. "Roger, you took me out of that terrible place... You helped me get back home."

"You remember." A heavy sigh.

"Dr. Porter told me parts of what happened—showed me my hospital records. It helped bring back the rest. I think he... wanted to confuse my memory. In his eagerness to plant the seeds of mistrust in my mind, by proving you'd hidden something from me, Porter hoped I wouldn't recall what he himself had done."

"Dr. Porter. You mean Archibald Porter?"

"Yes."

"My traitorous assistant. When did you speak with him?"

"At St. Ivy's. Just days ago… I was an inmate again."

He must have heard the tremor in my voice.

"What? No! Why didn't you tell me sooner?"

"How could I? We've had far more pressing concerns."

"What happened?"

A disk of light breached the edge of the oculus, shining into the ancient hall. The moon. I recalled Porter's words. *Lunatic.* No, it was not the word, but the place. It was a different from the other memory. It was recent.

Porter stood in front of an outlandish machine, resembling a huge armillary sphere, strung with maniac wires. The moon shone above us through a cracked windowpane. The room was a ruin, like an abandoned house, stinking of death. A bright flash of white.

Lost in the memory, I had not answered him.

"My God, Violet. Tell me what happened. Did he hurt you again?"

"I don't know. Yes. I can't remember at least three whole days. Several more nights. Evelyn Crane is a nurse there. She said Porter extracts the blood of patients like me, as well as other Fae and Changelings he's abducted, to produce the drug Tears of the Moon. She said his electro-shock therapy treatments cause memory loss, so we all forget what he does to us." My voice cracked on those last words. *That's how I'd forgotten everything ten years ago.* It was more than just the trauma of it all.

"I sent you through that portal only to protect you. I would've gone with you, but I was captured." Chains rattled. "I swear, I'll kill him! If by some miracle I live past this day, I will hunt Porter down. I don't care what it costs me."

"No! Don't say that, Roger." I recalled Cynbel's words. *You don't know the weight of an oath sworn in the realm of the Fae.* "Tell me what happened between you and him ten years ago. A few of the memories came back to me recently—of my first time at St. Ivy's. I remember you confronted him, and he threatened you. Is that why you left?"

"I left because I had no choice. After I discovered what he'd done to you as well as other patients, I made a formal complaint to the hospital's board regarding Porter's ethics and demanded he be removed. But he had friends in high places, and he retaliated. He planted false evidence in my laboratory and accused me of causing the death of one of our patients; one which he himself had caused. To my colleagues, the accusation alone confirmed their fears and prejudice against me. They suspected me of practicing sorcery, because my work involved the sciences of mesmerism and herbalism. They were right in that. I used magic in my treatments, but I harmed no one. To them, I was nothing but a charlatan witch. By contrast, they viewed Porter's barbaric misuse of electricity as scientific daring. They forced me to resign and, to avoid dragging my family name into further scandal, I left the country, returning to a monastery where I'd once found solace. I remained there until only a few years ago when I came home to my dying father and… you know the rest."

Roger rattled his chains and shouted into the hall. "Do you hear me, Rulers of Aes Sídhe? You must grant me vengeance! My enemy has harmed the woman I love, a daughter of the Summer Courts. Release me. Let me kill him, as your honor code demands! Afterward, I will face your judgment."

His echoing shouts went unanswered. I squinted through a lens of unshed tears. The ambient light grew brighter. I looked up to see the black sky give way to red and orange. The shadows of the bronze sphere shifted and intensified, following a changing light source. Dawn approached in rapid time.

"How is this possible?" I asked.

"The Queen is here. She brings day with her into this world of night."

Clouds which might have borne snow transformed into veils of color in the Southern sky. An indigo night sky full of stars, crowned with a full moon, lay to the north—an impossible division in the heavens. A tableau I might only have seen in antique illustrations or engraved on a clock face. Here it was real—if this place were not just a fevered dream.

"Violet, promise me. If they grant you one request, may it be mercy for your own life. Your freedom. Not mine. Not even your father's."

"Roger Gale, are you so eager to throw away your own life? Do not forget what we fight for."

His chains rattled, but before he could answer, a bell rang through the hall. Doors opened in the four corners of the room. Through the Easternmost doorway marched uniformed soldiers. After them followed stately figures arrayed in bright red, gold, and orange. Flowers, jewels, and living foliage decorated skin of many hues.

When the procession approached the center of the hall, they turned clockwise, joining others entering from the four corners. Silently the Fae circled, some lingering farther out. Cynbel, dressed in indigo and black, led a group of the King's guard. The pale knight's face was half-translucent in the half-starlight sky, as if he were divided into one real and one unreal person—a mirror of the split heavens.

Others wearing green, scarlet, or amethyst joined the circle, until a spectrum of color, rendered in many patterns, surrounded us. As one, they stopped and turned toward the center of the hall, where Roger and I were chained.

One tall Fae, with ears like a rabbit's under a headdress of black silk, tapped her wooden staff on the resounding stone. She lifted an arm covered in tawny fur and said, "Let Winter approach in his Court. Let Spring, Summer, and Autumn attend."

In unison, they turned and faced the exterior of the room. I could not see the King's entrance, but through the far doors, a regal woman entered, followed by two figures wearing matching robes. One carried a golden banner emblazoned with a red lion, the other a white banner with a gold falcon. The leader's golden-orange gown shimmered in the light of her dawn, like iridescent butterfly wings, though she had no wings of her own. Her hair and eyes were dark, her skin bronzed from the sun, with features so like Mother's. She wore a crown of gilded and living flowers—roses, peonies, poppies, and sunflowers. She could be none other than the Queen.

The audience parted before her, and she took a seat in a golden throne to the Southwest. She only glanced my way, but I made eye contact. Did she recognize me as family?

Another Fae wore a vibrant crown of autumn foliage and layers of copper and green. Darker skinned than the Queen, he was also human in appearance, unlike so many in the crowd. He approached a bronze throne in the Northwest, followed by attendants wearing headdresses of a gibbous moon, and carrying the green banner of the stag. A woman wearing a tiara with one circular black jewel, like a new moon, stood near me, directly south. Another woman in a plum-colored gown wore a coronet of crystals and flowers; she took a seat on her throne of living quartz, beside attendants who wore the crescent moon and carried the banner of a gray wolf on black. The Winter King, wearing silver and a cloak of midnight sky, led an entourage which carried the banners of both a white unicorn on a field of violet and an indigo dragon on black. He must have taken the silver throne to the Northeast, but chained where I was, I could not see.

A bell chimed eight times. The rabbit-eared Fae tapped her staff on the stone and spoke. "Let the High Courts of Faerie now be unified in our purpose. Winter shall state the nature of his summons."

The hall became quiet. Only the wind whistled past the dome.

Boots tread the stone floor. Arimos swaggered into the center of the hall, radiant in his own aura. The Winter King glanced at me. Sadness pooled below the frozen surface of his eyes—was it for my chains, or for what would soon come to pass?

He turned and spoke to the crowd. "I have called us together, Kindred of the Four Winds, to decide the fate of these two before you and one other. What crimes they have committed on Otherworld soil are only an echo of trespasses they and their human families have made against the Courts. Bring out the third accused."

The crowd parted to the orderly marching of guards, as a group led in another manacled prisoner. He wore a white blindfold but did not appear harmed.

"Father!"

"You're here, Violet?" His voice sounded hale, giving me courage.

"We are."

"Silence." The guard beside me shoved the tip of a sword inches from my skin.

"Lord Arimos," said the Queen. "We will not suffer these two any further humiliation. Unchain them from the stone. They will stand before us in their Houses."

Four guards approached and unfastened my manacles, forcing me to rise on shaky legs to meet the half-phantom face of Captain Cynbel. He grabbed the chain between my wrists with his transparent hand and led me near the Queen's throne—the falcon banner—before he returned to stand beside Arimos. The Queen did not but glance at me. If this noble woman held any joy at meeting the child of her sister, I saw no sign.

I couldn't see Roger, but my father stood nearby.

The glint of gold at my feet proved to be another medallion set within the stone floor's mysterious concentric lines. The relic contained an amber-colored jewel—beautiful, but dull and without inner fire, just as all the others I could see.

"I demand an audience of the Reliqua." Arimos raised a hand. "We shall summon the High Council. Let them be a witness and a voice in these proceedings."

The Summer Queen stood. Autumn and Spring rose from their thrones in unison and approached the center of the room.

When Arimos took his own position in the Northeast, at last I could see Roger. He stood, surrounded by guards in front of the King's throne, beside the dragon banner. They had washed him and given him fresh clothes, but his face bore new bruises. The sight brought physical pain to my heart. He met my eyes before another two guards moved between us, blocking my view.

Around the central stone, the four rulers spread their arms toward one another. Arimos turned the outermost ring of the giant armillary sphere; he focused that same lens I'd touched only hours ago.

Autumn rolled the glass orb into position to catch the light. The Queen turned the large prism. I could not see the spectrum they cast on the top of that granite block, but I had done so myself yesterday, with less light.

They each drew a chain from around their necks and slipped rings from their fingers. I glimpsed brilliant jewels. The Queen's was vibrant orange and yellow. Arimos' ring shone violet-blue, and his pendant black. As one, they set these into the holes in the stone's face.

When the last piece clicked into place, the machine shimmered. Seven rays of the spectrum, with one invisible band in darkness, spilled like liquid light through carved channels, such as I had witnessed before at the Welterwood Circle. When the light reached the floor, it intensified. Arteries of color pulsed through stone canals, illuminating each jewel set into the snow-dusted stone—stars amid threads of nebulae. Around me gleamed golden orange, yellow to my right, red on my left, and so on until the jeweled spectrum circled the entire hall, like my painter's color wheel. Murmurs of admiration and wonder rippled through the crowd. Perhaps it was a rare event, even in this world, to see four High Court rulers gathered together.

Spring, with dun-colored fur on her delicate face, rotated another ring. Clockwork mechanisms inside the stone base whirred to life. The ring's revolutions sped up until it appeared as a spectral sphere. Light played over that illusory canvas, as if a hidden cinema camera cast a moving picture. Instead of flickering monochrome, these images flowed in muted color. Human men and women, dressed in clothing of many cultures, moved through an opulent room. A dark-skinned man with gray hair and beard, who wore a coat of vibrant geometric patterns over a black waistcoat, stepped closer to whatever device captured his image on that side of the world.

"Lord Chancellor," said Arimos to the sphere. "Greetings from the Winter Court."

"King Arimos." The man answered in a voice distorted by space and distance, like an old phonograph. "Queen Ariadne. Princess Selene. Prince Raymond it is an honor." He bowed. "We greet you from the Reliqua High Council. Suffice it to say, we are saddened by the nature of today's business."

A woman appeared in the projection. Evelyn. She wore a formal burgundy gown and a ceremonial sword hung from her waist.

"Are they alive?" Evelyn demanded. "What have you done with Roger and Violet?"

"House Crane," said the Lord Chancellor. "You will observe protocol." He turned again to the Queen. "Forgive our emotions, Your Majesty. The stakes of this trial are high."

"Be assured, Lord Chancellor," said the Queen, "the prisoners are safe, and we shall strive for the good and true verdict."

Autumn, named Raymond, spoke. "Winter shall read the formal accusations."

Arimos drew a scroll from his cloak but did not unroll it. "Before I begin, I wish to remind the Courts that over a century ago, the heir of House Gale illegally killed a unicorn, an insult to my throne and banner. Against my protests, this poacher was allowed to keep the alicorn, the bloody spoils of his crime."

"Winter," said the Queen. "We require no history lessons. Nor will I allow my rulings, past or present, to be questioned."

Arimos bowed his head only. "No doubt the judgment of this Court is wise and merciful, but perhaps humanity does not deserve our trust." The King pointed at Roger, "These *humans* have since debased that most pure of relics, and your benevolence, with their foul deeds. Even now, this *trophy* is being used not to heal, as was the Queen's directive, but to harm."

The Winter King unrolled the parchment and read. "The counts against these three are five. First, the human Errol Morgen did knowingly conspire with the Reliqua to steal a living tree from my sacred garden; Second, Roger of House Gale did cut down this very tree; Third, Lady Violet, in aiding the escape of my prisoner, did knowingly use illegal magic to attack my Captain of the Guard; Fourth…" Arimos looked up from his scroll, and moved closer to the holographic sphere before he continued, "Roger of House Gale did violate the terms of the Treaty by using the alicorn in his possession to develop an insidious potion which gives ordinary humans the ability to use Faecraft, at the cost of innocent Fae lives; and Fifth, the Reliqua itself is complicit in the aforementioned crimes, because they have profited from the illegal trade of this potion for years."

Arimos raised a hand in proclamation. "Therefore, by Treaty Law, we of the Winter Court must call for the execution of all three who stand before you."

CHAPTER 25
THE UNICORN'S MAGIC

xecution? The King was as cruel as his servant Cynbel.

Roger turned to the Queen but kept his eyes averted to the floor. "Your Majesty, Violet is innocent of any crimes. We only defended our lives."

"The human will remain silent out of turn," said Raymond.

"Please! No harm must come to her. She wouldn't even be here if it weren't for me."

"Another word and you will be removed from these proceedings." The King gestured to Cynbel, who marched forward with several other guards. They surrounded Roger with swords drawn.

"This is outrageous!" The disembodied voice of the Reliqua Lord Chancellor boomed through the spinning brass sphere. "You summoned us to witness the charges against one of our own, yet now the Reliqua itself is on trial? What proof have you of such allegations?"

Evelyn paced the floor in the holographic council room.

"Yes. Explain yourself, Lord Arimos," said Ariadne. "You called for this trial because a sacred tree was killed. I presume you have good reason for this insult against our human allies."

"I do, my Queen." Arimos gestured for one of his guards.

"We shall see." Ariadne turned to my blindfolded father and asked, loudly enough for the hall to hear, "Errol Morgen, you heard the formal charges read against you. How do you answer?"

My father began, "Your Majesty, I did conspire to fell Helena's tree, in order to complete her dying wishes. For many long years, I schemed how to carry out such an impossible task. It's true, I used this Tears of the Moon potion to get here, but I did not purchase it from Mr. Gale. In my desperation, I asked for Gale's help to cut down the tree. That much I regret, for he wouldn't be here on trial if he hadn't been arrested while I got away. Nor would my daughter be in jeopardy if she hadn't come looking for both of us. Have you no heart, Ariadne?" He gestured with chained hands. "I'm the only reason they are both here now. I'm the only one you should punish."

"Well said, Errol. Time has given you wisdom. I remember the arrogant pup who stood before me those many years ago, so sure of his right to defy our traditions in the name of love. Now you offer yourself to us willingly, do you?"

"I do. To spare my daughter and the man she loves. Please, will you let them go, Ariadne?"

"Their time for judgment is not yet at hand." The Queen turned to Roger. "Roger of House Gale, it is now your turn to answer the charges. Why did you cut down this tree, knowing it was forbidden?"

"Your Majesty. I felled the tree because we could not complete your sister's dying wishes without it. I studied the Treaty law regarding the inheritance of Faestones, and I believe Violet is the rightful owner. Having just escaped torture at the hands of King Arimos' soldiers, I had little reason to think I could negotiate with them for the tree, one they had been content to let wither and die rather than harvest as custom demands. Furthermore, I would do anything for the woman I love. I wanted her to have this gift from her mother. I saw helping her father as the only way to do so."

"I see." The Queen did not sound convinced, if it was not disappointment. "Pity you did not think to come to us first. The tree of an exile is doomed to wither, and its magic consigned to be reabsorbed back into the earth. Arimos was right in his actions. However, we did not know my sister had a daughter. I might have ruled in her favor."

"Forgive me, Your Majesty. Even if your laws cannot."

"How do you answer the second charge, House Gale?"

"I can assure the Courts, I have nothing to do with this potion, Tears of the Moon, nor its manufacture or trade. I've never used the alicorn for any untoward purpose. If others in my Order are involved in this scheme, I have no knowledge and cannot speak for them."

"He has drunk the wine of truth," said the Queen. "So, there can be no falsehood in his words. What evidence have you of this second charge, Arimos? Why was he tortured at your hands *prior to* felling this tree? Even as a prisoner, he is still my servant. The Treaty protects him."

"Gale was injured when he resisted his capture, but my men did not mistreat him."

The Queen's brow knit. "House Gale? What have you to say? What happened?"

"On the fifth day of Equinox Bridge, Lady Violet and I were aboard the airship Minerva when we were set upon by soldiers of both the Spring and the Winter Courts. I did not want her identity to be discovered, lest she be compelled to stay in this realm against her will. I opened a doorway to send her home, but before I could follow, I was detained by Winter Court soldiers. They took me aboard their airship, held me immobilized with the toxin of an Arawn spider, and tortured me. When we arrived in Wyvern's Rock, I escaped their custody. After that, I found Mr. Morgen, and we conspired to liberate her mother's tree from Arimos' garden."

"Liberate." Arimos laughed, but he turned to Cynbel. "So, you admit you hid lady Violet's identity from the Courts." He and the Queen exchanged a weighted glance. "Once you discovered the identity of her mother, you were required to inform us, which you did not. As to your allegations of torture, the truth is, you escaped after being interrogated by my trusted advisors. Justified it was, for they learned your true involvement in these crimes regarding the alicorn's misuse."

"That is false. They asked me nothing of the kind. They only—" Roger was silenced at sword-point.

Undaunted, Arimos raised his hand to address the crowd. "The Courts heard him confess to the Queen's niece, just moments ago, that when he was employed as an alienist in the human village of Seastone, he knew which patients, like her, had fairy blood. House Gale, how did you know which of your patients had fairy blood, and why did you seek this information?"

"I can usually detect it in auras. Failing that, a simple blood test, one I invented for this use. It allowed me to better understand and thus cure their ailments."

"The blood test was your own invention. Did you not then use that very science to develop a method of extracting Faelight from your patients? Yes or no."

"I... Yes." Roger sounded anxious, either from the questions, or because Cynbel and his elite guard stood by, threatening. "You must understand. My methods were harmless and effective; only used on the willing. Most were humans who had wandered or been stolen into Faerie, and having returned home, found their minds and senses altered in undesirable ways. Some, like Violet, had Fae ancestry and did not know how to cope with life in the human realm. In these patients, my treatments drained away their tormenting visions or voices, by removing the magic of Faerie from their auras. It did not help in all cases, but for many, my work was a blessing."

"Did you not resign when the death of one of your subjects was discovered?"

"I was not the cause of that death, but it's true I was blamed for it and forced to resign. I suspected my assistant, Dr. Archibald Porter, of framing me for the death he himself had caused, but I had no proof. Before I left, I burned every journal and destroyed every piece of equipment in my laboratory. I swore to take the secrets of my methods to the grave, and so I shall. Just as I have sworn to kill Porter for harming Violet. Release me. If Porter is the one behind this evil, I will stop him or die trying."

Arimos ignored his plea and gestured to the Fae standing near his silver throne. One of them stepped forward, carrying a domed tray.

The Winter King continued, "My sources tell me that Gale did not, in fact, destroy this work, but went on to devise a potion which grants humans temporary use of Faecraft, made from this very extracted magic. Whether he is involved in its present manufacture or not, he made it possible. To feed demand for this profitable drug, hundreds of Fae and Changelings are now slaughtered every year."

The soldier with the tray approached and bowed. A female soldier. I found that fact an odd comfort, even in this desperate state. The Winter King lifted the dome and took up a small glowing vial—a bottle identical to what I'd held just days ago.

"My men purchased this sample on the streets of the human village in Seastone. My sorcerers tested the potion and detected the presence of unicorn horn. No doubt added to make the extracted Fae blood more palatable to human consumption. The only recorded source of alicorn powder for hundreds of miles around that village is the reliquary of House Gale. Such facts must present as more than mere coincidence. Our law demands justice and swift retribution. We must destroy this contagion in the human realm before it spreads. House Gale must be stricken from our Treaty, and their lights removed from our sacred halls forever."

Murmurs and exclamations of surprise rippled through the crowd. All I could see was the memory of tubes attached to my arms—flowing through them was not blood, but light. Faelight. I had thought it a nightmare, but no, it was a memory—not even a delusion brought on by the drugs, or Porter's electro-shock therapy. His *special treatments*. But Roger was not involved in any of that. I was sure.

The Queen said, "The Summer Courts have also heard rumors from the human cities concerning this Tears of the Moon and its growing misuse among humans. You are not the only one with far-reaching eyes and ears, Lord Arimos."

"I meant no disrespect, my Queen. I only fear what this drug will do to the balance between our realms."

"I share your concerns, Winter. However, we've yet to determine this threat's origin. Do you have any tangible evidence linking House Gale to these crimes? So far, we have heard only circumstantial connections. Bring the vial to me."

My heart sank like a stone. I had seen evidence. The notes in a storeroom below where Porter held me prisoner. Yet Roger said he'd destroyed his research. What was I missing?

The Queen passed a hand over the bottle, and its hue turned from green to dark red. "There is much sorrow in this glass. Suffering." She clenched the glass in her fist and turned her golden-brown eyes once again upon Roger. "Winter is right in one thing—I sense the unicorn's magic within, be it only a trace."

"Did you give this Dr. Porter the alicorn in your possession?" Arimos demanded of Roger.

"No… However, I sold a few grams of the alicorn powder months ago. It's possible the man was working for Porter, though I had no reason to suspect him of wrongdoing. I didn't ask his name."

"No, of course not. For the price he paid, I am sure no names were required." His glacial eyes blazed.

"The man came to my apothecary, claiming his brother was dying from exposure to poison. I only sold him enough for a cure and didn't question the honesty of his motives."

"Hmph." The Winter King shook his head. "Did you sell or give anyone your method of extracting Faelight from living half-breeds? Perhaps in a similar fit of compassion?"

"No, Your Majesty. As I told you, I destroyed all that work."

The Queen asked, "Could this Dr. Porter have stolen your work without your knowledge, when you were colleagues?"

Roger was silent for a moment before he answered. "I don't see how, Your Majesty. I warded my laboratory. Sealed every journal and logbook with a Babylon cypher. If anyone had entered the rooms and opened my files, they would've seen only unintelligible scribbles. Only a powerful wizard could break those protections. Dr. Porter was nothing of the kind."

"Perhaps Dr. Porter had help." The voice came not from inside the Winter Court hall, but stretched thin and distorted across the vastness of space. Evelyn.

"Please elaborate, House Crane," said the Queen.

"Lords and Ladies of the Sídhe. Your Majesties." Evelyn bowed. I envied her strength and commanding presence. "This Reliqua Council has undertaken its own investigations into the matter of this Tears of the Moon, since we noticed an alarming uptick in incidents involving the unskilled use of Faecraft. We have since discovered the source of the drug's production.

"For the past several months, I've been employed as a nurse at St. Ivy's Asylum. My goal has been to gain intelligence for the Reliqua on the activities of Dr. Porter, as well as any connection with his former mentor, Roger of House Gale. Recently, I've had the help of Septimus, a Changeling of Clan Greenrock, also employed there, himself having followed a shipment of stolen Fae and Changelings delivered into Porter's hands not months ago. We've found crates of the drug in storage below the hospital. We've seen documents concerning its manufacture, but have not yet been able to enter the compound where it's produced and where the Otherworld prisoners are held. Only a few of Porter's staff are allowed access. Septimus had just been granted clearance two days ago. I've not had communication with him since—a fact which greatly concerns me."

Evelyn looked at the floor, hands clasped behind her back, before she continued, "I can also testify as to what I have *not* found. I've seen no proof that House Gale is involved in Porter's current operations. However, it appears not all of Gale's old work was destroyed. I found a few notes and diagrams, seeming to describe the extraction of Faelight from living patients, written by Dr. Gale over ten years ago. Also, I've found hints at a larger picture. Lady Violet can testify of a certain antique Reliqua cabinet kept in Porter's archives, which contained, until days ago when she helped me retrieve it, a portal stone long considered lost. She used this very relic to travel to your world."

"Lord Arimos, do you have this relic?" asked the Queen.

The Winter King gestured to Cynbel, who broke ranks with his fellow soldiers and left the hall.

Evelyn proceeded with her account. "In hospital storage rooms, I've found a growing collection of occult antiques—grimoires and spell books, wands and talismans, a few bearing the marks of extinct Reliqua Houses. I've witnessed the delivery of such crates to Porter's offices. He's on a quest to acquire anything related to Faecraft."

The half-ghostly knight returned, bowed to his master, and offered the medallion to the Winter King.

Arimos lifted it up. The jewel now glowed as it had done in my hands under moonlight, if not brighter blue. He said, "The Reliqua has demonstrated only that they cannot police the illegal use of their own relics. Their corruption and negligence are more widespread than we feared." He stormed past me toward Ariadne's throne, bowed, and offered her the medallion.

The Queen inspected the jewel, which took on a more turquoise-gold hue in her hands than it had in Winter's.

"House Zuria. Lost but not forgotten." She closed her eyes, as if communing for a moment with the stone, before she said, "Have you anything else to tell us, House Crane?"

"Yes, Your Majesty. I've detected active magic in various places on the hospital's grounds. Wards. Energy vortexes. Presences. Porter himself has shown little inherent magical ability, so we reasoned he must be working with a skilled accomplice or an Otherworld ally. No doubt he also consumes the drug he manufactures, in order to work Faecraft. I've encountered a shadow entity there more than once. Possibly a Shade. The morning after Violet escaped, I nearly captured it using a basilisk's eye, but it eluded me and fled the institute's grounds."

"If it is a Shade," Arimos said, "this only proves human magic and deception is at work here. No doubt the doing of House Gale. You yourself admitted Gale's old research still exists. Therefore, he lied to this Court about destroying it."

"A Shade?" I asked, my heart sinking like a stone. "What does that mean?"

"The creation of black magic," Arimos answered. "Necromancy. A violation of the Treaty. Shades are the souls of the dead become puppets, conjured within a shadow, and bound to serve the whims of their dark masters." The King glared at Roger, who could not answer for the sword tip leveled at his chest.

"No, Your Majesties," I shouted over the murmur of the crowd. "It wasn't Roger." *It couldn't have been.* "I too saw this evidence that House Crane has explained, but those documents were not in Roger's handwriting. Someone must have stolen and copied his work. Listen, I can testify that it's Dr. Porter who is harming people. I was his victim, and I escaped. Others weren't so lucky." I remembered the man who had stared at me in Commons. We carted out his dead body the next day. His glare had felt peculiar. Did he have fairy blood? An instinct told me he wasn't the only one.

"Lady Violet will remain silent until she is called upon," said one of Selene's attendants, who wore a lunar headdress.

"I cannot!" I straightened, despite the weight of my chains. A sharp pain tore through my back, but quickly subsided. The audience gasped and murmured. I faced the Queen, trembling fists balled to steady my purpose. "Your Majesty, King Arimos promised me I could testify on their behalf."

The Queen didn't speak, but she raised a hand to halt the advance of Arimos. I did not realize he had approached me until I turned to follow her gaze. A bluish glow reflected within the King's polished armor as he drew near. The glow emanated from my skin, as it had done only once or twice before.

I glanced over my trembling shoulder and beheld two arcs of purple light. Wings.

Like a refraction through water, they were ephemeral membranes of light. Faelight. Brightest in the center of each veined wing, this arc of color was not the complete spectrum—only blue through to darkest Violet.

My new awareness of them ached. A limb long asleep for lack of circulation. I flexed a muscle I'd never yet used, awakening a surge of power through every nerve. Weightless, I rose from the ground, but my chains held me low.

Roger gazed upward at me, transfixed. His love radiated to me, as if I were a flower turned toward the sun.

My father could not see, his head still covered with the white cloth.

In the crowd, someone laughed. Cynbel.

Arimos reached out and grabbed one of my chains. He dragged me back down, buoyant as a balloon. My weightless feet touched cold stone.

"Truly, you are Ariadne's kin, if even your diluted blood will emote such a hue. Now, dear Fae, there is no way for you to return to the human realm. You have become one of us. Before the stars move another degree," Arimos glanced to the open oculus above us, half night and half-day. "You will complete this transformation."

"What?" Both my father and I yelled at the same time. He added, "What has happened to my daughter? Are you all right, Violet?"

"She's grown wings," said Roger, with sadness behind the wonder in his words.

"Oh, no!" Father shook his covered head. "Then it's too late. I blame you for this, Gale. You should never have allowed her to come here. Surely…. she wasn't prepared. She didn't know the risks."

The Fae wearing the new moon crest gestured to the guards, who in turn placed the tip of a sword into my father's shoulder. I prayed it was merely enough to intimidate.

"I knew the risks." I pulled my chain from Arimos' grasp and faced the Queen. "But I can't stay here, Your Majesty. You don't understand."

"The magic of the Courts is ancient, my niece. You stand upon sacred ground. The Faestones within this ancient hall, imbued with the power of your ancestors, have quickened your blood. You must now live here as one of us, as you should have all your life, if your family had not hidden you from us. You cannot go back."

Glancing at my fellow prisoners, I said, "I only came here to save them. Let me testify on their behalf. Please."

"First," said the Queen, "you must answer the charges presented against you. Did you use the summoning brush's magic to attack the King's Captain of the Guard?"

"Yes." I faced the Summer Queen in her glory, under the divided sky. "I did so only in self-defense. Cynbel's men attacked us without provocation. Roger had given himself up with no fight. Cynbel slayed my comrades in cold blood."

"I see." The Queen turned to the King's guard. "Captain Cynbel, is this true?"

"No, Your Majesty. If she speaks what she thinks is the truth, it is only because her memories are confused or ill-informed. My master's orders were to apprehend the fugitives and capture your niece alive. We were met with resistance. I countered with necessary force. Regrettably, lives were lost." The pale knight clenched his fists—one solid and one translucent, reflecting starlight like glass. One eye appeared as flesh and blood and the other an ethereal mist. Even half of his white locks were clear—like the tentacles of a jellyfish.

"If you don't believe my words," I said, "look into my mind—my past. If such a thing is possible, surely it is for the Lords and Ladies of the Sídhe. I offer my memories to you, if it will show you the truth."

"Lady Violet has already admitted to this Court," Arimos gestured to the crowd, "that she cannot fully remember her last several days. Therefore, she offers no evidence that it was not Gale himself who perpetrated these crimes in the moments she has forgotten."

"So... I must recall those missing days. They will prove our innocence." I turned to the queen and asked, "Can such a thing be done?" I might not want to know what I'd forgotten, but I trusted my heart wouldn't lie.

"It can," said the Queen. "Although not easily. The process will drain your physical strength, and you may experience pain and shock, especially if you've forgotten what you have to protect your psyche. Nor can we see what you did not. If you were unconscious during that time, this effort will do little good. Do you understand?"

"I do. I will allow it." But my heart thudded with a sickly weight.

The Queen's eyebrows knit in concern, before she regained her mask of regal passivity, and raised a hand. "I will need a powerful telepath to begin the link. Lord Arimos, are you willing to assist?"

"Yes, my Queen." Arimos stepped forward and bowed.

"The King is to read my thoughts?" I asked, perplexed. "Surely he won't speak the truth of what he sees, if it suits not his purpose. Not moments ago, he called for my execution." My new wings itched to take flight.

"You will not speak so of my master!" Cynbel interjected. "This is pointless. She will not cooperate. This effort will be a waste of time. The human is guilty and must pay."

"And *you* speak out of turn, my servant."

The ire the King had shown his captain melted to a surprising kindness, if not pity, when he turned to me. "You have nothing to fear from me, daughter of Helena." He lifted an open hand, as if swearing an oath, or sensing vibration.

"I am guilty." Roger raised his voice. "I confessed to felling the tree. This alone will convict me. There's no need for this invasion of Violet's mind. I beg Your Majesty. Spare her this pain and indignity."

"Her testimony may exonerate House Gale," said Ariadne. "Your family's star on our map may continue to shine," she gestured to the jewels in the floor.

"You will still execute me."

"Perhaps."

"Roger," I said to him, "it will prove your innocence."

"You don't need to do this, Violet. Not for me."

"Don't you understand? I need to remember what happened."

His only reply was a nod, but his sorrowful eyes stayed locked with mine.

The queen turned to me. "My niece, one member of each Court will witness your memories, myself included, as well as Roger Gale, since he stands accused. You need fear no deception from Lord Arimos. Though there are risks. Is this acceptable to you?"

"Yes." I swallowed.

"Let us proceed." The Queen gestured for one of her attendants. "Bring a seeing bowl. House Gale will join us here."

They poured water into a leaf-shaped bowl and set it before me. Arimos waved a hand, and the liquid froze. The four rulers of the Fae Courts encircled me, and I dared not meet Roger's eyes when they brought him close, for fear of losing my resolve. Motionless, we stared into the mirror of ice.

I waited for an eternity of mere seconds before Arimos touched my forehead, drawing my attention like a lightning rod. His inhuman eyes held mine. I swam in those aqua-black depths, aware part of my consciousness was being peeled back, like a shedding skin. Someone placed my left hand atop the bowl of ice. I must have fluttered my wings, for a breeze rustled my hair.

My eyes became heavy. Physical awareness compressed. Space warped and collapsed, like I'd dived into deep ocean.

I was only distantly aware of someone shouting out my name.

A name I did not recognize...

CHAPTER 26
THE PROMISE

 cat howled. Hissed.

Sand gritted in my mouth. Water in my nose. Tumbled rocks, slick with oil and dirt, slipped through my fingers. I coughed up sea water and inhaled the odor of fish and sea trash. It was night, and my eyes couldn't focus on the dark shore.

How much time had passed?

I remembered jumping from the airship into the gateway spell. The mermaids. Scrambling up to a rocky jetty. Maggie chasing them away. Then a rock struck my head.

This was only a memory, a place in my past, yet the pain was no less real as I recalled a man's boot connecting with my thigh.

"You alive, wench?" Laughter and a wheezing cough.

The cat screamed.

The man kicked at the water and whistled. "Scat, beastie! Before I drown ye."

I floundered in the muck and sand. A wave crested the rocks. Seawater lapped my wet clothing, running into my nostrils.

More laughter in an age-cracked voice. "Your lucky day, eh? Least you ain't dead!" He kicked me again, this time in the shoulder. "Not yet."

My vision blurred. The world was red. My eyelids seemed sticky.

A shout, followed by a gunshot.

The man above me cursed. Cataract-covered eyes glinted in the gaslight from the docks. It was the old fisherman who lurked by Roger's shop, but his shadow on the water was *wrong*.

"Get away from her. Don't make me aim this time." The voice of a woman grew louder as she approached.

"Just offering to help the lady, ma'am. Weren't me that did it. Found her this way." His shadow stretched. Twitched.

"Then unfind her!" The woman chambered another round.

A wash of sensations enveloped me. I was lying on a folded blanket, staring into a small hearth fire. Wet, shivering. Wrapped in a quilt.

I turned my head, and the pain nearly split me in two. My back felt like it had been hit with a hammer in a few places. I struggled to assess my surroundings.

Feathers peeked out from patterned cardboard boxes. Hats and fascinators topped head-shaped display forms. Veils draped beside stacks of gloves. Baskets of ribbon, lace laden shelves, and bolts of wool. This had to be Mrs. Tremble's millinery.

Footfalls sounded on the wooden floor. "I've found some dry clothes might fit you." A woman's voice. "Let's see if we can get you cleaned up before the doctor comes to have a look."

"What… what happened to me?"

"I'm afraid I can't say. My name is Constance Tremble. You're in my shop on Harbor Street. I was closing up tonight and heard the commotion by the docks—frightened away the riffraff who must have hurt you. You need a doctor, so I called one. He's on his way now."

"A doctor?" I tried to move to get a better look at her, but the pain in my back would not permit.

"More important your wounds are looked after first, dear." She sighed. "I know who you are, Miss Morgen. The missing girl the whole town's looking for. You and that no-good apothecary who took you. If I called the lawmen first, there's no telling how long you'd wait before you saw a proper physician." She frowned. "Truth is, I would have done the same, even if your doctor didn't ask me to call him straight away if you were found."

A knock at what sounded like a glass-paneled door.

"Dear me, that was fast."

She left the room. I shifted again, despite the pain, and touched the ruffled silk at my neck, drawing back fingers wet with seawater. I still wore the blouse and trousers which once belonged to Roger's sister, Felicity.

The flood of memories wrenched me forward through time's currents. They strapped me to a gurney inside a moving vehicle. No, I was rolling, supine and immobile, through a long hallway. Iron everywhere! The metal burned my blood and bones. A man leaned over me to study my face. Porter. I tried to cry out, but I could not form a word.

Beside him in this memory walked a familiar orderly with a sickening leer. Philips. His shadow moved erratically on the tile wall behind him, like it had a life of its own.

Now I was lying in an opulent room on a velvet chaise. Philips tied a rubber cord around my arm before he took up an empty syringe. Dr. Porter faced a tall mirror. He grasped a silver pendant he wore, chanting as his fingers stroked the metal. A face appeared in the mirror. A face without features. My Shadow. That wretched void of light morphed into Cynbel's pale face, void eyes searching mine.

She's the one, it said.

The room blurred. I glimpsed a vial of my own red blood in the orderly's hand.

I clawed through darkness, trying to wake up.

I opened my eyes, and Arimos removed his hand from my face. I had only a second to fear Winter truly was that cruel, before I saw the concern and question in his eyes. He spoke my name aloud.

"I'm all right." I answered, finding my balance on shaky legs.

Arimos exhaled and turned to face his soldiers. "Guards, seize that Fae." He pointed at Cynbel, his eyes flashing bright blue. "This man is no longer your captain. He is a traitor to the Courts."

Cynbel ran, scattering the astonished crowd. Five soldiers broke formation to advance on their former captain.

Arimos shouted three magic words, and wind wailed past the oculus. Snowflakes tore from their roof side moorings, loosed in whistling torrents. A bank of heavy cloud moved through the divided heavens, veiling both night and day. Cynbel reached into the night with his transparent arm, grabbed the light of a star before it was shrouded, his form absorbing the starlight as he disappeared into the shadow of an ancient standing stone.

The Winter King closed his eyes, and when he opened them, the glow was gone. "I could not cover the stars fast enough. They are the source of his power."

When only torchlight remained, and the machine's lenses and crystals dulled, the hologram of the Reliqua council hall ghosted away.

Arimos' guards surrounded the standing stone. One of them shouted, "He's vanished, Your Majesty!"

"There's your traitor," said Roger. "Cynbel is Porter's accomplice. He must also be the Shade."

"In this much, we agree, House Gale," said the Queen. "Cynbel must be dealt with. But where has he gone?"

Arimos paced, aglow with his rage, like lightning in a summer storm. "Find him! He will be rent asunder by four wyverns!"

"Your Majesties," said Roger, "I know little about their kind, for I have never worked such necromancy. But I have read that a Shade can attach itself to a living host, as a shadow, in order to journey through the human realm, unhindered by the constraints of the celestial clock, as are most of us. They can slip through the Divide at any point shared by both worlds. Like that standing stone, which must have a counterpart in the human realm."

"It does." Arimos shook his head. "The thought crossed my mind. But how can Cynbel be a Shade?" He glared at Roger, mistrustful. "I have never encountered one with so many abilities. With a mind of its own. I did not know what kind of Fae my captain was, because... he claimed he had arrived in my country with no memory of his past life."

The Queen asked, "This man we saw with you, Violet. Was this Dr. Porter?"

"Yes, and the other is an orderly named Philips."

"I recognized Philips," said Roger. "He's the one I sold the alicorn powder to those months ago. I'm sure of it." His eyes sought mine, and I knew what he was thinking. *Tell them about your Shadow.* But I could not speak the words. Not yet.

"So let it be written in the records. We have seen evidence that Porter is controlling the Shade, Cynbel, who is a traitor to the Crown of Winter. Porter and his operations in creating this drug must be stopped. Cynbel must be brought to reckoning."

"Let me stop them for you," said Roger. "I swear I will see it done or die trying."

"You are still guilty, insubordinate human, by your own confession," said Arimos. "Treaty law must be satisfied. You cannot escape justice any longer."

"I await your verdict."

My father shouted from across the hall. "Ariadne, if you want to execute anyone for cutting down that tree, it should be me! It was my bloody idea. I took the first swing of the axe. But I got away and Gale didn't. I can't let this travesty continue." In a flash of movement, Father's chains hit the stone floor, and he pulled off the blindfold. Unshackled, he walked to stand before the Queen, amidst murmurs of shock from the crowd.

"How dare this profane human uncover his eyes in the Queen's presence!" shouted the Fae with the new moon headdress.

"This is sacrilege!" Another shouted.

"You called me brother once, Ariadne." He knelt before the Queen. "Or have you forgotten you gave your blessing to your sister's wedding? Even though you made her an exile."

"I forget nothing, Errol. Your impudence knows no bounds. I gave my blessing out of respect for my sister. I could just as easily have killed you for breaking our laws."

"Please, Ariadne. I implore you, spare the man my daughter loves. Take my life if you must, for I'm the only one to blame." Father knelt and bowed his head.

"Your Majesty," I said. "Helena was my mother. I have more claim to her tree than anyone else in this hall. My father and Roger only sought to return what belongs to me and my family. Yet it was the Shade who destroyed what we sacrificed so much to gain. We lost Helena's Faestone because Cynbel took the tree's ashes from us and spilled them into the wind."

"He did not tell me this," said Arimos. "I am sorry, Lady Violet, that I allowed such treachery to lurk under my watch."

"The grimoire," Roger spoke quietly at first, as though he were piecing something together. "When Cynbel captured me in the garden, he took a grimoire from us, one detailing the alchemical process for creating Faestones. Lord Arimos, did he surrender this to you?"

Arimos shook his head. "He did not. Nor did he tell me anything about such a grimoire."

"Then Cynbel, or Porter, must have a purpose for it yet. Perhaps he kept the heart of the tree, though he spilled the ashes. I could not tell."

"Whatever their plan. They must not succeed." Ariadne struck the end of her staff on the stone floor four times and raised a hand to silence the murmuring crowd. "We have reached a verdict. We have no proof House Gale is involved in these murders or the manufacture of this drug, and we find Lady Violet to be the rightful heir of her mother's tree, despite the subversive manner in which she sought to obtain it from us. Thus, our judgment is rendered. It is the will of the Courts. The lives of these three will be spared."

"Thank you, my Queen." Roger, chains rattling, knelt and bowed his head, and I followed suit.

Arimos walked to the armillary machine—silent and unmoving under the clouded sky.

"Errol Morgen," said the Queen. "You are a Changeling now. Even I cannot know how long you will remain in human form. You, who were once my sister's mate, may stay in the Summer Courts as a guest of my banner if you so choose."

Father bowed low. "I am forever grateful, Ariadne."

Ariadne continued, "Roger of House Gale, we have spared your life again on one condition. You must continue to fight for us. Your House must defend the sacred balance between our realms. First, you must stop these crimes perpetrated by your onetime colleague, Dr. Porter, as you have already sworn. You will destroy this threat by whatever means necessary."

"Yes, my Queen." Roger bowed his head and clenched shut his eyes. He and I could not be together if he could not leave the Reliqua.

"Furthermore. I will open a star portal and set protections on you such as I am able, so that you may return immediately. House Gale will once again be welcome at my stone circle, for you will need all its power to complete this quest, if you survive the crossing."

Grim but determined, Roger nodded.

"I must go with him, Your Majesty," I said, "To vanquish the Shade. I alone injured him before."

I had not noticed my wings had lifted me off the ground until my perspective changed. With a rush of air against my skin, I rose higher.

"I am sorry, but you cannot," said the Queen.

"Please, Your Majesty. I'm not afraid. I know this enemy. I must help those still in danger."

"My niece, I do not question of your bravery. No doubt you would fight with courage, but now you are transformed," she gestured with a graceful arm toward the wings holding me aloft. "Aside from our holy days, you cannot leave Faerie for longer than one moon's cycle per year, or you will perish."

"This can't be. I don't belong here. I must return… to my real life. To my home."

"I am sorry, but that life is finished. You belong in this world now, as you always did, had your parents not hidden you from us."

"Then make me human. Exile me, as you did my mother."

A murmur of surprise passed through the room.

"You know not what you ask, my niece. Exile will sever your link to Faerie forever. It will also affect your human side in ways we cannot understand until too late."

"I belong in the human realm. I want to be with the man I love. I want the life I left behind. I choose to be human." My boots touched the ground again. "More than that, I *know* Roger needs my help to stop the Shade. He can't do it alone. You must let me return."

"Lady Violet," said Arimos, approaching me, "You are not yet strong enough to face such an enemy. So much of your magic is yet to awaken. Would you trade a life of centuries in the royal Courts of your birthright, for an inferior mortal existence? One that could end in so swift a battle?"

"Yes." I only glanced at Father. He'd heard similar words from my mother long ago.

"If you return to the human world," said the Queen, "your powers will fade by the next new moon, in only three days. Before this time, you must either return to our realm, or sever the link with your sacred tree. If you do neither you will die. I echo Lord Arimos' concerns, my niece. I fear overcoming this enemy may be beyond your fledgling strength."

"Roger, I love you. I want to fight alongside you. Whatever the costs. Don't you want the same?"

"No." He wouldn't face me, but turned to the Queen. "I will not let her destroy herself for me. I cannot allow her to risk her life for my battle. Your Majesty, I must kill Porter and stop Cynbel alone."

"Come here to me, both of you." The Queen gestured to the guards. "Remove their chains."

With that weight removed, my wings made my body so buoyant my feet left the ground with every step. What would it be like to fly? If my wish was granted, I might never know.

We stood before the Queen. She beckoned to me. I stepped closer and bowed my head. She whispered to me, "My niece, I am glad to meet you at last." She leaned forward and touched my forehead. Warmth spread from her fingers to my injury. She brushed away the now-loosened stitches, and my skin was whole.

"Thank you," I said, my eyes pooling with tears. I stepped back beside Roger and took his hand.

The Queen beckoned Roger to draw near. She touched the side of his face with glowing fingers, and his cuts and bruises healed. Roger bowed and whispered his thanks.

"What is love but a heart at risk of losing what we hold so dear?" she said. "Even the most powerful of the Aes Sídhe can fall in battle. Answer me, House Gale. Would you still love my niece if she were merely human? Or have you sought this union because her power would strengthen your own magic?"

"I will always love her, regardless of who we become, or where we are in the two worlds."

Every word spoken here was true.

The Queen nodded and turned to me. "Lady Violet, you need not give up your powers for love. You can still be with your human a few days each year, for the many centuries you both shall live. Would that not be enough?"

"No, Your Majesty. And this battle cannot be won without me. I can't explain it, but the Shade and I are connected. We've always been. I don't know why, but he has haunted my nightmares, my waking terrors, for as long as I can remember. I alone wounded him when he attacked us here. You must let me return, or Roger will be defeated, and this evil will persist."

The Queen closed her eyes, though she remained attentive, as though she viewed a scene far away.

Roger gazed at me with both longing and loss. I took his hand.

"So be it," said the Queen. "There is indeed old magic at work here. You are connected to the Shade, though I cannot yet name how. Gale, she is right. She must go into battle with you." The Queen paused, meeting Roger's eyes, then mine. "There is a way both of you can become stronger for this task. I cannot require it of you, but I offer it for your own choosing."

"How?" I asked.

"A bonding. A blending of your magic through an oath of love. Not unlike a marriage in the human world, or a handfasting, though they are not the same. It will strengthen each of you, for these precious few hours before the moon wanes. It could help you win this fight."

"I will. Yes." I did not hesitate. My heart leapt in my chest.

"And you, Gale?"

"Yes. I will." He spoke above a whisper. Tears stained his cheeks, and he squeezed my hand.

At the queen's gesture, a girl dressed in leaves and yellow feathers approached and wrapped a green silk ribbon around our joined hands, from my forearm and around my wrist to Roger's. Tendrils of power entwined us, uniting my energy with his, filling me with desire. For him. For life.

Yet a grim task had united us now. I steadied my heartbeat with a purposeful breath.

The Queen spoke with raised hands. "These words spoken by Roger of Reliqua House Gale and Lady Violet of the Faerie Summer Courts, together in this ancient hall, heard by the living and the dead, shall not be forgotten. The promise of love and loyalty to each other is given, even as they are both willing to sacrifice for the other, so they will be called to do time and again. I give you my blessing and this gift. May your life together be filled with purpose."

Roger laced his fingers through mine. Had we given our wedding vows? *A word spoken in the realm of the Fae*, indeed.

Surely there was still time enough for a proper engagement on the human side of the universe. One had to plan for such things. When one wasn't trying to rescue loved ones from execution.

"You must seal this oath with a kiss," The Queen smiled.

When I turned my face to Roger's, the rest of the room, the crowd, the looming threat of our task, all disappeared. I kissed him, a little more chastely than before. His warmth and love radiated in return. A magic passed between us, lips to hands to beating hearts, as full of life and purpose as the discovery of a new world. I would have stayed in that moment with him for a thousand years.

The Queen turned her gaze from us to Arimos. "King of Winter, is it not customary for the Courts to bestow gifts at such an auspicious occasion?"

"It is, my Queen."

"These two are heading into battle. I can see nothing more fitting to give my niece than the silver summoning brush which once wounded her enemy. Before her magic fades, Lady Violet may need its powers once more. As for House Gale, return his ring, as it was long ago granted to him in this very hall when he was first pledged to our service."

"Done." Arimos gestured to his attendants. Two bowed and left the room, likely heading to Arimos' treasury.

The Winter King, regal and luminous, approached us, though his eyes held sadness. "You must kill the Shade or banish him to this realm and I will kill him, for I, bearing up the magic of Winter, cannot leave Faerie. Beware his power." He drew from his cloak the same necklace Roger had once given me. "Here lady, I believe this also belongs to you." He placed it in the palm of my hand. "These crystals grow in my kingdom. Deep in the earth, their power is a living heart of our land. An ancestor of House Gale crafted this talisman here long ago. Fitting it should have come to you now." He glanced at Roger with ice in his unfathomable eyes.

"Thank you, Lord Arimos." We both bowed.

The Queen spoke to me. "Before the next new moon rises in three days, you must perform the rite which will break your link with this world, or you will perish on human soil. You must bury two nails of iron and two coins of silver around your own sacred tree—the source of your magic. Afterward, you will be human for the remainder of your mortal days. Once done, it can never be undone. Do you understand?"

"My tree... But I don't know where it grows."

"Surely you do. Every Fae must sense her tree."

"How can I find it?"

"I know where it is. I will tell my daughter." Father couldn't hide his sorrow. "My Queen, may I converse privately with her?"

"You may." She turned to me. "Now is the time to say your goodbyes, before you must leave this world forever."

I nodded. Words seemed useless.

"We will open a star portal," she said, "to send the two of you home. Violet, you must protect your human mate, for outside of an Equinox Bridge, the journey between worlds is perilous to their kind. Now we must prepare. You have but a few minutes." She struck a spherical stone against a wooden block, like a gavel.

The rest of the crowd murmured as in recess. Roger stepped away to give my father and me privacy, such as at was in the center of the crowded hall.

My father drew closer and took my hands, speaking quietly. "When your mother was exiled, she was allowed to take with her a few rowan berries from her own tree. We tried for more than a hundred years to have children. I'd given up, but still she kept them. When you came to us at last, one seed sprouted. Your mother didn't know where to plant it. She could not return to Faerie to give birth, as custom would normally have it. So important a choice could not be made lightly. The answer came to her in a dream. We moved to a quiet village near the Queen's Welterwood and located the field of sleeping violets beside a stream that she'd been shown. It was the elder Mr. Gale who helped us set protection spells and bury talismans around the young sapling, and he swore to guard our secret." Father glanced at Roger, then back to me. "We used to take you there for picnics when you were small. Do you remember?"

"I remember. Then it's…" *The same rowan tree I've painted so many times*, I wanted to say, but Father placed a finger near his lips. Many ears were listening.

"When you find that place, your tree will call to you. It always did. Forgive me, Violet. I wanted you to be human so badly, but I never wanted you to sacrifice so much."

"I've already forgiven you, Father."

He wiped a tear from his face. "I'm sorrowful that we lost the final gift your Mother meant for you to have."

I wanted to say it was fine, but that wasn't true. I could never understand his loss, because I had only just begun to know love.

"You have much wisdom, my daughter. You will succeed." He kissed my forehead.

"Thank you." I hugged him, wishing it could last forever.

He took my hands. "Make me one more promise. Tend to your mother's garden. Even if you sell the house, please see it's cared for. Visit every year on her birthday, if you possibly can."

"I will."

After a farewell embrace, the Queen beckoned to me.

"Lord Arimos," said she, "It is time."

"The stars are agreeable."

Roger and I were led to the machine where we had been chained, now facing one another. Arimos gave me the silver-handled brush and returned Roger's ring.

"Roger, heir of House Gale," said the Queen. "A true heart beats within you, though it has long been lost in darkness, and it often cannot see past its own rebellious nature. Now mercy is granted to you yet again. Do not let us down."

He bowed. "I will serve you with honor, my Queen, and I will protect Violet with my life."

She turned to me. "Trust who you are, my niece. Your strength will not fail you."

"Thank you." I also bowed. I wanted to spend more time with her; Ariadne, my mother's sister. But now I could never return to this place.

Roger took my hands. He was anxious, a rare emotion to read on his face.

The four rulers of Faerie surrounded us. Arimos, eyes aglow again, gestured to the sky, and the few remaining clouds scattered. Starlight cascaded through rings of glass and bronze, focused and projected toward Roger and me, like the beacon of a lighthouse.

Roger, his face now a dark silhouette against blinding light, was my anchor. We leaned on one another; my retinas stung through closed eyelids. He trembled, but held me close. I knew instinctively this magic was too strong for any human, even one like him. My wings sprang out in a protective shield around the two of us. He took the shelter I offered, giving me strength in return.

Our bodies dissolved into nothing.

Suspended within time, space, and starlight, a comet-like aura encircled us. We sailed through endless night, my wings like a cocoon. We caught our impossible breath together, cheek against cheek, here in the void among the stars.

A force akin to gravity pulled our two bodies through windless heavens. Then all became still.

The soft patter of rain on my cold skin brought me back from a dark void. Muddy water filled my mouth.

I smelled vegetation, soil, and earth. I tasted rainwater. A sharp pain tore through my back.

I was alone. Roger was gone.

CHAPTER 27
To Be Alive

I lay on muddy ground. I blinked but could barely see. Had I stared too long at the sun? Or had I lost my sight in the darkness of space? I shook off a weight like deep sleep.

Raindrops chilled my skin. Ancient oak branches swayed overhead. It was night, but gray lined the horizon. The star portal transported us here—wherever this was.

Where was Roger?

Tracks led through the fallen leaves toward me. Mud covered my boots. I must have stumbled here myself.

I shouted for him through the wind and rain. My eyesight adjusted; I could see more clearly in darkness than I ever remembered. Was this the Welterwood?

I scrambled for purchase on the wet ground and stood. With a step, I staggered but caught myself on a fallen Waystone. Yes, this was near the Queen's Circle.

Ancient granite pulsed beneath my fingers. Vibrating with a life so different from animal or vegetable, it was little wonder I had never noticed it before.

My wings were gone. The skin on my back was whole, but the pain was raw and unexpected. I had used them to shield us as we crossed the distance between worlds. Had they burned away?

Here in the rainy ordinary world, I wished my silk Winter Court dress was more substantial. I drew out my crystal pendant. The stone glowed like a firefly. I found the silver brush still tucked under my chemise. I would test my magic as soon as the risk was acceptable.

I walked toward the monument, calling for Roger.

The Waystones shone like a ring of earth's living bones. In the center, evidence of my previous excavations remained below a fresh layer of mud. Wind gusted through treetops with the sound of waves crashing on cliffs. I stopped to listen. The trees knew dawn was near—an odd realization.

A moan. I hurried toward the voice, pulling a glamour around me to match the forest. I found Roger lying beside a steaming crater. He'd dragged himself alongside two fallen monoliths, finding partial shelter from the rain.

"Violet." He reached for me. "Is that you?"

"It's me." I knelt and touched his face. I released my glamour so he could see me. "Are you all right? Your skin feels hot." And his breathing was shallow.

"I awoke, and you were gone."

"Never." I brushed damp locks of hair away from his gorgeous eyes, leaning closer. "You're stuck with me now, like it or not."

He touched my cheek, smiling. "Does that mean you'll marry me? Here... in the human fashion, that is."

"If that's a proposal. Yes."

I traced the contours of his lips. The heat of his breath on my wrist awakened nerves down to my toes, igniting desire which had only grown with our love. Now the pull of a new magic entwined us, just as our hearts had sought to beat alongside one another for so long.

I slid my fingers through his hair. He uttered a quiet groan, the vibration in his chest low and delicious.

"Oh, my Violet."

I kissed him, tasting rain and earth and spice.

He broke the contact and spoke softly, stroking my back. "I can't bear to think of what you've endured these last few days. I should never have left you alone." He grimaced. "I swear, I'll—"

Another kiss silenced him. "Listen. I'm stronger than you think."

His eyes searched mine, and he exhaled, as if releasing some weight. "I know."

I nuzzled his neck with the tip of my nose, trailing soft kisses, tasting rain, and the spice of his skin. "I want you." My own whispered words surprised me but gave me courage to kiss him again, claiming more from this love.

He groaned, breaking away only to draw ragged breath. "The feeling is mutual. Though... the spirit is willing, but my flesh is weak. In fact, I'm sure my leg is broken."

"What?" I sat upright and laid a palm on his damp trousers. "Where?"

"Just below the knee."

I traced the lines of his limb until he winced.

"There. My tibia. As I'd feared."

Heat of inflammation soaked through his wet clothing.

"Can we take off your trousers? I need to see what it looks like."

He smirked. "I'll admit I'd imagined this moment somewhat differently." Roger unbuckled his belt and together we slid the sodden cotton from his legs.

"You imagined disrobing for me?"

In answer, he only smiled.

I did my best not to let my eyes linger on those sculpted muscles, revealed below his tight-fitting underclothes, or any other bulges he might have tried to hide with the tail of his shirt. Attention focused on the damage below his knee, I could not miss the improper alignment of the bones. That he wasn't screaming in agony was a wonder.

I bit my lip and laid a hand near the break. "Can you move it at all?"

Roger flexed his knee, testing injured muscles. He shook his head. "I'm afraid I won't walk unaided for a while." He pointed to the crater. "We must have fallen hard. Are you sure you're uninjured?"

"I'm fine. Perhaps you cushioned my fall."

Roger laughed and checked his side. "Damn. I think I've cracked a rib too."

I furrowed my brow and slid my fingers over his chest. "How bad is it?"

"I've endured worse. If only we could rest here for a short time. The magic of the Queen's Circle will help my strength recover. It's been so long since I've walked this sacred ground… not since that blackest of days—" He'd closed his eyes, and when he looked at me again, they held a flame of hope. He touched my cheek. "To be here with you now—this is like a dream."

"Yes." I stopped to listen to the forest. "For the moment, we're alone. Only animals are nearby for perhaps miles. Nothing with harmful intentions. We can rest. We both need it."

He glanced at the forest canopy. "You can sense that? How?"

A good question. I'd not considered how I came by that revelation. I closed my eyes to concentrate. "I can hear the… silent voices of trees. The vines, the shrubs and the grass. Even the birds and the insects. They're calm."

"You still have your magic." He looked away, no doubt thinking of my sacrifice.

"Well." I tapped a finger on his chest. "You'd better have off with the rest of your clothes so I can get a good look at everything."

Before he could protest, I began unbuttoning his shirt and pulled that over his head, along with his undershirt. My fingers explored his skin, the lines of his ribs, the curves of his attractive pectoral muscles.

"We'll need to make a splint. Can you help me find any suitable... branches? Ow."

I'd found the injured rib. His breathing deepened and slowed.

He said, "Press gently. See if it moves."

I did, and he gave a sharp exhale. I felt no shift in the bones, but somehow sensed the hairline cracks.

"Nothing too bad, but... oh, that hurts. Maybe more than the leg."

"I don't know if my magic will work the same way here in this world, but perhaps I can heal you, like before. Let me hold you." I slid closer and folded him in my arms.

My cheek rested against his, my hands on his injured side. Our heat joined through the thin wet fabric of my Winter Court gown. The curves and planes of his chest. The rhythm of his heartbeat. His breath beside my neck. I pressed a hand on his back, behind the cracked rib, the other at his side, just below his heart.

I concentrated on the broken bone below my fingers, willing my light to enfold the injury. In the realm of the Fae, I had not questioned how it worked; the healing had simply flowed from me to him. Here, the magic pushed against the sluggish material of reality, like trying to sail against the wind.

Yet... a new source called to me. The ring of standing stones. In my mind's eye, I beheld a rowan tree, crowned in colorful light. I received their currents of energy, and power flowed through my veins, as if I were a living conduit.

Roger whispered. "Whatever you're doing, that feels so good."

"Good."

"You're glowing again, my love."

I opened my eyes to see my fingers lit from within and surrounded by a violet-white radiance.

"Do you think it worked? Do... you have less pain?"

"Yes."

My light reflected in Roger's eyes, revealing tears.

I kissed him. He responded with renewed fervor, pulling me closer. Desire pulsed through every heartbeat. After a breath, the reconnection of our lips sparked another surge of delight through my body. I wanted more. I had to remember the poor man's leg was broken.

I pulled away, shivering in the chilly autumn air.

"I don't know if I can heal your leg, but I'll try. Here, we must straighten it first."

He clenched his jaw as he shifted to lie back.

I laid my hands over the injured bone, willing tissues to heal and repair. I drew upon my newfound sources of magic, like water from a secret well. That hidden light flowed from my heart through my limbs and fingertips, pulsing bright with life, into Roger's leg. His veins and bone became illuminated from within, as if he himself were Fae. The break knit back together impossibly fast. I gasped, fearing I'd done too much.

This time, he initiated the kiss, pressing me closer in the rush of that preternatural warmth and renewal that flooded us both. We held each other until the light faded to normal reality, elated and wonderful as it was.

Something grazed my cheek, startling me enough to pull away from his lips. A tuft of newly grown grass. I laughed. The moss and grasses surrounding us had all doubled in size.

"I'm grateful I still have my powers. We'll need them again, before our battle is done." I touched his face.

"We will." Roger stroked my unruly hair, brushing damp locks from my eyes. "Can you sense the power from the stone circle flowing to you?"

I reached to touch the granite of our shelter. "Yes. It's like... I've never known what it means to be alive. Awake. Until now." To be *Fae*. If only for a little while longer. "My rowan tree also speaks to me. It's a source of magic, like the stones, but different. As if... it knows a language only my soul understands."

"A rowan. Like your mother's?"

I nodded, wiping away an unbidden tear.

He held me close. "The mysteries of the sacred trees of Royal Fae are a closely guarded secret of Faecraft. I didn't know your two lives were so connected. I'll admit, this new knowledge is unsettling. Regardless, we'll find a way to protect your tree."

"At least I'll sever my connection to it soon. I hope that means I will no longer be vulnerable if it's harmed."

"Violet. I cannot ask you to sacrifice so much for me."

"You know I've decided this." I hid my face against his bare chest.

"You can still change your mind and return before the new moon. You are not yet exiled." He stroked my damp hair. "You saved my life. I am eternally grateful to you—for loving me. I will always love you. Even if you decide to live out your centuries with these newfound powers. With your wonderful wings."

I feared my wings were already gone, but I didn't want to tell him.

"If I remained Fae, I couldn't live here in this world. I'd only be able to see you for a few days each year."

"I could never ask you… to live like that."

Better to leave him for good. I couldn't speak the words.

"But what if I chose it? Would you still be mine? Or would you leave me?" When he didn't answer, I said, "Come on. Let's get out of here. If you're so keen on rejecting my advances. Can you walk now?" I moved to sit up, but he caught my hand and drew me back.

"That's not what I mean. Of course, I am yours. Always. And I'm not rejecting your advances."

"Then what are you afraid of?"

"I don't know how our story will end."

"Does anyone?" I stroked his cheek. My fingertips brushed his soft lips, the hint of stubble on his jaw.

"I suppose not." He pulled me closer and kissed the side of my neck, sparking a shiver of delight through my entire nervous system.

"Besides…" I gasped. "I'm a woman of Faerie. I believe I'm expected to carry the hero off into the woods to have my wicked way with him, at least once, before he completes his quest. I've read that story before." I combed fingers through his hair.

His kisses graced my collarbone, mouth trailing lower, blazing fire on rain-wet skin.

"True." He began to unbutton my gown, as if he'd read my mind. "However, I believe *you* are the hero of this story, my lady love." He kissed the swell of my breast through my wet chemise. "After all, you just charged into a dangerous new land to mount my daring rescue."

"Oh, I like the sound of that." Cradling his face in my hands, I whispered in his ear, "Please let me seduce you now, Roger Gale."

"Yes, my love."

Sheltered by the ancient stones, we removed the remaining soggy layers of fabric between us, and lay beside one another in a bed of moss and discarded clothes. He stroked my damp hair, gazing into my eyes, as though he was just as spellbound. Our whispered words, *I love you,* silenced by kisses. We drew each other closer. Closer. Skin against skin. I wanted to enshrine this moment within my ecstatic heart.

I didn't notice we both glowed, wherever we touched—brightest at our hearts, until he hesitated, cautious eyes asking if I was all right.

In answer, I kissed him, grabbed his hips, and slid my fingers around those shapely muscles, slick with rain and sweat, urging him to resume.

We carried one another higher—bodies deliciously tensed before my world of sensation exploded into bliss. Weightless. His touch was my only grounding to this earth. My awareness expanded—to the drumbeat of the rain striking the ground, the magic of the ancient standing stones, the golden sun cresting the horizon, the boom of distant thunder over the sea. We were part of it all. All was within us.

Out of breath, we rested; the lines of our demarcation blended. My hand fell to the damp ground beside my face, and he slipped his fingers through mine. A tendril of vine swirled around our wrists and burst into flower.

After we'd dressed again in our wet clothes, Roger knelt before me, tying the laces of my muddy Winter Court boots.

"How do you feel?" He kissed my knee, enticing goosebumps.

"Wonderful, but damp. And you?"

He laughed. "Likewise."

I offered him a hand up, and he sat on the granite stone beside me.

"I should be exhausted, but I could take on a dragon." He poured out the rainwater from his boots before slipping those on.

"Luckily, we only have to capture a Shade."

Roger's brow furrowed and he faced the ground, lost in thought.

I tucked my silver-handled brush inside my bodice once more—since my flimsy Winter Court dress had no pockets.

The rain had slackened as the morning grew brighter. Only a sweet-smelling breeze shook droplets from the trees. We walked the old trails made and maintained by centuries of Seastone's pilgrims, away from the ancient monument.

"Dr. Crane mentioned using a basilisk's eye to capture him," I said.

"Useful, but that would only be a temporary banishment. We mean to kill it, so we'll have to sever the link with its source. In this case, Porter, or some talisman he created. We destroy that and we weaken their power."

Or destroy Porter, I could see he meant to add, though he wouldn't voice the thought.

"A silver amulet," I said. "On a chain around Porter's neck. I saw it before and sensed it was evil, but I'm not sure."

He faced our path ahead, expression heavy with concern. "I'm puzzled as to why you alone could wound the Shade before. Why it seems to have targeted you, all your life."

"Maybe I wasn't his only target. If he's been working with Porter to make this drug, perhaps he seeks out those able to see him. Those with fairy blood like me. To bring them to Porter."

"I don't know." He shook his head. "You said you saw it first when you were a child, of nine or ten, correct?"

"Yes. That was in the Welterwood. I saw it in the... water. I've been in hospital many times since."

"Porter was a physician at General before he came to work for me at the Institute years later. He could have found you back then, I suppose, but at that time he knew nothing of my work, for I'd not yet invented it. He wouldn't have had any means of extracting Faelight to make this drug. One way or another, he's possessed magic all along, and hidden it from me, if he's been commanding the Shade all this time. But why? I'm missing some connection."

"The Queen said Cynbel and I were linked."

She's the one, Cynbel had said in that memory Arimos had helped my mind recall. It gave me chills.

Roger put an arm around me as we walked, his eyes on the path ahead, lost in thought. "We must warn Evelyn that Cynbel is here once more. Likely with vengeance on his mind."

"Evelyn. You and Dr. Crane are close, aren't you? She's put her life on the line to investigate you. She testified at your trial. Do you two have a... history?"

"I see." He smirked. "Would it bother you?"

"Well, no..." Yes, probably.

"Yes. Although not that sort of history. House Crane and House Gale have long been close, as we are the only two Reliqua families on this island. We've worked together, hunted side by side. We're friends, and I trust her, although we both know she hates me, and not without cause. Moreover, she was never all that interested in men." His expression shrouded again.

"Oh. You mean she loved your sister."

He nodded, his gaze cast to the ground. "She will never forgive me. Just as I can't forgive myself."

We walked on in silence for a moment. I hadn't meant to cause his thoughts to stray to his sister's death. I took his hand and kissed it. That earned a smile from him.

I asked, "A monastery, huh? Did I hear that right earlier?"

"You did, indeed."

"Were you a monk?"

"No." He smiled. "Though I've always been somewhat of a hermit."

"A hermit," I teased. "What did you do there?"

His expression became somber again. "I served the temple as an herbalist and learned much of their ways and medicine. Those wise teachers, and the mountains themselves, saved me from darkest oblivion. More than once. In fact, that was the place where first you visited me in a dream."

"You'll have to tell me that story sometime."

He nodded. "When Father wrote to me, I knew it was time to come home, and I'm glad I did."

"So am I."

He brought my hand to his lips to kiss my wrist, causing my pulse to race. "I've never felt anything quite like... what we just shared."

"Oh?" I didn't want to be so embarrassed.

"Ah. Well, I mean..." Roger must have blushed. He stopped and pulled me close to him. "I've never been in love like this, it's true. But this is more. A power connects us, like I've never experienced before. It must be the Binding. Was it the same for you?" His fingers glided through my hair, enticing new goosebumps.

"Yes." I kissed his cheek. "Although..." I couldn't believe I was about to speak these words. "I don't have much basis for comparison. There was only one other time. Years ago, and it was... I've tried to make myself forget."

Roger tensed. "Do I need to hunt down and kill anyone else?"

"No. It wasn't like that." It might have been if I were to be honest with myself. "I suppose I was... young and foolish, and I paid for it. I never saw him again."

"The rotten bastard. Don't say you were foolish. Such a thing is never a woman's fault." He held me close, cheek against my forehead, stroking my back for a restful moment. "Who was he?"

"Nobody. Someone I met in Seastone's art society. Forever ago."

"Another artist?"

"Worse. A patron."

He groaned. "Are you sure you don't want me to kill him? Make him wish he were dead, perhaps? Turn him into a newt—that sort of thing?"

"No." I laughed. "Could you even do that?"

He arched an eyebrow.

We continued again, hand in hand. The morning wind brought wayward bands of cloud in from the sea, sweeping glittering raindrops from the trees.

After we had walked some ways in silence, I pointed through the forest ahead. "This is the direction I traveled before. From the institute. It's several hours' walk, but we can find a road if we head that way."

"We have no weapons. Even with our magic, I don't like those odds. I have equipment back at my shop which could help us. Assuming Porter's not already destroyed the place."

"We do have a weapon." I drew out the silver brush. "I'm just not sure if I can use it in this world."

"I can help you try."

"Yes, let's." I lifted the brush and scanned the surrounding woods. "I will think of something harmless to paint."

If I deepened the gold on those autumn-clad trees, it wouldn't be much of a test. Perhaps I'd conjure a dragonfly. Could I render the illusion of life? I thought I might attempt a rainbow, there on the canvas of sunlit cloud to the west.

"Wait." Roger wrapped me in his arms and sang three magic words beside my ear. Energy danced between us. A palpable charge, like an electromagnetic wind, flowed around and through me—through both of us, for I could feel the quickening through his blood along with mine. We were a vessel with new sails unfurled. "Now. We're ready."

"A protection spell?"

"And a good excuse to hold you." He kissed my earlobe, and it gave me gooseflesh. A frisson of magical awareness swept through my body, stimulated by his. I settled into his warmth. He distracted me too much, but it all felt so good.

I closed my eyes and stretched my consciousness into the forest. I envisioned my rowan tree. A stream of power flowed into me—us. I sensed the amplifying magic of the Queen's Circle. Roger's power and intention joined with mine. Our Fae Court Bonding. Would it be enough of an edge to defeat our enemy? I wasn't even sure I knew what I was doing.

I lifted the brush, bristles gleaming.

Before I'd painted one stroke, I perceived an unspoken alarm. The forest stood on alert. Trees and animals whispered urgent news, from one mind to another. A chain of inhuman voices grew inaudibly louder. Thousands spoke of *danger*.

"Something's coming." My hand holding the brush fell to my side, a magic charge still bristling along with goose bumps on my skin. "It's big. Traveling this way. And swiftly."

As if I had a magnet in my head, I could locate the threat. I pointed.

Roger scanned the horizon. "From the northwest. The institute?"

"Yes. Let's go."

We ran in the opposite direction, veering from the trail. Single file, we pushed ahead through thicker brambles. Thorns tore at my ankles and arms, the thin fabric of my gown. The sky darkened with clouds, and rain pattered leaves overhead.

We stopped to catch our breath, leaning on one another. A doleful howl echoed through ancient oaks.

"Wolves?" asked Roger.

"I encountered a pack of them here before, but I never felt threatened."

"Good to know. Can you sense the creature? Have we gained any distance?"

I closed my eyes and listened. The surrounding trees sang in gratefulness for the rain—a beautiful silent sound, but it clouded my search for distant alert calls. *There.*

"It's still in pursuit, but farther away. There are more. Humans. Dogs. I'm not sure. Come on."

We renewed our haste through the tangled forest until we found an animal trail leading to a grassy clearing. Distant thunder boomed. Lightning danced on the dark horizon.

Not wolves. The battle cry of baying hounds. Roger heard them too.

"If we can find a stream," I said, "we'll hide the scent of our tracks. I did this before."

"In a lightning storm?" Roger glanced at the sky. "Not if that front comes much closer."

We'd only run some twenty yards through the clearing, when a wretched noise echoed through the woods. A wolf's howl and a bear's roar mixed with the keening of a man. So close now. We renewed our haste.

A loud crashing sound came from behind me. I turned to see the earth break apart under Roger's feet.

The ground swallowed him whole.

CHAPTER 28
THE BARROW

oger!" I ran through the rain toward the place where I'd last seen him.

The ground gave way under my foot. My leg sank into a void, and I scrambled backward. Darkness opened below, as chunks of earth—sodden and netted with forest roots and moss—fell into the hole. The cave-in revealed stone masonry—dank, moldy blackness like a tomb. I crawled to higher ground, scanning for any sign of him, calling his name.

"Violet. I'm here."

From beside a pile of rubble, his hand reached for me.

"Are you hurt?"

"I don't think so. I got lucky." The dust had cleared, and I saw his wicked grin.

Even now, he would joke. I exhaled in relief. "Thank heavens!"

He scaled the rubble, which must once have been the roof of this subterranean room. With shaky balance on shifting stones, he stood to reach through a shaft of light.

"I'm afraid I can't jump that high."

"I'm going to get you out. Hang on." Could I paint a ladder solid enough for him to climb? In this realm? I was doubtful. But I had to act quickly.

"Careful. This entire ceiling may be compromised. I can't see far, but the space feels large."

I cast about for inspiration. A nearby oak supported ivy vines. I ran and pulled a tendril from a lower branch, tugging it toward the pit. Just as I had done before, I connected with the vine's life force, willing it to grow.

The leaves fluttered, as if stirred by a breeze, but nothing else happened.

Roger said, "Your brush is like a wand. A tool for directing one's intention. It may help focus your power."

"Right."

I drew out the brush and began to paint. I pulled the green of the ivy's reflected light, painted its path through the air down into the underground cavern. Incredibly, the plant followed those lines of color, lengthening and bursting into vibrant leaf. Green tendrils descended into the cave.

As the ivy grew, my limbs became heavier. I sank to one knee as the vegetation I had coaxed into off-season rapid growth gave its last burst of energy.

"Move back from the edge. I'm going to try…" Roger's voice silenced as the ground below me buckled.

Rock struck rock, and earth slid away under my feet. I clung to the ivy, slowing my fall, but I landed hard enough to knock the breath out of me.

I coughed, shifting to sit up on uneven stones. Through the swirling debris and raindrops, I shouted into the dank darkness of this tomb, "Roger, talk to me!"

"Violet. Are you injured?" The haze settled, and he was sound, gazing back at me through the quickening rain.

"No. Are you?"

"I'm fine. Thank God you're unharmed. Can we still climb up?" He scrambled over the rubble toward me.

I tugged on the ivy, but the remaining vine snapped and fell into the pit, showering us with debris, though we dodged most of it.

I wiped rain and dirt from my eyes and lifted the brush. "Well, I still have this."

Roger placed his hand on mine. "You must save your strength. First, let's see where we are." He snapped off a portion of the broken vine I had summoned, about as thick as a wand, branched with new leaves. "I've heard legends of ancient ruins still hidden on this island, but I never knew any aside from the Queen's Circle existed in the Welterwood. Certainly not any barrows like this."

He whispered a spell. In the darkness, an emerald pulse of light ignited the ivy wand in his hands; a cold green flame appeared at the tip. An unearthly torchlight.

"Fortunately for us, ivy has many uses…. Aha!" Roger pointed into the newly revealed space. "We may have a way out."

"A tunnel?" I saw little through the swirling dust and rain.

"Better."

He took my hand, and we proceeded over piles of dirt and fallen masonry.

"There is a Wayportal here. Look. A magical doorway on the wall, like in Egyptian tombs. It looks ancient. In fact…." He raised an eyebrow. "Hmm… I'll have to guess at our latitude and longitude. We could find ourselves below ground in Cairo if I'm not careful."

When we reached the walls of the chamber, the ivy light illuminated mysterious symbols carved on every stone. If they were Fae, the script looked different. Perhaps it was an extinct human language. The lines glimmered in the darkness as if alive, reflecting all colors of the rainbow, so faint at first I almost missed them. I gasped. We were the first people in centuries to behold this sight. Wherever we approached with our green-blazing torch, petroglyphs shone with inner brilliance. I touched a wall; below layers of dust, the lettering around my hands pulsed bright violet. *Like my wings had been.*

"A writing hidden to those unable to see. This must be some ancient dialect of High Fae, but… I can't read most of it. The syntax is strange. I wonder how old it is?" He walked along a line of characters, torchlight illuminating a group within a circle. "Ah. This is familiar. I believe… I've seen something like this before. Long ago."

"Where?"

"It's a long story. Remind me to tell you sometime."

"I have a feeling you owe me quite a few tales, Mr. Gale."

"Indeed." He smirked. "I look forward to regaling you with all the sordid details of my life, but first, let's get out of here."

We approached a grouping of symbols which formed an arched doorway in the solid wall. Behind us, rain cascaded down a stairway of fallen rubble. Lightning flashed, revealing for an instant a circular tomb. I thought I glimpsed the remains of a sepulcher on the far wall, before thunder boomed.

"Is this Wayportal like the Fae Roads?"

"Yes, the magic is much the same. On equinox, we use Wayportals for travel to and from the realms of Faerie, like your father's mirror portal. Other times of the year, they are linked one to another here on Earth. I *believe* I can take us to the doorway at my shop."

"Would this be the one in your rat-riddled basement?"

"The very one. Now, are you ready for this?"

"I was born ready." I smirked.

Roger lifted his arms to either side and intoned a spell in the language of my Fae ancestors… our ancestors, for Roger's blood was linked to the Winter Courts, I had to remember. The resonant words awakened something primal in my heart. I chanted alongside him, knowing the ancient syllables almost before he spoke them. The space in front of us shimmered, like a reflection on water. He took my hand. A jolt of power surged between us, as if we had connected two wires in an electrical circuit. He sang the words of an incanta-tion while tracing symbols in the air. They appeared on the wall—one within the border of the door, three on the arch, two on either side, and one by the floor.

From outside the tomb came the cry of hounds. Too close. Then, an un-familiar bellow. Was it the low moaning of storm winds, or was it the call of that beast which had chased us?

"We must hurry," I said.

"They can't follow us through without magic. Do you see the door now in your mind?"

When I closed my eyes, the rest of the barrow disappeared, while the doorway before us remained. Within that dark void, bright symbols like he'd drawn appeared, yet their colors were reversed. An afterimage. "Yes."

"Reach for the handle and open it. Together we must focus—"

A crash behind us—the sound of rock striking mud-slicked rock. Another section of the ceiling collapsed. Roger tugged my hand, and we sprinted away from the landslide, turning in time to avoid a low stone shelf, if it was not a sepulcher.

I dropped the ivy wand. Green light flickered to blackness.

The bay and bark of hounds echoed through the wind and rain. A roaring scream pierced the dust-filled chamber, coming from the opening above. My blood froze.

I could not see the Wayportal. Newly fallen debris blocked our path.

Roger knelt and palmed a stone in each hand, whispering under his breath.

I drew my paintbrush. A glowing sphere of Faelight appeared at the bris-tle tip. Like I'd dipped it in radiant ink.

Another howl echoed through the barrow. Dust cleared, revealing snarls on rain-soaked canine faces with shining eyes. Three dogs stared at us from the pile of rubble—black Pinschers like those employed at the institute for grounds patrol. One growled. The animal's shadow looked bigger than the others'—different from the creature's shape.

All three turned and ran back the way they'd come, as if their master had recalled them.

I gasped, in a mixture of shock and relief. "Why did they leave?"

"I don't know, but it wasn't a dog which made that scream we heard." Roger dropped the stones. "Did you see that shadow?"

"Yes. It's how he… Cynbel… moves through this realm, isn't it? Attaching himself to people—or animals."

"I believe so, yes. A Shade can also transport through mirrors and other two-dimensional spaces, as you know. Quickly. We might reach the Wayportal if we go around the other side. It's still draining my energy."

We picked our way through the ruined barrow. The doorway came into view once more. The forest had gone silent, yet the trees whispered. A monster neared.

"We must clear the threshold." Roger hefted away debris. I added my strength to the task.

A crash behind us. A horrifying, unnatural growl. The hair on the back of my neck stood on end. I turned to look and beheld a nightmarish foot, like the claw of a vulture and the paw of a lion. A leg appeared, followed by five more—gray-green, like a corpse's skin under the matted coat of a drowned rat.

Roger lifted one of the larger stones, whispering a spell under the sound of the rain.

The massive, arachnid-like creature slid down the pile of debris. Its abdomen terminated in a horridly human torso, which swung a pair of furless arms through the rain. Set in the too-human face were an insect's compound eyes and a slit-like mouth with protruding mandibles. An exoskeletal carapace covered its back.

The monster leaped, evading Roger's first volley. A segmented scorpion-like tail whipped through the air.

I raised my brush like a sword. I had only a split second to wonder if I was going mad, before I connected to my power, and the silver-handled brush glowed in my hand. I slashed through the open air—for no other way to explain it—painting a wound. The bristles touched no canvas at all, not even the monster's sickly green flesh, but the stroke cut deep as a blade.

It yelped and pressed an all too human hand against its dead-gray breast, trying to staunch the flow of greenish fluid from the gash I'd imagined. It screamed. The hideous sound reverberated through the barrow and shocked our eardrums. Roger pummeled the creature's head with another magically altered stone, impacting with a visible shockwave. The monster roared and sprang to higher ground, scorpion tail thrashing.

Roger drew a geometric shape in the air with an outstretched hand, his ring glowing.

Screeching, the chimera lobbed a chunk of the ceiling at us.

We couldn't dodge fast enough, but the projectile struck a shimmering light shield and fell to the ground, just inches away. Roger and I clung to one another, gasping.

"I can't keep the door open much longer. Go. I'll lead it away!" He dashed toward the creature.

I yelled after him, but he'd already caught the thing's attention.

"Go now, Violet!"

The monster's tail whipped toward him. I slashed with my brush. Invisible impact connected mid-motion. The creature screamed. Its tail dripped foul fluids from the gash opened by my brushstroke.

It sprang toward me, moving too fast for such a hulking thing. My new Fae reflexes proved the advantage, and I rolled clear of that scorpion's tail. The stinger cracked the stone beside my face, like a shovel striking buried rock.

Before I could draw a counterattack, the monster turned a clawed hand on Roger, knocking him down. Roger stifled a cry. Crimson striped the white of his shirt. He stilled, limbs and head limp against the ground.

I screamed in fury. The brush became a spear directed at the enemy's heart.

Something knocked me down. Pain shattered my right thigh. Shockwaves wracked my whole body. The stinger. I caught the hazy image of a hooked barb pulling away, red with my blood.

The chimera issued an ear-numbing screech. My strike had only severed one of the hideous arms. Six legs maneuvered to lift the monster's inhuman torso higher, oozing noxious green blood from its shoulder wound. It shrieked, front legs twitching. When its terrible compound eyes locked on me, they flashed with *darklight*.

My limbs were paralyzed with poison. Where I'd let it fall, the magic brush lay on the ground, out of my reach. My vocal cords could not even form a scream as the injured beast scuttled toward me, enraged.

Terror could not unlock my frozen muscles. Time stretched for eternity while my mind grasped for any means to fight back.

The ivy. A few tendrils cascaded from the broken ceiling.

Answer me, I begged the vines. *I, a daughter of the Fairy Summer Courts, need your help.*

They answered.

Like stealthy serpents, the vines coiled around the monster's stinger, encasing the thorax in a living net while it thrashed, eyes glinting with bloodlust.

More of the ruin collapsed. Roger staggered into my distorted vision. He lobbed a flaming stone at the horror's chest, and it roared in anger, catching fire.

I called for Roger. He grabbed the brush and placed it in my hand, wrapping my cold fingers around the silver handle. I channeled all my fury and slashed the glowing bristles through empty air, though my numbed wrist only moved it an inch.

The creature's flaming head slid away from its neck. With a rattling thud, it tumbled down the rubble and came to a stop near our feet, oozing noxious fluids.

The body's dead weight slumped within a tangle of vines. One by one, the remaining stones above gave way under the strain, cracking into our prison room like an avalanche.

Roger lifted me up, carrying me against his wounded chest. Trembling and immobilized, my vision worsened. I could see only flashing light and Fae script as we dashed toward the Wayportal, dodging falling rocks. I closed my eyes and pictured the gateway on my mind's canvas.

We stepped into the wall.

CHAPTER 29
YOUR MANY SINS

eow."

I felt the comforting vibrations of a purr.

"Puck," I whispered. *Is that you, little one?* I wanted to speak it out loud, but my voice was not cooperating. The room spun. My pulse thudded in my ears.

"I found him upstairs." Roger's voice. "Once I coaxed him down to see you, he's not left your side, not even for more food."

I tried to move, but my muscles shivered. Fire ran through my veins. Pain registered everywhere, from my toes and fingers to my spine, even in my teeth, when I gulped for a breath. I could hazily remember being carried through a cold, featureless expanse, neither night nor day, until a bright light enveloped us. He'd laid me on a cot, in a room I didn't recognize, and I must have gone to sleep.

I could not focus, but my eyes found my lover's shape in the lantern light where he sat beside me. Dried blood on his torn shirt. I wanted to ask if he was all right but could hardly draw breath enough for a whisper.

"Easy. You've been poisoned." Roger pressed my hand in reassurance. "You saved our lives, Violet. I'm sorry I couldn't protect you from this." His jaw clenched; the open wounds on his chest still wept.

"You need help," I managed to utter.

"Shh. You more so than me."

Only then did I realize my right leg lay exposed up to my thigh, which was swollen around a painful puncture injury, like a giant bee sting. Roger pressed a cloth to my inflamed skin.

"I've applied a drawing poultice. These herbs helped drain much of the poison, but I'm not sure what sort of creature that was, so we're fighting an unknown venom. I regret I don't possess your same spontaneous healing ability, but I'm doing everything I can."

I groaned. He wrapped strips of bandage around my leg, tying the padding in place, before he turned to a nearby shelf.

Puck purred beside me. I coerced my numb fingers to move enough to stroke the kitten's soft fur.

"I think he must have come in days ago." Roger gestured to Puck. "Probably with the police searching for us. The place is a wreck upstairs, but they left this room mostly intact." I willed my eyes to work and caught the sight of him pouring liquid from a kettle into a teacup, if but for an instant.

I blinked, and thought I glimpsed a vision through a window behind Roger, of a Roman vineyard in the evening, like a Dutch Italianate painting. I wondered if we were outside until my unruly eyes focused. It was a mural, containing a cleverly hidden false door, made to resemble part of the romantic ruins. The perfect way to hide a magical portal in plain sight. A figure in silhouette walked along one pastoral valley ridge. I blinked again, but the figure was gone.

On a table beside the cot, Roger set down a teacup decorated with clover, filled with fragrant, amber-colored tea. He brought a small bottle closer to my inspection. It contained a few drops of glittering liquid.

"This is a solution of alicorn powder, a cure for all poisons. I'm afraid a few drops were all I had left here at the shop. It may not be enough, but it should help neutralize the remaining venom." He stirred the bottle's contents into the teacup and set that to my trembling lips. "The rest is on your wound. I will retrieve more from my house as quickly as possible."

I gulped the potion, tasting of rose petals and honey mixed with vinegar. A gritty texture thickened the cool floral tea, like sandy blood.

Before I swallowed the last drop, the medicine both warmed my chills and cooled my fever. I gasped.

"I… I think it's work—" From behind closed eyelids I beheld again a flash of light. Like the first time I touched the unicorn horn.

A vision of white fur against living green. I ran through a forest on four legs. A young man with dark hair and green eyes knelt beside a young woman with hair of dark chestnut. She cradled my head in her arms, with tears in her eyes, so like her brother's. The boy drew nearer, a dagger in his outstretched hand, polished steel gleaming in the sun before it plunged for my throat.

The image of the boy dissolved into the man beside me. Those same viridian eyes, ever youthful but no longer filled with innocence, hid a century of wisdom forged in tragedy. In that quality, I recognized something akin to my own sorrow. I loved that damaged part of him, before I knew the violence at its source.

Roger laid the back of his palm against my forehead. His eyebrows knit in concentration. "Violet, talk to me. How do you feel?"

"Better. Thank you." For the moment, I said nothing else. I touched his leg. He still wore the same trousers given to him in the Winter Courts, muddy from the ground where we had held one another after making love.

Exhaling in relief, he brought my wrist to his lips and kissed my pulse.

I threaded my fingers through his hair. With every breath, the potion restored more sensation to my numbed limbs. My vision cleared. I laid chilled fingers on the side of his face. The low strum of some latent awareness fluttered in the back of my brain. I could sense... his emotions. Could almost read his thoughts. A poem veiled only by the hesitant turn of a page.

"Something else bothers you," I said. "Tell me."

His shoulders slumped, eyes pleading, as if he begged for a chance to keep silent. "That monster was not natural. Not from either of our worlds. It was... made, like a golem or a homunculus. I sensed dark magic from the beast, as well as some sort of... inhuman science. Borne from the mind of a depraved vivisectionist."

He shook his head, staring at the floor. "If Porter stole my old research, and created such an abomination, I fear..."

Movement within that vineyard scene drew my eye. I thought I glimpsed a figure walking along a picturesque path. Beside me, the kitten ceased his purring.

Roger closed his eyes and rubbed the back of his head. "One evening eleven years ago, I sat in my laboratory, reviewing my notes. On my desk was a beaker of extracted Faelight, now cloudy and inert—toxic, devoid of detectable magic, as it always became not hours after extraction. I had opened a window, and in flew a beetle toward my lamp. The insect struck the glass chimney hard enough to propel it into the beaker of liquid. It sank to the bottom as though dead. Hours later, I heard a shuffling sound coming from inside the beaker. The beetle emerged, spread larger wings than before, and flew toward the now-closed window, to tap like mad on the glass.

"I approached the insect, sensing a weak magic field. Dark energy. I captured it and discovered its anatomy had changed. The ordinary dung beetle species which had entered the room had mutated. Altered proportions. An enlarged head. An anthropomorphic quality to the new limbs. Even its eyes glowed red. Horrified, I destroyed the unnatural creature with fire, and resolved to do the same from then on to every drop of Faelight I extracted. The dangers posed by this new discovery were great, yet I reasoned… I couldn't put an end to the aid I provided my most desperate patients. I thought I could manage the risks." He rubbed his neck, facing the floor. "I should have burned all my notes then and there. I don't know when Porter stole them from me."

"Arimos was right. You were hiding something from us at the trial."

He exhaled and shook his head. "I never lied. I didn't think this information was relevant. The fact is, I destroyed that work before I left, and I have nothing to do with this… Tears of the Moon. I didn't see any other connections, or didn't want to see. Until we encountered that chimera monster."

I recalled the bodies I'd helped the orderlies truck out of the hospital before I escaped.

Puck issued a low howl. A cry of caution and warning as the young cat stared at the painted wall, his tail twitching.

The shadow within the mural grew. It approached the foreground— walking through the stone ruins. I blinked and lost sight of it within the painted shapes.

Roger stood and paced, arms crossed over his bloody shirt. "The Winter King was right. I *am* to blame. All those people…." He faced me, anguished. "All those deaths? I only wanted my work to *save* lives. Am I truly so cursed?"

"Roger!" I pointed at the wall. "Something's here. In the painting."

"What?"

He stood and grabbed a pair of Spectrocles from the table beside him, donning those as he turned to the mural. "What do you sense?"

"More like what I saw. Wait…"

An energy. Opposite to my own. We were two poles of a magnet. Both of us connected to the Otherworld's power. But if I was a force of good magic, this was evil.

"It's by the ruins." I pointed. "In the shadow of that column. Don't you see it?"

He adjusted his goggles, sliding a blue lens over one eye. "I do now."

Puck hissed and dashed from my side, disappearing somewhere in the cluttered basement.

Roger grabbed a dagger from a nearby desk and whispered the words of a spell.

Within the mural, the Shade's outline quivered. Expanding, it infected the painted landscape's color with roiling blackness.

"Brace yourself."

Roger cut a large pentagram into the air with his blade, then a series of geometric symbols in points around the writhing shadow. One by one, they plucked the surrounding energy fields, like vibrating guitar strings. The words of his song resonated with the sigils, growing louder, until I covered my ears. Their combined force struck like the crack of a whip.

As quickly as the sound wave crested, the spell passed over us, and the room quieted.

The silhouette of a man, near now to life size, froze within the painting's foreground, and dissipated like smoke. The mural returned to normal.

Roger set down the dagger, pushed the Spectrocles to his neck, and his eyes sought mine.

"I'm all right," I said. "It was Cynbel. I'm sure."

"I've only blocked him from using that doorway—temporarily." Roger offered an arm, and I took it. "Can you stand? Our enemies know where to find us now."

I stood and braced myself with his strength as another wave of dizziness tested my limbs. "Where's my paintbrush?"

"It's gone. We must have dropped it somewhere."

"What? No." Had I let it slip through my fingers so carelessly?

"We can search for it later."

"We can, indeed," spoke a voice which did not belong.

I gasped.

Porter stood on the wooden stairway leading down from the upper level, wearing a bowler hat and tan frock coat. Two other policemen, along with Sgt. Smith, trained rifles on us.

Roger raised two open hands, as if in surrender. I did the same.

"How did you get in?" I knew he meant, *get past my wards*.

Porter laughed, fingering a chain at his neck. That strange silver pendant he wore hidden below his shirt. "Through the doors, of course. Keep him in your sights, gentlemen. Shoot this madman if he moves." He drew a revolver from his coat pocket, eyeing the chambers and spinning the cylinder before aiming at Roger.

"I don't want to kill you in front of my patient. Her mind could not stand the shock. But I'm sure you appreciate the delicate nature of her constitution, do you not?" Laughing, Porter descended the creaking steps.

"Archibald Porter, you will pay for your many sins. Know this to be true."

"Perhaps, but not today."

Another man followed Porter, an orderly from the institute, carrying a medical kit the same pea green as his uniform. More guns trained on us, drawing nearer at my every fevered heartbeat. We were trapped.

Porter lowered his revolver and approached. "Ah, but it *is* good to see you, Dr. Gale. How long has it been? Ten years? I think you've not aged a day, in all that time. You might even look younger. Quite remarkable. You'll have to share your secrets with me sometime." His laugh was a miserable wheeze.

"What… do you want with us?" A wave of dizziness passed through me.

"My dear Miss Morgen," said Porter, "You've been kidnapped yet again. The police and I are here to rescue you from this evil man's clutches, once and for all."

"That's not true! Don't listen to him, officers. Mr. Gale has never harmed me. Dr. Porter is the one who imprisoned me against my will. I escaped. Now he wants to ensure I never tell the world the truth of what he does in that hospital. Do not allow him to manipulate you, men of the law, with these lies."

One of the policemen, gun still aimed at me, asked, "What's she on about, doc?"

"Hmm." Porter licked his lips. "Knowing these individuals as I do, I suspect the female victim here has fallen in love with her handsome captor. Not unthinkable when you consider he's been manipulating her with hallucinogens and preposterous fantasies." Porter sighed, walking toward me. "I'm afraid it will now take much more work to cure the unfortunate Miss Morgen. In fact, we may be too late."

The men drew closer, aiming weapons at us.

"Officers, hear me." Roger raised his voice. "This woman needs immediate medical attention. She's been poisoned. I have the only antidote at my house. Please, let me retrieve it and help her. Afterward, you may take me into custody. I give you my word."

"Poisoned? By what?" asked Sgt. Smith.

"I don't know what kind of creature it was. It had a scorpion's stinger but was far too large to be natural."

They snickered.

"Ah, yes," said Porter. "I too have heard this charming bit of local folklore. The Institute's grounds crew swear they've witnessed all manner of misshapen monsters in the surrounding forest. I'm sure Miss Morgen must have heard such tales from the other lunatics—giving your lies more credibility—another layer of control over her mind, as she allows you to administer the 'cure' for this imaginary poison. Is that not so?"

"You know it is not. Please. I'm begging you, Archibald, if you honor any trace of your Hippocratic Oath, allow me to retrieve the antidote or this woman may die."

"That, I will." Porter did not lower his gun, aimed at Roger's chest. "Officers, in the interest of saving my patient, escort Dr. Gale to his estate. Let him bring this antidote to me in person. Every last gram in his possession.

He will comply without resistance if he cares for this woman's life, as he claims. Is this understood, Gale?"

"Yes."

"Meet me at your old laboratory. You have three hours." To the officers, he added, "Gag him and keep his hands bound. Give him a sedative and bring me that ring he wears. Don't let him speak a word, lest his silver tongue beguile your feeble minds."

Porter's entourage laughed, but Smith nodded, as if he understood more than the rest. Panic clawed up my throat. The room tilted on its axis, and the floor rushed upward.

Roger caught me. "Stay strong, my love," he whispered. In our embrace, Roger's deft fingers slipped a small object into my bodice. Spherical and cold, like glass.

Roger gave no resistance as they pulled him from me at gunpoint. I could only watch, drawing painful breaths as they handcuffed him, taking his ring. One orderly jabbed a hypodermic needle into his arm.

"No!" I didn't have the strength to resist them, or the sting of another needle.

In my fading vision, I glimpsed an unnaturally dark shape below the shoes of Sgt. Smith. His shadow fell at odd angles to the others, as if it wasn't cast by the same gaslight.

Philips snapped heavy manacles on my wrists. Iron.

I cried out in pain. The metal seared my skin like a brand. I couldn't breathe.

The shadow below Smith writhed. A two-dimensional tentacle licked the uneven surface of the brick basement floor.

On my arms, the iron burned. On the floor, the Shadow squirmed.

CHAPTER 30
MEN WHO SPECIALIZE

dreamt of flying. Arms outstretched, hands open, fingers splayed. No... these were real wings. Membranes of tangible light strained against heavy air. I jolted upward. Swam through the atmosphere. Up to the eternal stars. Gravity a forgotten shackle. I reached the dark plateau dividing two worlds. I flew higher, finding a void of nothing, only another unbreachable boundary.

The universe contracted. I clawed and kicked at a quicksand of writhing shadows.

I coughed and opened my eyes to a dim room. The light of a dying evening seeped between the bars of a lofty window. I lay on the filthy padded floor of some isolation cell.

When I tried to sit up, my limbs would not obey, bound around my torso. I rolled to one side, fighting panic at the pressure on my chest.

Straitjacket.

Under the new restraints, I wore the same dress I'd been given in the Winter Courts. The same muddy boots. Could I have been asleep for the whole day? It was late morning when they brought me here.

The stench of the padded floor, combined with the pain in my bandaged leg, nearly made me sick. I forced myself up, every nerve and muscle burning. The venom of the monster I'd slain must still be taking its toll. A lightning pain cracked through my head. My ears rang.

Could I heal myself, as I had Roger's injuries? I closed my eyes and reached out to my tree, the stone circle, but... sensed nothing. Their power slipped my mental grasp. Something blocked my magic, or perhaps I couldn't use that ability on myself.

"I need help." I shouted at the locked door. "Please!"

I maneuvered myself closer to the door and kicked.

My only answer was a pitiful moan, doubtless from another cell. What part of the hospital was this? Even the dreary women's ward was not so unkempt. Stained paint rippled over decaying plaster walls. Someone had partially hacked away a sagging tin ceiling to allow for new pipes. None of the gaps looked big enough to fit through, even if I could climb that high.

"What was it you taught me about straitjackets, Father? Part of your act—the madman escape. You showed me the trick once when we found your old trunk of stage props."

Talking to myself again, but I was only reliving a memory, wasn't I? Perfectly sane.

I strained against the canvas, hoping I was thin enough within the bulky thing designed for a man. Soon I had my wrists unbuckled from my waist, but a longer strap still connected them. Now the painful bit—flipping my arms and shoulders through the unnatural motion of front to back. I managed, in part because the scorpion's poison inured me to the pain. Hands free, I shook off the wretched thing and kicked it away.

The door was locked. I tested the iron bolt, searing my fingers, but it held. I tried the straitjacket buckles, but they were not shaped to pick this lock.

Roger left me something. I patted the ruined silk of my bodice, glad to find the small orb still tucked there. I drew it out for inspection in that lonely shaft of light.

If I'd expected a Waysphere, I found instead a shiny surface of dark, veined gold. When I turned it in my hand, a thin, inhuman pupil stared back at me, dulled by a nictitating membrane of rock.

A petrified basilisk's eye. Evelyn had said she required one to trap a Shade. Roger had given me what I needed to help her. Or did he expect me to know how to use it myself? I slipped the stone eye into its hiding place between my undergarments and skin.

Shouting, I pounded my fists on the padded door, but doubted anyone heard me over the hiss of steam through rusting pipes or the low resonance of some mechanical-room engine. I retrieved the straitjacket and slammed its metal buckles into the door, hoping the noise would generate attention.

I listened. Nothing. After another barrage, keys rattled at the iron lock.

Quickly, I backed into one padded wall, flattening myself against the molding oilcloth.

"I'm invisible," I whispered, praying I could still make my glamour work.

Dim light bent along my skin, painting me in the horrid wall's colors.

The door creaked open, and two uniformed men walked in, carrying an electric torch.

"What the…" Yellow torchlight panned the room. "I know we locked her in here. She been moved?"

"Don't think so."

The other man picked up my discarded straitjacket. He squinted up at the barred window.

I inched toward the door. My boots left indentations in the padding, which I prayed were unnoticed.

"You calling me a liar?"

"Nobody gets outa these rooms on their own. She had *help*."

"Let's go. If we don't find her, Doc will kill us!"

They rushed the door. One of them brushed my torn shirt sleeve.

I held my breath and lifted the keyring from the guard's belt as he passed by.

"Wait," he said. "You hear something?"

I flattened myself on the padded wall. My fingers burned from the iron keys, but I gripped them together so they wouldn't jangle. A quickened pulse swished through my ears. If I missed my chance to reach the door…

"Nah. You're drunk. Come on."

I darted through before it slammed shut. Crouching beside a crate, I blended my appearance to that new pattern while the men stomped down the hallway.

"You check that wing. Every room. Find that bitch, or we're done for." He slammed his nightstick against the porthole window of the next cell. The sound of wood on metal bars rang through the corridor.

My wounded leg throbbed, though no doubt it would be worse if not for the alicorn medicine. I might already be dead. I tore a strip of cloth from my skirt and wrapped it around my hand, to shield it a bit from the sting of the iron keys.

"Look sharp, loony! Inspection time."

A wailing *Nooo!*

Who were these people locked in here? Others like me? Did they all have Fae blood?

When the guard fumbled for his missing keys, I sprinted down the hall and ducked into the shadow of an open door. I painted the image of that guard's face over mine and wrapped the illusion of a hospital uniform over my own soiled dress.

I peeked through the barred glass window of another cell door. A boy of seven or eight years stared back. Skin and bones inside a worn patient's gown, with hair filthy and matted. The child crouched in the corner. Innocent draw-ings were carved into the leather padding of the walls. He stood and lunged for the door, teeth barred, hissing. His skin was vivid green, like Changelings I'd seen in Faerie.

What had Porter done to these people? To me?

I caught my glamour's reflection in the window glass. An incorrect face looked back through my eyes. When I dropped the disguise, the Changeling child must have recognized what I was—a creature like him.

"You." He pounded a small hand on the door. "Let me out."

Trusting in perhaps a foolish impulse, I unlocked the door.

"We have to find a way out of here," I said, but the boy dashed away into the dark.

Donning my disguise once more, I checked every cell. Inside the next, a pitiful old man, human-looking and frail as a ghost. I unlocked his door, not stopping long enough to wait for him to leave.

I limped to the next cell. Inside, an emaciated female figure lay on a cot. The woman's hair had been shaved in uneven clumps. She did not move or turn her head when I swung her door open.

I ran from door to door, fumbling to find the right master keys, unlock-ing them all. When I reached the end of the passage, I turned to see most of my fellow inmates had emerged from their cells. We would all find a way out.

The doors opened to a perpendicular corridor like the one I'd just left, bisected by more bleak hallways. How large was this place? We seemed to be underground.

Heart pounding and hands shaking, I quickly unlocked more cells. A creature the size of a dog flew out of the next. I flattened myself along the wall, preparing to run, but it did not attack me. It floated, using bat-like wings and a seeming reversal of gravity to stay aloft. Its head resembled a dragon's, perched on a longish neck. Intelligent eyes studied me. Its scales were silver-blue, like the wyverns in Arimos' kingdom.

"Thou be-esssst a Fae?" It spoke in a croaking hiss; tiny hands with sap-phire claws gestured with the question.

"I am." I sensed no hostile intent.

"Blessss thou for helping esssscape. We musst kill the foul humans. Ssssteals usss from the homelandsssss. Harms ussss."

A crashing boom issued from the last cell on this block. In that second I turned to look, the wyvern had disappeared.

I approached the door, my hands trembling. A guttural growl shook the walls. Glowing tawny eyes, larger than a horse's, stared at me through barred glass. This was a magical creature. I sensed *her* trying to tell me something.

I had not noticed another of my fellow prisoners had stopped to rest beside me. "She's a root spirit. One of the Ancient Ones." The man coughed.

Startled, I recognized Septimus, or rather, Ace. His eyes flashed gold, skin flickering from brown to crimson, as if he were having difficulty holding his human glamour disguise. He wore hospital uniform pants and a cotton undershirt. Bandages wrapped his abdomen and side.

"Septimus!" I near-shouted the whisper. "What happened to you?"

He shook his head. "Porter's experiments. Let's get out of here. Quickly."

I turned back to the root spirit's cell. "We must help them escape first."

"Yes, but this one's too dangerous."

I touched the door, and the creature moved closer. I felt the intelligence of this beast. She didn't have words, but images flashed to my mind—thoughts not so different from a tree's. "She says… she can help us."

I unbolted the lock and leapt out of the way as the steel door slammed open. On green, serpentine vines slithered a creature the size of a bear. Green feathers, or leafy scales, covered her head and torso, with bark-like skin on her legs. Flowers sprouted for hair around a large deer-like head.

One forelimb had gone pale, like a log burned to ash, yet to crumble; no doubt an injury.

Sniffing the air, the root spirit turned jewel eyes on Septimus before it fixed them on me. I stood motionless as it straightened on hind legs, standing as tall as the corridor's ceiling. She roared and sprang into a lumbering run. When she came to a dead end, she didn't turn, but slammed one tentacle arm into the wall, while the pale limb hung uselessly at her side. She struck again and bellowed.

The wall cracked.

"What's she doing?" I glanced to see Septimus bracing his weight on the wall. He didn't look good.

"I don't know."

Dozens of our fellow ragged inmates, human and non-human alike, formed a group behind Septimus and me, watching the spectacle.

The wyvern hovered in the forefront, and spoke as if in a riddle, "The stonessss don't lie. There's an exit nearby. Corridorssss of the blind onessss."

The root spirit's lively tentacles tore at the plaster. She shattered concrete blocks with limb and shoulder. Vines curled and slithered into the new hole. Cracks expanded as branches grew. In seconds, the creature broke through the wall. Her extended vines snapped away and continued to grow, sprouting green leaves and bright coral flowers in the dim electric light. On three working legs, she limped through dust and debris, disappearing into another dark space.

The wyvern shrieked and flapped its wings. It followed her into what proved to be a rough tunnel dug through the earth.

Septimus coughed and brushed the settling dust away from his face. "This was not dug by machine, but by hands. The creature knew this was here."

I wiped the sweat and dust from my eyes. "Corridors of the blind ones. Who are they?"

"I don't know, but… I can smell outside air." He winced, pressing a hand to his side. A few spots of blood seeped through his bandages and shirt. "This tunnel must lead to the surface. But there's no telling what else is in there."

Our ragged crowd poured through the new opening in the wall.

I walked to Septimus, who had not yet moved. "Let me help you. My magic can heal your wound." I hoped.

He shook his head. "Not down here. Porter has too many active wards— to keep his prisoners from using their powers."

"But I can still use my glamour."

"Not the same. Glamour is natural camouflage. I can use it too, and Changelings have no Faecraft."

"Then come on." I slipped an arm around him and we negotiated chunks of broken concrete toward a path of rocky soil. The root spirit's new vines clung to walls like a mining tunnel, but no other artificial supports held up the ceiling. My ears popped. The ringing faded the farther we moved into the tunnel.

More humans, Fae, and Changelings ran or flew past us as we limped through the underground meters. Septimus's eyes shifted to their golden aspect, faintly gleaming, but he held his remaining human glamour—perhaps this helped him see better in the darkness, like my own newly awakened Fae senses. We followed the root spirit's leaf-strewn trail through the dark maze until we discerned moonlight ahead. The tunnel broke into a subterranean structure, like an abandoned cellar from the old hotel days. Night sky poured through a decaying roof, revealing piles of dirt and shelves of dusty crockery. In the bones of a rotted stairway, earth and rock had been packed to form a natural ramp. Footprints of our fellow escapees showed the way out.

I helped Septimus climb. Before we exited into the exposed night, we stopped to rest. For the moment we were alone, so I briefly updated him on the events which transpired in the Otherworld, my quest to defeat the Shade, and our capture.

"The captain of the Winter King's guard?" Septimus shook his head. "He was once part of a feared Changeling clan. A bloodthirsty band of brigands and criminals. He came into the King's military service years ago after he was taken prisoner but rose through the ranks quickly. I've heard tales of his cruelty. If Cynbel is indeed a Shade, he's a powerful one." He stroked his stubble, thinking. "Yes, that explains how Porter has gathered so many Fae prisoners, if he's had such help."

"Why does Porter steal them? I thought he made the drug from the blood of his human patients, ones with Fae ancestry like me."

"That's how it started, but he learned beings from the Otherworld are a more profitable source. And he's developed a way to revive dead human flesh. He chooses these Fae and Changelings for the magic traits he desires, and uses their blood to reanimate his cadavers, creating his... abominations. I'd entered his lab to investigate when they captured me." He laid a hand on his injured side.

"Let me try to heal you. We must be past the wards by now."

"Maybe." He looked up at the moonlit cellar door.

I moved closer, hand hovering by his bandages. "What did they do to you?"

"Took something... I think. Must not have been too important." He winced as I pressed gently on the wound. "Porter became obsessed with vestigial human organs—and Changelings. So he told me. I can't remember much else." His skin flickered from his human shade to the bright red hue of his true self. He shook his head, returning to human appearance. "It's strange. I can't relax my glamour. Must be the pain."

I closed my eyes and willed a connection to my tree. The effort was like punching through water.

"Don't waste your strength, Lady Morgen. You will need it."

"And you need my help." I strained—there it was. My hands began to glow. Not brightly enough. "I'm afraid you'll have to remove the bandage."

Underneath bandages badly in need of replacement, an ugly row of sutures wrapped his midsection, the skin angry and oozing. I blenched, furious at the evil of this place, which we had both endured. I channeled that compassion and outrage into my magic, calling my tree and the old power of the Queen's Circle to help us.

My fingers shone brighter. I sensed at least one organ had been removed. I visualized the tissues healing, renewing. I asked for more from my source, and it flowed through me until my power dwindled. My light dimmed, and I slumped against the cellar wall.

"Miss Morgen." He gently shook my shoulder.

Septimus's anxious eyes were a human shade of brown.

"I'm fine. It will pass." *I hoped.* Had the monster's poison, rather than the wards, caused my difficulty? I didn't have enough energy to try again on myself.

"Thank the Gods." Septimus smiled, touching his renewed side. "I'm in your debt, Lady of the Summer Courts."

"You saved me earlier, remember? Now we're even. Pity the sutures are still there."

"Easily removed—later. Let's get out of here before someone else comes down that tunnel."

He grabbed the keyring I'd discarded and helped me stand. A wave of exhaustion hit me—the cost of using so much magic. We continued up the earth ramp and emerged into a section of overgrown grounds. In moon shadows, we crept along the tree line beside the open yard and stopped under cover of a hemlock grove, surveying the guards stationed in front of the old groundskeeper's cottage I had seen before with Mrs. H. Only a few newer outbuildings hinted at Porter's below-ground alterations. I rested against a tree trunk, still short of breath.

"Four, maybe five men." Septimus peered through a screen of branches. "There should be a truck around back we can reach. Deliveries come and go often out here. Even at night. If we hurry, we might make it off the grounds before they discover prisoners are loose. We'll get you somewhere safe, then I'm coming back to free the rest of them."

"I'm not leaving. Not without Roger. The police are bringing him back to Porter. He might already be inside."

He sighed in frustration. "Let me go see what I can learn. You stay here. Keep hidden."

"Are you kidding? You're still in no shape to take on—"

"You're right. I need a different shape."

He knelt and placed one hand on the ground. His arms shimmered briefest red. His hair glimmered golden-bronze for an instant, but the color didn't hold. He remained in human form.

"Something is wrong. I can't transform."

"You must still be too exhausted from your injuries."

He sat on the ground and shook his head. "No, this is…. different. My senses are dulled. My hearing, smell, night vision. Nothing is right. Even my glamour seems to be… stuck."

"Can a Changeling become human again?"

"No. If we're away from the Otherworld for too long, we simply die. I've never heard of one losing their powers first. Porter must have done something else to me. I don't know what."

Before I could think of a reply, the sound of engines approached. Wheels rattled over the wooden bridge.

Two cars drove into view. One of them was a police paddy wagon. In the glare of headlamps, I saw a hooded man in the backseat of the first vehicle.

"It's Roger. I'm sure." I didn't know how this new bonding between us functioned, but my heart sensed his nearness.

Men with rifles met the convoy. A man in a tan frock coat stood under the covered portico, cast in the dim gaslight. Porter.

Steel doors swung wide. Sgt. Smith and three other officers exited. Philips got out of the second automobile. Two policemen dragged Roger, shackled, toward Porter. They removed his hood, but he was still gagged. They had changed his clothing or allowed him to do so. Men shouted and laughed. I was too far away to make out any words.

"I have to get closer," I whispered to Septimus. "I'll use my glamour."

Before he could protest, I dashed through the shadows and crouched behind a boxwood hedge bordering a low brick wall. I glided meters along the row, camouflaging myself.

"We meet again, my old colleague." Porter's voice. "Providence has re-acquainted us tonight. You and I will once more be working closely togeth-er. Ah, it will be like the old days." He laughed. "After all, I am your best student."

Roger shouted, but the gag muffled his words. A guard kicked him in the shin. Roger staggered, catching his fall on one knee. My heart felt the pain alongside his. He glanced in my direction, with the briefest change in his expression. Had he also sensed I was nearby?

"We brought what you asked."

Two men placed an object at Porter's feet. They pulled back a piece of burlap to reveal a glass and gold box like a small coffin—the same reliquary I'd seen at Roger's house. Within, the unicorn horn lay on its bed of silk. Roger's most valuable possession—the constant reminder of his deepest shame.

"Excellent. Tell the press you found the nefarious Gale and his innocent victim both dead. By the time the papers go to print, it will be true."

"He says you'll need him alive to open that lock."

"Nonsense, bring it here. I will show you how to open a box made of glass."

"Suit yourself. Damn thing ain't no kind of glass we ever seen. Like steel. Go ahead. Try and crack it."

Porter laughed.

Roger, despite his chains, stood.

"Come, officer." Porter gestured. "Let me illustrate why you failed. You are dealing with matters not, shall we say, in your jurisdiction. Certain things are best left to men who specialize."

I risked leaning forward to get a better view.

One man lit an electric torch and held it over the mad doctor's shoulder. Porter knelt and stretched his arm above the reliquary. His shadow hand cut a stark line over the limestone drive. Shadow fingers passed into the glass walls of the reliquary. Shock showed on the other men's faces at the sound of breaking glass.

Porter stood, dusting shards from his skin, and held the alicorn aloft. "Now, what were you saying, Sergeant?"

"Nothing, sir."

"Very well." He pointed to the shattered reliquary with the tip of the horn. "Please consider what's left of that container as my thanks. The gold is genuine. Melt it down and you'd have nearly a year's salary for each of you here, I'll wager. No need to tell your police chief unless you're inclined to cut him in."

"I think we can handle this quietly."

"As always, officers, I find your discretion most heartening." Porter turned to Roger as another group of hospital uniforms approached. "I must attend to pressing business. Gentlemen, I bid you a good evening."

"Boss?" said one of the newcomers. "The girl's gone."

"What?"

"Escaped. Along with the rest of the freak show on wings three and four. We need to get to safety."

Roger shouted through his gag, straining at his bonds. Two men held him back.

Porter drew an object from his coat. The edge of a knife reflected cold gaslight. Porter lunged toward Roger, blade in hand.

CHAPTER 31
EVIL REFLECTION

o!" I didn't think. I leapt toward them.

Iron hands caught me and held fast.

One orderly pinched my wrist until I was sure the bones would break.

I called upon my magic and begged nearby plants to come to my aid—to wrap their living vines around my captors, freeing Roger and me, but they did not obey. My will strained against an invisible force; a pulsing hum grew louder in my ears. These must be powerful wards.

"Ah, here is our runaway. Excellent. You saved me the trouble of torturing your paramour into helping us locate you. How I do love efficiency." Porter brought a knife to Roger's head.

"Don't you *dare* touch him! I'll—"

The orderly slapped a meaty hand over my mouth and nose. I couldn't breathe.

"Or you'll what, Miss Morgen. Turn me into a toad?" Porter laughed. "This delusion of your fairy powers is a persistent one. Fortunately for you, I know the cure. One developed by the good Dr. Gale, of course." He sliced through Roger's gag in one clean movement. "With a few of my special… improvements."

Roger spat away the cloth. "Let her go, Porter! Your man is suffocating her!" Roger turned to the police. "Officers, can you stand by and watch this? Are you not sworn to protect innocent citizens?"

A roar echoed from behind Porter. A tall and twisted form emerged into the lamplight. Like the chimera beast we had battled before, if not more grotesque. Once-human arms hung from knotted shoulders—asymmetrical, as if from different bodies. Torn, bat-like wings bent over the slumped posture.

The policemen cursed and stepped back.

"How about it, men?" said Porter. "Does anyone wish to aid our damsel in distress?"

Each officer withstood the doctor's gaze in turn. He pointed at me. The orderly removed his hand. I sucked in cold air and coughed.

"Violet!" Roger's eyes burned with green fire. "Are you unharmed?"

"Yes." I lied.

"Very well. Let there be no further delays." Porter lifted the unicorn horn into the yellow gaslight. Gone was the relic's pearly luminescence. In Porter's hand, the horn had become a mundane arrangement of once-living proteins, like the trimmings from a horse's hoof.

Porter's shadow did not track with those of the surrounding men. The doctor strutted forward, approaching Philips. He shook his hand. I blinked, but it was no trick of the light. The Shade passed from one man's feet to the other.

"Go. See that preparations are underway." Porter placed the unicorn horn in Philips' black-gloved hands. The relic's color dulled even further to a dead gray. Porter consulted his pocket watch before he glanced at the crescent moon. "Quickly now! There is little time."

Philips, his extra shadow, Sgt. Smith and the other two police officers returned to their vehicles. Two other hospital orderlies followed.

"Foul corruption." Roger's chains clanked as he strained. "You bring shame to this profession. You will not live until morning, Porter. Your evil will be cleansed from this earth."

"Come now. There is no call for theatrics. You disappoint me so, my mentor. But isn't that the way of all things?"

A needle stung my upper arm. *Not again!* I struggled, kicked, but my limbs became as heavy as lead. My eyelids slid closed, and they lowered me into a wheelchair.

From behind us came a resounding roar. An enormous beast crashed through the underbrush and emerged into the open, red flowers crowning her head.

"The root spirit," I whispered.

Someone cursed. "Big mama's loose."

She reared up on hind-legs which resembled tree trunks. The chimera moved to intercept. An unreal sight made more surreal by the sedative snaking through my veins, compounded by the monster's venom.

Gunfire erupted, but I couldn't see what happened. They pushed me toward the door of the groundskeeper's cottage. Another monstrous bellow. The men shouted.

"Get them inside." Porter yelled. "Now!"

"It's too dangerous, sir. Too many have escaped. We need to get out of here."

"No. We take the risk. The prize is worth it. Shoot anything in our way and lock the doors."

Porter's men rushed me into the house above the dungeon where I'd just been imprisoned. The walls muffled the gunfire. Through brief windows of mental clarity, I glimpsed my surroundings. The cottage's antique décor had once been innocent of these horrors. Traces of its past domestic life remained—a well-worn settee, a fireplace long unused, a cracked umbrella urn. They wheeled me through a vaguely recognizable drawing room, through a hall papered in half-remembered floral motifs.

We traveled up a small elevator. Only my wheelchair, Porter, and one orderly fit behind the openwork iron bars. I endured the ironfear, even under the sedative haze. Roger and his handlers must have followed, but I could not see or hear him. They rolled me through a bleak archway under peeling paint.

In this room, a sickly sweet odor invaded my nose. Formaldehyde and rot. Filthy sheets draped ominous shapes on worktables. A steel tray contained one severed arm, riddled with stitches, immersed in a pool of noxious ooze. Behind it all pulsed the malevolent rumbling of some machine's engine.

I might have vomited from the stench if the drug had not distanced me from it all, like a bad dream. *I had been here before, not long ago.*

Porter and the other man lifted me from the wheelchair. They dragged me, boots scraping a greasy floor, toward a monstrous metal contraption. Like a barber chair surmounted by gyroscope rings, lenses and prisms encrusted the complicated armature. Steel implements and surgical tools dangled from chains.

My eyelids grew so heavy. For a moment I imagined I was back in the Winter Courts, by that brass machine in Arimos' hall. This might have been its evil reflection.

The rings slid aside, and they placed me within the iron chair. I could neither move nor scream.

"No! Archibald. I beg you. Please." Roger's voice sounded so far away.

They spun me around until I faced the man I loved across this grotesque room. An orderly kicked Roger to the floor, chains clattering. They secured his shackles to a support beam, while another clamped metal bands around my wrists and forehead. Ice coursed through my blood; fire singed my skin.

This was not steel, but iron coated in silver. My chair shifted to face a large open window in the roof above, but I could still glimpse Roger in my strained periphery.

A sliver of moon shone through the clear night.

"Leave us—all of you," Porter commanded the orderlies. "Secure the other escaped prisoners. I can't afford to lose them. Now!"

"This madness will fail," Roger shouted.

"Do you not recognize your own work, Dr. Gale? Several generations removed in advancement, of course." Porter grabbed a large glass lens, positioning it between my sight and the sky above. "On a much larger scale—as was necessary for any truly efficient extraction." The mad doctor looked up, adjusting a series of dials.

"What have you done?" Roger strained at his chains.

"Moonlight gives the quickest results, but starlight works to a lesser degree. I've had disastrous outcomes in daylight, just as your notes predicted."

"I destroyed those notes. My equipment. Everything."

Porter rotated another section above my head until it clicked. Magical symbols marked the brass rings at regular intervals. Fae script. Glyphs of sorcery such as I'd seen in Roger's books. Lenses brightened and enlarged the silver moon before my fixed gaze.

"Did you think such valuable knowledge would simply disappear? No. I took… preemptive measures. Your work has proven quite lucrative for many important people. Luckily for me, I'm the only one who can keep up the supply for our niche demands. This gives me, as you might say, much creative freedom in this town. Call it another of your legacies, Dr. Gale. Of course, I had outside help. An enlightening partnership, I assure you."

"Please don't harm her. I'll do anything you ask."

"Indeed, you will. Tonight, I need your assistance once again, my old colleague. In fact, we shall complete a black-magic spell which you yourself commenced long ago."

Roger closed his eyes and began to chant.

Porter laughed. "Your ridiculous incantations are a waste of breath. Do you think me a rank amateur? I have ensured no unwanted conjurations interfere with our work in this place." He inserted large needles into my forearms, connected to rubber tubes. The puncture wounds were just below my elbows—alongside healing scars made by the same procedure days ago.

I tried to scream, but uttered only a sedated moan.

From across the room, Roger continued his monotone chanting.

"Half-breeds like her are a scourge on both of our races." Porter pulled a lever and the sound of the machine's engine changed pitch. "Though I can't fault you for your lust." Looming over me, Porter ogled the low neckline of my Winter Court gown. I wanted to stab him with a nearby pair of surgical scissors, but my limbs were bound and paralyzed. "Yet she has a higher purpose. When we are through with her, what's left will fetch a price far greater than your alicorn. You shall see."

Porter drew a knife from his waistcoat pocket. The blade came to my immobile face, flushed cold. He cut a lock of my hair.

The metal around me reflected an eerie glow. My reflection on his eyeglasses became obscured as a misty layer of blue-violet luminescence encircled me. Faelight.

"Such power! A pity this will be her last extraction." Porter's maniacal laugh cut through the mechanical noise, until he added, "Though, were it not for your most recent trip to the Otherworld, I would've had to wait six months to get another full yield from this one. We nearly killed her last time. What a tragedy that would have been, without knowing her true worth."

Roger's chants became like the verses of a resonant song, an edge of desperation in even that controlled music.

Porter drew a gun from his waistcoat and aimed it at Roger. I strained, trying to kick him off balance, but my knee only managed a twitch. Silver-coated iron bit into my wrists, searing my nerves. The sedative dulled every muscle.

"You will be silent! Or I will cease to find this demonstration amusing!" He locked the hammer in place. "Do you understand, Dr. Gale?"

No answer. Only the sonorous words of Roger's magic, under the hiss of steam and the grind of gears as my chair lifted.

Porter pointed the gun at me, laughing before I rose too high to see him. Closer to the open window above, I tasted sweet night air mingling with the room's chemical rot.

So badly did I want to sleep. I pushed against that urge.

"First, we drain every precious drop of her magic. We only need her body to finish the spell. We will add her ashes to those of her tree, thereby creating a dark Faestone more powerful than anything humans have commanded in centuries. One which contains the power of your own curse. Oh, I must thank you for locating the grimoire as well. My associate and I have been searching for years for this spell. Do you see how our stars are so beautifully aligned?"

Now too high to see either of them, the myriad reflections of the moon and the glow of my own light surrounded me.

Roger ceased his chanting, as though he had given up. "My curse has nothing to do with this! You've stolen and corrupted my work, but I take no part in your evil."

"Have you not yet determined who this creature is to you? Where the source of her own magic grows? Too incredible." He laughed. "Perhaps you do not wish to see it, hmm? You know we often blind ourselves to the obvious. Ah, but that you found each other at long last... I do love a good tragedy."

"Violet's tree is the source of her magic. But if it grows... *No*. The Queen would have told me."

"The Queen's rule is nearing an end. And now, my erstwhile mentor, take heart, for *your many sins* will be reborn as a weapon of fantastic magnitude."

Searing cold rushed through my limbs. Magic poured out through my veins. Yet I felt not the same elation as when I called that power on my own. This use was anathema to my will.

Roger yelled something I could not make out under the machine's noise, if it was not my own muffled senses. Pain numbed all else. Breathing was a battle. My life was draining away.

I cast my gaze to the sky, past the machine and my own fractured reflections, to the waning moon. A shadow moved at the edge of the domed glass. I recognized three-lobed leaves. Ivy.

So tired, but I had to fight. A distant chanting called me back. Roger's spell. His resonant voice sought the boundaries of Cynbel's wards, widening cracks in the magic. They snapped. I gasped for a breath of fresh night air.

Roger shouted, "Now, Violet!"

The power of the forest rushed to me, like blood into a limb freed of its ropes.

I called out to the ivy covering these walls. She answered, whispering disgust at what the humans had done to her home. At my silent command, she spiraled tendrils through the ceiling's opening. Leafy vines corkscrewed, blocking the moonlight. I asked the ivy to break the mirrors. Vines whipped to obey. A shield of new leaves cocooned me—protection from the shrapnel.

Far below, men shouted. I could not distinguish voices under the noise.

Curling wisps of green sought my skin. Branches levered the cuffs holding my wrists, cracking the cold iron hinges. I was free. I yanked out the needles attached to those hideous surgical tubes. No time or energy to inspect my wounds. I unlatched the braces from my head, unbuckled my feet and swung out to grab the ivy. It swirled into a seat, and I trusted this old wood spirit who whispered she could bear the weight.

Mother once told me plants never lied.

In my leafy gondola, I rose into the air above the machine, pressing the wounds on my forearms closed with glowing fingers, fighting the sedative.

If only I still had my wings.

Gunshots rang out—louder than the destruction I'd unleashed. A ball of yellow flame burst from within the dust and falling debris—I could not see the source.

Another barrage of gunfire. A vine exploded beside my head. I directed the ivy to lower me quickly.

The ivy spirit I'd awakened now raged. She burst through grungy windows, shattering glass, wood, and iron. Tendrils found cracks in the brick and a section of wall gave way, crashing into the courtyard below. Light from the brightest stars shone into the wretched room before clouds of dust eclipsed all but the stench.

My ivy snapped. I tumbled to the floor, but she softened my fall.

I wiped my eyes to see Roger and Porter on the floor, scuffling. Porter held a gun in one hand, and Roger's neck in the other. Roger pinned the gun hand to Porter's side, but his strength was fading in the struggle.

I called the vines. They snaked towards the men. I balled a fist in midair and the tendrils constricted around Porter's arms and torso. The shock made Porter lose his grip. Roger rolled away, gasping, and grabbed the gun from the man's slack fingers. He stood and shot Porter in the chest. Again.

Porter's body went limp within the tangled vines and a cloud of gun smoke. Dark blood pooled.

Roger crouched beside me and dropped the gun to the floor.

He helped me sit up. Fire had blackened and singed the cuffs of his torn white shirt, as though he'd burned away his chains. His skin was scratched, but unsinged. He wrapped me in a hug.

"Are you all right?" I brushed a lock of his hair, damp with sweat, away from a bruised cheekbone. My fingers were so numb I could not feel his skin, but this embrace was a refuge from the nightmare.

"Yes. Are you, my love?"

"I don't know. My legs… and hands are numb."

"She'll die tonight. Her tree will soon be felled."

We turned to face Porter, who heaved a ragged cough, still bound in the ivy.

"You of all men know you cannot stop this kind of ritual once set in motion." His grimace showed blood-slicked teeth. "Fortune smiles upon you once again, Dr. Gale. With a Faestone containing the magic of your own curse, combined with her magic, imagine the power you would hold. Don't let her sacrifice be in vain. The moon has not yet set."

"Damn you! I'd sooner see you in hell."

"Hell?" Another drowning laugh. He spat blood. "We are already living in hell. But I will soon be free." Porter's hand reached under the fabric of his shirt.

No. I clenched a fist. The ivy vines constricted around his neck, slick with blood, and Porter's laugh became a wheeze. The realization unsettled me—that I could delight in another's torture. Even this man's.

Roger placed a hand on my shoulder. "Violet. You must not kill him. Let me bear this guilt alone."

I exhaled. My vines relaxed their hold.

"Foolish half-breed. His kind are nothing but hunters, and you are his greatest prize."

Porter's eyes closed behind dusty spectacles. He drew out a chain from behind his shirt collar and smeared blood on the mirror amulet. He whispered a word and the talisman pulsed with darklight.

Roger thrust his open hand forward, and with a word of command, an invisible pulse struck Porter like a physical blow, knocking the bloody amulet from his fingers.

In an instant, the air temperature plummeted, and I heard the crack of ice.

"It's too late…" Porter's voice bubbled into silence. The focus in his eyes dimmed, and his head slumped on a limp neck. Lifeless.

Roger helped me stand, retrieving the gun. Together we walked to the unmoving body.

Roger knelt and checked for pulse and breathing. "He's dead."

He pulled a ring from Porter's finger—his own Reliqua ring they had stolen from him. He spoke a word over it, and the stone flashed indigo before he slipped it back on his finger.

From a nearby pile of surgical tools, he retrieved a rusty scalpel and began unbuttoning his waistcoat.

"What are you doing?" I asked, drawing closer.

"Certain materials, black silk among them, can act as insulation against magic." With the scalpel, he cut and ripped away a section of his waistcoat lining. Holding the cloth in his hand so as not to touch the amulet, he snapped the chain from Porter's neck, folding the object carefully within. Using an index finger, he drew a symbol above the cloth bundle in his other hand. It shimmered with darklight.

He shook his head. "The talisman is still bonded to the Shade's magic. But…"

"You said we should destroy it."

"Yes." His brow furrowed. "But now that Porter is dead… the Shade should have lost its anchor to this world. Should have already gone back to sleep. Something's wrong."

He stood and turned to me, beautiful eyes pleading. Tonight, I saw clearly the Faelight he'd possessed behind that gaze all along, like a distant star on a moonless night.

He slipped the cloth-wrapped amulet into his coat pocket, his expression again unreadable. "If we are to rout him, this talisman may yet prove useful."

What was he hiding? I didn't like it. "Porter said my tree is in danger. How did they know where it was? Did I tell them when…?" I glanced again at the body lying in a crimson puddle and suppressed a wave of nausea. "I don't remember, but I've been in this room before. Perhaps more than once."

Roger drew me close, exhaled a weary tremor as his arms encircled me. "You never deserved this." I sensed the fear he tried to hide.

A bizarre thought struck me with sudden clarity. Roger and I had been linked to each other our whole lives… or at least all of mine. It all had to do with his curse. I didn't understand, and I wasn't sure how to judge it either. Yet I read the truth of his heart. Every touch spoke of genuine love. I prayed that was enough, but I was beginning to doubt.

I said, "We must stop them from cutting it down. Or else…"

"We will."

CHAPTER 32
WITHOUT ITS SOURCE

nother section of the laboratory's roof gave way to the ivy's work, crushing a table of beakers and surgical instruments. We covered our faces against raining debris.

After only a few steps, exhaustion hit me like a tidal wave. I staggered. How much life had the machine drained away?

Roger caught me, his own touch cold. Leaning on each other, we struggled through the rubble, past the ruins of the extraction chair. A piece of discarded tubing still glowed with the residue of my fairy blood. "There," I pointed to a small glass container which had survived intact. "That must be my Faelight." Another beside it lay broken, oozing luminous liquid down one of the machine's brass instrument panels.

Roger collected and stoppered the unbroken vial. He placed it in my hands.

"Keep this safe, but don't drink it. It will last longer if you keep it near your heart. If it fades, the magic is lost."

I tucked the warm glass between my corset and chemise. I recognized the magic as my own, even out of body.

A wall of shelving gave way. We ran through dust and darkness, over fallen detritus, toward the main doors, blocked by vines and ceiling boards. I added my dwindling strength to the task of heaving obstacles out of our path.

Another gunshot rang out. The bullet shattered a board beside Roger's leg. He grabbed my hand. Together, we ducked for the cover of an upturned steel table. He drew the revolver from his waistcoat, peered around our shield, and gasped.

I risked a glance.

My ivy vines slithered to uncoil from Porter's body, but not of my accord. They lifted his corpse from the floor, growing and lengthening as they lassoed the walls and ceiling for purchase. Porter's head swiveled unnaturally wide. A dead smile, near agape, drooling blood. The vines puppeted the lifeless flesh enough for it to take a wobbling step.

"The Shade," Roger whispered. "It must be."

Roger fired the gun; two rounds in the corpse's heart and one in the head before the revolver's chambers clicked empty.

"She knows my name, Human." Clotted fluid oozed from the bullet hole in his forehead, but the bloody lips smiled. Unblinking eyes as black as Cynbel's fixed on me. His voice was a ghastly mimicry of life. "Yes, she knows me. She and I have been close for a long, long time."

Agape at my living nightmares, I could not speak for the shock.

"Long I lusted for your death, half-breed. For your tree drained my strength." Blood bubbled through Porter's dead mouth when he laughed. "I wanted to kill you. Just as I made this sorcerer's sister jump to her death. But your mother's wards stopped me. Then I learned what you would become. I waited. Watched. Until your magic was full. Now the harvest has come at last."

"The Welterwood hears me!" I shouted. "We will stop you. Even if you kill us."

Porter's dead body raised a pale hand. Nearby vines coiled like ropes around Roger and me. I pleaded with the ivy, but under Cynbel's control, she no longer heard my unspoken commands.

Roger whispered another spell. A current of air swirled around us. I caught the odor of smoke on the wind. Foul things burning hot. Chemicals. Yet I could see no fire.

The basilisk eye. My fingers went to that small stone kept under my clothing. Still there, beside the vial of my extracted light.

The cadaver laughed, lumbering closer to us; a marionette of lifeless flesh on its trellis of vines.

My numb skin rose into gooseflesh.

"Porter was an incompetent fool—calling me here when the ritual had begun. But I am free of him now." He spat blood from a drooping mouth. "We have little time. This forces me to take drastic measures."

"Gale! Lady Violet!" Evelyn's voice, though I could not see her. "Stand back."

A loud crack of gunfire was followed by a burst of yellow-white flame. The explosion knocked Porter's corpse off its feet. My ears rang with the percussion.

Evelyn stormed through a haze of smoke. Still wearing her nurse's uniform, she aimed a large handgun at our enemy. The thing broke from the ivy and slithered under a fallen steel surgical table.

Our restraining vines loosened. Roger and I shook free of the tendrils and stood.

"Are both of you unharmed?"

"We're alive," I said. "Dr. Crane, I have a basilisk eye." I handed the sphere to her.

"Excellent. Gale, do you remember what to do?" She clenched a fist, and the eye shattered in her black-gloved hand.

"Yes. You take the north."

She nodded and dashed into the shadows.

Porter's corpse advanced on us with an unbalanced gait and eyes like two bottomless pits.

"Stay behind me." Roger moved to intercept, leading with a salvaged surgical knife.

"I will not harm your body, wretched human. I need you intact. My rightful place is within your flesh."

"Never." Roger shouted. "I will not be your puppet."

"Oh, my foolish creator, do you not know me?" The Shade raised its arms as if in supplication. "I am the record of your deepest Shame. The shape of your very own Sins. It is why I suffered you to live all these years, after your sister paid the price for both your transgressions."

"No! I… I never summoned you."

"Your unholy actions were my genesis. I am the Shadow you cast on the mirror of spilt unicorn blood. You created me through your evil, even if you did not speak the words—"

"No." He clenched his eyes shut.

"You and I will reintegrate. Curse and Cursed. Together we shall wield a Faestone made from the ashes of your lover's tree. We will be unstoppable."

The knife in Roger's hand trembled. He inhaled, spoke a magic word, and traced a symbol with the point of the blade, slicing a burning trail of Faelight to complete the spell. This mirage hung upon the air, a transient banner. Raw power cracked through the atmosphere like a wake. Roger shouted another command, directing that force toward the Shade.

The corpse laughed and raised a hand, bloodlust in abysmal eyes. An inverse reflection of that same sigil appeared before him, drawn not in light but in darkness.

Now I understood. If light existed, there must also be its opposite. There could never be one without the other.

"This cannot be true. You are not of my Making. This must be deception." He sounded desperate to convince himself of that statement.

And if it were true, what did that mean? I shuddered.

All the shadows in the room warped and twisted. Lines of blackness lifted, seeped like paint from a wet canvas, and pooled around the cadaver's undead fingers.

Roger raised his right hand above his forehead—an edge of desperation in the tone of his incantation. His arms trembled with restrained tension, or with fear. Light swirled within his open palm.

The Shade launched its weapon. Gathered darkness opened into a writhing net above our heads.

With a word, Roger's magic became a shield, like the glass-thin surface of water reflecting an unseen sun. Thick shadows hit this barrier and oozed to the ground—dissolving alongside a brilliant arc of light.

Roger staggered, but I caught him. Our hands braced on the fallen debris, our bodies trembling from exhaustion, leaning on one another.

Cynbel howled with an inhuman voice. The corpse cupped its face with pale hands.

"Now," Evelyn shouted and rushed toward the howling monster, fist clenched like she carried an invisible weapon.

"Close your eyes." Roger spoke beside my ear before he dashed away.

Evelyn traced symbols in the air. She held her magic words like notes in a song—her voice higher than Roger's baritone. Their spell crackled with electric charge. Another bright flash of light—like red and green fireworks. My eyes stung under half-closed lids.

Porter's corpse fell to the tile like a bundle of wet laundry, and I risked a look. Above the body, tangible shadows coalesced into a black orb, which imploded into a strand of smoke.

Evelyn knelt beside the body. She traced a sigil in the ashy remains of what must have been the basilisk eye.

"Cynbel's gone?" I asked, staring at the now-lifeless body of Porter. "Is it done?"

"No. We only weakened him. Sent him back to the Void between worlds. For now." Evelyn wiped a hand through the symbol she'd drawn and blew the ashes from her palm.

Roger and I braced one another to stand. He turned from my gaze. I fought a wave of dizziness.

"Cynbel means to finish what he started. To complete the ritual at Violet's tree. He will soon return for us." Roger clenched a fist and stared at the corpse—with a dead look in his own eyes.

"Is it true? Is the Shade of your Making, Gale?"

"So it appears." His face had become ashen.

"If we survive…" Evelyn stepped closer to him, her brow furrowed, jaw set firm, but I could see she was holding back a stronger emotion. "You know I must inform the Council of this."

"I won't stop you. Right now, my only thought is to reach Violet's tree before they can cut it down, or she will be killed. Nothing else matters."

Evelyn exhaled and wiped sweat and grime from her face with a uniform sleeve. "We cannot allow the Shade to create a dark Faestone. He would control too great a power in this world. He must be stopped. At all costs." She glanced at me in sorrow. They knew something they weren't telling me. She paced, eyes darting from Roger to the floor, her arms crossed. "Everything in this room must be destroyed. None of these abominations can be permitted to live, for they will infect other life on the island. I will take care of that. You must finish what the Queen commanded of you, Gale. Destroy it. Unfortunately, I believe Violet must go with you. She is part of this magic."

"The Council?" Roger asked. "Were they informed of the trial proceedings after our connection was lost?"

"Perhaps, but I've been out of contact for hours. Septimius filled me in. Outside just moments ago."

"Septimus?" I asked. "Is he safe?"

"Yes. He's gone to release the rest of the prisoners from the underground wings of this complex. I came here to find you. And it appears my timing was perfect." She exhaled and shook her head.

Roger seemed dazed. In shock.

She put a hand on his shoulder, and he did the same to her. They shared a moment of intimate connection that might have made me jealous, if I had not feared what it meant. She nodded, as though she understood some unspoken message, confirming she could trust him. He heaved a breath, his sorrow palpable.

My heart sank. All I could do was go numb.

She set her eagle-like eyes on me. "Do you know where your tree grows?"

"Yes. In the Welterwood. I'll lead us there."

"Good. That's not far. Especially by air." She turned to Roger. "Can you still fly a Steam-Dart?"

"Never as well as you, Crane."

"I know where Porter keeps a few behind the maintenance wing. Follow me."

Evelyn led the way toward the room's main entrance. Every step brought a wave of dizziness and pain. Roger offered me an arm, and we climbed through piles of rubble.

Evelyn heaved an upturned gurney out of our way and pushed open the double-doors. Thick smoke hit us like an oily rag. Heat rushed from the dark hallway. Fire surged toward us—hungry for the new source of air.

Evelyn slammed shut the metal doors, coughing through the smoke. Flames licked the glass viewing portals. "There must be another way out."

We retreated from the blaze and scanned the room.

Roger signaled. "We'll climb the outside wall."

Flames crept under the door. Smoke thickened. One row of laboratory specimens caught fire. Jars of formaldehyde popped in the heat, exploding the inferno in new directions.

We ran to the opening in the exterior wall, ripped asunder by my ivy. I called to that vine with my waning strength. She answered, sending forth tendrils to form a ladder.

Evelyn began to descend that living staircase. I followed behind her, but a lightning bolt of pain struck my back. I collapsed on the floor beside the ivy grown precipice. Spasms shook my limbs, and I couldn't speak.

Evelyn climbed back up and sat next to Roger and me while the worst passed.

Roger cradled my face in his hands. "What happened? Talk to me."

"I don't know... Something's wrong." Something worse than the utter defeat I heard in his voice. I closed my eyes and exhaled a tendril of awareness, listening. Seeking.

The shape of my rowan tree against the indigo night sky. I shook with iron-fear. Iron nails pierced my body.

I coughed. The smoke had thickened, smelling of burning chemicals and charred organic remains.

"It's my tree. I can feel... they've hammered iron nails into its trunk. They are starting the ritual. We'll never... get there in time."

Roger pounded the floor with a fist. "We must! We will." He glanced behind me. Red and yellow flames danced in his tear-glossed eyes. "Can you climb?"

I shook my head. "No. I have an idea. There's a faster way. The Wayportal... we found. In the barrow. It was near the valley where my tree grows."

"Yes. That could work." He turned to Evelyn. "Do you have a traveling relic?"

"Fortunately, yes." She pulled a bracelet from her wrist and gave it to Roger, who pocketed it, eying the encroaching blaze. "We'll need a large enough reflective surface." She stood and searched. "Pity none of Porter's giant mirrors are around. At least none I can see in this rubble."

Roger coughed and pointed. "We'll use a surgical table."

He helped me stand and gave me his clean handkerchief to shield my nose against the smoke. We hobbled to a section of the room lined with cloth-draped tables and haphazard trays of medical equipment. Evelyn over-turned a bigger one, dumping its grim contents. A corpse of unnatural shape thudded to the floor. She used a blood-spattered cloth to wipe brown residue from the steel surface.

The shock of where I stood was too much. I didn't see a vat of arms soak-ing in some foul green liquid meters away. I didn't smell the sadness of decay and the hellfire of chemical smoke. There was no row of severed heads with skulls sawed open to reveal dead-gray brain pincushions for rusty clamps. Nor did I recognize a body I'd carted out of the main hospital days ago—the shrunken, suture-ridden cadaver of the young man who had stared at me in Commons. No. None of this could be real.

Despite the heat of the encroaching flames, my cheeks flushed cold. My knees trembled and my vision narrowed. My stomach turned.

Roger squeezed my hand to comfort me, and it helped.

Evelyn had propped the table upright, like an unhinged door. The brushed-metal mirror, reflecting our blurred forms in the burning laborato-ry's reflection. She began a spell. Currents of energy shimmered around her.

"Can you stand unaided for a moment?" Roger asked. "I must help her draw the sigils."

I nodded and grabbed the edge of another surgical table for balance. What did I care that a greenish dead hand protruded from a filthy shroud?

The two Reliqua warriors began their melodious chanting in words of magic power. They synchronized the tone of their voices, stimulating the surrounding currents of force like powerful magnets.

Evelyn stood with her hands raised, as if she were a tuning fork for this new nexus of energy they summoned. A faint glimmer of light formed be-tween her inward-facing palms. Roger drew shapes in the air at four points around the door. The symbols flickered into the visible light spectrum, be-coming solid tracers of light. Geometric figures combined with elegant Fae letters. I tried to mark them in my memory, even if I didn't quite understand their meanings.

Another chemical vat exploded, rattling the filthy steel implements on the table beside me.

Roger turned to me, shouting through the roar of flames, "Visualize the destination in your mind. Your magic will help us build the link."

I closed my eyes and pictured the underground cavern—the glyphs we had awoken in the walls. The cascade of rubble we must scale.

A rush of aetheric current rose the hairs on my neck—like someone had thrown open a window to a spectral breeze. I opened my eyes to see a new doorway of light formed on the steel table.

Something grabbed my wrist. The green cadaver hand!

I yelped and pulled back. Clawed fingers squeezed like a vise.

The thing on the table convulsed as if in seizure. Its shroud slipped away, revealing a hideous patchwork of human and non-human limbs. Skin the color of pond scum. A bloated woman's face. Eyes white and dead as a three-day-old fish opened and turned to me. She gurgled, "Sister. Pure." A ropy tongue snaked out and probed the skin on the back of my hand. I recoiled in mute horror. Rows of shark-like teeth drooled. The tongue slid up my arm, licking the needle's wound. I pulled with my remaining strength, but the grip was like iron.

Evelyn shouted to me, "Duck!"

With a tracer of yellow-white light, an augmented pistol blast knocked the monster back. It released its hold and scuttled from the table. Evelyn fired again; the luminous ammunition revealing her aim was true. The creature squealed and flailed mismatched arms before it stilled.

Another human-sized experiment sat up and pulled the cloth drape from its huge insect eyes. Sutures zigzagged the chimera's neck, oozing oily liquid. It bellowed. Evelyn shot it in the torso, silencing the horrible cry, yet it still twitched.

"Go, you two! Get out of here. I will save the living prisoners, but these revivified abominations must be destroyed." She fired again, reached into her nurse's apron, pulled out an ammunition cartridge, and reloaded.

Still holding me up, Roger grabbed Evelyn's forearm as we passed. "Godspeed, House Crane."

She returned the quick gesture—a warrior's grip. "And to you, House Gale." Evelyn's voice cracked. "Get her out of here, Gale. I'm trusting you. Protect her."

Evelyn turned to me. "Protect him. May the forest be with you, and the Goddess watch over you both."

Her words seemed to steel Roger's nerves, and he regained a little composure, though not enough to ease my anxiety.

Roger and I limped toward the shimmering mirage, and grasped the handle formed of arcane symbols. The ethereal doorway opened; a plane of reality hinged upon itself. Fresh air swept my face, the smell of moss and rock.

Inside, beams of pale moonlight illuminated fallen rubble in a dark space. The barrow.

We crossed the impossible threshold. My boots crunched sand and stone.

Through the Wayportal, we knelt to catch our breath, holding one another. The glimmering doorway faded behind us, returning to the ordinary wall of a tomb. I wiped my cold face. It was dark enough here to see a glow through the thin fabric of my ruined dress. I thought at first it was my crystal pendant, but I couldn't remember where I had lost it. No, it was the vial of liquid light tucked next to my skin.

Roger touched my cheek. In a voice laden with fear and sadness he couldn't hide from me, he asked, "How do you feel?" and placed two fingers on the side of my neck and my wrist, reading my pulse.

"Dizzy. Exhausted. But my leg is healing." I didn't tell him I could still sense the iron nails piercing my tree. Like ghost knives, they stabbed an invisible second skin. "It's not far. There's a valley with a stream running through it. A single rowan—"

"I know... where it grows." He squeezed my hands. "The one you painted."

"Many times. I never knew what it was to me." I used to think the thing looked lonely, growing through those rocks, gnarled and twisted. Picturesque in a rugged way.

"I'm so sorry." The heartache in his voice was more than I could bear. "None of this should ever have happened to you. I'll make it right." He kissed my wrist and guided my hand to the side of his face.

I tucked my head against his neck. He stroked my hair. Yet, we had no time to rest.

Too soon, we stood and surveyed this ruined underground chamber— the cave-in we'd caused just days ago. Through a breach in the stonework ceiling, moonlight revealed granite rubble, littered with fallen forest leaves, and marked with rivulets of mud.

"The monster's remains are gone." Roger helped me atop a lager flat stone, and he climbed ahead, gazing up through intermittent moonbeams.

"I wonder how they managed that trick?" Ahead of us, the tumbled stones and earth were blackened, as if charred by a fire. That might have been where the beast had fallen when I severed its head.

Withered vines trailed into the cave, leaves brown and curling.

Roger pulled on one, and it held. "I think these are strong enough to climb. Let me try first."

He'd ascended nearly to the opening when the vine snapped, crashing to the chamber floor. He jumped in time to catch a ragged stone's edge and heave himself over the side.

I walked toward him through a swirl of dust and debris.

He stood, gazing down at me; his face was in shadow, sculpted lines and dark hair silvered by thin moonlight.

"Is there another vine you could toss to me?" I couldn't waste my dwindling strength here, with our battle yet to come.

"No." Roger wiped a hand over his eyes, and I caught the glint of tears. "Violet. Please stay here until daybreak. Ask the forest to protect you tonight. Use your magic to escape when it's safe. If you go with me now, the Shade will destroy you. I can't let that happen."

"What?" My blood turned to ice. "I'll not hide here like a craven. I will fight."

"Would you kill even me?"

"Roger, what are you saying?"

"The math is simple. A shadow cannot exist without its source. The Shade must be reabsorbed by the magic of its origins. I must allow it to use my body so that I can destroy both of us. There is no other way to kill it... now that it has become so powerful. You know we must stop this monster. We have no choice."

I clenched a fist and shook my head. "No. That can't be right."

"It is."

"Evelyn knew this?"

"Yes. Please. Let me... say goodbye. When I'm still myself. When I can still protect you... from myself."

"Roger, you can't! This is wrong!"

"I love you, Violet."

He turned and limped out of my view. A black silhouette against the inky night.

CHAPTER 33

TOWARD THE LIGHT

❦

T his *was* wrong. I felt it to my bones. The math, as Roger said, did not add up. I could not let him walk to his death. Not when I could fight.

I couldn't give in to despair either, or panic, though they closed in on me, colder and darker than the air of this tomb.

I had to find a way out of this pit.

Could I risk using enough magic to call more vines? I reached out, but the connection slipped through my mental grasp, and I didn't have the strength. Porter's machine had drained too much. The iron nails in my tree were constant pressure and pain, while that chimera's dark poison lingered in my veins. Small mercy the sedative's effects were fading.

I drew out the glowing vial of extracted Faelight, holding it like a lantern. How did one even use it out of body? The darkness of the cave receded. Injured leg throbbing, I navigated the ruin. Fallen stones and heaps of earth. Slicks of mud and curtains of dead vines. The Wayportal slept once again. I was certain I didn't have enough energy to open it by myself, if I could even remember how. Could someone else—or *something else*—come through? Probably. Another reason not to tarry here.

The more I dwelt on Roger's desertion of me now, the more my cheeks burned with fury. Anger was easier than acknowledging the horror of what he'd said. That he must kill himself to stop Cynbel.

I rested with a hand on the damp stone wall, pulling in shallow breaths. A draft, tasting of moss and forgotten subterranean spaces, chilled my fevered skin. I hobbled toward the darkest shadows and discovered an archway. My light revealed a long corridor, narrow and strangled with roots from the forest above. I could not see far. Perhaps it was only a dead end.

I cast one more glance around the chamber. No other options. Then a faint glimmer of greenish-blue light caught my eye—like a firefly resting on a stone.

I approached, kneeling beside the mysterious light. A clump of something like fur protruded from the mud. I hesitated, but reached to touch it. Under the wet sand, my fingers found a silver handle.

"My summoning brush."

I wiped it on my skirt, but the bristles were still caked with soil. On a nearby stone, a pocket of rainwater mirrored the crescent moon through the cave-in opening. I swished the glowing brush tip through the water to clean it, breaking the sky's reflection into a dance. I watched in silent awe as the pool illuminated, nearly as bright as the liquid light I carried.

Drink.

The word came from everywhere and nowhere. Many whispers in unison, like the voices of the Welterwood's trees.

The water will restore your health.

"Who are you?" Was it the voice I had heard in my garden that night before father disappeared?

Drink and see.

I had no reason to trust this message, but no reason to doubt it either. This was only rainwater, after all.

I cupped a handful of lustrous liquid and drank. The water tasted sweet on my parched throat. I didn't realize how thirsty I had been. I reached for more, but my fingers froze at the sight of a face.

Not a human face. It rippled on the surface—gleaming white in an indigo sky. Two doe-like eyes. A spiral horn pointing toward stars. The unicorn.

You have seen me in your dreams. The unicorn's eyes did not blink, and its mouth did not move. *We are connected, Daughter of the Forest.*

"I don't understand."

I am the guardian of the Welterwood. The form that once was, the shape of this beast, cannot return. That body was destroyed, but my consciousness remained, as it will until the last of the trees are gone. I was filled with rage and sadness, forgetting what I was. I sought only revenge, taking on his hateful human shape. But through the life of your tree, through your love, I grew again toward the light. The Welterwood has found its protector again. In you.

"What do you ask of me?"

Do not fear. Be swift. You must undo the curse on my forest. The wizard will fail without you, for he believes a lie.

"A lie?" I closed my eyes and knew. If the unicorn had run through my most blessed dreams, the Shade had haunted my darkest nightmares. "The shadow is not his. It's yours."

When I opened my eyes, the face was gone. In its place was only the bright crescent moon. The rainwater pool no longer tasted like wine, but stone, sand, and sky. I drank another three handfuls.

I stood, finding balance again. My footsteps steady—my breathing stronger. The enchanted water must have indeed restored me. I checked my arms, but the wounds left by the hospital remained.

Holding the brush like a weapon, I ventured into the dark tunnel, with a bottle of my own dwindling Faelight for a lamp.

The space narrowed. Air rushed through. My light was only strong enough to reveal a few steps ahead. I scarcely squeezed between tree roots and stone. When I came upon a solid wall, I bent to check every corner and found no other openings, only worn petroglyphs like those I had brought to life at the Queen's Circle. If I were not about to die, I might have stayed and traced each one, recording them for study. Enigmatic shapes surrounded a circular petroglyph—perhaps lightning bolts or rays radiating from some source. No, they must be roots, and mirrored above were the tops of trees.

I found a dead end, yet air flowed in from an opening I missed. Backtracking a few paces, I lifted my light to inspect the dilapidated stonework ceiling. A promising shadow led me beside a cluster of protruding tree roots. There I glimpsed the starlit sky. Was the gap wide enough?

I tucked away the brush and climbed a living ladder of roots. As I ascended, a figure eclipsed the ribbon of starlight. Something swift-moving and heavy. Footsteps loosened particles of dirt. I covered my light, hoping it was not yet noticed. The creature snorted a visible breath; catching a scent on the night.

The brush. Could I still use it for a weapon?

I leaned forward to get a better look at my foe. A howl. This was a wolf, its pelt golden-brown, faintly lit with auric haze.

The wolf's large yellow eyes found me through the opening in the rocks, lit by the moonlight. Familiar eyes.

"Violet, is that you?"

The wolf moved aside. A human silhouette. I lifted my lamp and saw Septimus.

"Yes. I'm here."

"Thank the Gods. Stand back, Lady. We'll open the way."

The wolf began digging at the soil around the tree's root, revealing more sections of starlit sky.

Soon the hole was wide enough, and Septimus helped me climb. I emerged into a clearing beside an old oak.

The wolf, too large to be a natural animal from this world, eyed me quizzically.

"She's a fellow Changeling. She helped me move the other prisoners to safety. The ones who could escape…" He shook his head, and I knew he'd seen enough horrors of Porter's madness, just as I had. "She sensed your magic and led me here."

"We've met before. At the Queen's Circle. Thank you both." I bowed my head. "We must get to my tree as quickly as possible. They're trying to cut it down. If they do, I'll die." I pointed in the direction of the clearing I knew so well. "That way."

The wolf gave a yelping bark, but in my mind, I understood the words, *If you can't run, I will carry you.*

"I can run."

My two legs proved not as swift as the wolf's four. I missed my wings. I had only known them all too briefly before they were gone.

The forest thinned into a grassy clearing. An echoing crack rang out. Gunfire.

Stay down. The wolf growled.

I located the shooter—a glimpse of movement in the distance. A gray-green uniform I could never forget.

"Philips!" Septimus shouted. "Don't shoot!"

I yelled, "Porter's dead! It's over!" Though it wasn't, and Philips had to know.

A delirious laugh. "You stupid bitch! This is all your fault. And you, Ace. Freak of nature. I should've killed you already."

He fired again. The shot bounced off a tree beside me. Then another.

On instinct, I dipped the silver brush in my vial of light and painted a vine coiled around Philips' hand.

The vines in the nearby trees surged with preternatural vigor toward him. He screamed. Thorns and brambles encircled his arm with the speed of striking serpents. The gun fell to the ground.

I approached my vegetation encased captive, bound to the forest floor.

"Enough," I whispered to the vines, and they slowed to a crawl. "Keep him here for a while."

Philips coughed. His bloody hands shook. His crazed face was spattered and smeared with blood and sweat. "Porter said it would spare me, but he lied! They're all dead. He killed them. I couldn't stop it!" Philips struggled against the vines, but they tightened around him. "It would have killed me too, but Porter called it back…" Philips uttered a moan, so miserable I pitied him. "He should have let it kill me."

I picked up his discarded gun and gave it to Septimus, who checked the barrel. "Only two bullets left."

The wolf ran to join us, hackles raised as she growled at Philips. *Let me kill him.*

"No. He can't hurt us now."

From his prison of vines and brambles, Philips laughed—a tortured sound. "We'll all be dead before the night's done."

The Changeling wolf howled and leapt into a run.

When I followed her, a wave of heat and dizziness hit me. I sank to the ground, resting in a crouch.

"What's wrong?" asked Septimus.

Pain stung my feet, crawling up my legs like ghost flames. "They are… burning my tree."

Septimus helped me up, and we hobbled onward, the wolf leading the way.

Soon, enough of my strength returned that I could run again. Every step felt like walking on hot coals. More wolves joined our party, pacing alongside us through the night forest.

A crash echoed through the woods from behind us. The wolves growled and yelped in alarm. Hackles of fur rose along their backs.

I could sense her before she was in view. "The root spirit."

"It's all right." Septimus spoke to the pack. "Don't be afraid."

She rose on two legs and greeted us with her formidable roar. The trees beside her burst into buds of spring green. The brown grass grew with renewed life below her step, like the basilisk's effect on its surroundings, only in reverse. Her injured arm, however, was still ash.

Her mind had no language, but she gave me impressions of friendship. The desire to help. Empathy for what we'd suffered.

"Thank you, friend." I spoke to her as she approached and sniffed my hand. "We're nearly there."

The fire at my roots and the nails in my trunk spurred me onward. The wolves quickened their pace, disappearing into the forest's moon-shadows. I lost track of their movements when acrid smoke hit my nose.

My face chilled. The hair on the back of my neck stood on end.

The trail broke into a familiar rocky clearing, lit by more than the thin sliver of a moon. Magic collected in this hollow like wine in a bowl, reflected and concentrated by a layer of mist. Or was it smoke? The miasma thickened alongside a stream I had painted or sketched so many times. There, in the shrouded distance, the source of this eerie illumination was my rowan tree. Haloed in blue-gold Faelight, the twisted trunk smoldered. I was too far away to judge the damage, but someone had extinguished the fire moments ago.

"It's still alive," said Septimus. "It must be."

Three wolves stood alongside us. One growled, baring its teeth.

I turned to follow the animal's line of sight and gasped.

A dead body—wearing a hospital uniform—lay beside the trail. Another just ahead, bloodied. More lay beyond—so hidden in shadow one could take them for stones.

Philips had said *he killed them all*. What did he mean? The Shade? Philips had been its host when Porter sent him here to begin the ritual.

Through the cold air came a low animal groan. The crash of underbrush. One wolf ran toward the sound. Veiled in fog and smoke, an unreal outline broke into view—a beast sewn together with the tail of a scorpion, the torso of a bull, and forepaws like the twisted arms of a man. As tall as an elephant, pale and dead-fleshed, it raised a clawed, human hand in the moonlight and bellowed. The malevolent sound echoed through the forest.

The beast turned, sniffed the air, and rushed toward us.

Septimus aimed his gun and shot, striking the chimera in the head.

The massive beast screamed as blood gushed from an eye. It reared, flashed a row of shark's teeth in a tentacle-bearing maw, and advanced.

Septimus fired his last bullet, but the creature dodged. "Shit."

Another chimera, twice as tall, screamed from within the darkness and pushed the heavy mist with massive bat-like wings. The root spirit lumbered toward this new enemy, roaring.

A black wolf snarled and leapt at the first monster, catching it by the hind-leg. The chimera thrashed onward, shaking the animal's grip.

I drew my brush and dipped it into the dwindling vial of Faelight. "Stay down!"

But Septimus had charged ahead to meet the enemy, alongside two more wolves. The pack attacked with tooth and claw, while Septimus leapt onto creature's back. With bare hands, he tore at the remaining insect-like eye. The creature shrieked and struggled, exposing its belly to the wolves' quick strikes. It landed a return blow to one wolf, sending the animal flying.

Unsure if it would work, I slashed through the air as if my brush were a sword. Gleaming bristles cut through the creature's distant skin. It screamed and reared, clutching an injured arm. Septimus jumped free.

Eyes riveted on this nightmare target, I lunged forward, directing the brush tip toward the creature's patchwork torso, like thrusting a dagger. Yards away, the monster bellowed and fell, shaking the ground like a downed tree. A wolf rushed in to finish the kill.

This was too much power. My fingertips went numb around the silver handle. I staggered closer to the beast, nearly choking on foul-smelling air.

Riven gray belly flesh steamed, oozing greenish-black blood. At the cut, Faelight residue swirled with gore, evidence of my unearthly weapon. Like water, magic seeped deeper into the wound, pooled, and brightened. The monster's chest expanded, as though with breath. Could it have survived? Terrified, I backed away. The wolf beside me growled, hackles raised.

The chimera's body cavity heaved. Something inside struggled against a prison of dead flesh. A tentacle, washed in lustrous green blood, snaked out of the wound, followed by a clawed hand.

Another wolf ran to my side. Brown fur bristled along the animal's spine as it growled and snarled.

Behind the wolves' voices and the sound of tearing flesh, I heard Septimus' shout.

"Lady, get back!"

Nearly identical in shape but smaller, a monster, slicked with gore and oily phosphorescence, emerged from the fallen chimera. It reared up and howled.

Another sibling clawed its way from the dead parent. And a third. They sniffed the air and screamed through tentacled maws. Most appalling, no sutures connected their anthropomorphic arms to bovine body or insect tail—no evidence remained of their surgical origin in Porter's laboratory. My own magic must have completed this grim transformation.

I stood, horrified.

A hand on my shoulder brought me back. Septimus. Without a word, we dashed in time to avert the first creature's bellowing charge.

The other two followed.

"We can't outrun them." Gasping, I knelt and touched the ground. "Stop them!" I yelled, willing the forest to hear my voice.

Brambles and vines heeded my call. Vegetation entwined two of the creatures in a leafy web. The third broke free of a thorny vine and lunged for Septimus, but halted mid-air amid the sound of rapid gunfire.

Iron bullets rained from above, tearing into the monster. I ducked.

Wind bore the clatter of engine noise and the smell of spent fuel. A dark silhouette of rigid wings—moonlight glinted metal. The glider-like aircraft disappeared over the treetops.

A loud cry came from behind me—another chimera joined the fray. How many of these things had Porter brought to unnatural life? For what purpose?

Compound eyes found me crouched among the grass and brambles. The beast charged. Again, I drew my silver brush with trembling hands. I had no other weapon and nowhere to run.

In a brushstroke, I severed one of the chimera's human-like arms. It lifted a monstrous head and screamed. I steadied my hand to deliver another blow.

"No!" Septimus stretched a hand toward me. "You'll damage your soul if you use your magic for evil."

"We're dead if we do nothing." I dipped the brush again in the liquid light.

"Ask the forest." He drew nearer, gasping. "It can stop them. They do not belong here."

I eyed the creature's surroundings, looking for an answer, but finding only another horror. The dead-gray arm I'd severed twitched where it lay; my Faelight, like phosphorescent paint, pulsing through its veins. The clawed hand opened. Fingers elongated, shifted, morphing into insect-like legs. The severed limb swelled into an abdomen, thorax, and stinger—a smaller copy of its parent. Above, the injured monster screamed and swung its scorpion's tail. From its arm-wound emerged a slimy tentacle—growing until its frenzied excesses collided with the ground.

Overhead, the Steam-Dart had returned to the fray. Gunfire blasted in bursts of blue light. Ammunition tore into the foe. The creature wailed as black fluid gushed from a chest wound. With its new tentacle, it lashed out for the glider and tethered a wing. The aircraft completed a swift arc to the ground, exploding into flames. The monster followed, toppling with a guttural groan before it stilled.

Septimus ran toward the burning crash.

With a screech, the severed arm charged me on its finger-legs.

I lifted my brush and slashed a pattern of horizontal and vertical lines through the air. If this experiment failed, I might not live long.

As though traveling new roads my mind had mapped, living vines spiraled from the forest floor with lightning speed. Branches stretched from the trees, weaving a physical net. The creature tore and clawed at the trap but couldn't break free.

I approached. In the few minutes since the severed limb acquired unnatural life, the thing had grown a head. I raised the brush like a wand, bristles aglow with residual paint. Solid black eyes, within an elongated crab-like face, tracked my hand's every movement. The beast calmed.

Was it possible I could control this monster I'd created?

The fleeting notion vanished when, in a crash of fury, the root spirit flattened the creature with her good arm. Its flesh blackened and melted into the ground.

Grateful for her aid, and not a little terrified of her power, I backed away. She eyed me now with a questioning energy. Her foliage-fur quivered. Red and orange blooms withered and dropped from her crown. She turned and ran into the mist and smoke.

A wolf howled, followed by another. I identified the call for aid, though I did not know whom they called.

Septimus shouted over the distance and the roaring fire.

I ran toward the downed aircraft. My friend carried a body away from the flaming hull, knelt and laid her on the ground. When I got close enough, I sighed in relief when she stirred.

"Evelyn!" I hugged her. "Are you injured?"

"I'm fine." She slipped her aviator goggles down around her neck. "I saved a few patients. Most of his... experiments were too far gone..." She shuddered.

"Death can be a mercy," said Septimus.

Evelyn nodded and wiped her eyes. "Where is the Shade?"

"I don't know," I said. "Roger left to fight it alone before we arrived here. He must have stopped the ritual."

"So I see." Evelyn glanced from my smoldering tree some distance away, toward one of the bodies lying face down in the dirt.

"Can you walk?" Septimus offered her a hand.

"Yes." Evelyn grabbed a rifle from the ground beside her and stood. "I lost the other weapons in the crash." She reloaded with ammunition from a pouch belted to her waist. She'd ditched the nurse's hat in favor of an aviator's cap but still wore the somber black uniform dress and white pinafore, charred and torn though it was.

Smoke from the glider fire subsided. Evelyn limped, and Septimus braced her as we proceeded toward the distant tree. The Changeling wolf paced beside us. Another sniffed at one lifeless chimera. Gray-green flesh had begun to rapidly dissolve. Blackened ooze, smelling of formaldehyde and rot, exposed pale, metal-studded bones.

We approached one of the first creatures my brush had spawned. The monster hissed and thrashed from inside a cage of vines and branches. Evelyn raised her rifle.

"Wait!" I lifted a hand, but she fired a glowing round into the monster. It whined, twitched. She shot again.

The beast collapsed. In seconds, the gray corpse melted into putrid black.

Evelyn lowered the smoking weapon and turned to me. "We can't allow any of this evil to survive."

"This creature was made by my hand," I said. "Not Porter's."

Evelyn appraised me with a look of what appeared to be, if I didn't know better, fear.

A scream broke through the palpable darkness. The inhuman sound was of such a tortured pitch, for another sickened heartbeat I didn't recognize it.

Roger. I ran toward him.

Chapter 34
The Rowan Tree

ll the violets which bloomed here in spring were now dormant. Only moss and sparse grass dotted the moon-silvered ground. I ran along the rocky stream to the bend where my rowan grew, crowned in a bluish-white halo of smoke and mist. Ribbons of living bark remained on the charred trunk. Pale branches reached for the stars. A few leafy twigs, laden with autumn gold, supported berries red as blood. Others were blackened and withered. The tree smoldered, just as spasms of pain wracked my body. I couldn't see Roger in the gloom and smoke.

I sidestepped a freshly dug hole, deep enough to expose tree roots. On the ground beside it, moonlight revealed shards of glass, or perhaps fragments of rock crystal. Once charged with magic, but now broken. Had Mother buried these here to protect me?

Evelyn grabbed my arm. "Wait. It's a containment spell. Don't cross it." She pointed to a red radiance not yards away. The mirage was so thin I might have missed it in my charge ahead.

Inside that circle, a shadowed figure stood beside my tree. Roger's hand opened to me, a gesture of warning. "Get back!"

In his other hand, he held the unicorn horn, like a gleaming wand pointing down to the ground.

"Roger! What's happening? Where is the Shade?"

"Stay away! I can't ke… keep it here much longer." His voice was strained, like he fought to speak the words.

The wolves beside us growled.

I blinked, and Roger stood closer. Though he had no blood on his hands, his white shirt was stained with red, torn open, and his coat and waistcoat were gone. Lines and symbols marked his chest, alongside the cuts the chimera had given him the day before. He wore Porter's evil medallion. Eyes so unnaturally dark, face shadowed. He was now the one possessed.

He paced closer, laughing, but it was not Roger's laugh. The sound burdened my heart with a terrible mixture of fear and protectiveness.

He shook his head and groaned. "Do it, Crane. This is the only way. Now! For Felicity."

Evelyn raised her rifle, chambered a round, and aimed it at the man I loved. "You saw the bodies. He cannot control the Shade. It's too late to save him."

"No! He didn't kill them!" I moved to intercept, but she sidestepped. "Don't—"

"Forgive me." She pulled the trigger and the weapon fired.

Roger staggered, clutched his chest, and fell.

I ran, heedless of the magic barrier between us. If Evelyn's bullet had crossed through it, I could too.

Septimus yelled, "Stop! You'll be trapped—"

I crashed through a membrane of red light. A sound like a swarm of bees swallowed the rest of his words. I entered a space of cursed ground.

Below my feet, the granite bedrock silently cried out. Inaudible whispers and images. Memory of sorrow. Red splattered snow of an endless winter. The unicorn's blood had long ago soaked these stones. This ground had reclaimed the creature's body after Roger and Felicity took their trophies.

In the center of this tragic place grew the source of my magic. I drew near my rowan tree. Our life sprouted from a seed of my mother's own rowan. Planted in the very spot where she'd dreamed it must grow.

Roger clutched at his chest with one hand, braced on the rocky earth with the other. He pulled back bloodied fingers and laughed in a voice not his own.

Gaze fixed on the ground, he swallowed. "This… is justice. But you—you should not be here."

"Roger." Those had been his own words. I crouched in front of him, hoping to block Evelyn's line of fire. "Where are you shot?"

Now those eyes dilated, almost full black. Cynbel did not turn to look at me, but pointed his hand downward. The blood on his fingers shimmered, transforming into shadow. With a puff of breath, he scattered black dust to the wind.

"The wizard thought to destroy me, just as he once created me. But I have proven more powerful than my origins."

I scooted back.

Cynbel stood. "Humans will always be weaker than us. Your mother knew this, yet she defiled her royal bloodline, giving birth to *you*."

"Fight him, Roger!"

He grinned, under too much shadow. "Oh, your lover is still here. I can read his thoughts and his… memories." He exhaled. "Ah, now there's a nice one. Pity those were your last moments together in this life. Take comfort, for I will remember them forever."

Cynbel lifted a hand, holding the unicorn horn perpendicular to the ground, pointing downward. The wand shone with a corona of bloodred light.

The Shade whispered foul, inhuman words through Roger's lips; not the language of my mother's people; this was some dark reflection I had not yet known. My charred tree burst anew into scarlet flame. Just as my mother's tree had burned in the Winter King's garden with a blue and green fire.

The heat seared me from within. A scream escaped my lips. I pulled in ragged breaths, clenched a fist and soon the spasms of pain stilled—my every sensation numbed, and I watched the scene of my own impending death as through someone else's eyes.

Wind loosed tendrils of smoke, choking the crescent moon.

Forest treetops rustled in violent song. Firelight danced through the clearing and surrounding woods. Suspended from Roger's feet, a shadow writhed across the granite, in tempo with the flickering flames, out of sync with Roger's own movements.

Roger's face dissolved into Cynbel's. His dark hair grew longer and faded to dead white. His green eyes deepened to obsidian pools. A glamour disguise, showing the true enemy. He smiled.

My fingers shook as I drew out my container of dwindling light and dipped the brush into ethereal paint. I willed the image of a dagger to mind, like one I'd seen in a long-ago nightmare. My hand and brush fluttered through the air, forming a weapon. The mirage shimmered and took on mass, transforming air and light into temporary matter. I grabbed the dagger's hilt before it succumbed to gravity, finding the weight real enough.

"Do you think your illusions can harm me here in this world?" Cynbel moved aside the torn fabric of his shirt, exposing Roger's skin marked with lines of ash and dried blood. The silver amulet shone with darklight. The bullet wound above his heart wept dark red in the firelight, though the bleeding looked to have slowed. How much time did he have?

He took a step toward me, open hands wide. "Kill him if you can. It will only hasten my full control over this body."

"You will not defeat us."

Cynbel laughed.

I lunged, not for Roger's living flesh, but for the shadow at his feet.

My dagger struck rock. The pool of oily darkness rippled like water.

The Shade cried out in pain.

I sliced at the vile outline. Cynbel fell to his knees.

The phantom knife crumbled to dust in my hand. On the rock below lay the silver-handled brush—white bristles of unicorn mane tarnished with dirt and blood.

I checked my fingers. Not my blood.

A flash of inner light blinded me for an instant; seared my mind's canvas with a vision. No, another half-remembered dream. A festering madness I had tried every day of my life to forget.

A shadow with spindly, transparent limbs crept from the corner of my room to loom over my bed. I lay frozen in paralyzed terror. Only a whispering breath escaped my lungs when I tried to scream. The thing rasped a dagger of a word, which I still could not remember, though it was my long-forgotten name. The Shade infected my mind with a grafted memory, one I'd I never seen with my own eyes. A hand reached into moonlight, holding a knife. The same one I had just painted. Roger's hand, long ago, when he was so young. A pool of blood as big as a mirror reflected the light of a half-lit moon. Reflected a man's trembling outline.

But this was no memory. I cried out and struck the red-soaked rock with my bare fist. Roger had fallen here when Evelyn shot him.

Desperate, I tore at the shadow's outline on the wet granite. The slick darkness stung like acid. I withdrew fingers stained with blood, but otherwise unharmed. Yet a sickening numbness, like the weight of sleep, crept from my hands into my limbs and body.

I stood and willed a step backward, but my foot wouldn't budge. I tried to lift my brush, but my arm hung limp and useless. The rowan tree cracked and burned, searing through my numb awareness, as though my own skin were aflame. Yet I couldn't move.

My muscles were frozen. Like in my nightmares.

"When your mother planted this rowan on the ground of my genesis, I sensed you draining my power—altering me. Oh, how I hated you. I tried to kill you, but I could not cross the barriers she had erected. I tried to lure you into my world, but you never followed. Yet the Fates smiled upon me. For your love of my vile master, and your father's greed, proved the perfect bait. Now your powers are awakened, and the time has come. Do not fear.

Soon your pain will end. You will be with him—with us—forever. And your magic… will become our muse." He laughed.

"No." A weight of sadness crushed my heart, like it came from somewhere outside of me, even as the fire burned through my tree's remaining life. *My Muse.* I had called Roger that once or twice. It had upset him.

Was Roger there in Cynbel's hideous words? Hadn't he and Cynbel been connected all along? Had Porter been right? Porter, with his infernal theories and his damned documents of my personal history. Had he told me the truth about the good Dr. Gale?

I trembled. *No.* I trusted my heart didn't lie.

From behind me came a muffled scream, followed by gunshots. I could not even turn my head to see my friends.

"It is too late. You will all die."

I called out with the last of my strength. "Hear me, spirit of the Welterwood! Help us."

Of its own accord, my awareness twined through the roots of my dying tree, far down into the rocky earth. Deeper still, into the bedrock where gemstones pulsed with power. The crystalline heart of the forest thrummed an ancient song below our feet, one my soul recognized.

A storm charged the clearing with a furious wind. Raindrops fell. Red light from my burning tree glossed the landscape. Outside the circle of Roger's containment spell, swift wolves cut toward attacking monsters. Another barrage of gunfire drowned out battle cries, both human and animal.

A whisper came in the wind, like the sound of wings. Whether it came from within me or without, I couldn't tell.

Thunder cracked. My invisible bonds broke, and I lunged forward.

Cynbel's glamour vanished, just like my conjured knife. Returned was the face of my love, eclipsed though he still was. He fell to the cursed stone, clutching his bleeding side. His shadow squirmed in the flickering firelight. The Shade yearned to be free of its fleshly tether.

The unicorn horn lay between us, in a pool of crimson rainwater.

Cynbel could not move fast enough now, in Roger's injured shell.

I grabbed the horn. Power like ice and fire cracked through my veins. I did not yet have the training to use a magic wand, like Roger and Evelyn. But how much different was it from a brush?

Now I understood. If I was to vanquish the Shade, it must know its true source.

Beside Roger, I knelt and stretched out the wand. Dark water churned in the growing storm. Below my hand, it solidified, becoming like obsidian.

Roger's altered shadow danced along this shining surface, cast by the firelight of my dying tree. A grim marionette, the Shade struggled to pull free. Roger's ashen face strained—he held the creature there, attached to his clenched and trembling fists, like he knew what I must do.

I shouted. "Behold what you truly are!"

Colors and light glimmered into this reality, brushstrokes at my command. I painted a memory—the unicorn, gleaming with ethereal light, on the black mirror's surface.

The image took life, walked through that two-dimensional landscape of another world, and passed through reflected firelight. Under mirrored pre-dawn stars, the unicorn slipped below the holographic moon and met that shape of Roger's shadow, once cast upon his darkest night. The unicorn's image reared and stabbed the Shade with a brilliant horn.

Stone cracked. Ice fractured. The dark mirror shattered.

Shards of ice struck my exposed skin and began to melt.

"How... is this possible?" Cynbel's voice was strained.

Before us stood the unicorn. Be it real or only glamour, my painting had become manifest in this three-dimensional space. The creature of light strode forward. Gleaming hooves splashed through rivulets of bloody rain. Bright blue Faelight streamed from a horn translucent as pearlized glass—the spectral twin of the wand I held.

"Awake and remember!" I raised the horn above my head, where it gathered starlight. "Your nightmare must end!"

Roger collapsed on the ground. A shadow lifted away from his limp body—an inky copy split through a dark prism. The Shade's eyes fixed on mine—two cavernous pools in a face sculpted from indistinct darkness.

It stretched an arm toward the unicorn.

I remember now... The Shade glided forward. *No. I am... afraid... for this to end.*

An end is only a beginning. The unicorn lowered its horn and paced forward. *We are one.*

Light and dark converged. Raindrops passed through spectral flesh as the unicorn absorbed its wayward shadow.

A blinding flash of lightning stuck the ground not a mile away, perhaps near the Queen's Circle, followed by the sharp smell of ozone. When my vision had recovered enough to see, the unicorn was gone.

My tree still burned, steaming in the rain, but the containment field around us had disappeared.

The wind howled. Then came a sound like a train, the snapping of tree-limbs.

A whirlwind blasted into the clearing, leaving a trail of bare soil in its wake. Rain and forest debris swirled in a wriggling column. It roared in our direction.

I threw myself to the ground beside Roger.

"Protect us!" I held the alicorn wand aloft and scribed a gleaming arc above our heads. A shield of light, like sunlight over a lens, illuminated for an instant the bloody stone where we lay. Roger's pale face, his cold body, didn't move.

I bent to cover him as the torrent approached. Raindrops stung like needles. My hair whipped as if pulled by vindictive spirits. The wind's roar became a screeching hiss, almost as loud as silence.

It passed us by and crashed into my rowan. I thought it might hasten the tree's destruction and thus my own death. My fingers gripped Roger's wet shirt, his hair. He lay motionless. The twister shrouded my tree in writhing darkness.

The whirlwind thinned, casting a million gold leaves into the Welterwood before it disappeared. The rain stopped. Night sky paled to gray through parting clouds.

The storm had doused the unnatural fire, but the branches of my tree were charred, foliage blackened. Surely it would not survive.

"Come back to me, Roger." I touched his neck but could not tell if the pulse I sensed through numbed fingers was my heartbeat or his. I pressed my cheek against his chest, listening for a sign of life. His skin was so cold. Mine burned with phantom fire.

I closed my tear-filled eyes and covered him with my warmth—my will. "Please come back."

A heartbeat. A breath. My own heart leapt in response.

He gasped and whispered, "My love." He laid one trembling hand on my head. "I failed you. I tried to protect you. Your tree. Forgive me."

"Roger, I'm still here." I sat up and stretched the wand above his blood-soaked shirt. "Be still. Let me use magic to heal you. While I have it."

"No. If you have any strength left, you must save your tree." A ragged breath. "You are the only one who can."

"There's too much damage." How much longer did I have before my life also faded?

"No… it's not too late. Do you still have the liquid Faelight?"

I sat up and retrieved the vial from my bodice. "Only a few drops."

"It must be enough. Pour it on a living root. Quickly, before the sun rises and its lunar magic fades."

I kissed his cold cheek, stood, and limped toward my tree. The charred wood yielded up tendrils of smoke into a gray sky. Embers at the trunk's base echoed my pulsing pain. With inadequate balance, I sidestepped remains of fallen branches. I passed through veils of mist and smoke, drawing near the trunk. I saw no clear bark. All was burned, save a few desiccated branch tips. The sap must have boiled, destroying every root from inside. Tears streamed from my eyes, mixed with sweat and rain.

The unicorn's horn had become so heavy—like iron. It would have slipped through my deadened fingers, so I tied it to the sash at my waist. Another smoke-filled breath strengthened my shaking hands with resolve.

The Changeling wolf ran to me. Her golden-brown eyes searched mine. *Don't despair.*

She sniffed at the charred soil, pacing alongside me. We circled the tree, looking for anything alive.

The ground steamed in serpentine rivulets, radiating out from the trunk. I knelt and scraped away soil, finding roots hot enough to sting. I uncovered another. Where once had been the living wood, pale ash sloughed away, revealing spent coals.

Was I too late? Overhead, dawn grew brighter. My strength waned. Yellow light shimmered like jewels through rain-wet bracken, glimmered in puddles captured by ancient stones.

Close by, the wolf yelped and pawed at the strewn ashes. I crawled to meet her and helped her dig down to damp soil. The wolf's paws struck wood, peeled away the root's bark in thin green stripes. Alive!

When I drew out the vial this time, I gasped. *Empty?*

I held it up into the light. Clear liquid clung to the bottom, but if any luminescence remained, I detected none. Sunrays broke through the forested horizon. Warm, like the promise of new life on cold, night-weary skin.

"My light," I whispered. "This is all I have left. Please. It must be enough."

Remember your shadow.

It was not the wolf who had spoken. If this message had come from the unicorn, or from the Welterwood, or from a memory, it mattered not. With the rising sun at my back, I leaned over the root, casting my own shadow on the ground. That living outline contained all my nightmares and dreams. All my hidden, ugly parts which no longer gave me shame. All the unfathomed depths I no longer feared.

On this dark stage, behind reality's curtain, the liquid flashed with pale violet light. When I held the vial close to my heart, it glowed like a thousand fireflies.

I poured it over the root. Pulses of light like a visible heartbeat seeped into the wood. Blue-green luminescence traveled through the tree's lifelines, under mud and ashes, to the central trunk. Green crept like moss up the blackened bark.

I drew out the alicorn wand and held it like a brush. The crack of power through my arm only steadied my resolve.

I traced outlines of branches from memory, gathering color from the fading stars and the waking dawn, pulling down light from an ever-flowing source. Faelight spiraled upward from the earth, through the root I'd watered, to meet this light directed from above, transmuting our damaged remains into new life. Shimmering leaves budded and unfurled. Flowers burst open and formed clusters of crimson berries.

Time froze. My pain vanished, leaving enraptured weightlessness.

When this world's gravity returned, I knelt in warm mud. Chill wind whipped through my damp hair, smelling of smoke.

The horn was gone.

So was my tree.

Only a pile of gray ashes and coals marked where it had once stood.

Perhaps for only a little while longer, I was still alive.

The fingers of my filthy hand uncurled; where I had once held the alicorn wand, an opalescent pebble flashed with myriad hidden hues. I lifted it into the morning light. Infinite patterns of color refracted through crystalline veins. Within that matrix, a vision of the unicorn galloped through an ethereal forest.

This was a Faestone. The unicorn's.

A gift freely and truly given. Keep it with you, Lady of the Summer Courts. Protect our forest.

"I will." I tucked the stone under the fabric of my ruined dress, where the vial of light had rested not long ago.

You must send them back. All those my shadow stole into this world. I will help you, and I will protect them as they cross.

I stood, finding my legs stronger. I dashed to Roger, who lay on his side facing me, hand clutching part of his torn shirt to the bullet wound. Atop the stony ground where long ago he'd spilled the unicorn's blood, he now shed his own. He had once taken a life to save another's, though it had failed. Now he had been willing to give up his own life to save mine.

I knelt and caressed his cold cheek.

"You are glowing," Roger whispered, "my Violet."

I looked at my normal, pale hands. "No, I'm not."

He kissed my wrist. "I don't mean like that." His smile, despite the wounds of this battle, told me he would survive. Only when I sensed we were not alone did I find the will to pull away.

Evelyn waited until I nodded my assent before she knelt beside us. "Please forgive me for shooting him, Lady." It was not until she said the last word, did I realize Evelyn was speaking to me, not to Roger. She bowed her head, as Roger had bowed to the Queen of the Fae.

I tried to process this contradiction in Reliqua protocol, and said, "It's all right. You were only trying to protect us."

Septimus sat beside her, grim-faced. We all turned to stare at the smoking ruins of my tree. No one spoke until I asked.

"How long will I live without it?"

Evelyn shook her head. "I've never seen anything like this. I can't say what magic is keeping you alive, even now."

Roger said, "The new moon rises tomorrow tonight. Perhaps, if you return to the Otherworld before—"

"No. Without a tree, I would perish there just the same. I belong here."

He squeezed my hand. Tears glossed his eyes.

Evelyn wiped her cheek. Septimus stared at the ground.

"Listen, everyone. I'm not dead yet. Somehow… the unicorn's magic has changed me. Don't give up hope. I haven't. There is more we must do. Before this forest's curse is truly broken, the balance must be restored. All the Fae and Changelings Porter stole into this world must go home. Their energy must return to the Otherworld where it belongs."

"Spoken with wisdom, Lady of the Summer Courts." Septimus nodded.

Roger took my hand and laid the silver-handled brush in my palm, with pride and awe in his eyes. "You will need your wand."

I stood on shaky knees. "We must open a portal at the Queen's Circle once more. Quickly. The moonlight will soon fade. Will you help me, Dr. Crane?"

"I will." She stood. "Indeed, we must all leave here. Soon Porter's men will come looking for the others."

They would find the bodies. It didn't help matters we couldn't trust the police. I would win that battle too, when the time came.

"Septimus, I must ask a favor of you."

"Anything."

"Will you get Roger to medical treatment at once?"

He nodded.

"Please don't let him convince you he can suture himself."

Roger shifted to sit up, wincing. "Don't worry. I'll be a model patient."

Septimus put an arm around him, and they stood.

We left the clearing together, but Evelyn and I headed north along the stream, while Roger and Septimus traveled south, back toward the institute—the quickest way to get help, despite the risks. They disappeared from the range of my backward glance through the woods. In the distance, an automobile engine rattled to life.

The Changeling wolf walked beside me. *I will help gather them all together.*

"Thank you," I told her. "Please bring them to the Queen's Circle."

When the wolf ran off, Evelyn asked, "How will they make it through outside of Equinox Bridge? Even if you're able to open the gateway? Some maybe be powerful enough, but others..."

"The unicorn promised to protect them." I glanced at the waning moon.

She nodded. "Then the forest's guardian is still here." She smiled, but I saw the pain behind it. She wiped her eyes and faced the wind.

Wolf voices joined in a chorus. Their song echoed through the clearing, over the sea cliffs, to the ocean.

We wound our way through the forest until we reached a footpath—soil, stone and root worn by generations of pilgrims.

A gray fox wreathed in ethereal blue light joined our procession. A stag with silver horns fell in step beside Evelyn. Wings rustled. Dark avian shapes wove through bare tree branches at either side of the path—a flock of large birds; in my Fae blood I sensed their Name, but I knew no human equivalent.

The ancient monoliths lay ahead, radiant against the shady forest. Overhead, the fading crescent moon shone in a violet sunrise, veiled with clouds of rosy gold. *Let it be enough.*

"I will try to strengthen the doorway," said Evelyn.

I placed the Faestone on the altar, as I had done before, and blue liquid light seeped through the petroglyph lines.

Evelyn lifted her arms and began an incantation—her voice a clear note in the autumn morning. She drew energy from the stones, gathering the charge in her aura, swirling power in the space between her open hands, as the magic of the old gateway awakened once more.

From behind us came a roar, but the sound carried a peaceful intent. I turned to see the root spirit scattering birds from the trees.

More wolves broke into the clearing, driving creatures before them. Many I recognized as those we had freed from Porter's prison. The blue wyvern. The boy with green skin and shark teeth. A slender tree on two root-like legs—I had not seen her before, but three more like her emerged from the woods, followed by a swarm of firefly-like pixies. Soon, the grassy field teamed with

Faerie life. From all I sensed a desire to return home, and the forest's own hope and trust in me.

Evelyn finished a circumambulation, hand raised in magical command. A circle of light flashed around the stones, following the direction she had walked. The monoliths emitted a low tone in concert, like a giant bell.

The unicorn's consciousness gave me the words of power to speak, the symbols to draw in the shimmering air. I let the magic flow through me, too elated to be terrified.

I lifted the silver brush and painted a diaphanous arc of light from one side of the circle to the other. A rainbow. The air underneath shimmered like glass—a mirror reflecting the Otherworld forest.

I raised my glowing brush. "It is time. All must return home."

First the Otherworld birds and bats flew through. They entered the circle of stones and slipped out of this reality; the sky in Faerie filled with their retreating shapes. The wyvern followed, then the swiftest of the beasts. The Root Spirit lumbered across this threshold between worlds. I dropped to one knee, as fatigue enveloped me, yet I kept my wand aloft.

Overhead, the moon disappeared under an advancing line of cloud. A boom of thunder rolled through the forested hills—lightning like a glimmer of lanterns behind a silvery curtain. The hair on my forearms stood on end. A magnetic charge pulled me in some indefinable direction, or everywhere at once.

I spiraled through a universe of causes and effects, like every atom composing earth and stars and life, yet I was not adrift. I was buoyed, by my magic and my will.

I looked to see the unicorn standing within the archway, if it were not a mirage. Distant, like a beacon on a far-away shore.

When I blinked, the unicorn's image became a shadow. The unreal outline—made of not one but many—broke apart and rose like a column of smoke. Silhouettes of myriad creatures advanced on the Otherworld doorway. A flock of birds burst through into human air. Eagles. A species I'd not seen in this forest since I was a child. Smaller birds came next, and animals of all kinds. Once they thrived in the Welterwood, before its curse. They belonged here, just as their counterparts belonged in the realm of the Fae.

When the last field mouse had crossed through, I lifted the brush and struck through the symbols I'd written in the air, sealing their power. With the last of my dwindling strength, I closed the door between our two worlds and sank to my knees in exhaustion.

The brush fell to the ground.

CHAPTER 35
A FRESH CANVAS

I dreamed of my rowan tree. It grew in the charred and blackened Otherworld soil where the unicorn's horn first transported me—the mirror version of where it once grew in the human world. Its roots healed the blighted ground, bringing life anew. But it seemed unprotected. In the dream I could not approach it. A force like liquid gravity held me back. Then the bark and branches, the leaves and berries, ghosted away into mist as it had done just days ago.

I awoke in my own bed and rubbed bleary eyes as the dream retreated.

Had I sent it through the Divide somehow? Is that why I was still alive? Perhaps the magic of the Welterwood had found the only way to save my tree, since it could no longer live in this human world. But what did that mean for me?

Such were my thoughts as I took in the sea view from my bedroom's open window, framed in fluttering lace. Home. I inhaled the salt smell of the cool autumn air, the perfume of flowers. A hint of spice was like the familiar bouquet of a certain beloved apothecary shop, which often clung to its owner's clothing. I whispered his name, wishing I could summon him so easily.

A vase of roses, asters, and chrysanthemums sat on my bedside table. Amid the flowers, tall rowan branches bore clusters of red berries and white petals—blooms out of season. Beside them lay the silver-handled paintbrush given to me in the Winter Courts, along with the crystal necklace Roger had given me on my birthday. "Oh." I reached to pick it up. "I thought I'd lost this."

"It was at my shop. We left it there after our escape from the barrow."

"Roger?"

"I'm here, my love."

I turned to see him sitting in a chair beside my bookshelves, an open book in his hands. He wore a fine suit in charcoal and sky blue, sans coat, and over his right arm and shirtsleeve, a sling.

He closed his book, and with obvious discomfort, stood and hobbled towards my bed. He tarried a few paces away until I reached for him. He took my hand with his uninjured one and sat on the bed beside me. His face bore healing bruises, and he wore a small bandage above his left eye, but his smile was no less a beautiful sight.

"You're making house calls now?" I smiled. Alone in this room with me, his presence roused memories of our intimate moments, yet he did not draw near enough.

"Your Mrs. H allowed me to watch over you this afternoon while she rests. I'm glad you are finally awake." He kissed my hand, warm lips lingering on my skin. I yearned for more of his touch, yet something held him back. He asked, "How are you feeling?"

"I'm fine. Just tired." Then I processed what he'd said. "Finally? How long ago did we defeat the Shade?"

"Nearly four days."

"Right. The new moon has passed, hasn't it? And I'm still alive. Somehow."

Evelyn had driven me home in an automobile that must have belonged to the institute, and I was too fatigued to wonder why I didn't fear its iron. Home again, Mrs. H had helped me bathe and dress for bed. I half-remembered waking moments, attempts at tea and scant meals; Mrs. H helping me move about or tend to hygiene for hazy minutes before I succumbed again to the constant need for sleep. At last, when the worst seemed to have passed, I'd glimpsed a waxing crescent moon through my window, though I'd wondered if it was a dream.

I touched the sling on Roger's arm. Could I heal him like I did before? "How is your injury?"

"The gunshot wound is mending well, thanks to Septimus and a few of my herbal preparations. Time will heal the rest." He leaned closer and kissed my forehead, and I inhaled the delicious smell of him, wishing we were truly alone.

I curled one hand inside his, and with the other, combed my fingers through his hair. He stroked my hand in reassurance. I gently touched his side, the bandages beneath his linen shirt. I closed my eyes, but I could not find my source of magic. There were no wards blocking me. It was just *gone*. In the silence, I saw he understood.

"We still won, you know." I exhaled. "We defeated Porter. And the Shade."

He tried to smile. "Yes."

"I thought I lost you, Roger. But here we are. We survived this madness, and I never want us to be apart again."

"Nor do I." A glimmer of hope flashed through his weary eyes before sadness replaced it. He gazed out the window.

"But… what's wrong?"

"How can you love me? Have I not been the monster who tormented you… all your life? Was it not my actions which created the Shade? Even unknowingly… I…" He shook his head, jaw clenched. "On top of my other sins. I am responsible for every death Porter caused in the name of my work. Does that not make me just as evil? I cannot allow what I am to corrupt you. I must protect you. Even from myself."

His words sent ice through my veins. Was he so broken that he would forever fall on his sword? I would not let it happen.

I touched his face, bringing his tear-glossed gaze back to mine. "No. It was not you who hurt me, Roger Gale. Your work, long ago, may have set the course in motion, but you are not responsible for the choices Porter made. Or even Cynbel's. When you discovered this evil, you defeated it. You were willing to give up your life to stop it. That's all any of us can do. Do not forget the people you cured before your research was stolen and corrupted. All the lives we saved from Porter's grasp. You have sought absolution, and you have been granted it." I squeezed his hand.

He wanted to believe me. "I can never repay you, Violet. You have given me life itself, and at too great a cost. Yet I fear I'm still cursed. I fear…" The words choked in his throat.

A weight pressed on me. "Don't yield to fear. Fear will destroy us, but love… Love is our salvation. Do you not love me?"

"Yes." His answer unequivocal, and a smile broke through his clouds. "With all I am."

"Then let that be enough. Do you remember… You told me never to give in to the darkness. All those years ago. That fear was only an illusion of our own making. You gave me a mantra. A spell to clear my mind of fear."

He breathed an almost-laugh of relief. "Did it help?"

"More than you know." I curled a finger and smiled. "Come here."

He knit his brow in concern as he leaned closer, but I pulled him to me and placed my lips on his. His answering fervor, his muffled moan, was assurance that we could fight this enemy of his despair. We would make our love enough.

Caressing his cheek, I broke away to whisper, "Let's be married soon. I don't want to be apart from you any longer."

His questioning eyes searched mine. "You still wish to be my wife? Knowing what I am?"

"Do I have to propose to you? Please marry me, Roger Gale."

"Yes, my Violet."

Another lingering kiss.

"Besides, you're going to teach me all about this human magic of yours. Now that it seems my Faerie powers are gone."

"Gladly. Though I'll warn you, it's a heap of study and memorization. Rather more dull at times than people expect."

I laughed. "In your library, I'm sure it would be quite the pleasure."

By his raised eyebrow, I know he didn't miss my double meaning.

"Ah." He sat up and patted his waistcoat pocket with his good hand. "Aside from that, I'm not convinced your Faerie magic is gone. Here." He drew forth a pebble.

I'd almost forgotten. "But that's not the same stone…"

It was the right shape, but its opaque surface held only a dull, gray-blue sheen. Like any ordinary beach stone.

"Because it's in my hand. I believe its magic was meant only for you."

When he placed the stone in my palm, a vibration stirred within, like the resonance of a silent bell—or the flutter of tiny wings. The pulse ended as quickly, leaving behind a clear jewel, filled with threads of swirling luminescence.

I laid it beside my heart. Light seeped from the cracks between my fingers, like I held a star.

"What is it like?" His brow furrowed in unease.

"It's… invigorating. Sunlight after a cloudy day."

When I closed my eyes, I felt as though a second part of me flew over the treetops, ran along the forest floor, grew roots into the soil, unfolded new leaves toward the light. "This must be part of the Welterwood's magic. It's connected to the animals and trees—every living thing it shelters. What the unicorn protected." *And what I must now protect.*

When I withdrew my concentration from the Faestone, the link faded.

"I don't know how I am to guard the Welterwood, as the unicorn wished. I don't know what the task will require of me."

"In any and every way I can, I will help you." He brushed a wayward strand of hair from my eyes. "Only promise me one thing."

"Yes?"

"Don't use this stone every day. With magic so powerful, you could lose yourself within it. Never forget who you are, Violet. Who you were before all of this. The woman I fell in love with. Always remain true to your own inner light."

I set the stone on the table beside my silver brush, and its light faded. It appeared like an ordinary gray pebble once more.

"I remember long ago, when we were painting, my mother said that in any artwork I must always remember the light source, and my own was always the most important. I didn't understand her then, but I do now."

My eyes settled on the rowan branches, and if they didn't deceive me, a faint halo surrounded the flowers and leaves. But that was impossible. My tree, at least in this world, was gone.

"Where did these branches come from?"

"The rowan tree in your garden. The one we saw together in the Otherworld version of this place."

My mother had rooted that cutting so many years ago—a branch taken from an unknown source. It had first grown in the vase beside my sickbed. She had known its nearness would help me heal.

Roger beamed a knowing smile.

I was about to inquire as to his thoughts when we were interrupted by a knock at my half-opened door. Mrs. H cleared her throat.

"Come in, Agnes," I said.

I turned to see her holding a tray of tea.

"Oh, Wonderful! You're awake." She strode into the room, wearing a smart navy suit she'd made not a year ago. At her side followed a familiar black kitten, fuzzy tail and ears alert. He mewed when he saw me.

"Puck!"

He ran to us and hopped up on the bed.

Roger said, "He's been another of your constant companions since I brought him here two nights ago. I daresay he's as much in love with you as I am."

I kissed Puck's tiny head, and he purred, settling into the blankets beside me.

Mrs. H set the tea tray on a bedside table. Though she raised an eyebrow at Roger's proximity, she smiled at me. "I had a feeling you'd be up soon and would need refreshment."

"Thank you. How very thoughtful."

"This is your favorite personal brew." She poured a cup. "From our favorite apothecary shop, of course." She stirred in a spoonful of honey before she offered me a fragrant cup of russet-gold.

"Which Miss Morgen will soon own," said Roger, scratching the kitten's tiny chin.

"Oh?" Mrs. H's baffled look melted into a grin.

"Yes, Roger and I are to be married."

"Oh, my! Congratulations, my dear. To both of you. Bless me, this is fantastic news! But…" Her expression fell.

"Do you not approve?" I sipped the delicious tea. Perhaps that was the moment I first knew I loved the man, when I realized he could make such a wonderful thing.

"No, dear. I'm quite happy for the both of you. It's just… with Mr. Morgen gone to the Otherworld, and you to be married, what should become of this house? Of Travers and me? We had enough of a scare when the Institute tried to take the deed from us. Luckily, they didn't have time to finish before, well…"

"Oh! I'd forgotten. I'll hire an attorney if I must—"

"There's no need," said Roger. "I've had a few days to tie up loose ends. Porter had not yet filed any paperwork regarding your legal status with the courts, so it won't even appear on your record." The kitten mewed and Roger scooped him up. The wriggling creature purred. "Listen, Mrs. Holstead…" His tone bespoke eagerness to change the subject. "I see no reason Miss Morgen should be parted from either you or Mr. Travers. You're her family. This house need not be sold. If there is a concern of finances—"

"I will not sell the house," I said. "I'd like to keep this place running, and I know just how to do it. In fact, we may need to hire additional staff." The seed of this new idea had been dormant within me for so long. It was time for it to germinate.

I swung a leg out of bed and planted a bare foot on a tattered old rug. Roger offered a hand as I stood. Puck jumped down to the bed.

"Oh?" said Mrs. H. "Oh. My dear, let me fetch your dressing gown."

I noticed, perhaps too late, that my nightgown might be construed as too thin for present company. Nor did I miss Roger's approving smile before he turned and paced away, pretending to inspect another of my paintings. Soon enough, Mrs. H brought me one of Mother's old robes. I rarely wore it, considering it too beautiful for everyday use. I now recognized the Otherworld artistry I had always admired. I slipped my arms through fine lace sleeves lined with amber silk and tied the gold sash around my waist.

"Well?" Mrs. H prodded.

With a fortifying gulp of tea, I turned my gaze on the wallpapered walls— the fading yards of vines and stripes, peeling at a few of the top seams, where the roof had leaked two winters ago in a bad storm. The house would need work, but I visualized it transformed, even now, like I'd cast the glamour spell myself. Fresh paper, paint, and plaster. My old bedroom furniture would be removed, in favor of sofa or two, to view the paintings.

"We shall turn this house into an art gallery. A place to showcase new artists who might otherwise go unnoticed. Like so many of the young women I teach."

"A brilliant idea." Roger took my hand. "I hope you will also continue to teach, as long as you wish."

"Thank you, I intend to."

"Oh!" Mrs. H clapped. "What a perfect location for a gallery! Right here by the seacoast. You could even have your engagement party here. In the garden, perhaps in the spring. Or, no, this fall. I can see you two don't mean to wait. Not to mention, the sooner we get the word out about the new gallery, the better."

I swigged the last drop and handed her an empty teacup. "Furthermore, if you would consider it, Agnes, I'd like you to oversee the gallery business. To be part-owner with me. What do you think?"

"Oh, Vio— Miss Morgen, I don't know what to say. I'd be honored!"

"Wonderful. We shall have to put our ideas together soon."

She clapped her hands. "Oh, this is such good news! I must go tell Mr. Travers." She took a few steps, stopped, and turned around. "Bless me! I've almost forgotten. Mr. Gale, did you tell her yet?"

Roger smiled and shook his head. "No. I was saving the honor for you, Mrs. Holstead."

She grabbed my hands with her trembling ones. Her eyes went wide. She was giddy.

"What is it, Agnes?"

"It's your mother's rowan tree! In the garden beside the angel statue. The night before you came back home, it began to... well, to shine. The next day it was taller and covered in new spring branches and flowers, here in October of all things! I knew without a doubt it was the work of the Good People, the... *fairies*. It's done the same the last three days and nights. Now it's twice as tall as before you left. No one's ever seen its like. Not Mrs. Tremble, not the ladies from the Sisterhood, not the solicitor, or the parson. Oh, don't worry dear, we all respected your privacy. Not a soul's been allowed on the second floor of this house except for myself or Mr. Travers, and of course Mr. Gale and that nice Dr. Crane. And... most certainly not the police. Not since that first day."

"The police?"

Her jovial expression all at once sobered. "Well, that may have been my fault. Dr. Porter told us you'd run away from the hospital. At first, they wanted to know if you'd returned home, and… you understand, Travers and I didn't know what had happened to you. We were worried. Then they came back again after you did." Anxious, she looked at Roger.

"I answered their questions. Assured them you were safe and saw to it they left swiftly. I can be persuasive when necessary."

"No doubt you can," I grinned, yet I didn't like the worry I'd glimpsed in his eyes. "However," I added, "at least a few of the police were working for Porter. They looked the other way when he harmed people. For years. In exchange for a cut of the profits. I don't think they will just let it go."

"Nor do I. We'll face that battle when we must. Philips is in police custody. It seems he's confessed to the murder of several orderlies. Just as I also confessed to shooting Porter in self-defense. If there's to be a trial, we have truth on our side, as well as the testimony of Evelyn, Septimus, and other hospital employees who will attest to Porter's crimes and our kidnapping at his hands."

Mrs. H sighed. "You've both been through so much. I'm just glad you're safe."

Agnes drew me into a hug, and when she pulled back, she had tears in her eyes. "Oh, you were telling the truth. What you said at the hospital—about your mother, and your father. About the… Otherworld. I believe you now, Violet. I'm sorry I ever doubted you."

"It's all right Agnes. How could you have known? Even I didn't at first. Now, will you take me to see this tree?"

"Yes! Let's all visit the garden. I'll find Travers." She knelt and called for Puck, who came scrambling into her arms. I would have competition for the kitten's affections, and it warmed my heart.

Roger took my arm. "After you, my love."

We all descended the creaky wooden stairway, my strength returning with every step. I envisioned the old house as it would soon become, full of paintings and new purpose, while my own life with Roger was a fresh canvas, awaiting the scenes of our future. For as many days as we would share, I would fill them with wonder and passion.

We passed by a hallway mirror, now uncovered. In the silvered glass, I glimpsed the reflection of my own shadow. A fleeting memory of an old fear, before it was gone, scattered by the light of day.

THE END

A Note From Cristen E. Rose:

Thank you so much for reading this story! Readers like you are why I persevered through the writing, rewriting, editing, and publishing stages of this alchemy to bring this book to light.

Did you know reviews are invaluable to indie authors? If you have enjoyed this book, please let others know so they can find me too. Consider leaving an online review. Thank you again and have a magical day!

ACKNOWLEDGEMENTS

This book started with a dream I had about ten years ago. The dream began almost exactly like the first chapter, but ended with a download of symbols and images which gave me clues about the rest of the story. I woke up so affected by it I knew I had to write it all down. I would find those dream symbols again as I drafted the rest of the book, "pantsing" my way through the plot without an outline. It took me ten years because I wasn't an experienced writer, and because life threw me major challenges along the way, which made me take some years off in the process. Rewriting this thing many times made me stronger, and I'm so grateful to all the people who helped me untangle this mess.

To my fellow high-school students in the Writers Exchange, thank you for kindling this writing obsession of mine way back when I still had all the time in the world, and giving me an excuse to dress up as Mina Harker for that kick-ass Halloween party.

To Mark Winegardner, my college creative writing professor, thank you for assigning all those dry literary short stories (some pretty fun to read anyway), and for teaching me the basics of good writing Craft way back then before I even knew what the hell I wanted to say.

I wouldn't have gotten far in my writing endeavors without my first writing critique group, The Outcasts, whom I met through the Tallahassee Writers Association. Mary Andrews (a.k.a Zelle Andrews), Jeff Bauer, Robert C. Frink, Andre Smith, Jolene Fine, and Jayne Wallace (aka J.T. Austin). You all suffered through the early versions of this thing like champs, and I thank you for your advice, friendship, and laughs over all those plates of artichoke dip. Robert, your Bizarre Travels never failed to entertain, and your notes were always encouraging. Mary, I have enjoyed working with you on book covers over the years as your career has bloomed. Jayne, wherever you are now in this wide universe, I hope you know how much you helped people back here on Earth. I still have the notes you wrote in the margins of my drafts, (and a few of our scandalous emails). I'm grateful you found Roger as intriguing as me, even when he was a bit flat in those early days. We miss you, girl!

There are so many other people I need to thank for helping me with this writing obsession of mine. Su Riley, thank you for being a fan of this story and supporting my writing from the beginning. Linda Sturgeon, thank you for staying up late with my story "because you got into it!" Heather Whitaker, you helped me see my prose issues more clearly in our writing conference critique session, and your Twitter Spaces workshops taught me so much. Laura Zats, whom I met at an amazing conference—even though we didn't end up working together, your interest in my story way back then was what I needed to continue this journey through some difficult years. Jessica Morell, you are truly a master at your craft. You saved me (and the world) from a terrible first version of this book! I am so grateful you spent the time to help me understand the structure and pacing of a good story, and the value of building a story-specific lexicon. Our work together helped shape all my future writing.

And then, the querying years began. (Oh, if I only knew then what I know now, etc.). I'm still glad I went through the process, because I learned a ton about the industry, and found some amazing friends in the Twitter #WritingCommunity which made the whole thing worthwhile. Anna Bowman, you believed in this story enough to paint some gorgeous fan art! Thank you so much for being an outstanding writer, artist, and beta-reader. Holly Riddle, your notes on the book were so helpful in my revision process. Alexandrina Brant and D. C. Lockhart, you helped me catch some issues with those critical first chapters. I appreciate you all and everyone I've met through the Twitter #vss365, #RevPit, and #amwriting communities.

And to all those who volunteered to read this thing before it was published, you are champions. To my friend Will Ferguson, champion fantasy novel fan, your notes on an early draft helped me see the things that worked and didn't, and your encouragement meant so much. Rhett DeVane, you are a legend, amazing lady. Thank you for helping me shape up those first chapters, for being an ARC reader, catcher of typos, and for inspiring me with your amazing career. To Elisabeth Staab, my friend, ARC reader, and fellow appreciator of gorgeous book cover models, I can't begin to thank you for all the years of support and encouragement. You are my indie-author mentor, and this book wouldn't be here without you. Katie Clark, your amazing photography skills helped me look good on this book's back cover! And to the fabulous M.R. Street with Turtle Cove Publications, your help and advice was instrumental in helping me to set up my publishing company, Happy Cat Press.

A very special thank you goes to my amazing editor Joan Leggitt with Twisted Road Publications. Your professionalism and eye for detail helped me get this book in its final best shape, and gave me the confidence to release this baby out into the world.

And to my magical mentors, Chic Cicero and Tabatha Cicero, I owe you such a debt of gratitude for opening my eyes to the real magic which enlightens this world and enriches our lives.

Finally, I want to thank my wonderful husband John, for encouraging me to keep going with this writing obsession so many times when I wanted to quit, for being my muse and inspiration for a certain handsome magician hero, and for sticking by me all those nights when I tapped away at my keyboard, lost in the world of my story.

One last note: my readers should know that my sweet kitty Tesla (named for the steampunk inventor well before the car was a thing) stepped into my life just a little after Puck wandered into this story. He soon became my constant writing-buddy (when he didn't push my laptop out of the way for more attention) and eventually inspired the Happy Cat Press logo in this book.

Afterward

This book began with a dream and took me ten years to finish, though I had put it aside off and on for long periods of time in that process. I began the draft a year before I was to begin my real-life journey through the world of ceremonial magic. My own tale often paralleled themes in Violet's story as it came to me over the following years, and I think these pages capture some of the energy of my own experiences, though I hope only that it proves entertaining fiction. It should be noted that the magic described in this book, while influenced and inspired by my studies of alchemy, Hermeticism, and ceremonial magic practice, is wholly fictional—invented and embellished purely for this fantasy world. Though the mythology of Ireland and Great Britain inspired the fairy tales of generations of my ancestors, and while the Faerie of Violet's universe hints at real myths and legends of the Sidhe, the Reliqua and Seastone only exist in the pages of my books.

This text has undergone many alchemical transmutations through the drafting process. I scrapped and rewrote the entire thing at least twice, and subsequent scenes received many rewrites before they reached this stage. If I transformed the base lead of my original ideas into anything like gold is for readers to decide. I hope to write better books as I continue in the pursuit, and I happen to know that Roger and Violet's sequel is shaping up to be fun. (Hang on to the end of this book for a way to stay in touch with me if you want to be notified of my future projects.)

I also wanted to address the mental health themes in this book. My readers might imagine that I know many of my protagonist's struggles from the inside out. Only some of them I do literally, and the rest figuratively. I also have family members whose experiences helped inform the direction taken by this plot. No doubt writing Violet through her journey was therapy for me, as I wished for more ways to help the people in my life going through hospitalizations and treatments. An extended family member of mine also survived their experience with 1950s-era electroshock therapy. I always found this fact remarkable, myself only aware of that treatment through fiction such as the 1985 film, *Return to Oz*. The rest I tried to fill in to the best of my ability through research. For my glimpse into the practice of antique psychology that Roger and Porter might have known, I explored Dr. Mesmer's theories on animal magnetism and hypnosis, and relied upon C.G. Jung's essays on topics from synchronicity to archetypes. Jung's infamous, *The Red Book*, which describes a series of inner journeys to a realm much like his own private Otherworld, proved visually inspiring as well. I came across the book *Ten Days in a Mad-House* by Nellie Bly, an astounding first-hand account of a young journalist's experiences in a Victorian-era New York mental institution. The audiobook is open-source on LibriVox, and it is well worth the listen.

My fiction is written for entertainment, but I hope it conveys the message that help is available to those dealing with mental illness. Above all else, I wanted to show Violet and Roger and their struggles in a positive light, and I hope that if you are reading this and you identify with them, that you understand you can win. Real world drama is not so cut and dry as fiction. We don't have three-act structures for the challenges we face every day. In real life, there are rarely any moments in which you know you've overcome the enemy, broken the curse, or restored the balance. But the tide can turn in sometimes unnoticed increments, and clarity can come in moments of reflection. We can win the minor battles every day, by choosing to do the best of our ability with the resources we have, and forgiving ourselves when we can't. Small choices can add up to positive change, not just for us, but for those around us. And yes, there is a magic within you that you can awaken, that can help guide you through the darkness—it is the light of your own soul.

Reach out for help when you need it. If you or a loved one are in crisis, or are dealing with suicidal thoughts, please call or text the 988 Suicide & Crisis Lifeline at 988, or visit 988lifeline.org.

KEEP IN TOUCH WITH C. E. ROSE

STAY TUNED FOR THE EXCITING SEQUEL TO APOTHECARY 709...

I'm hard at work crafting the next part of this story. If you'd like to be notified when it's ready to read, as well as stay up to date with my other projects, please find me on my website or connect with me on social media:

www.cristenerose.com

facebook.com/CristenERose

instagram.com/CristenElizabethRose

Twitter: @CristenERose

The Happy Cat Press
GAZETTE

Sign up for the *Happy Cat Press Gazette* to stay informed about news and happenings in the world of my stories and art. We will only deliver a few of these esteemed publications per year, so we promise we won't make a mess in your inbox!

Sign up at:
www.happycatpress.com